Burning Buildings

By

Mark E. Scott

CHAPTER ONE

I could not pinpoint the exact moment she no longer wanted to touch me, the moment she lost interest in my physical presence. I imagined it happened over time, but who knows? Did it come to her as an epiphany, or was it more like the drip of a leaky hose over a patch of dirt, slowly eroding the ground beneath? These were my thoughts as I hit the snooze button a third time.

I didn't really need the alarm, however. My customary early morning panic had woken me long before the clock had the chance to do so. The panic, the product of a gnawing, self-indulgent questioning, had stalked me for months. But the questions themselves had become meaningless, an empty premise for which no real answer existed or mattered, and my dwelling upon them had become self-destructive. And while I was sure the weight I was feeling was more than age and fatherhood and eighteen years of marriage, there was something more, something I was just starting to put my finger on. An unenthusiastic existence.

It was useless to dwell on unhappy thoughts. Even more useless was lying on my back in a semi-dark room, staring at the ceiling, thinking those unhappy thoughts, so I rolled out of bed and into the bathroom. Once vertical I was pleased to note that, despite my marital woes, I was still catching morning wood. With my tumescence yet to subside, I took a moment to give myself a once over in the mirror, hesitantly assigning myself a B minus. I still looked decent for a middle-aged guy, and though I had experienced some stress related weight loss I actually considered it a plus. But the spreading furrows from the corners of my eyes brought down my overall grade. My auburn hair was still full and, well, auburnish, and my eyes clear. When viewed objectively I thought I looked okay. It was the internals that were a mess. I could no longer remember the last time I felt unburdened. Even the origins of my morning rituals were lost to antiquity. Brush my teeth, urinate, gargle, shower, dry off, brush my hair, take a vitamin. . . blah, blah, blah. In more lucid moments I understood these supposed burdens to be a good bit of what husbandhood/fatherhood was all about. Indeed it was what I had signed on for; maintaining a stable household and creating a safe environment for the kids while planning for the future. And while I love being a father, and (much of the time) had loved being a husband, only recently had I come to appreciate the intensity of my rut and the attendant boredom. Childhood memories revolving around the intense monotony that accompanied long car trips and the tedium of clothes shopping trips with my mother were easily recalled, but those times didn't hold a candle to the torpidity I had come to experience in my adult life. In the moment, lest I be overcome by my mirrored image, for sanity's sake I stopped staring at myself and returned to my morning ablutions, making a mental note to apologize to my Mom for my being an ass while she was trying to shop.

By the time I was ready to go to work I carried little hope that my day would hold anything more promising than a stray phone call from a new client or the usual busywork passed down from on high. While the best part of my day was coming home to the boys, dwelling on the drudgery of my time between leaving and returning home slowed my steps and movements. Grudgingly I pulled on my pants one leg at a time, awkwardly hopping around to avoid stepping on our border collie's tail as she bounced around me in full attention-seeking mode.

Though mostly emotionally retarded, it was apparent even to me that I had succumbed to the belief that life no longer held many surprises. Well, at least not the personal kind. The kind that have nothing to do with government secrets, the stock market, or international affairs. Because while there always seemed to be a new war or famine with which to concern myself; gone forever were first kisses, spontaneous travel, and the unexpected physical and mental challenges that seemed to regularly present themselves when I was younger. No more love letters. Even my morning stiffy, though still appreciated for its dogged regularity, could feel

3

somewhat too usual. What was not appreciated was the lack of opportunity to satisfy its insistence.

I bent over to tie my shoes while it occurred to me that all the decisions I had made prior to now had led to this singular, crappy moment. Here to a sexless marriage and a wife who by her own admission been pissed off at me for at least eight years. (On the bright side I had a job with few opportunities left for advancement, a reality which actually worked to reduce my stress level.) Had my expectations been too high? Was I lacking ambition and/or drive? Did I have a spare shoelace to replace the one I just broke?

Dressed and girded, I made my way down the stairs and into the kitchen. The house was quiet. Our boys, Trevor and Alex, had already been shuffled onto the bus by their mother and were on their way to school. Despite everything that seemed to be going wrong, Trevor and Alex represented the antithesis, and occupied the best part of my soul. I'm sure Kim felt the same. The poison of our difficulties would not easily leak into that relationship. Earlier I had awakened the boys and, by routine and mutual agreement, handed them off to their mother after they were dressed. I then returned to bed to catch a few more minutes of shuteye. In the family room Kim was asleep on the family room couch. The family room had become her bedroom and the couch her bed. It had also become her office, her arts and crafts area, her entertainment center, and her escape from me. For the last two or three years she had only slept in our marital bed when she felt sorry for me, or when she needed to use the alarm clock. At some point she discovered her cell phone rendered the same service as the alarm clock and so no longer needed to set foot in our bedroom except to get dressed. It had not always been so. Before the boys were born, and for some years thereafter, much of our marriage was spent in anticipation of being alone together. But things began to change when the care of small children began to chew into our alone time. To alleviate the situation Kim took a cue from prior generations of mothers and established an early bed time. Even if we didn't have sex we at least could relax together. But despite her efforts we still managed to lose track of each other. Things slip away when you're not paying attention.

This morning I chose not to wake Kim before leaving for work. It was easier than getting her up and faking our way through a discussion of the day to come. Rather than go through the motions of two people who aren't sure if the other really gives a damn, I snuck out to the garage as quietly as I could. Though the sound of the garage door opening would most likely alert her to my exit it probably wouldn't matter. We had become somewhat impervious to one another.

I drove south to my office in Florence, Kentucky, using the travel time to unproductively dwell on our situation. We lived in the northern reaches of Cincinnati, about twenty-five miles from work, so I had time during the forty-minute commute to contemplate life and its mysteries. I would have had even more time if the snow from the day before had not been plowed so efficiently by the county and city workers.

Part of me was certain that Kim and I still cared about each other, and on many levels. I was sure that had either of us died from some debilitating disease or in a fiery car crash the surviving partner would have been genuinely sad. It was the small things that presented a problem. The niceties we still managed to bestow upon one another no longer flowed from the desire to display affection and caring. Instead, they had become the perfunctory behavior of two people who once cared for each other but who were now just struggling to remain civil. Kim, a nurse by profession, spent her days helping her father take care of her ailing mother and ferrying the boys from activity to activity. I spent mine hiding out at the bank. While I encouraged Kim to return to nursing, I simultaneously (and somewhat hypocritically) appreciated the fact that she handled all matters at home, leaving me free to do other things. At the same time I resented her lack of financial contribution and she, quite naturally, was similarly annoyed by my self-serving resentment. Indeed, Kim maintained that one of the core reasons for her lack of desire, at least for me, was financial pressure, even though our somewhat weak monetary situation had been a hallmark of our marriage since its inception. Only later did I come to understand that she was intentionally holding something back from me so not to be hurtful, and that perhaps even she didn't fully understand her reasons for no longer wanting me.

Kim had always been a head turner, and I still found her alluring despite a concerted effort not to. Years of gymnastics, beginning at an early age, had sculpted Kim's thin frame and had

5

made her strong and though she regularly denied it, two pregnancies had failed to ruin her figure. She had changed in other ways, however. Or so I thought. While I would not describe Kim as overly adventurous, in her younger years she had been more open minded and daring than the person still asleep in our family room. And during the last few years Kim's tendency to agoraphobia had become dominant and seemed to blot out her flirtatious nature. Rarely did we go out socially, and she began to reveal how her feelings had evolved to the point that she was unbearably uncomfortable with men admiring her physique. Clueless to the reasons for her discomfort, I spent an inordinate amount of time dwelling on the subject and discussing it with my shrink, Therapist Jim. When regaled with tales of my rejection and frustration, he countered with questions about our relationship and past experiences. To me, he was "the ultimate" shrink, brutally honest and a tad foul-mouthed, at least for a professional counselor. I liked him from day one. Under questioning Therapist Jim reassured me that I was not going through a mid-life crisis, a condition of which Kim had regularly accused me of suffering. After all, my age put me squarely in the middle of my expected life span. She had only to put two and two together and a mid-life crisis was an obvious explanation for my over-active libido and the desire to regularly prove my virility. The conversation with Therapist Jim went something like this:

Me: "Well, Kim says one of the reasons she's afraid to have sex with me is that if we do have sex then I will want even more, at which point she'll be having more sex, which is exactly what she doesn't want."
Therapist Jim: "Hmmmm... Does that sound rational to you?"
Me: "Well, yeah, in a way. But....in another way no, not really. Like, I enjoy steak, right? And I would definitely eat more steak, you know, given the opportunity. So I guess I see her point there. But I doubt the steakhouse owners would be upset if I ordered more steak. In fact, they'd probably take it as a complement that I liked their meat enough to want more."
Therapist Jim: "Yes, one would think so, wouldn't one? You know, Jason, I think you should ask yourself, 'How is it my problem that she won't sleep with me?'"

Me: "Well, isn't it obvious? It's my problem because I'm horny and she won't sleep with me, and her not sleeping with me doesn't make me any less horny."

Therapist Jim: "Do you think it's possible you're using sex as a way to mask some other, deeper feelings of loss?"

Me: "Nope."

Therapist Jim: "Really? It's not possible you've experienced the realization that you're not number one in Kim's thoughts? That perhaps you've taken a back seat to someone else in her life?"

Me: "Nope. Well, I mean, how the hell do you even know if you're number one in someone's life? Or, who that number one person might be?"

Therapist Jim: "There's a simple way to figure that out. You say Kim spends a lot of time at her parent's house helping out with her mother. Ask yourself, if you and Kim's mother were in a burning building and she could only save one of you—whom would she save?"

Me: "Hmmm... Probably her Mom?"

Therapist Jim: "Okay, then. Doesn't that tell you that you're no longer number one in her life, and even though you may not have thought about it in those terms that, deep down, you knew it anyway and that you're really suffering?"

Me: "What the fuck?"

Therapist Jim: "Yes, exactly. What the fuck?"

Therapist Jim had forced me into an unpleasant revelation. He never beat around the bush, perhaps because he felt I lacked the mental acuity to arrive at these conclusions on my own. Or maybe he was just being respectful of my time. Regardless, I was paying him to side with me and so expected his support, and I suppose I was getting it, but Therapist Jim's buoyant tone did little to counteract the gut-wrenching pain that accompanied the epiphany. The experience taught me how big a deal therapists make about your spouse being number one in your life, and focusing their allegiance on the immediate family—an observation reinforced during marriage counseling a few days later, when Therapist Number Two asked if I wanted to share that revelation with my wife. I agreed, and when I recounted the burning building scenario, pointing out that I believed Kim would save her mother first, the following conversation ensued:

7

Therapist #2: "So, Kim. Who would you save?"
Kim: "My mother, of course! She's in a wheel chair, for God's sake. Jason's able bodied and should be able to save himself."
Therapist #2: "So, then, Jason is absolutely right?"
Kim: "Well, yes, I guess so."

At the time I wasn't sure how much more proof I needed that our marriage was in deep trouble, but apparently that was all the proof Therapist Number Two needed. She abruptly ended the session and referred us to another therapist whom she believed better qualified to deal with our perverse situation. She explained he was a "full-on" psychiatrist, not just a doctor of psychology like her. The psychiatrist specialized in psychoanalysis and sex therapy. She did not elaborate on the sex therapist aspect of the referral which, given the subject matter, I found disappointing and somewhat anti-climactic. But I imagined it had something to do with Kim no longer wanting to do "it" with me. She did explain that she felt it possible to save the marriage, but only with another therapist at the helm. Kim and I were understandably stunned by the referral and subsequent confession from Therapist Number Two that she felt unqualified to deal with our situation. I mean, how fucked up were we that eight years of college education proved unequal to the task? To make matters worse, she cut short our time, but under the circumstances I felt it bad form to ask that the hourly fee be prorated, and so did not bring it up. Instead, we left in a daze and had an uncomfortable lunch at Cracker Barrel, arriving home shortly before the boys got off the school bus. It was not a good day.

My commute complete, I concluded my musings as I arrived in the parking lot at the main branch of Northern Kentucky Bank and Trust, where I exited my vehicle and hoofed it to my office on the second floor. At the time I was Chief Credit Officer for the bank, which was a fairly small operation consisting of twenty-two branches and about 175 employees. I had been in banking nearly twenty years before accepting this new position three years prior, leaving a larger bank for what I considered a step up the corporate ladder. Being Chief Credit Officer was often simultaneously boring and exciting. The boredom was comprised of the minutiae of credit

8

policy, federal regulations, and making sure the bank didn't go bankrupt by making shitty loans. The exciting part was visiting customers. Factories and work sites was fascinating. It's like watching a show on how things are made.

My office looked exactly as I had left it, except the trash had been emptied by the cleaning elves that came every night after the humans departed. The elves had also vacuumed and shampooed the carpet. As far as I knew, no one had ever seen the elves and they were somewhat of a mystery. By the same token, no one doubted their existence as the trash cans were empty every morning and the carpet immaculate. What was not empty was the desk occupied by my administrative assistant, Emily. I believed Emily to be in her early-twenties, but for reasons unknown had never asked. She seemed a diligent-enough worker for someone in that age group, which in my experience meant spending about equal amounts of time working and texting or updating one's status on various and sundry social networks. Though not quite as punctual as my previous administrative assistant, nor was she as severe in appearance or manner. And this morning she didn't even look hung over.

"Morning, Em," I said cheerfully. Emily Snodgrass had been with me for a year, since the retirement of my last assistant, the ruthlessly efficient and imperious Rita Standwoegen. During Rita's reign it was understood that she knew everything that went on at the bank and that nobody wanted her as an enemy. Luckily, she took me under her protective wing early on and saved my ass a number of times from what potentially could have been career ending decisions. How I made it as far as I had without her was beyond me, and in the end I was sorry to see her retire. Things never ran as smoothly after her departure. Rita had spoiled me and now poor Emily was forced to stand in her shadow, forever being held to an impossibly high standard.

"Morning, Jason." Emily smiled up at me. It had taken three months of constant reminders to get her to address me by my first name. "Mr. Kubrick" sounded so god-awfully formal, and hearing it from someone who was (probably) in her early twenties made me feel old, a classification I decided to resist until I turned eighty, at least.

I hung up my overcoat, the chill of the frigid January

morning still clinging to the wool, and poured myself a cup of coffee. When Rita Standwoegen was with me I never got my own coffee. She was old-school in this regard, and each morning brought in my first cup. Rita was always at her desk before I arrived, and she made it a point to know my schedule—two items of discipline Emily had yet to master. In my defense, I have never *required* anyone to bring me coffee, but I considered it a perk that Rita did it as a matter of course even over my objections. But Emily was easy on the eyes. Everyone said so.

Monday was full of regular morning meetings. I don't know if this tradition evolved from the desire to get the week planned first thing or from a need to appear busy while the staff focused their attention after the weekend. Though I found them of little value, over time I had adopted a laissez-faire attitude toward these weekly meetings, eventually letting go of the resistance I had felt as a younger man. Listening to others drone on when more productive things were going undone was something for which I had little tolerance. But the preoccupation with my marriage status had thrown me off my game and needed to make a conscious effort to remain fully engaged, to be a "team player." Still, while my willfully positive sense of engagement helped make the morning meeting schedule less oppressive, it did little to make time move faster.

During the second teleconference I felt the need to visit the restroom. I had learned over time that, due to the miracles inherent in modern technology, it was possible to leave a teleconference without anyone knowing I was gone so long as I timed it properly. So I waited, knowing that at the appropriate moment I could put my speaker phone on mute and walk out, but also that I would need to act swiftly and decisively.

"Hey, Em." I called out as I opened my door.

"Yes, Jason?" said Emily, looking up from her computer screen where she was either reviewing daily overdrafts or shoe shopping online. I couldn't be sure which.

"We need to go to Plan Charlie."

"You bet" she replied matter-of-factly, then rose from her desk and seated herself in the chair I had just vacated.

"I'll be right back."

Under the directives of Plan Charlie, Emily would sit in my

office until I returned or until the meeting appeared to be heading in a direction where my input was required. At that point she would, as swiftly as possible, alert me so I could return to the phone. Our system: Alpha stood for coffee/snack, Bravo for private phone call, and Charlie for bathroom break. We had developed the code over the last year and it generally went off without a hitch. Emily always knew where to find me, and I never left without my cell phone. For the system to work Emily needed to pay close attention to the teleconference which wasn't an easy task and, at times, could be a stumbling block. In such instances the system could quickly break down. For her part Rita would never have allowed me to slack off in this way. Had she been a willing participant, however, Rita's diligence would certainly have assured a smooth functioning of the system. Emily, on the other hand, had been trained in a different way and at a different time. She viewed our system as an inside joke, albeit a stressful one if she found herself caught off guard.

I had come to believe that Emily Snodgrass was responsible for my wake-up boners. Granted, it could just have been a morning spike in testosterone or the result of an urgent need to urinate, but lately I had caught myself daydreaming about her. Despite not knowing her age I had learned a lot about Emily during our year together. According to the office rumor mill Emily was a tad promiscuous and not very choosy about her boyfriends. This, of course, wasn't necessarily a long-term problem. Being, I assumed, somewhere in her early-twenties gave her the opportunity to make bad choices and still have plenty of time to recover. And though the slight air of sultriness she exuded was not lost on me or on the other men and women on the second floor, my overriding desire to not further destroy my family or tarnish my career was enough to prevent me from acting on fantasies which had become more persistent as my marriage headed south. Besides, as far as I knew she was probably around half my age. For better or worse Rita Standwoegen, with her all-business demeanor and style of dress, had never inspired me this way, which of course made it easier to keep my nose to the grindstone. For all I knew Rita may have been a raging nymphomaniac; but, if true, that particular idiosyncrasy never manifested itself at work. She may even have had a great body, but it was impossible to tell what was really going on beneath her padded woolen jackets and multi-layers of silk and cotton. All I can say with certainty is that Rita was not fat.

I returned from the bathroom to find Emily sitting patiently in my chair, staring at the phone and listening as intently as she could. She was dressed in a sleeveless cotton blouse that nicely hugged her curves, and a pair of polyester trousers. Her hair was pulled back behind her ears, which sported four piercings each. Her only physical flaw appeared to be a minor case of acne she had yet to shake from her teen years.

"No problem, Jason," she assured me as she vacated my chair. "They never noticed you were gone."

"Story of my life." I returned to my seat with mixed emotions about not being missed during my five to ten-minute interlude.

"Let me know if you need anything else" she said, and strolled out of my office and back to her desk.

My timing impeccable, I sat down just as it was my turn to weigh in on a loan request. After sagely imparting words of wisdom on the client's chance for success I was greeted by an unnerving and resounding silence. I was convinced that either everyone was enraptured by my credit musings or that they, like I, had reached the limits of patience but were afraid to respond lest any stray comment keep the meeting going for a fraction of a second longer than necessary. Assuming it was the latter, I signaled I had nothing else to add and suggested we end the call. The wave of relief rolling back to me through the phone was palpable.

It was now lunchtime, and though I had piles of work to peruse and act upon I decided instead to go to the gym. Sitting at my desk all morning had put me in a fog and I needed the exercise to recharge my batteries and release some stress. I grabbed my suit jacket and veered out into the maze of cubicles, informing Emily of my destination as I slid past her desk and waived to my boss, Stephen Keefe, on the way out. The distance to the gym was minimal but to get there I had to maneuver through one of the busiest intersections in Florence, which at least tripled the time it would have taken the average crow. In the days of my youth Florence had been a sleepy burg, its only claim to fame being a water tower with the phrase "Florence Y'All" written in bold white lettering. The tower originally advertised "Florence Mall" but had been changed, I assumed, either by the city fathers or by some enterprising and, most likely, inebriated high school students. I wasn't sure which and never thought to ask or investigate further. The only time I, or most Ohioans, had the opportunity to enjoy the folksy play on words was when we passed it on the highway. In those days the mall itself was not a shopping destination for any self-respecting Buckeye, but in years hence Florence had become a thriving business hub and now the traffic sucked.

I arrived at the gym in due course, scanning the room for motivation while noting I was not alone in my desire for lunch time release. Luckily for me, there were a goodly number of attractive women casting about who would adequately serve as a mental steroid for the day's exercise experience. Despite its awful name, The Fitness Outlet was a modern and well-kept facility with a lot of regulars and on the way back to the locker room I was greeted with nods and winks by a number of gym rats who either maintained the same workout schedule as mine or, perhaps, never left the gym.

I quickly changed out of my suit. The pace of the clothing change due not only to the fact I allotted myself just one hour for lunch, there was also the matter of the Old Naked Bastard. True to his assigned moniker he was, indeed, old and naked, and always seemed to be so. He was also astoundingly creepy, sitting as he was on the edge of his towel in his birthday suit, saggy testicles hanging off the edge of the bench in full view of everyone unfortunate enough to have to use the restroom. Judging by the leftover cream on his face, I assumed and hoped he had just finished shaving as any alternatives were too horrible to imagine. But for now he was just sitting naked, balls descending toward the floor, watching ESPN on the flat screen with rapt attention. Having no desire to engage Old Naked Bastard in conversation or catch his eye in any way, I surreptitiously slipped into my gear and snuck out of the room.

I took a spot on the floor to stretch, an act that allows for five or ten minutes of self-reflection and work out planning. It occurred to me, during the self-reflective portion of the stretching, that I could not continue in my marriage in the same manner to which I had become accustomed. I needed do something, and soon. But, since I could do nothing about my marriage at that moment, I headed to the darkened media room where I could run on the treadmill and watch a movie.

The stationary running/biking/stair-stepping room was kept

13

dark to make the movie easier to watch and always seemed to be a few degrees warmer than the open areas of the gym. For this reason an oscillating fan was kept running at all times in one of the corners. So, between the noise of the fan and the noise of the machines in use by the stationary runners, bikers, and stair-steppers, it was traditionally difficult to hear the dialogue in the movie, a problem overcome by the display of subtitles at the bottom of the screen. Regardless, I found it difficult to run on the treadmill whilst simultaneously reading the text. This distraction caused my balance to shift unexpectedly, doubly so if the movie happened to be an action flick, which was the case at the moment. Things were flying around the screen and getting blown up. The otherwise simple act of shifting my focus between reading the dialogue and watching the screen was not so simple and the loss of balance resulted in a lot of squeaking as my running feet wandered off the treadmill and got caught between the moving belt and the stationary frame of the machine. For my tell-tale squeaks I received embarrassed smiles and an occasional expression of concern from other fellow stationary travelers. Still, I managed to finish three miles in due course without sustaining permanent physical injury. By the end I was good and sweaty with fresh endorphins lightening my mood and clearing my head. Now I was ready to take on the more strenuous battle of wills that occurred whenever free weights and my ass muscles came to grips.

I felt fortunate but also slightly disappointed that a number of bars and weights remained unused, thus allowing me to pursue the second half of my workout instead of cutting it short. Steeling for the light-headedness and shortness-of-breath awaiting me, I loaded the bar with weights and proceeded to torture myself. It was a love/hate relationship. I carried on with the dead lifts not for personal motivation, but for the desire not to shame myself in front of the attractive pair of women working out in close proximity. Involved as they were in their own routine and conversation, they probably hadn't even noticed me. Still, as I recovered my breath between sets, I was given the opportunity to admire them in the mirror without appearing too perverted.

After showering and changing I headed back to the office. Outside the car it was cold but sunny and I entertained the idea of playing hooky for the rest of the day, but my pile of work was calling me. The natural high with which I was rewarded for a strenuous workout could be accessed for good or for evil, either making me a more productive employee or, alternatively, someone who could enjoy a sunny afternoon away from work. In either case I knew Kim was home alone, which eliminated that option as a location where I could comfortably ditch work for the balance of the day. I loathed the thought of trying to make conversation and attempting to fill the empty space with the sound of our voices. Nor did I imagine she would relish the idea either. Of late we had adopted an avoidance policy, which largely involved neither touching each other nor saying anything which could later be used in a court of law.

Bearing this in mind, I entered the bank committed to productivity and to finishing the review of at least two loan requests before the end of the day. By late afternoon, however, my energy level was flagging, as was my ability to concentrate. As a result, the words and numbers laid out all over my desk began to blur and I found myself reflexively checking the status of the stock market and surfing the Internet for interesting news stories, or at least news stories that were more interesting than actually working. These supremely unproductive activities were occasionally interrupted by calls from other bank employees or by questions from Emily. Compared to the demands of other employees, Emily's interruptions were less stressful as they mostly involved questions about what should be done with various pieces of paper that had managed to find a way to her desk. I mostly welcomed the interruptions, viewing them as an opportunity to do something useful and, despite my lethargy, by the end of the day I had actually completed the review of one loan request and helped Emily clear off a corner of her desk. After wishing Emily and Stephen a good night, I withdrew from the second floor to my trusty Malibu for the ride home. It was after five-thirty and the sun was sinking quickly as the evening air grew colder. Entering the highway I gunned the engine and merged with the northbound traffic, employing the "smile and wave" technique I had learned from my father as a sure fire way to abate the ire of other motorists as I wedged my car between theirs. Soon I was pleasantly positioned in a lane where nearly everyone was traveling at a speed we all agreed was appropriate.

15

Kim and I enjoyed a strong relationship for at least ten years. I can still remember how good it felt to be with her before everything soured, and the memory of the gusto of my feelings for her just five years earlier seemed to intensify the sense of isolation and emptiness that had become the norm. That gusto had eliminated the ache and yearning common to bachelorhood, something which cannot adequately be defined until the feeling is gone. As I drove along I reflected on what it felt like to drive with Kim sitting next to me, always wanting to reach out and touch her. It was so good to sit together with her hand on my leg, wondering if she felt the same. Such were the simple pleasures that had been taken for granted. Only too late would I realize that physical contact was not the cause of our connection; it was the reflection and reinforcement of it. In time, and partially due to our inattentiveness, the ties that bound us together began to fade until all that was left was the memory of happiness. The resulting emptiness was devastating, a painful reminder of lost love and joy.

Only very recently had I come to understand this, but by then there was little I could do to alter the situation. When I still believed our marriage could be salvaged, I dragged Kim to the marriage counselor despite her objections in the hope that an expert could fix what we seemed powerless to repair. But while therapy helped us to identify our problems—and offered me a number of darkly humorous anecdotes to share and recall later—it also, ironically, served to sharpen our differences. As a result we became even more aware of how far apart we had grown. Still, part of me believed we could find a way to stay together, and that Kim desired the same thing. But as I felt our relationship slipping away I kept reaching back for something solid to hold onto, not realizing that what I was trying to grab had disappeared. Since the beginning I had relied on Kim's guidance and strength whenever we drifted into rough waters. Now, without her guidance, even small pleasantries—like sharing a greeting when we entered the house—were subsequently eliminated. We kept up appearances for the boys and for our neighbors, but our life together had been hollowed out. Things were not going to end well. Dueling pistols at dawn would have provided a more honorable conclusion.

It was dark by the time I arrived home, and I prepared myself for the conversation with Kim which now was long overdue. She always said that if we ever got divorced that I would have to be the one who asked, but neither of us was guilt free.

CHAPTER TWO

I glanced around the neighborhood while the garage door finished opening. My neighbors were walking their dogs, getting their mail, and shoveling the leftover snow from the last storm. Ours was a cookie cutter community of medium sized, two-story homes on eighth-acre lots. I had grown up in similar neighborhoods. Kim, on the other hand, had grown up with horses and acreage and frequently suggested we move to such a place. The closeness of our neighbors made her claustrophobic, and when she wasn't talking overtly about moving she still made a point of showing me pictures of mini-farms for sale. None of the mini-farms we could afford were located in our school district, where the boys were thriving in their respective schools. I would remind Kim of this as a way to slow her roll, so to speak, but while I was intrigued with the thought of living in the "country," I was not enthralled with the idea and had grown tired of talking about it. Kim knew this but she was equally tired of living in a subdivision, and within a few hours or days the subject would come up again.

I could hear the television as I walked through the door that separated the garage from the foyer leading to the family room. By the sound of it, the show blaring from the set was something from the Nickelodeon lineup. I was okay with this. The only channel safer for preteen viewing was Disney. My older boy, Trevor, had taken to watching the occasional show involving frank depictions of sex and violence, like *Law and Order* and *The Secret Lives of Teenagers*. While I understood he was hurtling uncontrollably into puberty, I still found it difficult to get comfortable with him viewing this type of subject matter. But, not wanting to be the asshole, rather than banning these shows Kim and I would, on occasion, watch them with him so we could intervene should anything become too graphic. We were also available to answer questions, should he feel the need to inquire. Trevor was a good student and talented athlete and appeared to be adjusting well to his new body hair and burgeoning attraction to the fairer sex. We just wanted to make sure he understood that there were crazies out in the world who were doing things most everyone else considered abnormal. And that he shouldn't try these things at home. At least not until he had his own place.

Both of the boys greeted me as I walked in and set my briefcase down next to the couch. Although their greetings were not as effusive as they had been at a younger age, I was pleased they at least still acknowledged my homecomings. I don't know the algorithm that determines the size of the greeting a parent receives based on the age of the child, but I am sure it exists and that it demonstrates a diminishing return over time. The running-up-to-Daddy-for-a-hug upon his return home had been replaced with a sullen "Hey, Dad," and a determination not to change focus or alter their line of vision. At age ten Alex still displayed a bit more joy at the greeting than his older brother, but that joy was quickly fading. I blamed peer pressure.

"Hey, boys!" I sounded a bit loud as I battled the TV for auditory supremacy. "Can you turn that down a little?" The show *Drake and Josh* was on the flat screen, a show I enjoyed watching at least as much as the boys. It was well written and funny and both main characters had excellent comedic timing. Trevor was lying on the couch and Alex had positioned himself on a horizontal axis across the arms of the recliner with the foot rest fully extended despite the fact that it wasn't serving its intended function.

"Sure, Dad." Alex responded for both of them. He currently had control of the remote and therefore the power to grant my request. The battle for the clicker must have occurred before I got home and Alex seemed firmly in charge which, as the younger brother, must have been quite a coup. He turned the volume lower as I removed my overcoat and hung it in the closet.

"Where's Mom?" I asked. And then, "Alex, please don't lie in the chair like that. It'll loosen the frame." I don't know why I bothered to explain the 'why' behind the request. Alex wasn't going to care until he owned his own furniture, and maybe not even then.

"She's upstairs getting our soccer stuff ready." Trevor's voice wafted over the back of the couch. I received no verbal response from Alex, but he did shift his position in the chair, which I took as a sign he concurred with Trevor's response to my query. I didn't bother to ask them why they weren't getting their own soccer stuff ready, assuming Kim had grown tired of asking them and finally just did it herself. This winter the boys were playing in an indoor soccer league and were on the same team, a small blessing when it came to scheduling. But the fact Kim was getting their things together indicated she was probably already in a bad mood. She would be angry at them but also at herself for having given in to their goldbricking. As I was in no hurry to verify my theory on Kim's emotional status, I wandered into the kitchen to examine the contents of the refrigerator. I stared at the full shelves for nearly a minute, but nothing beckoned to me so I took Kim's footsteps on the staircase as my cue to head up to the bedroom and change out of my suit. On the landing I managed to gracefully skirt around her and the net bags full of gear that she was carrying in each hand.

"Hey," I tried to sound cheerful.

"Hey back." Her greeting was just a smidge less sullen than the one I had received from the boys five minutes prior.

"What time's practice?" I had actually forgotten the boys had practice that evening but wasn't about to admit it. Practices for the indoor league were few in number as both space and time were limited.

"6:30. I thought we'd just order pizza when we get home." Kim and I had become accustomed to using as few words as necessary to convey information to each other and had grown competitive in this effort. Whoever had to request additional information or ask the other to repeat themselves lost the round.

"No problem," was my response. It was almost 6:30 and the three of them were heading out the door. Had practice been a little later I might have gone with them, but the rush to leave eliminated the option and left me free to enjoy a couple hours of quiet. What would I do with this gift of time? Masturbation was an option. I felt a bit horny, although I wasn't quite sure why. A pile of dirty clothes demanded attention as well. I could multitask.

The minimalist nature of interaction between Kim and me had become the norm, and on any other day the time spent together

20

after soccer practice and pizza would be equally as trifling. But that night would be different. Unexpected horniness aside, I was determined to bring the dreadful existence of our marriage to some sort of resolution. As I had for months, I agonized over the potential harm a divorce could have on the boys. Alex and Trevor seemed to perennially exist in some critical stage of development and, in my untrained opinion, upsetting their respective apple carts would most certainly result in at least one of them becoming a serial killer or a computer programmer, or both. From a purely financial perspective, of course, computer programming was superior to serial killing although both professions seemed to lead their victims to a life of loneliness and socially awkward behavior. I can't remember the exact tipping point at which my unhappiness finally outweighed theirs, but I do remember it took a long time to get there. As a child of divorce I knew how much it sucked to be that kid, and though I endeavored to keep rationalizations to a minimum and for all intents and purposes I seemed to turn out okay. At the very least, I did not spend my time hiding body parts; nor was I trapped under a desk in a cube farm running miles of cable and breathing dust mites. I hoped they'd be okay, and knew the chance of their getting through a divorce relatively unscathed would dramatically increase as long as Kim and I could find a way to be civil. Still, I wasn't confident. Outside of television I had yet to witness an amicable divorce—least of all between my own parents. But the chips would fall where they would. All either of us could do was pick up pieces as best we could.

The house emptied of humanity before I finished changing, so I took a moment to relish the peace before embarking on my labors. The dog and cat were still in the house, but they were keeping to themselves at the moment. I imagined they were enjoying the quiet as well. Once changed, I went back downstairs and started in on the laundry. With winter came bigger clothes, which translated into a larger volume of dirty clothes than the summer months, and the ever-present piles of dirty garments were testament to my belief that the boys went through at least three outfits daily. It was astounding. I sorted the newest batch, put in a new load after switching the first one to the dryer, and then took the dry clothes to the family room to be folded while I watched television. I had not forgotten my pledge to multitask, however, and snuck off to the bedroom for the requisite time. Afterwards I treated myself to a beer and a stick of string cheese.

It was habit to watch TV while I folded. It made me feel less lazy than just plopping in front of the boob tube doing nothing productive at all. After cruising through the million or so channels available from our local cable service, I settled on a local news station. Due to the cheap, regular attempts to manipulate my. emotions through embellishment and overblown teasers, I normally can't bear to watch the local news, nor even the national and international news. Part of me is passively waiting for televised news to die out altogether, but it was January and I wanted to check on the weather.

"Looks like another big storm is set to hit the Tri-State!" said the weatherman somewhat gleefully, his jaw set as he stared into the camera. In Cincinnati weathermen and women can get as frenzied over two inches of snow as they do over a blizzard. I was sure it was the same face he would use were he announcing the advent of a nuclear war. "More on this story after the break"; and the station went immediately to commercial. I found the anchorman's deadly serious delivery sickening, but decided to wait out the break to see if we were really in for a storm or if his announcement was designed only to keep me viewing through the commercial. It turned out to be the latter, of course.

After finishing the cheese stick I dove into the laundry basket. Each folded piece of clothing was assigned to a pile on the couch, with, one pile for each human in the house. The couch-cum-folding table had a flowered print covering that I detested. Kim had picked it out as she had every other piece of furniture in the house, with the exception of my lounge chair, which had received few compliments over the years. Perhaps it was a tad hideous, but I felt its comfort made up for its unsightliness. While I was physically present for the purchase most of the furniture in the house, years earlier I came to understand that Kim asking for my opinion was a mere formality. The final decision was always hers. I assume the same scenario plays out in most marriages, unless the husband is a metrosexual or closeted gay. I also believe the same holds true for weddings, and that that's probably for the best. I can't imagine trying to choose flower arrangements or center pieces without my skin crawling, though I do maintain the capacity to pick out a nice suit or tuxedo.

I was deep into the basket when the anchor announced the resumption of the news, or what the producers considered "news." It turned out the weather crisis consisted entirely of a forty-percent chance of half an inch of snow which, I guess, would really be a crisis if there were orange groves in Cincinnati. Pronouncements such as these usually meant we'd either get six inches of snow overnight, or the city would wake up to find itself in the middle of an Indian summer. Perhaps I'm becoming a crotchety old man, but anecdotal evidence suggests weather reporting has become less accurate as meteorologists increasingly rely on computer modeling for the forecast. It is an irony that the person reporting the weather will tell the audience that the high temperature of the day will be thirty-five degrees, even as they report the current temperature at forty. Regardless, I received the information with a grain of salt and promptly filed it in the "useless" folder of my brain, next to claims of impending, catastrophic global warming and half the stock market predictions I read throughout the day. After completing the task of folding and working myself into a lather over the current state of the media, I sank into my ugly chair and dozed off.

The sound of Kim and the boys returning from practice woke me from my catnap. The boys were arguing over who was better at "bending it like Beckham"; and, judging by the clenched look on Kim's face the disagreement started long before they got home.

"You don't curve it as well as I do!" Trevor yelled at his younger brother.

"Yes I do!" Returned Alex, with like volume and ferocity. "You're dumb. Your kicks always go straight!"

"Boys! Get upstairs and change into your pajamas," I bellowed louder than the situation required. In my defense they had startled me from a good nap.

"Thanks." Kim sounded exasperated. "They've been doing that all the way home. Did you order pizza?"

"No, sorry." I admitted. "I fell asleep."

"Fine; I'll do it myself," She responded with the same level of exasperation she displayed concerning the boys' argument. If Kim had not been abiding by our current habit of conversational terseness it's likely her statement would have been more biting. I imagined something like "Fine, you lazy asshole! I have to do everything else around here so why should I expect that you could do something as simple as order pizza?!" A year or two earlier I might have insisted on ordering the pizza, a small courtesy on my part, but not now. And it sounds awful but the reality was that I no longer cared if she was pissed off and no longer felt any responsibility for it. After years of bearing the brunt of her frustration, whatever it happened to be, I had learned to let it go. It wasn't that I didn't have any fight left in me; I just didn't see the point. There would always be one more task I should have undertaken (or taken over); one more gift I should have given; or, one more consideration I failed to make. I could do little more to bring her joy and, true or not, felt Kim held me responsible for both her happiness and mine. She never said this directly, of course. She found other ways to express her displeasure, like making sure I was in earshot of conversations in which I was the object of her derision. The upshot is I think she had reached a place where she was so unhappy that there was no way to keep it inside of her, and since her complaints appeared to be falling on deaf ears she did what she could to get through to me. Take this conversation from a party we attended a year earlier:

"You're right." Kim's volume amplified as I shot past her. "All that fairy tale crap we read when we were young girls is useless. There are no princes out there waiting to save us, not that we need them at all." She meant 'men,' of course; or, more specifically, her husband.

Then there was the conversation she and I had a month earlier on the drive back from the grocery store:

"Dad said Mom is really worried about us, but he told her not to worry and that we'd be okay."

"Really? She's never said anything to me." I sounded like an ass, but I prefer the direct approach. If Kim was trying to get my take on the status of our marriage she could have just asked. I knew my snide response was unproductive, but it took me by surprise and I've never been sure how to respond to that type of comment regardless. She was just probing, after all; sticking her toe in the water to gauge the temperature; looking for something positive. But I found it tiresome. It wasn't in me to give her what she was looking

24

for, which was really just a ray of hope. I wasn't strong enough to give it to her and instead unwittingly put another nail in the coffin.

The boys dumped their gear on the floor as they came through the door and began scrounging around the kitchen for a snack. As the pizza was going to take a while I joined them in their hunt. We settled on apples, which I sliced while Trevor and Alex reluctantly gathered their things to take upstairs, a triumph, and I only had to ask three times. With the task complete, the boys gave me an overview of the evening's practice while Kim disappeared to another part of the house.

"Hey, Dad, can we watch *America's Favorite Singer?*" Trevor seemed earnest in his request.

"Yeah, Dad, they have all the losers tonight." Alex went on to explain a special addition of the show featuring singers who, perhaps, had an unusual style or were just terrible singers.

"C'mon guys, isn't there something better?" I said, feeling I was walking a tightrope. I had conflicting emotions about certain aspects of the show. There were some wonderful singers, but the mixed bag included the deluded and, yes, the appalling. There was also the issue of judges being rude to those auditioning. At times I cringed watching some misguided or daft dreamer sing on as the judges roared with laughter. If I couldn't talk them out of it I wouldn't have stopped the boys from watching, though the idea of their inevitable schadenfreude made me uncomfortable. Saved by the bell, the pizza arrived.

I rummaged through my pockets as I headed to the front door, our dog Spot underfoot, to find the pizza man waiting patiently on the porch. To the best of my knowledge Spot had never eaten pizza, but to him a strange human at the door was always cause for celebration. I paid for the pizza and returned to the family, happy to be out of the chill that flowed in with the pizza. Over my admittedly weak protests the four of us (Kim had reappeared) consumed the pizza in front of the boob tube, watching the worst of American Idol. But, it was as comfortable a dinner as any of late, punctuated as it was with laughter and "pass the pizza, please."

Dinner finished and the show over, I herded the boys to their bedrooms; rarely a quick process. The boys had learned, like generations of children before them, that bedtime could be delayed by simply moving at a snail's pace. At times this behavior could become pernicious, depending on the moods of everyone involved. On this evening, however, the boys were mercifully compliant and agreed to have their teeth brushed and pajamas on by the time I went up to kiss them goodnight. I gave them ten minutes to complete these tasks and, surprisingly, they were already in their respective beds and settling down by the time I arrived. They hadn't shared a bedroom for years. I, on the other hand, always had a sibling roommate growing up and, perhaps selfishly, wanted them to share the experience. With four bedrooms available, however, over time it seemed ridiculous to resist their requests for individual accommodations. I looked at them lying quietly and missed them. I missed them because I wouldn't see them again until morning, and I missed them because their lives were about to change dramatically and it would be my own selfishness that brought about that change. Could I be more of an ass? I wasn't sure, but Therapist Jim sounded sure of himself when I initially broached the subject.

Therapist Jim: "Do you think your boys are getting a good look at a healthy marriage?"
Me: "No, of course not."
Therapist Jim: "Do you think they might have a sense of what's going on between you and your wife. Do they notice you don't sleep together?"
Me: "Well, probably yes. How could they not?"
Therapist Jim: "Well, it's nice to see you're at least as observant as they are, but you need to ask yourself if you want them growing up thinking that this is what marriage is all about. If the answer to that question is yes, then don't change anything." (Therapist Jim sometimes made me feel stupid, although I don't think he did it on purpose even though at times I probably deserved it.)
Me, sounding stupid: "Of course I don't want that, but I don't want them devastated either. If only there was a third path."
Therapist Jim, sounding fatherly: "I believe you've tried the third path. It was marriage counseling. How'd that work out for you?"

His point was that I was running out of options. He knew that our original marriage counselor had called it quits and referred us out. He also knew I made it Kim's responsibility to make the appointment with the psychoanalyst sex therapist because I wanted to check her interest level in trying to work things out. Of course, it was no surprise that Kim's interest level hovered around zero. A month had passed since I handed the referral slip to her and an appointment had yet to be made. When it came to the boys, though, none of that seemed to matter. I couldn't rationalize away the pain they would experience and was already grieving as I kissed them goodnight.

"Goodnight, Dad."

"Goodnight boys. I love you." I stood in the hallway between their rooms so they both could hear me.

"Love you too." They responded almost in unison. I could feel tears building as I lingered in the hallway. I held them back but lingered for a little longer, not wanting to lose that moment.

Back in the family room some show was being ignored while Kim typed away on her laptop. I wasn't sure on what she was working. It could have been administrative tasks for the soccer league, for which she was secretary. Or it might have been Facebook. I didn't ask. Instead, I quizzed her about our marriage:

"Kim, do you find any joy in our marriage anymore?" Not groundbreaking but to the point.

Kim looked up from her computer, appearing to consider the point. I'm sure the abruptness of the inquiry took her by surprise. We had not agreed to talk about our marriage that night as we had at times in the past. And there had been nothing leading up to it, like an argument or a lunar eclipse. She would not have expected me to raise the question without there being an obvious reason for it. It seemed to take several minutes for her to respond.

"What do you mean?" She said softly, muttering under her breath.

"I mean…do you find any joy in our relationship? Do you smile when you think of me? Do you think I'm funny or charming anymore? Do you look forward to the time I get home from work or do you dread it? Ummm… I guess I'm asking what it is about our marriage that you feel may be worth saving." I did not raise my voice and tried instead to be as conversational as possible. It was dirty business.

After considering the question she finally responded, but didn't answer the question. "What about the kids? They make me happy."

"They make me happy too," I responded. And it was true, of course, but as I said the words I could feel my heart breaking, just like dozens of times before. And I could feel her heart break, just like dozens of times before. It was terrifying and I felt like I might throw up. "But what is it about me that makes you happy, or about us?" I ventured. "I want us to be honest about this. You've told me you that you lack desire for me. You never touch me. We don't sleep together and everything I do seems to piss you off. It's obvious I can't or don't give you what you need. I don't understand why you think we should stay together." I had never said this before. It was too painful to admit. I was sincere but lacked the manic earnestness that dominated prior conversations about our relationship, an earnestness sprung from the fear of losing Kim. But despite its omnipresence, that fear had diminished.

"I know things will get better," Kim volunteered. This was a stock response. She relayed the sentiment with the grim demeanor of someone whose home had just been hit by a tornado.

"But how will they get better? Have you made an appointment with the new shrink?" I knew she hadn't.

"No," she replied, knowing I realized that she probably had not made the call. "I'm not going through that again, Jason. It didn't solve anything and just made us angrier at each other."

"You're right." She was, too. I just didn't know if it was relevant anymore. "Then how do you propose that things will get better? I'm asking because the situation sucks. How do you suggest we make it better?"

"Time."

"Time? That's your answer? You think time will make you want me again?" I could feel my heart pounding in my chest. I was confused, sad and pissed off all at the same time. The passiveness of her strategy for a happier marriage made no sense to me, and yet I had no counter. Time may help you forgive and forget, but how does it heal problems that have yet to be identified? God knows we needed each other's understanding and forgiveness, but neither of us knew how to go about granting or receiving it. Back then those two things were just lights at the end of a very long tunnel.

"I can't live like this, Kim. I need a real relationship with my wife, like what we used to have. If we can't save our marriage, then

28

we need to let each other go. Don't you want something better for yourself, too? Don't you want to feel that passion again?"

"If you're talking about sex again, I'm sick of talking about it. Why can't we just accept that we're older and have kids and it can't be the same as before? Isn't having sex twice a week enough for you?"

"I'm not just talking about our sex life, Kim." I didn't bother to point out that sex twice weekly was more than we were currently having. I pressed on. "I'd be fine with no sex if I at least knew you were still interested in me, but I'm tired of being rejected. You pull away when I reach for your hand or try to touch you. I don't seem to know the rules anymore, but I do know that this isn't good anymore."

"And I'm tired of talking about it, Jason." And she did sound tired. "I've told you before that if you want a divorce, then you need to be the one to ask for it. I don't know how to fix this, Jason. I wish I did. There's more going on than I can put into words, but I don't want to hurt the boys."

"Look, I don't want to hurt the boys either. But I don't want them to think that this is what marriage should be. I don't think either of us want them to think that it's normal for a husband and wife to sleep in separate rooms, and I'm sure they see how unhappy we are." Suddenly I realized this had become the same old conversation repeated *ad nauseum*. We were back in the old loop.

When Kim responded she was angry, her voice low and barely audible. "It's better than divorce, which will hurt them far more than our fucked up marriage."

I was in a quandary. True, there's no simple way for anyone to attain happiness all the time, but neither was I willing to accept the status quo. I wanted the boys to have a normal, loving home, and I was frustrated that Kim and I didn't share the same point of view.

"All right then, if this is what it takes…then I am formally asking you for a divorce." I nearly choked on the words. It sounded so absurd I struggled not to laugh, and I might have had I not had to fight the bile rising in the back of my throat. Somewhere in the back of my mind I pictured myself getting down on one knee, pleading for divorce.

There was a moment of silence before Kim responded. I knew she was carefully weighing each word. When she finally spoke it was with tears in her eyes. It was a moment of vulnerability, and I wrestled for self-control since my natural instinct was to reach out and hold her in my arms. Instead, I tried as gently as possible to convince both of us that a divorce was something we wanted and that I was ready to take that first lonely step. I pictured the innocent faces of our two young sons, stunned by the news they never would expect to hear. My mind was racing. The tears were rolling down Kim's cheeks and I failed to hold back my own. What would happen next? Could I really go through with it? I realized that once the words were out of my mouth there was no turning back, and I imagined all possible outcomes. For the very first time I felt real fear and turmoil as I sat fused to my seat, gazing at Kim as we wept.

"Will you go?" She asked softly, her voice choked up and trembling.

"Yes"

CHAPTER THREE

Our conversation ended there. I stood frozen by the wave of anxiety and revulsion washing over me. I didn't know what to do, what to say or where to go. Maybe everything that could be said already had been. Kim sat entirely still, staring into the lit gas fireplace. When finally I felt able to move I grabbed my coat and headed out of the house.

"I'm going for a beer."

The urge to leave the house was overwhelming. Safely ensconced in my car, I backed into the black night feeling stunned. I drove aimlessly at first, trying to decide how far I wanted to be from the house and, secondarily, how much beer I would need to come back to it. Finally I called my friend Arthur and asked him to meet me at O'Hearn's, a bar on the west side of Cincinnati which was just about equidistant between his house and mine. I offered to buy.

O'Hearn's had been around for years. Popular even on a Monday night, the bar and grille was not especially well lit and sported steeply backed booths which afforded those who desired it a decent level of privacy both of sight and sound from the rest of the bar. All in all a comfortable place where one could choose to be noticed or to be left in peace. When I arrived around ten o'clock O'Hearn's was half full and a quick scan revealed no one resembling my friend Arthur, so I took a seat at the bar and ordered a beer. Arthur walked in just as I finished my first sip of beer.

"Good evening!" Arthur said as he walked over to me and positioned his stocky, five-foot, nine inch frame onto the stool next to me. Despite the fact he had lived in the U.S. nearly fifteen years, the pleasant Cambridge lilt in his voice was still evident. And he could do an excellent Cockney accent when he wanted to entertain his friends or disguise his identity. "Have you got one of those for me?"

"Sure," I said. "What are you having?"

"I'll have what you're having." He replied with feigned formality.

Arthur Tolbert Smythe was, and is, perhaps one of the most interesting, people I know or imagine I will ever know. He is English but had returned home only once or twice since we met eight years earlier. When asked by me or others why he had not journeyed to England more often to see his family he would either ignore the question or give a rambling, almost incoherent answer, even when he was sober. Intermittent interrogations on my part seemed to indicate that Arthur's lack of welcome in the British Isles had more to do with legal issues than with family matters, a fact which, if true, would go far to fill in at least one piece of the puzzle that was Arthur.

"Cheers, mate." He quickly polished off half the contents of the glass.

"Cheers."

"So why are we here tonight?" Arthur surveyed his environment. "Trouble at home?"

"Why else would I be out on a Monday night?" I began to relax and took another drink. "I told Kim I wanted a divorce."

"Oh, did you now? How did that work out?" He asked.

"Don't know yet. Feel like shit, though."

I had come to know Arthur when he and I were working in different capacities at the same bank. He was a branch manager and my position as a loan underwriter had provided us regular occasion to talk business. While his creative rationales for extending credit were rarely sound I had always found them interesting, even more so after receiving an unexpected call from Interpol. It would later be revealed that I was one of a string of bank employees being questioned about some rather dubious activity emanating from his branch, but at the time the investigative process was being kept secret. Interpol, it seemed, in tandem with the FDIC and the Treasury Department, was highly interested in Arthur's loan portfolio and the ways in which he moved money around. In the end, whatever their interest in Arthur, Interpol and the other law enforcement agencies involved were either unable or unwilling to charge him with anything. The bank, however, did not hold its employees to the same evidentiary standard as the International Police, and Arthur was dismissed soon thereafter. Despite the cloud of illegality clinging to him I called Arthur post termination and invited him to meet me for a bit of liquid solace. We had been friends ever since.

"Well, then." Arthur opined. "I say we don't worry about it and get a little pissed." Pissed is a British word for drunk, one of the numerous synonyms for the activity I had learned from Arthur over the years.

"Why not?"

We spent the next hour or so in quiet conversation while I described my earlier encounter with Kim. Arthur had always been a good listener, a trait perhaps stemming from the fact that he rarely suffered from the inclination to discuss his own life. While he was always willing to talk about his children (a boy and a girl close in age to Alex and Trevor,) his wife Gladys (a dental assistant and native South Carolinian,) and even his workout regimen (two hours a day, four days a week,) any effort to glean information about his English family, his personal history, or how he paid the bills was rarely productive. On that evening he didn't seem especially talkative, at least not at first, and appeared content to listen to me ramble on about my marital woes while drinking beer that I purchased. This last part was standard, as Arthur never seemed to have pocket money. This was fine with me. For reasons known and unknown, I always felt like I owed him something anyway, perhaps because beer was cheaper than Therapist Jim and Arthur could be nearly as insightful when it came to human relations. Regardless, others in our group of friends had experienced this strange feeling of indebtedness as well. Since none of us could explain it no one seemed to mind that Arthur tended to disappear or take a phone call whenever it was his turn to buy.

"So what's next?" Arthur prodded me; and then "Did you notice the tall bird over there?"

I ignored the first question in favor of looking in the direction to which Arthur was subtly directing me. Swinging my bar stool around as cunningly as possible, I soon spied two attractive women, one brunette and one with auburn hair. A bottle of wine sat between them and they appeared deep in conversation. The one with auburn hair caught me looking and flashed a smile before she turned back to their conversation.

"Did you see that?" Arthur was grinning. "She wants you."

"Really? You got that from her smiling at me? That she wants me? So whenever someone smiles at me it means they want me? You smiled at me earlier. Do you want me, Arthur?"

Arthur was trying to talk and laugh at the same time. "She was basically waving you over. She's clearly interested. Don't be a putz."

For the whole of my life I have never been adept at reading womanly signals. Their communication style is foreign to me. Unlike most men, who as a group tend to be straightforward when it comes to verbal communication, women's speech often seems to convey more than the literal meaning of the words being spoken. The potential of hidden meaning raises the risk of dangerous pitfalls for someone such as myself, as I am rarely able to discern what is or isn't being conveyed. Of course, this isn't always the case. When women desire to be direct they seem more than capable, but this fact can lead to more chaos and confusion, as it is then incumbent upon the male to sort it all out. Of course, other women get it, which is how they always seem to know what's going on in your relationship before you do. Some men get it too, but these are the lucky few. The men who get it appear to have achieved a state of communicative nirvana of which Buddhist monks would be jealous. They live in a world of free-flowing information, more powerful than the internet, giving women the understanding they desire and getting as much in return. Arthur had been blessed with this power, although to the best of my knowledge he chose not to use it very often and when he did it was generally employed for good rather than evil.

"Go on now," Arthur was still yammering in spite of my sarcasm. "You've had a rough night. Go over and see if you can buy her a drink."

"Arthur, I'm married." This was true, of course.

"Barely," This was true also. "And if you don't go over and say hello one of these other blokes will and you'll feel like a git." Git translates roughly into "dumbass."

I looked around. The bar was still about half full and the male/female ratio was definitely tilted in the women's favor. I figured I was probably drunk enough to go for it, even though I was confident in the inevitable rejection.

"You can't go like that!" Arthur spoke with quiet emphasis, sensing my air of defeat.

"What do you mean?"

"You've got failure dripping off you. I can feel it. She's not going to respond to that. You've got to go over there like you know she'll say yes. Don't act like an ass but don't be a wimp either." He said, confirming my fear.

"Shit! Why don't you just do it?"

"Alright, you pansy," He was smiling. "Watch and learn."

He popped off his bar stool and walked over to the brunette. "My friend and I would like to buy you ladies a drink and engage you in some light conversation. Perhaps another bottle of wine for the four of us?" He glanced at me and nodded, wordlessly telling me that I would be paying for the bottle of wine. Arthur's accent and demeanor could be terribly endearing, and from my vantage point the two ladies seemed to find him as charming as he was attempting to appear and in less than a minute he waved me over. Through introductions I discovered May was the brunette and Elaine was the one who had smiled at me. May and Elaine worked together in project management at General Electric.

Arthur fell into conversation with May, leaving me to talk to Elaine. Elaine was tall and slim and willowy. Despite the cold weather, she sported short sleeves, exposing tone arms and smooth, ivory skin. It was difficult not to stare at her. Elaine was gregarious and had an off-beat sense of humor. I found myself talking easily with her, without a hint of awkwardness, about her life and mine.

"So, how's the marriage going?" She smiled disarmingly, nodding at my wedding ring.

"Not as well as one would hope." I demurred. I just met her after all.

"Can you be more specific?" She was still smiling, amused by my discomfort.

"I'll tell you what; if we're still here in an hour I'll tell you all about it." I demurred a second time. I didn't want to spend the evening figuratively, or literally, sorting my dirty laundry.

"Fine." With her fingers she combed her straight hair behind her ears. "And if we're still here in two hours, I'll give you my phone number." Elaine was a better flirt than me. More practiced. It was terrifying.

"So, now that we're settling in for a while, tell me exactly how you go about managing your projects." I was trying to sound smooth but wasn't sure I was pulling it off.

"Well," she feigned contemplation and held my gaze. "Mostly I do a lot of math and boss people around. I also spend at least half my day devising ways to make myself look good."

"Interesting. And what do you do with the rest of your day? Golf? Tennis? Drinking?"

"Well, drinking, obviously. And tennis on the nights I'm sober. I also devote a couple hours each day to looking busy and a few hours a month to helping the homeless. It's very rewarding work. Few people seem to understand the importance of looking busy."

"I couldn't agree more." Where had Elaine been hiding? "And how's the pay? I mean, if you don't mind me asking."

"Oh, the pay's amazing, especially considering how little I do to earn it." I would later learn the reality of her schedule, which left little time for tennis or golf. Or sleeping. "It's like winning the lottery every two weeks. How about you? What do you do all day?" She was the kind of person Arthur would describe as "clever."

"Mostly crush entrepreneurial dreams and entertain unclean thoughts about my administrative assistant. I also enjoy contemplating my naval and reading in the bathroom."

I made her laugh. "Sounds nearly as rewarding as what I do. Is it interesting?"

"Crushing entrepreneurial dreams? You bet! What kind of person doesn't like to sit in judgment of others and tell them when they are, or are not, deserving?"

"I'm sorry! I was referring to the unclean thoughts about your administrative assistant." She touched my hand, which suddenly felt warmer.

"Oh! That!" I feigned surprise, trying not to let the touching become too distracting. "Of course! I instituted a strict hiring policy after my last assistant retired."

"And what is the new policy?" She was still touching me.

"The new policy is that she has to be at least twenty years younger than me." She was still touching me. I felt my tongue thickening.

"And what's your reasoning for the policy?"

"Hmmm…good question. I suppose my reasoning is that the new policy is more in sync with my self-destructive death wish. My last assistant, Rita, was far too efficient and unattractive. I needed someone more distracting and less helpful. I've learned if I don't set traps for myself at work I risk becoming too successful."

"Oh my, God. You're a genius. I never wanted to be successful, either. But as hard as I try I can't seem to avoid it. I just keep getting promoted no matter what I do. You must teach me more." She was beautiful.

"I'd be happy to talk to you all night, if you think it will help." The wine was good and the conversation better.

Our conversation went on like this, on and off, for some time. During the off periods we actually managed to learn a few things about each other. I told her about the boys and my work. I also related (my version of) how my marriage to Kim had reached such a sorry state. I even shared some of Kim's complaints about me, either from a sense of fairness, or guilt, or both. I might even have been looking for some feminine insight, although none was immediately forthcoming. Elaine, like Arthur, was an excellent listener, but far more attractive. And while she would ask topical questions I perceived she was not one to offer advice when none had been requested. For my part, I found out Elaine Van Heusen was an only child, originally from Richmond, Virginia, and had married her college sweetheart soon after graduating from the University of Georgia. As she neared graduation she interviewed for and was offered a position with General Electric and moved to Cincinnati with her soon-to-be first husband. The marriage, however, would last only two years, due mainly to the fact he discovered he liked men more than he liked women. Though he had never been overly passionate she was still jolted by the revelation, having noticed no tell-tale signs throughout their relationship. They remained friends and still offered each other fashion and relationship advice. Elaine had yet to find husband number two.

The evening wore on in this way with no one at our table seeming to notice the midnight hour arrive and depart. We ordered drinks, joked, and told personal stories we hoped the others at the table would find amusing. Arthur's stories, of course, rarely involved anything more personal than a tale about the uncontrollable flatulence of his English Bull Terrier, Churchill. He also mentioned something about starting another import/export business involving Persian rugs, but I didn't pay much attention. He always brought this up this type of thing when he was drunk. As was usual with nearly everyone who first met Arthur, Elaine and May were alternately enthralled or dismayed by his chosen topics of conversation.

In spite of my wavering attention span I was grateful for the moments Arthur picked up the conversational ball, so to speak, because during those moments I was able to focus my attention on Elaine. Her expressive face alternately displayed either horror or joy whenever he managed to say something especially offbeat and funny. Feeling warm, happy, and secure, I was overwhelmed with the desire to touch her. And that posed a problem, and not just because I was married.

Unfortunately my personal history with women has been fraught with tragedy and misfortune. The tales of missed signals, lost opportunities, and a general cluelessness in my relations with the fairer sex had become legendary among my friends, and here's why: For every time I have gotten "lucky" there are ten stories of utter failure. Indeed, for me successful sexual encounters had nearly always been initiated by the female. Marriage had saved me from this vicious cycle of shame and regret, dwelling as I was in the safety and comfort of a monogamous relationship. Now, of course, the marriage had simply become my latest example in the string of failures. That evening, however, even I couldn't miss the attraction Elaine was displaying. It showed in the way she touched my hand and the way she would hang on my every word. I noticed the way she looked at me and the way her chair seemed to be moving inexorably toward my own. I noticed the way she smoothed some of my fly away hair with her fingertips and moved my beer away from the edge of the table because she was afraid I'd knock it off. Even I couldn't' miss the intimacy of her attention.

Despite my visceral joy at with what was happening at the table I found the need to excuse myself in order to take a bathroom break. To my surprise, I exited to find Elaine standing by herself in the little hallway outside the restrooms. I assumed she was waiting for me so, without forethought and quite uncharacteristically for me, reached our, put my arm around her waist, pulled her to me and kissed her full on. And then, hope against hope, she returned the kiss. It was deep and full. It was the kind of kiss that just makes you want to keep on kissing. So that's what we did. Wanting to feel every inch of her against me, I backed her against the wall and pushed into her. Her hands roamed down my back as I used mine to hold her face and neck. I was drowning in her redolence, aware of nothing beyond her and her body. But, after what I imagine was a few minutes, I let go of her. I had to. Elaine, with as much grace as possible, let me know she still needed to use the restroom.

Upon returning to the table we received no discernible reaction from Arthur or May indicating they noticed the length of our absence, which I found oddly disappointing. Elaine and I took our seats, which had again magically migrated toward one another, and returned to the conversation with Elaine resting her hand on my thigh. Unfortunately, within ten minutes of our return May was pointing at her watch and suggesting it was time to leave. As everyone but Arthur had to get up the next day for work, I did not fight Elaine's pending departure, at least not overtly. In my head I was screaming for her to stay. Elaine made the separation easier by pulling me aside and giving me her phone number.

"No pressure," She whispered in my ear as she slipped the paper into my hand. "I know you're having a rough time right now, but I'd love to hear from you if you can find your way to it."

"I think I'd like that, too." I whispered back, feeling really sure I was doing something wrong but not really caring.

There were hugs all around as the ladies took their leave. I watched Elaine walk away, wondering if I would ever actually use her phone number. Wanting to call her and actually calling her were very different considerations and I wasn't too drunk to realize I might feel differently in the morning, or even ten minutes later. But I had no plans to discard the enchanted slip of paper.

"Scotch?" Arthur's voice broke my meditation.

"Sure." I wasn't really sure I wanted the Scotch but to respond in the negative would have been ritualistic taboo. This was how Arthur and I always finished our evenings.

"Pretty bird, Elaine." He stated this plainly before flagging the bartender and ordering the drinks. "Good kisser?"

"How did you know?" Until that moment I had labored under the assumption no one had seen us.

"Went back to use the loo and there you were. Decided not to interrupt. I am a gentleman, after all."

"You think it's a problem?"

"Not for me. I wasn't fooling around on my wife tonight." He smiled. "I think you got more action tonight than you have in months, so maybe you'll sleep with a smile on your face. But you're still going to wake up in your house in a few hours."

I wasn't sure what he meant. Did he mean I should've worked harder to spend the night with Elaine or that I would soon feel guilty? I decided not to ask, mainly because I was fairly sure he meant the latter and I wasn't ready for reality to seep back into my evening. So we sat and drank the scotch, commenting on the evening's events and quietly girding ourselves for the short journey home. I paid the tab and again told him it was time to go.

"Already?" He feigned horror.

"Arthur, it's one in the morning. I've got to get some sleep. Besides, I'm not buying any more drinks tonight."

"Well...time to go then."

The night was cold and the clouds had begun to release their burden of snow. Arthur and I stood for a moment, enjoying the snow falling around us and the quiet beauty it was creating. I felt happy. I felt happy because the encounter with Elaine had served to diffuse some of the bleak outlook I had been nursing over the last year. It was just an inkling of feeling at the time, a sense that my ongoing state of dread might not be permanent. I suspected, however, and the suspicion would be confirmed over time, that the lightness I was feeling was temporary. I wanted to enjoy it as long as I could. Arthur's voice, clear in the chill air, again broke my moment of meditation.

"What's on your mind?"

"Who would you save?"

"What's that?" He had no idea what I was talking about.

"Who would you save, if your mother and I were in a burning building? If you could only save one, who would you save?"

"You, of course." He answered succinctly. "Can't stand my mother."

"'Night, Arthur."

"'Night, mate."

CHAPTER FOUR

I woke to the sound of the alarm. Confused and disoriented after just four hours of sleep, it took an herculean effort to drag myself out of bed to wake up the boys. Unlike me, Trevor had not spent the night drinking and jumped quickly out of bed in order to beat his brother to the shower. Alex, on the other hand, needed prodding.

"Five more minutes Dad," His voice emanated listlessly from beneath the covers.

"C'mon, Alex, get up and get ready." I was trying to be stern and he was trying to ignore me. He was winning. The house felt like ice, and I would have preferred to return to the safety and warmth of bed but that would have to wait until the boys were both up and getting dressed. Neither seemed to notice that I was hungover and had a stinging case of halitosis. When Alex finally managed to trek down the hall to the bathroom, I slipped quietly back under the covers for another fifteen minutes of sleep. My siesta was cut short, however, when Alex started shaking me five minutes later.

"Dad; today is delayed start. We don't have to get up yet." Delayed Start was a bi-weekly scheme designed to let teachers sleep in on hump day and to screw with parents' schedules. School would begin two hours later than usual.

"Oh, okay. Great." This morning *delayed start* meant I could enjoy another full hour of uninterrupted sleep and still get to work on time. Because of my work schedule, Kim usually got the boys up on delayed start days. "Why don't you guys go back to sleep?"

"We'll try, Dad." Turning to leave the room, Alex looked back at me over his shoulder. "You kinda smell, Dad." That, indeed, was the case so I did not protest his assessment, and reset the alarm for another hour of sleep.

The house had been dark and quiet when I returned home hours earlier. Kim, as usual, was asleep on the couch but my entrance didn't seem to wake her despite my movements being somewhat less than cat-like. No doubt she may have been pretending to be asleep simply to avoid talking to me, but since it was late the chances were slim that she was faking it. She didn't even move a muscle when I stumbled and sent a dining room chair sailing across the floor with a stray footfall.

The jubilation I experienced following the all too brief tête-à-tête with Elaine vanished all too quickly upon arriving home. I could not deny the reality that I was drunk, sleeping alone, and had to get up for work a few hours later. Still, as I slipped between the sheets I reflected momentarily on my chance meeting with Elaine. I had the magic slip of paper bearing her phone number stuffed in the glove compartment and knew I wasn't ready to throw it away. Nor did I necessarily believe I was ready to use it, either. I considered it a precious memento of the evening to be put in safekeeping for future use. Besotted, horny and alone, I decided it was best to hold off on any scrutiny until the next day, when my head would be clearer and adrenaline level back to normal. Plus I really needed some sleep.

All thought of Elaine was soon forgotten when the alarm resounded. The sixty minutes of sleep the school gifted me that morning passed in the blink of an eye and I was exhausted. Bathroom rituals complete, I showered away the stink Alex had so astutely brought to my attention, dressed, and kissed the boys before heading back out the door. To avoid any potential confrontation with Kim, I made certain to be quieter than the night before. I could hear her breathing as I tiptoed through the kitchen, skillfully managing not to kick any chairs. Though still shaky, I had sobered sufficiently to recognize the sea of confused and desperate emotion flowing between Kim and me . . . not to mention my indiscretion the night before. Now was not the time to discuss our future, or lack thereof. I left without disturbing the household and headed to McDonald's for a greasy breakfast and a cup of coffee. Past experience taught me the intake of both would eliminate the rumbling in my stomach and the pounding in my head.

43

With the sausage biscuit and coffee working their magic, driving with the window open was all I needed to clear away the remaining cobwebs. The cool air flowed over me as I drove and played back the mental tape of Elaine and me from the night before. Again I reprised the almost-sex scene with Elaine. If it was possible, I found thinking about touching Elaine nearly as thrilling as actually doing it. I found the idea any woman she would want to touch me, and be so open about it, nearly unbelievable. Over the last few years Kim had made it a point to remind me she had sex only because I wanted to, stating during one such conversation she would generally have preferred knitting to seeing me naked. Invariably I was conflicted by the premise. On the one hand I felt somewhat grateful for her sacrifice. But on the other I began to question that whole aspect of our relationship, horrified by the implication I might be an accidental rapist. Had it always been thus? How long had she been pretending to want me? The idea was dispiriting to say the least. Were there women who actually wanted sex? And was Elaine one of them? In the preceding months I would occasionally catch myself staring at couples holding hands, canoodling, or just generally enjoying one another's company. The couples in question often seemed oblivious to the world around them, focused only on each other. I felt envious, thinking if I observed them long enough I would learn their secrets. I never did, obviously. How long had it been since Kim and I were the happy couple being stared at by someone like me? Four years? Five? I suppose it could have been longer. The only thing I was sure about was that, according to Kim, it had been a long time. My lack of ability to pick up signals worked to ensure I would not notice things were going to shit, and my own culpability, until it was too late. But now here was this woman openly showing desire for me. Amazing! If Elaine was a woman who actually desired sex, would she have it with me? Was it possible she had already thought about it? I hoped, of course, that the answer was yes, even if I still wasn't sure if I would ever act on the notion. We were drunk, after all, so it was conceivable at the very moment I was imagining possibilities and feeling relief, Elaine was feeling regret. I didn't know, and couldn't know, unless I summoned the nerve to call her. I pulled into the bank parking lot thinking I would have to do just that. Elaine's number managed to migrate from the glove compartment to my shirt pocket.

44

Emily was not at her desk when I arrived on the second floor even though it was after eight thirty. I reassured myself she would be in soon, though her on-time record was more miss than hit. As an administrative assistant she didn't need to be as punctual as the branch personnel, but neither should she be wandering in and out completely at her discretion. Normally she was never more than ten minutes late. My boss, however, was already at his desk, which caused me some discomfort. I preferred to get there before Stephen to organize my day before he organized his, and also because it made me look good. Even if I was there only minutes before him, for all he knew my arrival could have preceded his by an hour or more. Lucky for me, Stephen was not a clock watcher. He expected his employees to do their jobs with minimal supervision. I waved to him as I passed his office.

"Morning, Stephen." He didn't like to be called Steve. He looked up from his copy of the Financial Times and greeted me. We had agreed a year earlier that I would maintain my subscription to the Wall Street Journal and he to the Financial Times so we could share papers instead of each of us paying for both.

"Where's Emily this morning?" He was a matter-of-fact guy, but that didn't mean he wasn't paying attention.

"She'll be in soon." I hoped I wasn't lying. Stephen wasn't keen on Emily's habitual tardiness, but since she was more my problem than his he just made sure I was aware of his frustration. Rita Standwoegen had spoiled him, too.

"Do you have time to help me with today's reviews?"

"You bet." I didn't, really, but knew he was expecting my help. "Do you need anything before I settle in?"

"No thanks. Computers are fucked up this morning. Looks like somebody tried to hack in again. IT's working on it but keep an eye out and save your work." As far as we knew this was the third time in as many weeks there had been an attempt to breach the bank's systems. We had reported it to the locals as well as our government overseers but nothing had yet been resolved. However, I was paying scant attention. I already had enough to distract me from work and I needed some coffee.

When I returned to my desk with the coffee I stared at the paper without really seeing the words. My concentration had disappeared when an unexpected wave of grief washed over me. I

45

had uttered the word "divorce" in an actual conversation with Kim. I put the paper down and turned away from the door, toward the window. The reality of it was overwhelming, and a vision of the boys popped into my head. There were tears streaming down their faces because Mom and Dad told them they weren't going to be married anymore. I found the vision horrifying. To children the world was and will always be exactly as it has been. For a moment I forgot to breathe. And then Emily walked in.

"Morning, Jason!" She was disturbingly cheerful.

"Morning, Em." My greeting was not effortless as I continued to stare out the window at the snow falling in the parking lot. "We're helping Stephen with some loan reviews this morning."

"Awesome!"

I wasn't sure doing loan reviews was "awesome" but I was sure I needed to think happy thoughts. With that in mind I turned back and forced myself to read the paper, which was always chock full of happy stories from all over the world. Ten minutes later I worked through voicemail and email, and at some point remembered the phone number on the magic paper. It was still in my pocket and, inexplicably, making me anxious, like I was having a panic attack or developing a brain tumor. My heart was racing, and given the volume of heartbeats emanating from my chest cavity it was only a matter of time before my ear drums started to bleed, weakened as they were from the morning alarm. I took the paper out of my shirt pocket and shoved it into my brief case. It would be safe there while I worked. Thankfully, my ruminations were interrupted by Emily.

"Stephen asked me to ask you if you're ready to get started on the loan reviews." She sounded nervous. Emily usually avoided contact with Stephen. Perhaps she sensed he was not happy with her.

"Tell him I'll be right there." I sent her back into the lion's den before grabbing a pen and paper and heading out. My coffee had gone cold so I left it behind.

Stephen and I began splitting the work as soon as I sat down in his office. The clouds were breaking, allowing the slanty beams of the winter sun to stream through the blinds across from where I was sitting. The beams were aiming directly for my face. It was yet another distraction and I was unable to find a comfortable position. Annoyed by my fidgeting, Stephen finally closed the blinds but the wooden slats couldn't completely hold back the irritating brilliance of the irksome fireball. Worse still, I began to find the pattern of light formed by the sun sneaking in between the slats vaguely hypnotic, thereby lowering my productivity even further. Fortunately, during one of these undesired reveries Stephen was required to accept a phone call. But rather than leaving his office to give him privacy for his call I instead stayed put and used the down time to contemplate Buddhism. Here's why: Buddhists and I both believe in karma, part of which concerns the idea that everything we do, good, bad, or indifferent, spins back to us on the wheel of life. For better or worse, my karmic wheel has always spun quickly. If I do something bad in the morning the universe often castigates me by that afternoon. Knowing this (and still somewhat hypnotized,) I sat wondering when/if the universe was going to punish me for kissing Elaine and, if so, just what form would the punishment take. Since it couldn't presently punish me by making my marriage worse or by giving me a hangover, I figured the universe would have to be more creative. But I would be admonished only if the judgment was against me, an outcome of which I wasn't completely convinced. I mean, I had already asked for a divorce, so was I really "cheating?"

"Jason!" Stephen's voice startled me awake. "Late night?"

"Yes, but I'm good," I said, still in a fog.

"How are things at home?" Stephen was nearly as up to date as Arthur when it came to my home life. He was a patient listener and enthusiastic sharer of personal marriage anecdotes.

"Sucks. Looks like divorce. Ended up out with Arthur last night."

"Arthur? Haven't they deported him?" He was, of course, being sarcastic since he knew that Arthur was one of my closest friends.

"Not yet. Any day, perhaps; none of us know where he gets his money."

"I'll start calling him James Bond, or maybe Austin Powers." He smiled before returning to his computer.

"He'll answer to either as long as you're buying," I offered.

"Alright, you've got your pile." Stephen nodded toward the files in front, indicating all personal matters were now off the table. "I need these by tomorrow."

"No problem." Happy to be back on my feet, I grabbed my stack and walked back to my office. But I lacked the necessary motivation to get the job done and knew it. The stack of papers just handed to me by Stephen lay before me untouched. Fearing another bout of inertia, I dialed Isabella's number to inform her about the evening.

"Northern Kentucky Bank and Trust!" Izzy's voice was abrasively upbeat when she answered the phone.

"Izzy, it's me. I've got an interesting story for you." I tried to sound conspiratorial.

"Oooh! I'm all ears."

Isabella D'Agostino and I had been fast friends since getting to know one another at the bank's annual officers' conference a couple years prior. Slim and reaching a height of five-ten in flats, her long black hair and olive skin made Izzy as exotic as her name. Izzy exuded a native sensuality that one tends to expect in movie stars but never in bank branch managers. She and I hit it off and our personalities clicked in a way that had only happened to me a few times over the course of my life and never with a woman. Our friendship chemistry was so apparent that the occasional work place rumor would crop up. But Isabella and I had never slept together. It wasn't that that the subject had never been broached. Indeed, the idea had surfaced on a number of occasions, but neither of us seemed terribly motivated by the thought. Perhaps we feared the consequences, whatever those would be. In topical conversations the fact I was married and that we (sort of) worked together had both been suggested as potential obstructions to a physical relationship, but it was most likely our friendship was just too satisfying to throw the sex wrench into the works. Regardless, we had never so much as kissed. We did, however, know just about everything there was to know about each other, which is why I called her. She needed to be brought up to date.

"Arthur and I had a few drinks last night." I began.

"You were with Arthur? Okay, you have my full attention."

I spent the next ten minutes giving her a summary of the evening, beginning with the declaration of divorce and ending with Arthur and me leaving the bar after our brief encounter with Elaine and May. Izzy did not interrupt. I learned from past experience if she whatever I was telling her did not hold her interest she would multitask, but in this case I knew I had her full attention.

"So what will you do now?" It was a simple question.

"What do you mean?"

"Dumbass. I mean, are you really going for the divorce? Will you get any work done today? Will you call Elaine?" She was frustrated. I had conveyed much information but no insight or conclusions.

"Well, yes, I guess, to all those things."

"Then you'd better get off the phone and get started. You have a busy day ahead. But, remember; tread lightly if you do call her. You've got lots of shit on your plate, and I hate to point out the obvious but you are still married." Izzy was blunt. "How about lunch tomorrow so we can talk. Besides your crap I think my new boyfriend is gay and I need you to help me figure it all out. And sweetie, I really am sorry about you and Kim. You probably don't want to hear this right now, but you're headed to a dark place, but I know you'll come out of it ok. Gotta go! Love ya!"

"Yeah...love you too." I replied perfunctorily, even though she had already hung up. Dark place and love ya? How do you say those two things together and hang up right after? But her comment was already floating around the universe and was not comforting. Izzy was twice divorced and so spoke from experience, while I had yet to be divorced even once.

I pondered her statement as well as the oddity of snow flurries in sunshine when my musing was again interrupted by Emily, who entered with another stack of paperwork from Stephen. Clearly I needed to buckle down and dig in for the rest of the day. There was no use in dwelling on eventualities which may or may not happen.

The snow fall picked up as the afternoon wore on and by the time I left work there was at least a couple inches on the ground, which meant my drive home would be fraught with jams, accidents, and attempts to dodge less confident drivers.

Traffic on I-75 was at a near standstill, so I decided to break the monotony of the traffic jam with a phone call. I dialed Arthur first, since his murky employment situation generally left him available to answer my calls but got no answer. I tried Izzy next but got no response there either. I thought about calling Kim, to let her know I'd be late. Despite our current state of limbo, I still needed to be courteous.

"Hello?"

"Hey, it's me. The snow is making everything crazy and I'll be about an hour late."   "That's fine." Kim said, sounding pleasant but detached, like she was only half-listening.

"Will I be late for dinner?" For some reason I found myself trying to get her attention.

"No. It's fine." She responded, sounding like a Stepford wife.

"Ok, see you guys soon." Kim and I had had such exchanges hundreds, if not thousands, of times. But now it was different. The quick trade of locational information no longer carried the sense of import or relevance it once did.

I hung up the phone, noting the tone of Kim's voice and also that I had moved no more than ten feet during the gabfest. Still bored and a tad demoralized, I decided to make another call. With one hand on the steering wheel I used the other to fish around inside my briefcase for the paper with Elaine's phone number and began to dial the number. But, a new wave of anxiety forestalled the hitting of the send button as I considered a myriad of disagreeable outcomes: The possibilities I imagined were:

1. Outright rejection.
2. Outright rejection coupled with anger.
3. The question, "Who are you, again?"
4. The question, "Who are you, again?" coupled with anger.
5. No answer.
6. Voicemail: *You've reached the voicemail of Elaine Van Heusen. If you were the drunk bastard I met last night at O'Hearn's, please do not call again. If you are not, please leave a message and I'll get back to you as soon as possible."*
7. Accusations of stalking.
8. A proposal of marriage.
9. Indifference.

Number nine would have been the worst, of course. With rejection or anger one at least has the opportunity to bow out gracefully. If met with indifference I felt sure to be left a stammering mess, grasping to find a clever way to exit the conversation whilst maintaining some shred of dignity. Astonishingly I dialed the number, even as my brain attempted to lash me into submission. More astonishingly, Elaine answered and even greeted me with a hint of excitement.

"Elaine? This is Jason...from last night." The stammering manifested immediately, like I was back in Junior High, trying to ask Rebecca Cundiff to the ninth grade dance.

"Hey, there! I was hoping you'd call." Despite her apparent sobriety Elaine's manner was as straightforward and refreshing as the evening before.

"And I was hoping you'd answer! Hey, listen...um...I really enjoyed meeting you last night." I didn't sound smooth at all. If I were to survive the experience Elaine would need to be as gracious about my stumbling delivery as Rebecca had been decades before.

"Me, too!" She paused. "But, honestly, that wasn't normal behavior for me. I don't generally go to random bars and make out with strange guys."

"Me neither. I mean, I don't make out with strange women. And never make out with guys." Holy crap! I sounded like a moron. "I'm sorry, Elaine. I can lose your number if you want me to. We've all done crazy things while under the influence . . ." I offered an escape because I thought she wanted one. It would be the first of many miscommunications between us. This time, however, I heard giggling from the other end.

"Oh, no! That's not what I meant. I guess I just wanted you to know that that wasn't normal for me. You know, I didn't want you to think I'm a slut or anything." She was still giggling. "But I really did enjoy meeting you. Especially the hallway part..."

"Great!" Now I felt exhilarated. She was somehow able to defend her virtue and complement me at the same time. I wondered if she could hear the relief in my voice. "Then would you like to get together again?"

"Absolutely, as long as you're really getting a divorce. Last night it didn't seem like it was just a line, but I was a little drunk. It wasn't just a line was it?"

"No, no. Everything I told you last night is true." Which is was.

51

"Well, then. When would you like to get together?"

"Ummm… how about Friday?" I generally kept Fridays open for work related issues that needed to be completed before the weekend.

"Friday would be great. Where do you want to meet?" I was blown away that our conversation had gotten this far, a moment I could not have imagined just days before. As I tried to think of a restaurant between our two places of employment, a stream of oily smoke began to pour from under the hood and tail pipe of the car directly in front of me in sufficient amounts to obscure my view. It was spewing like a volcano, and I found the contrast of white snow and dark smoke simultaneously entertaining and unsettling. I should have gotten out of the car to see if the driver needed help, but I elected to keep talking to Elaine. All the same I decided to share the moment with Elaine, hoping she wouldn't judge me. "Wow! I'm staring at a guy who looks like Santa Claus, and his car is about to catch on fire."

"Oh, no! Does he need help?"

"Probably; I see people stopping." But, I stayed on the phone with Elaine rather than join the ad hoc rescue party. By now smoke was billowing from the cabin and from every orifice the car had left to offer. By the time the flames engulfed the undercarriage the old man was safely behind the vehicle with the other observers who, unlike me, had pulled over to help. Soon the flames burst into the car's interior and exited through the windows, melting the glass and dissolving what little paint was left on the exterior.

"Wow!" I uttered under my breadth. "It's completely covered in flame!"

"Can you move away? Are you safe?" said, Elaine, with obvious concern.

"Yeah, I'll be okay here, but it's mind blowing—like a sign from God," I replied, half joking. Still, despite the resemblance to Santa Claus it could have been God on the side of the road, lit by the gentle glow of a car fire. But another part of me considered my relationship with Karma. Was the imploding vehicle a good or bad sign? After all, my car wasn't the one on fire. Still, maybe Karma just missed its intended target. Maybe it had a bout of snow blindness. Bearing this in mind, I made a quick choice while observing a runner carrying a fire extinguisher.

"So, tell me what you've been doing all day." There was nothing I could do for Santa that had not already been done.

I arrived home to a quiet house and found Kim sitting alone in the family room. She had taken the boys to her parents so we could talk. I had mixed emotions, hoping for at least a few days to allow the idea to sink in before making any major decisions. Kim, on the other hand, thought otherwise.

"Are you sure it's what you want?" She asked, evenly and without accusation.

"I'm sure." I suppose we were being mature.

"And you don't think there's any way we can work this out?"

"I used to think so...hope so, but not now; not anymore. Things have changed so drastically, and nothing good came out of marriage counseling. We're really not partners anymore, and I can't just turn off my desires the way you have. I can't expect you to live in a way that doesn't feel right to you, and it's not fair for you to expect that from me."

"I know" she replied, in a hushed voice, barely audible. "I just never thought we'd end up here. Remember when we promised never to divorce?"

"I remember."

I fought back the tears, but Kim let hers flow. The reality of this course of action and its consequences hit me in the gut. We were sitting apart, but now reached out to hold and comfort each other, too emotional to speak while attempting to make sense of the journey which had led us to this moment, the journey that had somehow gone so wrong. We held each other in a way we hadn't for years, letting our tears fall on each other's shoulders. Our bodies racked with pain and sorrow, we agonized over the choices we had made that had ultimately led to the death of our love, and to the end of our marriage. It was too late to say anything we hadn't said already.

CHAPTER FIVE

I had been sitting in Therapist Jim's office for several minutes, watching him shuffle papers on the table between us. My first thought was that Therapist Jim should not charge me until one of us started speaking. Only when he had the stacks arranged just so did he begin.

Therapist Jim: So, what's been happening since last time we met?
Me: Well, Kim and I decided to get a divorce and I met a nice woman named Elaine – all in the same day.
Therapist Jim: (Pausing.) Well…that's a lot for one day. Tell me about it.
Me: (I told him the whole story. I summarized but it still took about eight minutes.)
Therapist Jim: Interesting.
Me: (Feeling somewhat guilty.) Well, hell yes it's interesting. And devastating. And weird. So I guess you're probably thinking that I was compensating or something like that, like I was down emotionally so I came on to this girl to make up for feelings of loss. Is that where you're going? (Jeez! All the poor man said was "Interesting.")
Therapist Jim: No, not really. Actually I was thinking that's a lot to happen all in one night and was wondering how you were processing all of it. I was also thinking you might be triangulating.
Me: Hmmm. You might be right. I might be triangulating. But I won't know for sure until after you tell me what triangulating means.
Therapist Jim: Triangulating is when you put something between you and your problem that you can use an excuse for not dealing with your problem. (Now he was making a triangle with his thumbs

and pointy fingers.) See? In your case, you might be putting Elaine between yourself and Kim. By spending your energy on Elaine you have an excuse to avoid the issues between you and your wife.

Me: Hmmm. Interesting. But now that I know what it is, I'd have to say that I don't think I'm triangulating.

Therapist Jim: Why's that?

Me: Well, I didn't meet Elaine until AFTER Kim and I decided to divorce. How is that avoiding the problem? I mean, Kim and I haven't gone back to thinking about staying together or anything like that. We're still getting divorced, as far as I know. Besides, nothing has really happened between Elaine and me. We just talk…except for the one time at the bar the night I met her.

Therapist Jim: Have you and Kim moved forward on planning for the divorce since that night?

Me: Ah, well…no. I guess you got me there. I get the distinct impression she's leaving the pacing up to me, but I could be wrong.

Therapist Jim: And how often do you and Elaine talk?

Me: Well, yes, every day for the past week.

Therapist Jim: Hmm. So Kim's leaving the timing up to you…and you haven't pushed the process at all…in over a week. And during that time you have been talking to Elaine every day. So maybe you're talking to Elaine instead of talking to Kim. How would you interpret this?

Me: (Feeling flushed and stupid.) Look Doc, I'm in no hurry to tear the family apart. It's only been a week. I think I'm just letting the initial shock wear off before we take the next step.

Therapist Jim: Or you could be triangulating.

Me: Or I could be triangulating. (Damn him!)

We went on like this for another twenty-two minutes before moving on to my feelings about my job and how I felt my potential was being wasted, my feelings about living a celibate lifestyle, and my feelings about my feelings. I always enjoyed my time with Therapist Jim and learned early on that, unlike work, the process occurring in his office had little to do with quantifiable values or bottom line results, and that was okay. It was nice to have Therapist Jim explain what was going on my head, especially as the reasons behind my behavior were—and still are—generally a mystery to me.

55

Back then, one of the main questions was why my decisions did not always lead to behavior choices that would stand me in good stead in a corporate environment. I noted over the last few months that both my boss and Therapist Jim had pointed out some of my self-destructive tendencies. Indeed, I found these insights interesting and enlightening, but subsequently did little or nothing to change any of the behaviors that had been identified as self-destructive, even though I believed most of the identified weaknesses to be true. Of course, the choice to do nothing about my self-destructive behavior could have been considered self-destructive as well. But despite my failure to act I still had every intention of improving myself and becoming a "team player." I just needed to get past my issues with the "coach." Regardless, that day turned out to be a productive head shrinking session, and I left Therapist Jim's office in good spirits. And notwithstanding Therapist Jim's observations on triangulation, I still looked forward to lunch with Elaine.

When I arrived back at work it was apparent a pall had fallen over the second floor. At first I thought there must have been a run on the bank, but that would have been accompanied by a lot of commotion. I was walking past rows of tense employees with worried expressions, not bankers running around like the sky was falling. I wanted to find out what was going on but neither Emily nor Stephen were at their desks, so I decided to call Rita Standwoegen. Though she no longer worked at the bank, I doubted the fact that she was no longer an employee had diminished her ability to glean inside information. I could have asked one of the people milling about outside my office, but phoning Rita served a secondary purpose of not adding to the general stress level.

"This is Rita." She sounded just like she did when she worked at the bank. Professional.

"Hi, it's Jason. How's retirement going?" I felt a polite exchange of pleasantries appropriate before querying her about what was happening at her former workplace.

"As well as can be expected, Jason. I'm not exactly filling my time knitting doilies, if that's what you're asking. How are things with you? We haven't spoken for more than a month."

"I'd need at least an hour of your time to bring you up to date. Let me buy you lunch next week and regale you with the highlights." I would never lose touch with Rita. Certain people become indispensable in your life, and Rita was one of them.

"Well then, if you didn't call to update me on your personal life, then I imagine you called to ask about the computer hacking that occurred today." As usual, her voice betrayed no personal warmth although she always took my calls. Perhaps she was secretly in love with me, but that any latent sense of affection was deeply entombed.

"That's why I rang, but I didn't know what happened. You're the first one I called when I detected something weird going on. What happened?"

"From what I gather a determined effort was made to hack into the bank's secure network, and they would have succeeded had one of the IT people not shut down the system in time to prevent the incursion." Always matter-of-fact, Rita sounded as if it was the third or fourth time she had had this discussion.

"Stephen said something about hacking the other day. Does anyone know who was trying to get in?"

"No. The attackers masked their location by running the signal through some dummy addresses and unrelated servers. I heard the system was just brought back up twenty minutes ago. From what I understand they got further this time, and the assumption is that it's the same group that's attempted entry in the past."

"How do you find out all this crap, Rita? It's like you never left. Is that everything?"

"That's pretty much it. I understand they've added some extra security, but it's only a matter of time before someone tries again . . . and succeeds."

"Why so?"

"It's a small bank, Jason, running its own servers with limited manpower. If hackers can break into the Pentagon's system, they can certainly find a way to break into ours." I noted she still referred to the bank as "ours." The buck always stopped with Rita. We chatted a few more minutes and set a lunch date. Rita was a good friend, but she never got around to telling me what exactly she was doing with all her free time.

After the rush of adrenaline, precipitated by the hacking, the remainder of the afternoon seemed carefree. Most everyone on the second floor was given the assignment of checking customer computer files for signs of tampering, although most of us wouldn't have known it if we saw it. Unsurprisingly, no one found anything.

Other than the light snow fall, the drive home was uneventful. No ancient automobiles were afire on the side of the highway and I didn't spot God or Santa. Nor did I call Elaine. Though we had talked a lot the previous week, our lunch date was the next day and I was trying to "play it cool"—something I had never quite mastered.

"So what do you think you're doing?" Izzy asked abruptly from across the table during lunch at the International House of Pancakes.

"What do you mean?" I asked, knowing exactly what she meant.

"You've got unfinished business at home, so why are you messing with the other woman?" She sounded angry, and not angry, at the same time.

"I don't know, Izzy, maybe because she's awesome?" Izzy's demeanor indicated no acceptance of my social escapades, nor did she seem to find my marital status reason enough to be back on the dating scene. I opted not to explain the concept of triangulation to her and continued to plead my case. "It's like I can tell her anything. It didn't freak her out that I jack off three times a day. In fact, she found it interesting."

"Well who wouldn't?" Izzy was smiling now, but probably only because of the masturbation comment. "But what's your agenda here? You've only known her a week."

"I don't know, honestly. Nothing's happened and so far we're just friends, like you and me. Are you jealous?"

I replayed the conversation with Izzy as I moved through steady traffic. In our current state of estrangement I could never inform Kim about Elaine, even though we used to share everything with each other. In the happier days of our marriage, when trust was abundant, neither of us hesitated to share everything, or so I believed. Kim may have been hiding things from me and left me mercifully ignorant. But over time things gradually eroded, without me really noticing. I assumed it was the same for her. Somehow, we quietly reached a point where we no longer sought out each other's approval. The scenario reminded me of a movie I'd seen about a wife trying to escape an unhappy marriage, and felt murder a more viable option than divorce. To avoid detection she would administer just a little poison to her husband every day. It was a comedy, of sorts, and the amount of poison dispensed was just enough to kill a tiny part of him each day until finally his whole system shut down. Kim and I had been feeding each other little bits of poison for a long time.

Dinner was on the table when I arrived home. The boys talked animatedly about the events of the day, but few words passed between Kim and me. Instead, we each engaged the boys, who responded positively to the extra attention without understanding the reason for it. The meat loaf Kim had prepared was good, but I couldn't help wondering if any "extra" ingredients were added that I didn't know about. It was stupid, of course, because Kim was eating the same meat loaf and so were Alex and Trevor. The poison would affect all of us.

"Dad? Can I sleep in your bed tonight?" asked Trevor, with a mouthful of mashed potatoes. The boys knew that one side of the bed would always be available to them should they want to occupy it.

"Sure, honey. But you still need to go to bed early." I figured he still had a year or so before it would be too weird to sleep in my bed. Alex had a little longer.

"They have practice tonight," Kim reminded me as she rose to clear the table.

"I thought it was Trevor's night to clean up," but he was already attempting to slip away quietly.

"It is. But we have to get going." Suddenly she sounded exhausted.

"I can take them to practice," I offered, really wanting to help out if possible.

"No. It's ok. I've got to meet with the coaches and go over schedules."

Kim left with the boys soon thereafter and I found myself wondering what to do with the gift of free time. I thought about masturbating but couldn't find the motivation. Was I allowing a confusing and disjointed home life to interfere with my visceral desires? As a younger man it would never have made a difference, but already I was beginning to feel like a stranger in my own house. It had been only a week since we agreed to divorce, but the concept was settling in faster than expected. I grabbed a beer and plopped down in front of the television. The news was on and while watching the commentator report on some dumbass that got rid of his old flush toilets in favor of a contraption that composts your bodily waste, I randomly decided that wherever I ended up the easy chair on which I was currently positioned was coming with me. The easy chair seemed to make everything more palatable, even the newscast. I didn't think Kim would object.

When was the last time we had really connected, Kim and I? Five years ago? Ten? Before the boys were born, or after? I felt relatively confident we were still the center of each other's world for some time after the boys were born. If that were the case, then when did we lose touch and why? When had our communication broken down? I couldn't come up with an answer, but with the help of Therapist Jim what I figured out was that we weren't saving each other anymore. If one of us fell someone else would have to catch us, or else we'd just keep falling. It may have started with Kim, what with the burning building question and all, but I was well past the point where I wouldn't save her first either, at least not if offered a viable alternative.

The big day finally came. Throughout the morning I could barely contain my excitement and experienced a panic attack or two for fear of Elaine cancelling our lunch date. I reminded myself she was a busy person with myriad responsibilities and for those reasons could certainly rationalize our date out of existence should the need arise. And for that reason I refrained from calling her. If she was going cancel she'd be the one to pick up the phone.

The morning passed uneventfully and without a phone call from Elaine. It was cold and sunny as I drove to Cincinnati to meet her at Tink's, a restaurant in the Clifton neighborhood of the city. Tink's was small and had an excellent wine list. Its ten or fifteen tables were covered with white table cloths and placed at a comfortable distance from each other. The only problem was the absence of a parking lot, and street parking can be scarce in Clifton. I was forced to park three blocks away and brave the cold. To my delight Elaine was already at the door when I arrived. She smiled as we greeted each other. She was shivering.

"Why didn't you go inside?" I asked, holding the door for her to enter.

"It's a beautiful day," she responded with a grin, "and I wanted to enjoy the sunshine."

She was right. It was a beautiful day and getting better. Elaine was wearing a wool gray skirt just above the knee that showed off her long legs and knee-high leather boots. The black turtleneck was cotton and form fitting. She looked lovely.

"Would you like a drink?" I asked Elaine, unsure whether to order one for myself. Few business people drank at lunch anymore and I planned to go back to work after the meal.

"Sure. I'm taking the rest of the day off."

"Well, then. I guess I am too." I was beginning to relax. "What are we having?"

"Do you trust me?" she demurred.

"It looks like I'm just about to."

Elaine glanced up at the waiter, who had been hovering around the table, and ordered a bottle of wine. To this day I can't remember the name or the year, but it was red and dry and delicious. As she took charge of the wine ordering, I relaxed further. It felt good to sit back and let someone else run the show. I had picked the restaurant but Elaine was no wallflower, and her display of confidence was powerful and intoxicating.

"And what are we having for lunch?" I asked with a hint of irony, hoping the answer might be 'each other.'

"Well, let's see," she said while opening the menu. "I hope you're a meat eater. If not I'm leaving right now." She was laughing, but I think she meant it. "I say we have the filet medallions with new potatoes. They'll go great with the wine, and we can begin with a salad."

I was prepared to eat or drink anything she suggested. She was in charge and I found it all very seductive, whether she knew she was being seductive or not. I imagine she had at least an inkling of the effect she could have on men, whether she would admit it or not. The woman facing me was undeniably the same person I had met at O'Hearn's, capable of holding my rapt attention with little to no effort.

We finished lunch in good spirits. No doubt a product of good wine and food, the prospect at taking the rest of the day off, and the feeling we might be at the beginning of an adventure. I paid the tab and we walked out into the chilly afternoon air. The sky had clouded over again but it wasn't snowing. We stood for a moment fidgeting in front of the restaurant like two teenagers at the end of a first date. To put an end to the awkwardness, I took her hand in mine and began to speak.

"Hey Elaine, I know a nice hotel nearby." She squeezed my hand, and I had my answer.

"It's not exactly five stars, but it's comfortable and I think you'll like it."

I was trying to "be cool" while containing my anxiety and simultaneously slow my heart to a reasonable beats-per-minute.

"I think we should go," she said softly. "You know, since neither of us is going back to work. I'll follow you."

We walked to her car and she drove me to where I was parked. As she tailed behind I kept checking the rear-view mirror to make sure she was there and experienced another panic attack when I caught her talking on the phone at the stoplight. Was it work? Did she need to go in? The anticipation was killing me. I tried to focus on the radio but failed. The meager facility I had available was focused on getting to the hotel and imagining how things would play out once we got there.

When we arrived Elaine insisted on paying for the room, and I felt only nervous desire. My brain was no longer involved. Elaine handed me the key card when we got to our room and stroked my hand as I took it from her. Somehow we managed to enter the room together and get the door closed and locked behind us.

Then we undressed.

The feel of her nakedness against my body was heavenly and excruciating. Within moments we were locked together, still vertical but inseparable, and inching our way toward the bed. Everything beyond that moment was a blur of bodies in motion, moving to a rhythm of irregular beats and godly sounds that seemed to emanate from faraway. My desire was overwhelming. I remember the sweat and the hair pulling. I remember the smell of her and the attempts to crawl under her skin. I remember the exhaustion at the end. I also remember not wanting to leave the warmth of the bed, allowing the afternoon sun to bathe our naked bodies. Unfortunately that was not to be.

"Hey, listen," she almost whispered as we lay facing each other. "I got a phone call on my way over. I have to be in a conference call in about an hour so I have to go. Something about a product defect in China. I'm sorry. I know that's not very sexy pillow talk."

And poof! The bubble burst and reality invaded the room. We got dressed in relative silence and made small talk as I walked her to her SUV. I tried to be cheery as my heart sank and wondered if she was doing the same, but was unable to pick up on what she might really be feeling.

"Thank you." She said plainly as we hugged by her car. "I'm sorry I have to go. Will you call me next week?"

"Is that ok?" I asked, suddenly and characteristically unsure. Next week?

"Absolutely. Don't forget about me." She kissed me before opening her door and getting in.

I watched as she drove away, pondering the possibility of forgetting about her. It would certainly have been the wisest thing to do at that point. The prospect of driving home, alone, left me saddened. After my lecture from Therapist Jim (and subsequent firm-talking-to from Izzy) I knew our life—as we once knew it—had changed forever. Even though part of me hoped that Kim and I would reconcile, deep down I knew it was impossible.

As far back as I can recall I had a plan, or at least a general outline, for my life. Until now I had managed to ignore any incidents that didn't jibe with this outline and strategy. But life is messy and the mess is always stalking around, waiting for an unsuspecting moment to crawl in through a crack, uninvited. It seemed I had finally let the mess wheedle itself in, or at least I finally realized it. Meeting Elaine forced open the crack and had opened my eyes. For the first time I had a clear view of all that I thought had been missing.

CHAPTER SIX

Making love with you
Has left me peaceful, warm, and tired
What more could I ask
There's nothing left to be desired
Peace came upon me and it leaves me weak
So sleep, silent angel, go to sleep

Sometimes, all I need is the air that I breathe and to love you…

I wasn't sure but it was possible the Hollies were singing to me that Saturday morning as I drove the boys to a soccer game. One of the first things I noticed after the crack had opened was the effect music was having on me. Or rather, the effect it was having on me again. I seemed to be back in High School, where I felt everything and would listen to a song over and over again until the whole experience of it sank into my soul. The songs were almost always associated with girls with whom I'd had relationships of varying degrees of intimacy. By listening to the songs over and over again the chaos and torture invariably accompanying each unrequited love or soaring affection was sure to be ingrained in my psyche, becoming inextricably linked to that particular song. The Hollies' ballad brought back the memory of the first girl I ever loved that never loved me. There would be more after her, more than I can count with all my digits, but she was the first and therefore the most memorable. We never so much as held hands but the Hollies' description of innocent love and passionate love making seemed to fit the bill at the time. And now the universe, in the guise of the disc jockey at the other end of my radio, was telling me to relive that experience, but I wasn't sure why. Was I falling in love with Elaine? Was that even possible? I had only known her over a few short weeks. An escalating argument between Trevor and Alex interrupted my ruminations.

"I said I get shotgun on the way home!" Alex yelled at Trevor from the back seat. Trevor had beaten Alex in the calling of "Shotgun!" right before we left the house, and was thus resplendent in his joy at occupying the seat next to me.

"You have to call it!" Trevor yelled back at Alex.

"That's not fair!" Alex opined, omitting any supporting commentary on the nature of fairness in general or on the tradition of calling "Shotgun!" in particular.

"Boys!" I yelled sharply, admittedly a bit frustrated by their intrusion into my contemplation. "Hold it down. Alex, you can't call Shotgun on the WAY to wherever you're going. You have to wait until we're ready to leave again." At least this was my understanding.

"Why, Dad? Why can't I call it now?" He asked while Trevor snickered. Obviously the timing issue did not carry the same importance to a ten year old boy as it did to a man in his forties.

"That's just how it works, honey." I said, trying to induce calm. "That's how it's worked since the first Model T rolled off the assembly line."

"Well, then can I get an ice cream after the game?" Alex asked, inexplicably foregoing any questions about the first mass produced automobile.

"I want some, too." Trevor added.

"Well, Alex. I'm not sure what one has to do with the other, but I suppose it's alright." With the distraction of future ice cream, the boys let go of their debate and fell silent.

Peace returned to the vehicle but not quickly enough to allow any more thoughts on the subject at hand. We arrived at the indoor soccer arena and trundled inside, the boys taking every opportunity to climb over snow piles or kick chunks of ice around the parking lot. Without explanation Kim had decided not to attend the game that morning. I did not take issue with this, and decided to answer the inevitable "Where's Kim this morning?" questions with a simple "Sleeping in for a change." Since nearly all the adults in the arena would be parents I knew the opportunity to glean a couple extra hours of sleep on a Saturday morning would be appreciated, and received commiserating nods and smiles every time I answered the question.

The game went well for the boys. Undistracted by any concrete knowledge of what was going on between their parents (or apparently by anything at all) they threw themselves into the contest and by half time had scored three points between them. I watched the game but not with the usual gusto as part of my brain continued to process events from the day before, leaving barely half my brain to attend to the game. Through the pungent odors of pizza, popcorn and spilt soda I could still smell Elaine's skin. So while the crowd around me alternately cheered or groaned at the unfolding contest, I felt her feet pressing against my calves and the shape of her body beneath me. And despite Izzy's warning none of this made me feel guilty. And that was unexpected. I felt I should have felt guilty, and then felt a little guilty about not feeling guilty. But something in me must have thought I deserved it, deserved Elaine and our afternoon tryst. What I ended up getting stuck on was her sudden exit from our love nest. Being a neophyte to the "game," I wasn't sure if this behavior was common to the general population or if Elaine had been left feeling guilty herself, and consequently overwhelmed by an eagerness to escape as soon as it was feasible to do so. Nor did I understand the appropriate protocol as to any follow-on waiting period. Was I allowed to contact her first and, if so, when? Or should I wait for her to contact me? Being ignorant of such rules, I pulled my phone out and brazenly sent her a text message, a technology I had rarely used until that point but, under the circumstances, suddenly presented itself as the perfect form of communication.

"How are you today?" I messaged. It was certainly not eloquent but I was going for non-committal. To my joy and surprise I received a reply almost immediately.

"Good! How are you? I was hoping to hear from you today." Holy crap! Now what? I honestly didn't expect her to respond. The moment had the jarring sensation that normally accompanied someone answering the phone after I've fully prepared to leave a voice mail message. I was blindsided.

"I was hoping you'd answer!" was all I could come up with. And then added, "What are you up to?"

66

"Having a cup of coffee, watching a movie and thinking about yesterday... you?" She actually put the dot-dot-dot, like she was day dreaming. It was very distracting and the soccer game was coming down to the last few minutes, at least that's what less than half my brain was comprehending at the moment.

"At a soccer game. Almost done. Boys are doing well." My response was not romantic or dreamy. In fact, it was so unromantic and off topic I thought she might be insulted.

"So...when can I see you again?" Double holy crap!

Evidently Elaine had decided to overlook my fact based, simplistic response, but since all I had in my head at that point was "Uh......." I took a moment to think before responding.

Texting, while excellent for privacy, does not easily lend itself to eloquence or philosophical interpretations, both of which I suddenly felt need of. When could I see her again? Oddly, that question was absent from the litany of questions demanding answers all morning. In hindsight it occurred to me it should have been the first question I asked upon leaving the hotel. Of course, asking Elaine so soon after our little get together would have given away my naiveté' and lack of cool. But that wasn't why I didn't ask her, as we stood in the parking lot of the hotel, when I could see her again. The real reason had more to do with stunned silence. Regardless, I somehow managed to deftly avoid the appearance of pathetic neediness that most certainly would have sunk any chance of a second date. (The pathetic neediness would come later.)

"How about next week?" I finally texted back.

"Great! Let's talk on Monday after we look at schedules." I was ecstatic.

"Talk Monday then. Bye!"

"Bye!"

It was a quick conversation, and to the point. She wanted to get together again and that was enough information to sustain me through the weekend. I relaxed a bit more as the boys walked over to me carrying their gear bags over their shoulders. I was desirable after all.

"Hey! Nice game!" I believe I sounded a bit maniacal. "You guys got all your stuff?"

"Yeah, Dad." Alex answered for the two of them. "But remember, you said we could have ice cream." I had forgotten about the ice cream, but not on purpose.

"Right! I sure did. Let's go get some."

The three of us went to the concession and ordered ice cream. We had soft serve twists all around and talked lightly about the game's high and low points as we sat in the small seating area reserved for concession stand food buyers. Other than Trevor almost going over the wall during a particularly aggressive tackle, it appeared I did not miss any of the most exciting moments of the game and was able to recall them with enough detail to satisfy the boys that I had, indeed, been paying attention. To Alex's credit, he managed to beat Trevor out in the calling of "shotgun" for the ride home, wisely biding his time until Trevor had his mouth full of ice cream.

Arriving home, Trevor and Alex were excited to tell their mom about their victory. Kim was still asleep on the couch when we entered but awoke quickly once the boys started pestering her and pelting her with tales of missed shots and successful tackles. I sat across the room in the green arm chair, staring at the woman to whom the boys were speaking and wondering where my wife had gone. The mother was still there, however. As I watched her interact with her sons I wondered if, had I been more attendant through the years, I could have prevented us from reaching the point at which we now stood, she in her nightgown talking to the boys about the game and me across the room watching quietly. The space between us had grown so much larger than the ten feet of carpet that lay between us.

I like to fix things. I like to fix cars and plumbing and window screens. I like to help my friends fix their things. I feel honored to work on their machinery and problems when they deign to bring them to me. But I couldn't fix this without Kim's help. I needed her to hold the pipe while I attached it to the U-joint. I needed her to screw in the dry wall while I held the sheet against the studs. But this help was not to be forthcoming. My two hands were not enough to put everything back together and I didn't know how to make her WANT to help anymore. And Therapist Jim had as yet offered no magic ointment. None of my friends, colleagues or family members had been able to offer any helpful insight into how to repair the mish mash. I watched the three of them as tears welled in my eyes for the fate of Trevor and Alex, and perhaps for me and Kim as well.

Not wanting to cry in front of the boys or give them any clue as to what might be going on with their parents, I left the room. I wanted to preserve their innocence as long as possible. As I walked through the kitchen to head up the stairs I flashed back to the moment where we told Trevor there was no Santa Claus. He was in fifth grade. We had hoped to make it through his fifth grade Christmas before divulging a secret perpetuated by millions of parents worldwide, but he had finally buckled under the ridicule of class mates and asked us to tell him the truth. We did as he asked and a day of devastation was the payment for our honesty.

"Why do adults make that up? Especially because it just hurts when we find out the truth." He asked as tears streamed down his face.

"Well, honey, I think it's because it's nice to think that there's someone out there who gives gifts and expects nothing in return. And the kids don't have to do anything for the gifts but just be good kids." Oddly I was as unprepared for the question as Trevor was for reality. After all, I knew it had to come eventually but when it did it was worse than answering another age old question, "Where do babies come from?" He was sitting in Kim's lap and she hugged him tighter as he sobbed. But despite the rationale of his statement about the truth and his immediate feelings of betrayal we were eventually able to cheer him by bringing him into the Santa Conspiracy. Before he was even off Kim's lap he agreed to help us (and the rest of the adult world) maintain the illusion for his younger brother until such time as Alex suffered the same fate at the hands of his class mates. It was agreed the destruction of Alex's fantasy would not occur from inside the family.

Now, of course, the destruction of both boys' fantasy about relationships and the unquestioned acceptance of the longevity of love would come from the inside. They wouldn't suffer the birth pangs of truth at the hands of others in the know. Instead, they would hear it directly from the horses' mouths. There are worse fates, of course, but at the time I couldn't imagine one. I found the reality of the pain we were going to inflict upon them overwhelming. And this walked hand in hand with the reality there was nothing I could do about it. Or at least nothing I could do save a decidedly futile attempt to stay in a marriage that had proven unfixable. I rationalized the choice of divorce over the alternative by convincing myself I didn't want my children to think the marriage they witnessed every day was normal or healthy. That what they should expect in their future was quite different from what their parents had come to know. But what should they expect? What would their future hold? Would they walk through the rest of their lives with the belief, conscious or unconscious, that nothing lasts forever? Or would they instead react by fighting harder than I did? I wouldn't and couldn't know the answers for another twenty years, and I found it demoralizing. It's quite possible the boys would have preferred the unhappy marriage to no marriage at all. Looking for an escape hatch, I dialed Arthur as I entered my bedroom and closed the door behind me.

"Hello?"

"Hey, it's me. What are you doing tonight?" I asked.

"Whatever you're doing," he answered.

On Arthur's recommendation we invited our mutual friend, Johannes, to join us that evening at O'Hearn's. I had also invited Elaine via text message, but she begged off stating she had other plans. Over time I would learn when Elaine mentioned "plans" it could be any number of things. Book club, tennis lessons, a general social gathering, or a date were all possibilities. Elaine kept a busy social schedule. It confounded me at the time and I was impressed she ever managed to fit me into her schedule. I wanted to see Elaine, but if I couldn't Arthur and Johannes were probably the next best thing. Both were well aware of my recent history and therefore no time need be wasted relating any more than the latest news. Bringing them up to date on current developments could be completed over the first beer. As well, Johannes had recently divorced and was always willing to offer insight on his status, physical and emotional. Johannes also happened to be an engineer at General Electric, a fact I intended to utilize in order to glean as much information as possible about Elaine's status at the company. GE was a big organization, and I figured Johannes' extensive contacts within the company would come in handy to a light weight stalker such as myself. I had met Johannes through Arthur a number of years before, and like so much of Arthur's history had as yet been unable to ascertain the exact circumstances of their friendship.

"So how did you guys meet?" I asked Arthur one night.

"Oh, you know, through work." He demurred.

"Through who's work?" I pressed because, as far as I knew, Arthur and Johannes had never worked at the same company.

"He used to bank with us." Days later I would check into bank records for a Johannes Hausfeld and find no record of him as a customer. So I approached Arthur again.

"I don't know," Arthur evaded. "Maybe they deleted the record. Not my department."

I left it at that. I liked Johannes and felt it was best not to delve too deeply. Ignorance is bliss. I arrived at O'Hearn's to find the two of them already seated at a high top table. Johannes was a sports nut and, from what I could gather, a bit of a gambler. His ex-wife had never mentioned this as a point of contention within their marriage, but Johannes always tended to be more interested in outcomes and injury reports than in game highlights. But when he did win his joy was often translated into a round of drinks for his friends, an outcome which benefitted me and therefore should not be questioned too deeply. Johannes, much like Arthur, was the kind of guy you wanted with you in a tight spot, despite his occasional erratic behavior. I greeted both as I took a seat at the table but they were in the middle of a conversation so I kept my mouth shut until I learned enough about the conversation to jump in intelligently. My father called this the "five minute rule."

"So then what happened?" Arthur inquired of Johannes.

"That's when I grabbed my gun and chased them down the street. Didn't I tell you this story already?" Johannes looked somewhat puzzled. Unlike Arthur, I had heard this story before, which was probably why Johannes thought Arthur knew it as well. It was one of the worst days in Johannes' life. He and his wife had been having divorce-level problems and one night, unbeknownst to him, she snuck out of the house in the wee hours. Waking to find her absent from the marital bed he began methodically searching and, gun in hand, eventually found her on the street sitting in a car with another man. It was six in the morning.

"No. And I'm quite sure I would have remembered this particular story. Please, tell me more." Arthur was enthralled.

71

"Well, what I didn't know was that the guy she was sitting in the car with was a cop. He was a chicken shit, though, because as soon as they saw me coming he took off like a bat out of hell. I chased them down the street a little but never fired a shot. He brought her back about four hours later. I got the kids to school but I took the day off work so I could be there when she got back."

As I had the first time Johannes told me the story I failed to suppress a laugh at the vision of him in his underwear, brandishing a sidearm as he chased a car down the street. Random violence was not in his nature, which made the vision even funnier.

"Well, in his defense, I believe my reaction would have been the same. Facing down a gun waving mad man can be an unnerving experience. What happened when she got back?" Arthur had not suppressed his laughter either.

"Long story short, we decided to get a divorce. She packed her shit and moved out."

"What happened to her and the bobby?" Arthur asked. "Bobby" is British for "police officer." I think sometimes Arthur used certain words just to remind us he was English.

"I guess they dated for a little while but not for long. She's been through five or six guys since. She's got a revolving door to her apartment." Johannes said without malice, as though he were just stating fact. "What's up with you, man?" He asked, turning his attention to me.

"Oh, you know, same old shit. We're talking about divorce now."

"Damn. Sorry to hear it man. Kim was a good woman. She'd never pull the shit my ex did." Johannes focus still appeared to be on his ex-wife's antics.

"Maybe so, but she's not pulling anything with me either." I was trying to sound jovial but I wanted to change the subject. "How's work?"

"Not bad. GE just bought some jet engine manufacturer in Prague. I'm hoping they'll send me over for a few weeks to help get the transition started. Prague's a fun town." Johannes answered. He had been all over the world with his job and had picked favorites cities. "They're supposed to be setting up the transition team now. Then they'll send over engineers and project managers. GE's gotten pretty efficient at gobbling up other companies."

"Sucks for you, I guess!" I had always been a touch jealous of Johannes travel schedule. I made a note to see what the internet had to offer in the way of international banking positions.

"Hold on, mate." Arthur interjected. "Did you say project managers?"

"Yup."

"Hmmm. Just so happens our good friend here has become acquainted with one of your project managers. Appears he's gotten to know her pretty well, from what I gather." Arthur wore a wry smile, glaring at me but talking to Johannes. He knew about our lunch date. I may have been bragging.

"Who is she?" Johannes asked, turning toward me.

"Uh, her name's Elaine. Elaine Van Heusen. Ever heard of her?" Was my stalking plan beginning to fall into place?

"Nope. I can ask around, though." Johannes answered, dashing my immediate hopes of using him as a spy while simultaneously keeping hope alive. "How do you know her?"

Arthur chimed in. "Jason here has found someone to keep him warm on wintery nights, to play yin to his yang, so to speak. And she happens to work for the same company as you." "Really?" Johannes stretched the word "really" to a ridiculous length. "Well, corporate America is full of beautiful women. She is beautiful, right? You didn't snag yourself a mutant did you? She's got all her fingers and toes? If she doesn't it's ok, I won't judge you. I know you've gotten kind of desperate. I saw your boner when you first sat down."

"Whatever!" I wanted to sound as low key as possible but still felt the need to respond to Johannes barb. "She's actually very attractive. I may be desperate but I still have standards. I just wondered if you heard of her."

"Oh. Ok. Sure." Johannes looked at me with a dubious expression. "Like I said, I'll ask around, but I'll want to hear more about his later."

I let the subject drop to allow Johannes and Arthur more time to get caught up. Apparently neither talked to each other as often as both talked to me. Although taller than Arthur, Johannes had the same stocky build. And as far as I could tell women found him attractive. When Kim and I felt free to talk about such things, she once pointed out to me that Johannes had "puppy dog eyes." I believe the features of "puppy dog eyes" involve a certain type of droopy innocence and collectively induce the desire to hug, although the cause and effect have never been fully explained to me. I suppose when women use the phrase it's assumed everyone, or at least other women, in ear shot will know exactly what it means. In Johannes' case, the droopy innocence was probably a true reflection of his soul most of the time, unless you were sitting with his wife in a car in front of his house at six in the morning. I would imagine at that point his eyes reflected more a type of insane rage than a droopy innocence. Both images seemed to work for him, depending on the situation. The majority of the time Johannes was, and is, one of the most relaxed people I know. In the past I had been witness to the insane rage eyes, which is why I was happy Johannes was on my side.

"So are you seeing anyone?" Arthur asked Johannes. Having been married and faithful for nearly two decades, Arthur had a habit of living vicariously through his single male friends. Or, occasionally, his married friends.

"I was dating this intern." Johannes replied. "But she got transferred to Kansas. Good Catholic girl. Fifteen years younger than me."

"So....?" Arthur pressed.

"What?" Johannes was playing stupid.

"Damn! Do I have to ask? Did you bed her? Did you take her innocence? And what the hell do you mean by 'good catholic girl'?" Arthur was visibly frustrated by Johannes' stonewalling.

"No. I didn't sleep with her. Everything but." Johannes replied, defending his manhood against Arthur's onslaught.

"What does that mean?" I chimed in. "'Everything but'. What the hell does that mean? There's a lot of room there, don't you think? I want you to describe 'everything but' to us and not sound like you're sixteen."

"It means everything but sex!" Johannes was becoming exasperated by the attention being focused on his love life. "Damn! How much detail do you need? What? Are we back in high school? Use your imaginations, for Christ's sake. Why do you guys need to know every detail?"

"Mainly because we don't think anything really happened." Arthur said, grinning. "You said she was a good Catholic girl.

Well, that could mean all the rumors about Catholic girls are true or it could mean she follows the rules. Which is it?"

Johannes was probably too much of a gentleman (puppy dog eyes guy) to go into detail, or else he was protecting her honor. But Arthur and I had fun with it in the meantime. Since details were not forthcoming, for the next hour or so Johannes was forced to endure accusations of various and sundry sex crimes, splitting hairs on what sex is and isn't, and with trying to relive his virgin years. He took it all in good humor (mostly) and the subject of the intern was forgotten when he was sent a beer by a woman at the bar. Unfortunately for Johannes, the woman was at least 15 years his senior and this now became grist for more jokes about Johannes sex life.

"I don't know, Johannes," Arthur used his most formal British accent. "Seems to me you might be having a problem finding someone in your own age group. Have you talked to anyone about this? Sought any professional help?"

"Ok, we've had our fun." Johannes protested while he laughed. "You're just jealous because she didn't send you one, you dried up old limey!"

"Touche'!" Arthur replied. "But I suppose it would be nice for you to find someone aged somewhere in the middle." Johannes sighed in acquiescence to his current fate.

"You know, Johannes, my Mom is single. Do you want her phone number?" I asked.

"Alright gentleman," Johannes relented. "Let's move on."

And we did move on, or moved back to the business of catching up with the details of each other's lives. Well, as many as possible considering the company, the drinking, and an inability to stay on topic. Arthur was considering reviving his Persian Carpet import business and Johannes mentioned his next trip overseas was to be to Singapore. I had nothing much to add to this conversation. My days were spent within a thirty-mile radius of the building in which I worked. Boring by the standards to which I was being subjected. I could console myself in the thought that my children came first, which they did, and travelling might hurt our relationship. But both of my drinking buddies had children as well and somehow managed to work overseas trips into their schedules without permanently scarring their offspring. I found it a tad humbling to be reminded of how dull my job could sound in comparison with some others, at least in this aspect. While my friends were imbibing in the spirits and secrets of foreign cultures, I was reviewing financial statements. While they were learning "the language", I was determining how much money a company needed to advance their business. Even with the turmoil in my personal life, it appeared rather dry by comparison. In reflection it occurred to me we can't all be mountain climbers. And also that I had never heard of anyone getting paid to climb one.

Despite the relatively tame nature of my existence, I comforted myself with the secret of Elaine, the subject of which had yet to be revived by my cohorts. Even as we opined on the nature and potential availability of the female "talent" surrounding us, Arthur made no further comments about her, which was no surprise, and Johannes did not appear interested enough to ask any more questions. So for the rest of the evening I kept Elaine to myself. And during conversational slow periods I allowed my mind to relive the most prurient moments from the day before, which I suspect brought a ridiculous smile to my face. In one of these moments I found my cell phone vibrating anxiously in my pocket. It was text message from Elaine.

"Home now. Busy?" She inquired without using connectors.

"Out with friends." I sent back without putting too much thought in it. The beer was helping me defend against panic.

"Can u come over?"

Panic. Of course I wanted to see her, but how was I to slip out? What were the implications? It was all so new. I decided to lean on Arthur, whom I believed at least slightly more worldly than Johannes and a great deal more worldly than me.

"Umm...Arthur," I stumbled. "Can I have a word?"

Coming at him so abruptly, the question was received with inquisitive stares from Arthur and Johannes. I said nothing more as awkward silence fell on the table.

"Well, I've got to take a piss." Johannes gracefully left the table in order to give me a moment with Arthur.

"What is it?" Arthur asked once the coast was clear.

"Elaine wants me to come over. What do you think?" I could feel sweat beading on my forehead.

"Why are you still sitting here?" Arthur responded plainly.

"Well, you know, I don't want to leave you guys hanging. You know, this is sort of a guy's night out." What was I talking about?

"Are you insane?" Arthur was incredulous.

"Right. Understood. But I'll wait to tell Johannes goodnight." Always a gentleman.

"Off you go, you git." Arthur responded. "I'll make your apologies to Johannes."

"Well…alright then."

I grabbed my coat and texted Elaine on my way out of the bar. She was pleased to hear I was coming. She gave me her address and some helpful instructions on how to get there. It was only fifteen minutes or so from O'Hearn's so I had little time to prepare myself emotionally. As well, my car seemed to be driving faster than normal and as much as I tried to control the speed the vehicle would not obey the posted limit. In short order I arrived at Elaine's home, heart racing in with the engine.

Elaine's living space was a cottage nestled in the woods behind a rock-walled mansion. She would tell me later that the house was built as a servant's quarters. It was a two story, two bedroom affair at least a hundred years old and invisible from the road and to the random passerby. She had leased the building after her divorce after being forced, by decree, to sell the house in which she and her ex-husband had resided. The house was cloistered and without her instructions I never would have found the place. As carefully as was possible under the circumstances, I guided my ornery vehicle down a winding driveway. Anticipating my arrival Elaine turned on the exterior lights, which I could see through the bare tree branches but did little to help me negotiate the dark, single lane drive. When I arrived Elaine was standing at the end of the walkway holding a beer in her hand. It was for me.

"I thought you might like this." She said as I walked to her. "I remember the other day you said you like Rolling Rock and Guinness, so I bought some of both. I hope this is ok." It was a Rolling Rock.

"This is great!" was all I could think of to say. And it was. I admit I was a bit dumbfounded by her grace and the level of thoughtfulness being shown to me. Yet I also felt my confidence soar and I stopped questioning whether or not she truly wanted me there with her.

"Thank you." I took the beer from her hand and took a sip. With my free hand I took her by the waist, pulling her to me and kissing her as I had the first night we met at O'Hearn's. Releasing her waist, I took her hand and, quite literally, led her down the garden path toward the cottage. The front porch was enclosed and heated, and we alighted there long enough to remove clothing and begin love making. She paid no heed to the chance someone might see, and so I did not either. Despite the nakedness of the surrounding trees, there was little chance anyone would see us on the patio couch, although there was much to see for anyone with an interest. Leaving our clothing on the porch we eventually made our way into the house with Elaine now leading the way. I had no agenda but Elaine seemed intent on christening various pieces of furniture in the living room and kitchen, both of which had to be traversed in order to get to the stairs leading to her bedroom. The ascent was made laborious as our skin became slick and each of us refused to let the other go long enough to take even a step individually. I found it impossible to be close enough to her. Thus we ended in her bed, spooning our bodies together as the cold moonlight streamed in through the bedroom window onto our overheated bodies.

"This is nice," she whispered to her pillow as our breathing relaxed.

"Yes, it is." I whispered to her hair.

"Do you need anything?" She asked quietly.

Did I need anything? It was loaded question though I'm sure she didn't intend it to be. Did I need anything? I hadn't been asked that question in a long time. But at the moment I was completely satisfied. Her cottage seemed a haven from the rest of the world, a secret garden. Its woodsy isolation helped make it an island in the storm, a place difficult to find without prior knowledge or detailed instructions. As Elaine and I laid, calm and with bodies interwoven, I felt a rush of emotion for this woman who had unwittingly thrown me a life line. I realized how quickly she had become dear to me. Did she feel the same? I couldn't be sure and I didn't ask, afraid to break the spell with a question for which no simple answer existed even if it was an answer I wanted to hear. I let it go in order to stay in the moment, a perfect moment in which I felt utterly happy. I wanted the outside world to stay outside as long as possible.

"No. Nothing at all." I finally answered.

CHAPTER SEVEN

It turns out women are the keepers of my emotional well-being. I'm not sure if this is a good or a bad thing, but to a great extent I imagine this is true to for all men whether we want to admit it or not. And I do mean ALL men, because gay men have mothers and sisters to whom they look for encouragement as well. Certainly, we all want to please our fathers, which on some level tends to be a life-long pursuit whether we like them or not. But it's the women in our lives who drag us to the dance floor; they make us talk about things and think about things that have nothing to do with cars or carpentry or politics; and they teach us that giving in to our emotions isn't always a bad thing. Personally, I find the gift of their beauty and bodies overwhelming, let alone all the good and bad that can come with them. But we can't help but love them. It's genetic. It's fate. We are not given a choice. For me, at least since the onset of pubescence, women have represented a world of scary possibilities, potentially pleasant chaos, and gratifying loss of control. I have allowed them to bolster my dreams and/or crush them, often within the space of two or three sentences spoken at the breakfast table on a Saturday morning. I have looked to them for acceptance even when it wasn't forthcoming. I've looked to them to make me whole. And all of these expectations were completely unfair.

The thing is, I think it's quite probable women also feel all of these things about men. In fact, I find it hard to believe otherwise. After all no man, or woman, is an island. But as hard as I try to do otherwise I can only speak from my own, decidedly male perspective. And part of my perspective is as follows: Buried in their capacity to love and our desire to please them is a secret most men hate to admit – that the opinion of the women we love is more important than the opinion of all our male friends put together. Sometimes it doesn't even have to be a woman you love. It could just be a woman you want to love, or a woman you want to love you.

As I said, I believe the reasons for this are trapped in our genes. It probably also has something to do with survival of the species, but an education in business and finance doesn't do much to lend credence to my theory.

It's an understatement to say that the crack in my dome of existential safety probably already had a hairline fracture before I met Elaine. After all, things weren't going all that well in the most important love relationship I had going at the time. (I mean my marriage to Kim, of course.) And since things were unbalanced in that part of my life, Elaine's whirlwind appearance was all it took to turn the hairline fracture into a gaping rupture. So, for better or worse, what began as a trickle was in danger of becoming a flood. And I wasn't really conscious of it.

Of course, I didn't have to be. It was happening whether I noticed or not. So, without asking my permission, the crack went ahead and started to let in a different reality, a world of new potential, and all the confusion inherent to situations where one must make choices from a multitude of possibilities. Suddenly I was feeling things I had forgotten existed and even forgotten I could feel. What was I to do if I was, indeed, in love with Elaine? Or was it obsession? And what would that mean in the big picture? What actions, if any, should I take if either were the truth? It was all simultaneously exciting and painful because, not being a total asshole, I actually spent some time thinking about the consequences of various courses of action. And this, In turn, exposed the truth of my current existence. That was the realization I had been on the proverbial treadmill, running and running yet standing still. And the fact was I had been on the treadmill for so long I no longer recognized anything I hadn't been staring at for years. I hadn't let in anything new. So, much like an infant human or a puppy, both of which enjoy a rousing game of peek-a-boo, if I didn't see it then it didn't exist. And there was a lot I had chosen not to see. Suddenly I had all this new emotional territory to navigate and little experience on which to draw. Luckily for me, help was always right around the corner, metaphorically speaking.

Therapist Jim: So what's on your mind today?
Me: Funny. (I was hoping he recognized the pun in his question even if it was unintentional.)

Therapist Jim: No, really, you seem preoccupied. (He smiled while he said it so I did not feel the need to point out his attempt at low brow humor. I moved on.)

Me: Doc, do you think it's possible to love, or be in love with, more than one woman?

Therapist Jim: Of course. (He said this without hesitation, like he knew I was going to ask the question. He might have spent hours researching the topic before I walked into his office.)

Me: Really? It's that simple? You're not going to hedge around a little and start with something like "under certain circumstances...."?

Therapist Jim: Nope. I believe it's absolutely possible, and even probable, that we can be in love with more than one person. Why do you think it wouldn't be possible? (The bastard loved turning the tables on me.)

Me: Hmm. Got me there. Well, when you put it that way, I don't have an answer. I guess I just have this romantic and, I suppose, unrealistic view that we can, or should, only really be in love with one person at a time.

Therapist Jim: I would imagine that view is optimal if you're trying to avoid emotional distress in your primary love relationship, but that doesn't it mean it won't or can't happen. Are you talking about Elaine? (Sneaky devil. Why did he bother to make me talk at all? How much was I paying him to read my mind?)

Me: Of course. I mean, I don't think I've fallen *out* of love with Kim, which is confusing enough considering the impending divorce. Not necessarily, anyway. But I'm pretty sure I've actually fallen *in* love with Elaine. I just want to make sure I'm not fooling myself.

Therapist Jim: Well, you might actually be fooling yourself, but even if you are it doesn't mean you can't be in love with more than one person. Just remember that how you act on the emotion is far more important than the emotion itself, at least when it comes to the effect on you and those around you. (I had to appreciate his brutal honesty.)

Me: Hmmm. I think I understand what you're saying, but can you explain it anyway?

Therapist Jim: Well, *having* emotions doesn't necessarily affect outcomes. We all *have* emotions, but the course of your life is decided by what you do with them, not by the fact that you have them.

Me: Ok, well, that's pretty much exactly what I thought you meant. So, if I am in love with Elaine, what should I do with it?
Therapist Jim: What do you think you should do with it?

That was Therapist Jim for you. Simultaneously helpful and unhelpful. In hindsight it occurs to me I should have spent the rest of the session grilling him on the nature of love and what he really thought it all meant. But I didn't. I was too caught up in what some people, mainly those comprising a group of less critical thinkers than Therapist Jim, may have considered an obsession. This idea of Elaine as an obsession would, over time, occasionally occur to me as well, only to be dismissed out of hand. I mean, isn't love just a form of obsession? I'd like to believe the persistent desire to be in physical and emotional contact with another person is what most of us would identify as love, and only the cynical as obsession. But really, what do I know? I should have asked Therapist Jim how one goes about identifying the line between love and obsession, and in a rare moment of clarity made a mental note to ask him the next time we were together.

If I was on a game show and forced to answer the love vs. obsession question without guidance from an educated, well paid professional like Therapist Jim, I would respond thus: Love becomes obsession when one of the parties either never had or no longer has the persistent desire to be in physical and emotional contact with the other party. After that point the other person, the one whose feelings haven't changed, is called a "stalker" and becomes an object of ridicule. Of course, I realize my speculation is anecdotal and holds no clinical value, but God knows I had no desire to become an object of ridicule. I therefore decided that at some point I must test the waters, so to speak, with Elaine and make an attempt to discover the nature of her feelings toward me. At the risk of overemphasizing my spotty history of discerning the feelings of the opposite sex, I will say I did not relish carrying out this self-assignment. Certainly, if I could have found any way around it I would have undoubtedly done so.

Having spent the lunch hour with Therapist Jim, I returned to work to find little changed in the time I was gone. As far as anyone knew, no hackers had attempted to steal into our computer network over the last few weeks and today was no exception. And while I really had no desire to see the bank and its customers laid low by some smelly, unkempt computer geeks with too much time on their hands, the attempted break-ins had at least made things more interesting. Since then, however, the old routine had come back with a vengeance, leaving me with nothing better than to contemplate the pile of work on my desk. Through this contemplation, I discovered the most interesting thing about the pile was that no matter the strenuousness of my labors, it neither grew nor contracted in size, thereby rendering my work efforts meaningless. This thought drained me of motivation so I sat and stared at it. I was winning the staring contest when it was interrupted by Emily dialing in on the intercom.

"Jason, Kim's on the line for you." She was matter-of-fact. I was never sure if my marital situation registered with Emily. If it did she did not outwardly demonstrate any awkwardness about it.

"Ok, put her through, please." I responded in kind. Kim and I had reached a sort of détente over the past few weeks. Although nothing had changed between us, without any actual discussion we seemed to have mutually agreed to make the best of the situation for the time being. Making the best of the situation mostly involved staying out of each other's way and keeping each other abreast of our schedules. It also involved staying informed on anything affecting the boys, the latter being the reason for this particular phone call.

"Just calling to let you know there's no practice tonight. It was cancelled because the coach is sick." Her words were clipped and her voice business like.

"Ok. No problem. Thanks for letting me know. I'll be home at the regular time."

"Ok. See you later." She hung up.

I hung up as well and stared at the phone for a moment. It occurred to me the energy I was about to expend to discern the nature of my relationship with Elaine might be put to better use trying to figure out what had happened between my wife and me. This thought had been appearing regularly, only to be followed by the realization I had spent the better part of the last two years doing just that. It was a knee jerk reaction over which I exerted little control. Of course, by that time if I had been able to make an improvement in the course of my relationship with Kim it would already have been made. As it was, all my efforts in that area proved fruitless, at least as far as I could tell. So there I sat contemplating the implacable mound of file folders and trying to find the requisite motivation to reduce the height of a stack which consistently resisted reduction. To my credit, and with nothing better to do, I went ahead and started working. But after making an important decision or two concerning the financial future of one or two local companies, I decided to reward my resurgent work ethic with a call to Izzy.

"Northern Kentucky Bank and Trust, how may I help you today?" Izzy answered by the third ring.

"Hey, it's me. What are you doing?" I tried to sound conspiratorial.

"Working," she said. "The same thing you should be doing! Weren't you bitching just a few days ago that you felt like you were falling behind?"

"Well, yes...but I'm about to have a very productive afternoon and we haven't talked for a few days. This is my reward for being good....soon."

"Well, don't I feel special." Izzy stated with no small amount of sarcasm. "So what's going on? How was 'lunch' today?" She knew of my weekly encounters with Therapist Jim and was extremely supportive, just as I was about her regular appointments with her shaman, whom I referred to as "Therapist Jen." Not very creative, perhaps, but I liked the symmetry.

"It was all good. We contemplated the nature of love, the meaning of life, and our purpose in the universe. You know, the usual."

"And did you have an epiphany today? Did you finally figure out your place in the universe? If you did, I think you should share it with the world." Izzy responded. The sarcasm had been replaced by barely suppressed laughter.

"Whatever, Iz. You can laugh but yes, I had an epiphany. I've decided to determine exactly what's going on between me and Elaine." I sounded childishly defiant.

"Oh, really? Are you sure figuring out your place in the universe wouldn't be easier?"

"Of course not. Too many variables with the whole universe thing. If I stick to trying to figure out my place with just one person I should be able to figure it out before I die."

"Well, remember you're still talking about a woman. Most poets die before they figure out the first thing about us and I predict that one life is not enough time for you. Either you're underestimating her or overestimating yourself."

"I think you might be the one underestimating me." I said, still defiant. "Do you doubt my intelligence?"

"Oh, no way! Everyone who knows you gets that you're much smarter than you usually appear! But you're numbers smart, Jason, not chick smart. Understand?"

"I understand that's what you think," I chose to ignore the "smarter than you usually appear" comment for now. "Which is why I think you underestimate me."

"Sweetie, I know you're going to do whatever you're going to do no matter what I say....so good luck. And I mean that. Just be careful. I feel like you're really setting yourself up to get hurt and you know I only want what's best for you. I'm here if you need me." Izzy was sincere. And she really did mean it, which is why anyone would want her as a friend.

"I know that, Iz. And thanks. And you know what, believe it or not, I'm actually going to get some more work done before I leave today." I meant it, too.

"Sounds good. Call me later if you get a chance."

"You know I will." I replied and hung up. And to my own surprise I dug right back into work, determined to feel some sense of accomplishment before the end of the work day.

Listening to a top forty station and enjoying a wonderful sense of accomplishment, the last fragments of sunlight angled into the car, attempting to obscure my vision. I donned sunglasses and merged onto the highway, pleasantly surprised by the realization that the drive home didn't seem quite as lonely as it had for the past few months. While I always had my time with the boys to look forward to after work, this happy thought usually came handcuffed to a sense of dread. The dread had to do with any potential alone time with Kim. What would we talk about? How forced would the conversation, if any, be? Could we get away with simple communication, like "Do you have the remote?" or, if the television was already on, "Look at that dumbass!"? I imagine Kim shared this sense of dread as it related to my return home, although she had never communicated it to me. But for that matter I hadn't shared my sense of dread with her, either. We hadn't shared much of anything for months and months. Regardless, I found myself tapping my foot and singing along to a forgettable hip hop song with an otherwise good beat. As the song ended my phone buzzed. It was Elaine. Could this particular ride home have gotten any better?

"Hey, there!" She greeted me cheerfully. "Nice day today, isn't it?"

I assumed she meant the weather, which had given the tristate region a day of crisp air and plenty of sunshine. "Oh, beautiful. No doubt." I responded with a smile on my face. It was good to hear her voice.

"Hey…is there any way you can meet me for a drink on your way home? I need to talk to you about something." She sounded cryptic.

"No, Elaine. I'm sorry. There's no way I can do that today." I felt disappointed and a slight wave of anxiety passed over me. Was she pregnant? Was she blowing me off? She sounded too cheerful for either of those. "Is there any way you can tell me now?"

"Well, I guess so. But you probably won't think it's good news. In a lot of ways I don't think it's good news either." She said ominously and paused before continuing. "Umm…I'm just going to come out and tell you, ok? I've decided to take an assignment in Prague. It will probably last for a couple years. GE just bought a company there."

"What?" What did she say? Did she just say she was leaving for a couple years? Obviously Elaine was one of those people who just pulled the band aid off all at once. The implications of her statement struck me dumb. Looking back, I'm now sure that, at the time, I was better prepared for news of an unplanned pregnancy than being faced with the prospect of Elaine leaving the country. I had already begun to work her into my plans, so to speak, and this was one eventuality for which I had not calculated.

"Jason? Are you there?" I heard Elaine's voice on the other end of a tunnel. It sounded small and faint.

"Yes, I'm here. I'm…just a little surprised." I struggled to respond. "When did this happen? Did you know it was possible?"

"I'm sorry, Jason. I knew it was a possibility but I didn't think it would happen this soon." She went on to explain that in the last year she had been offered two overseas assignments but had turned both down. After her second refusal, she had been told by her boss that if she was offered another foreign posting she should take it and that opting not to do so would permanently damage her career. They wouldn't fire her for not accepting, but nor would they continue to promote her in the manner and frequency to which she had become accustomed. So, when the muckity-mucks asked her to help oversee the acquisition and transition of the aircraft company they just bought in Prague, she felt she had no choice but to take it.

"I am sorry, Jason. I really am. I didn't want to spring it on you like this. But, you know…we've only known each other for a few weeks and there just hasn't been time to tell you everything going on in my life." She said plainly. I would learn over time that Elaine made a habit of playing her cards close to her chest. This would not be the last revelation to take me by surprise.

"I understand, Elaine. Really. I don't like it, but I understand." I was trying to sound understanding. I was not feeling very understanding. Meanwhile I wordlessly fought the urge to fire bomb Prague, by all accounts a nice place to visit and not at all deserving of the animosity I was feeling toward it at the moment.

"Hey! Don't t' worry. We still have a couple months before I have to be there. And I want to spend as much time with you as I can. Ok?" Elaine was trying to sound cheerful. I was not feeling cheerful.

"Sure. Absolutely." I said without much cheer.
"So…speaking of getting together again...when would you like to do that?" Every fiber in my body was telling me I had to see her as soon as possible.

"Oh, sweetie. I'll have to check my schedule. I'll call you tomorrow, ok? I want to get together as soon as possible." Were her body fibers telling her the same thing as mine?

"Good. Great. Me too. Let's talk tomorrow." The smile had disappeared a few sentences before. Elaine apologized one last time, said goodbye and hung up the phone. Our conversation brought about a dramatic alteration in my mood and I no longer felt the confidence that had carried me through most of the day. Indeed, that confidence had been replaced with dread. I was well aware Elaine had begun to loom large in my own estimation of my existence, but I didn't realize just how much until the moment she told me she would no longer be a part of it. Her pending departure changed everything. Only moments before I was perfectly comfortable letting our relationship take its natural course. After all, I was still married. Now, however, that comfort had been replaced with a sense of urgency. What was my role in her life? What part was I playing? What did I mean to her? I was having high school flash backs again and not the happy kind. We had only been off the phone five minutes and I was fighting the urge to call her back. Instead, I went to the well. I called Arthur.

When I arrived home Kim had dinner on the table, where the boys were already sitting, waiting for me to walk through the door. I felt a rush of love for them as I sat down, looking at their beautiful faces and fielding questions from them about the availability of funds for video games or if we could see a movie over the weekend. The latter I promised we would do. I was less keen on video games but nonetheless did not completely close out discussion. The pure joy I felt at being in their company was extremely welcome and I was afraid I would spoil it if I gave them an outright "no" on their quest for a new game. Besides, it was quite possible I would actually buy it for them. I'm an old softie when it comes to this sort of thing and quite susceptible to a sustained, aggressive sales pitch. The boys had learned this over time and knew if I didn't say "no" they stood a good chance of getting what they wanted. We chatted lightly as Kim served the family.

"Dad!" Alex exclaimed. "Did you know Mom was going out tonight? And we get to have a baby sitter if you go out, too!"

"No, I didn't know." I said truthfully, trying to hide my surprise. I could count on one hand the number of times Kim had gone out socially without me during the course of our marriage. It was out of character but I chose not to question it. I had pushed her to widen her circle of friends for years and wasn't about to come off like a hypocrite at that point in our (non)marriage. Besides, she had apparently been nice enough to arrange for a sitter so that I could make the same choice if I so desired. Which I already had, of course. "And who's going to come over and watch you animals this evening?"

"Angela," Trevor's cheeks flushed as he answered. "She said she would make popcorn and we could watch movies." Angela was a senior in high school and Trevor had had a crush on her for at least a year.

"That sounds excellent!" I worked to match the enthusiasm of my sons. "And, thanks Kim, for thinking of me. Where are you headed tonight?"

"Just out for a couple drinks with some of the Moms." By "Moms" she meant "Soccer Moms."

"Well, this all works out. Arthur and I are going out for a couple of beers also." I commented as we all started eating. I had put Arthur on standby on my way home from work after talking to Elaine and was too absorbed with the Elaine issue to delve any further into Kim's business.

"Where are you guys going?" Kim, on the other hand, was apparently more curious than I.

"You know, the usual. We'll end up at O'Hearn's." The fact Kim hadn't asked where I was going in years didn't register until later. I just thought she was trying to show an interest. "And where are you headed?" I was being polite.

"Somewhere else," She was being evasive.

But again I chose not to question her further. The boys were excited and talkative and I was distracted by the knowledge of my new love interest leaving town for a couple years. At that point the details of Kim's evening seemed inconsequential. Besides, whatever concerns I had would be bounced off Arthur later anyway, so it was an easy enough decision to try to relax and enjoy a low stress dinner. The chicken teriyaki stir fry Kim had prepared was quite good and even Alex went back for seconds. As the boys cleared the table Kim informed me she would be exiting shortly, leaving me to wait for the baby sitter, who would be arriving within the hour. Despite my preoccupation the whole experience left me feeling rather unshackled and ready for the evening. I spent the next hour catching up with the boys and they seemed not at all unhappy to be left alone with Angela, who arrived on schedule. The corn was popping as I left the house.

Arthur was sitting at the bar in O'Hearn's when I arrived. Though it was getting closer to spring, the sun was still setting early and there were no traces of it as I walked in. Years before, as a result of intensive anecdotal research, I determined that bars filled up faster after sunset, at least in northern climes. O'Hearn's was no exception. Waiting for the sitter had cut me out of Happy Hour but the place was still nearly full. Luckily Arthur had reserved a seat for me at the bar. He did this by simply placing his jacket upon it. I had come to rely on these small acts of companionship from Arthur, and he could be counted on to provide them, especially in this setting. I believe this is so because he enjoyed sitting and drinking but did not enjoy sitting and drinking alone. With the unspoken but implied invitation I removed Arthur's jacket, handed it to him and plopped down. Upon planting my ass I was quickly served a Guinness, which had been pre-ordered by Arthur. It all felt very efficient and out character.

"Thanks for the beer."

"My pleasure, mate." Arthur responded. "After what you told me earlier I thought you'd be ready for one as soon as you got in. You'll be happy to learn Guinness is on sale for the evening. Dollar a pint. Should save you some money."

"So I bought this beer?" Why was I surprised?

"Well sure, but look at the money I'm saving you. I'll get the next round." Arthur was back in character. "So are we just here to drink or are you going to get back to crying on my shoulder?"

"Drink, mostly. There's really nothing more to tell. Elaine's moving to Prague and will be gone a couple years. And that's that. This whole acquisition thing isn't working out for me. Not that General Electric gives a shit about my feelings." I was attempting to amuse myself as well as Arthur.

"What acquisition thing?" Arthur asked.

"Remember when Johannes told us about GE buying that aircraft engine manufacturer in Prague? That's what she's going to be doing. I guess they send over a whole, big team to get everything going the right way. She's leaving within, like, six or eight weeks."

"What did you say when she told you?" Arthur must have ignored my response to his question about drinking or crying on his shoulder.

"What could I say?" I answered with a hint of exasperation and/or whininess. "What am I supposed to do? Tell her not to go? She told me if she doesn't go it'll probably ruin her career. I don't think I can tell her to stay so, you know, a year or so from now, after I get a divorce, and then after an appropriate waiting period, we'll start dating and maybe, just maybe, then we'll be together. It's all a little too vague to hang a future on, don't you think? She'd be nuts to consider staying, and even if she was willing I wouldn't want that

91

on my conscious. The problem is I'm really starting to feel something for her. I mean, damn, with everything else going on she's become the thing I look forward to… Other than our time together, of course."

"Wow! You've really all twisted up over this bird." Arthur paused from his beer to make the statement.

"It would seem so. But, look, I'm trying not to go overboard with this. That's why I DIDN'T ask her to stay."

"I get it but it sounds like you've considered it, which means in your head you're already on the road to crazy town, which means you're a hair irrational, which in turn means you're probably in love with her." Arthur's insight was usually best somewhere between three and six beers. Someday I'll figure out why I constantly underestimated him.

"Dude! Get out of my head! Were you eavesdropping on me and Therapist Jim today? How do you figure this shit out?" I wasn't really angry but Arthur was really staying on topic, which put him back out of character.

"I have an analytical mind," was his simple response before pausing to drain his glass. "Have you thought about talking to Johannes? Maybe he can spy on her for you. Maybe he can go to Prague also…" I'm pretty sure Arthur knew things didn't really work that way In corporate America, and assumed he was distracted by his empty glass or purposely playing the fool for his own amusement.

"Yeah, that's how it works." I said sarcastically. "I'll tell Johannes to tell GE that he wants to go to Prague, too…and then I'm sure they'll do what he wants and then he can give me daily reports. Sounds like a plan."

After signaling the bartender to bring us another round, Arthur turned back to me. "Sounds like I'm right. You've hung yourself up on this bird." He said plainly.

"Fine. I guess you could say that. Can't really tell you how it happened."

"Are you in love with her?" He asked.

"What? Are we really going to sit around and talk about our feelings?" I asked, smiling. Arthur had been my confidant for years but I found myself unexpectedly embarrassed by the directness and honesty of the question. "Is there a camera? Are we on Oprah?"

"Don't be a git." Arthur commanded, annoyed. "It's on your mind."

"Alright, Arthur. Fine. Yes. I think I'm in love with her. But how do I know if the 'feelings' are real or not? I've only known her for, like, two months. Therapist Jim says you can love more than one person but that doesn't mean I'm in love with her. Does it?"

"Well, I agree with Therapist Jim but feelings are feelings, Jason. It's not math. If you feel them, then they're real. Hell, prepubescent girls knows that much. My point is that if you think you're in love then you're probably in love, and that opens up a whole new can of worms that you're going to have to deal with. Maybe it's a good thing she's going to move away." Arthur sounded logical, like he was doing math.

"Arthur, don't you think we're getting a little touchy-feely here? Besides, how the fuck can her leaving be a good thing?" I drank my beer. I was getting fed up with the whole conversation.

"It can be a good thing because maybe then you'll get your shit together and either make things work at home or, if not, you can get moving with the equitable distribution of property." He ignored my touchy-feely comment.

"Well, maybe." I briefly pondered the probabilities of various, multiple outcomes and the resulting pain or pleasure of each, finally making a command decision. "You know what? Let's not worry about all that tonight. Let's call Johannes and see if he can spy on her in Prague. It'll be like a prank phone call."

"I was thinking the same thing." Arthur replied, coming to the same conclusion. We grabbed our beers and headed to the smoking patio to call Johannes.

As a phenomena smoking patios had cropped up at bars around the country as a result of the majority, non-smokers, telling the minority, smokers, they didn't want to be around their kind. Regardless, the good and innovative entrepreneurs of the bar/restaurant industry figured out a way to skirt the law: They added a patio to some part of the building where none had previously existed. During summer, the patios remain fenced in, open air affairs. During winter, however, many are enclosed with plastic or tarp, essentially adding another room to the bar. O'Hearn's patio is where we relocated to make the call to Johannes. Arthur and I were not smokers but other than residual smell on one's clothes have no

93

issue with second hand smoke. But there was less bustling on the patio, providing a better atmosphere from which to make a phone call. I dialed Johannes as Arthur and I settled in at a patio table.

"Hello?" Johannes' voice said from the other end of the phone.

"Johannes! It's me and Arthur. What are you up to?" I made sure to follow the social convention of checking on one's physical and/or emotional status before jumping in and asking them for a favor.

"I'm on a date with a hot girl. What do you need?" Johannes was rushing and though his voice sounded lighthearted he was not appreciating the disturbance. He'd not been on a date for three or four months.

"Oh, man! Never mind. It can wait for when you're not trying to get laid." I meant it, too. I didn't want to distract him from potential sex if, indeed, that was even possible.

"Don't worry, man. Give it up. What do you need?" He asked again.

"Ok, then. Here's the thing. Remember when you said GE bought that aircraft parts manufacturer in Prague?" I asked.

"Sure. What about it?"

"Well, I found out today that Elaine is moving there to help manage the transition. Do you know anything about that?"

"I know they always send a transition team. I'm not surprised she's on it if she's in project management. Why? You need me to do a little spying for you? Do you want me to get assigned there so I can keep an eye on her for you?" He laughed from the other end of the phone.

"Ah, well...yeah. Kind of..." I stuttered. I found Johannes' accidental prescience as bewildering as I had found Arthur's. "Any chance of that happening? And I'm not just asking because I've been drinking. I'm also asking because it freaked me out a little when she told me."

"Dude, you're funny! Ask me again tomorrow when we're both sober. I've got to get back to my date. She's got a great pair of legs and I want to see more of them. Buy Arthur a beer for me and I'll talk to you tomorrow." Johannes commanded and hung up. I supposed I should have felt slighted but I didn't. I was too empathetic when it came to the plight of the sexless and I wasn't about to deny Johannes his right to the pursuit of happiness.

"Well?" Arthur asked as I pulled the phone away from my ear.

"He told me to call him tomorrow. He's really bossy when he's trying to get laid." I said, feigning hurt feelings.

"Aren't we all?" Arthur said with a smile. "You know, Jason, I've been thinking."

"What about? Beer? Scotch?"

"Well, yes, I suppose…in a roundabout way. I've had a realization; an epiphany, if you will. It occurred to me that while O'Hearn's is a lovely dive and I always enjoy our time here, it might be time to expand our horizons. A la Magellan, we should see what lies across the sea, or at least across the street. In short, I've been thinking we should try another bar."

"Wow! That's quite a deposition. How drunk are you?" I asked jokingly and with a touch of disbelief. Arthur was a creature of habit and I, too, was a loyal O'Hearnian.

"Fairly," Arthur answered without irony. "But that's not the cause of my wander lust. I just think it's time. After all, there's a whole wide world full of drinking establishments out there that beg, nay, demand exploration and I, for one, would like to venture forth. Yes. It just feels right."

"Well then, who am I to stand in the way of a good epiphany? And you're obviously determined. So, where would you like to go?" I asked, trying to acknowledge the seriousness of Arthur's disclosure. Besides, I found myself excited at the prospect. Maybe a change of scenery would lift me out of my Elaine funk.

"Unfortunately, I haven't given that part nearly as much thought as I gave to my little speech. What say we just get in the car and drive around until we see a place that calls to us? We'll leave it up to Fate." Arthur waved vaguely to the horizon, or where the horizon would be if we could see it.

"Alright, fine. No problem. Let's leave it to Fate. But let's have a couple more here in case Fate leads us to a more expensive bar."

"Sound logic, Jason. It's hard to predict where the furies will take us this evening. Let me buy you a round right now!" My jaw dropped as we made our way out of the patio area and into the bar interior, where Arthur did, indeed, buy me a beer.

Initially, our search for Eldorado yielded nothing more than pleasant conversation and a re-acquaintance with the bar scene on the west side of Cincinnati. As a result, we were gently reminded that O'Hearn's was, in fact, the most inviting watering hole on our side of town. Ignoring this we pressed on, eventually spying a place the existence of which we had been heretofore unaware and so therefore must have been brand new. Regardless, the simultaneous exclamation we shared provided sufficient motivation for me to pull into a parking space. It was called The Hot Spot and from the exterior appeared to be clean and well kept. Although this untainted appearance originally filled us with dread regarding the potential cost of libations, our fiduciary fear was not sufficient to prevent us from proceeding.

The lighting inside was dim, forcing new entrant's eyes to adjust from the bright exterior lights before being able to see clearly. Without really waiting for this to happen, Arthur and I made our way to the bar, which was to our left as we entered. It was stacked two bodies deep so we took the time in line to study the beer selection, which was disappointing. It wasn't nearly as varied as O'Hearn's and the draft selection was full of the standard light beers and mass-produced pilsners. I looked at Arthur and he gave me a quick "no" nod. We would have to default to mixed drinks. I made it to the bar first and played it safe with a rum and coke for each of us. It was busy and I didn't want to stress the bartender, who looked young and unchallenged in his skills as a mixologist, thereby reinforcing my belief The Hot Spot was brand new. Once we had something to do with our left hands, we made our way further into the joint. For me, the first thing to stand out was the abundance of male groups and female groups but few, if any, mixed sex groups. The second was the techno music and the big, overstuffed furniture populating the open floor plan. The third was the dance floor, where a number of same sex couples were dancing. Being one who doesn't like to jump to conclusions (or perhaps just clueless,) I did not at first assume it was a gay/lesbian establishment, at least not until I looked at Arthur, who clearly mouthed the words "gay bar." Since Arthur and I are/were not gay (or lesbian,) we probably should have left immediately, but we had just bought drinks and our sense of thrift easily overrode our sense of sexual discomfort, which was negligible regardless. Getting hit on by another of your own sex could be somewhat ego reinforcing. So, while we didn't go as far as holding hands in order to fit in, we did share an unspoken conclusion that we would stay until our drinks were done. It was during these few minutes that I received an unexpected elucidation concerning my marriage.

As we hovered about trying not to be too conspicuously heterosexual, I reminded myself that just because the women were probably lesbians didn't mean they wouldn't be nice to look at. Indeed, there were more than a fair number of women upon whom my gaze could be pleasantly cast. Unfortunately, and to my complete surprise, one of them happened to be my (quasi)wife, Kim.

I didn't notice her at first, probably because she was lip-locked with another woman on one of the overstuffed couches lined up along the walls. Wrapped around each other as they were, Kim's face was hidden from me by the back of her partner's head, and did not become visible until the pair took a break from their little game of tonsil hockey. I believe I actually did a double take and then looked at Arthur, who had seen everything. Within seconds he was spiriting me out of the bar.

CHAPTER EIGHT

I've come to believe that if one lives long enough that one would, eventually, come to view as commonplace what the less experienced view as unique. In spite of this belief (or perhaps in support of it) it is obvious my forty plus trips around the sun had not yet dispensed a sufficient amount of time for me to reach this point if, indeed, it could ever be reached. As a result I am also convinced that life is truly full of surprises and, with any luck, always will be. Had I been conscious of this truth that evening I suspect I would have been simultaneously surprised and not surprised by the surprise of my wife swapping spit with another woman. And while the choice of bars was fairly random, I had only myself to blame for this enlightening discovery as it was a direct result of Arthur's and my decision to venture out into the unknown. Had we stayed put, had we decided to remain safely in the beery cocoon that was O'Hearn's, this little bit of information would most likely have remained hidden from me for an extended period of time. Perhaps forever. But this was not to be and my day kept getting better, or at least more interesting.

So how was I to react to this? Should I have put it down as just another nail in the marital coffin? After all, did Kim's sexual preference really matter to me anymore? Or would I dwell on it like Russian poets dwell on suicide? The development was compelling enough to warrant some thoughtful examination. It certainly would explain her sexual indifference toward me (unless I was the one who turned her gay, an admittedly egotistical revelation.) At first I wasn't quite sure which way things would fall. But I am not a Russian poet, and am actually quite the opposite. I am, indeed, rather shallow, and by the time Arthur was deftly shoving me into my car I was already leaning toward the "nail in the coffin" scenario, most likely as a way to avoid having to really examine the issue

AND avoid any unnecessary confrontation with Kim. Or with myself. Or both.

On the other hand, knowing something you didn't really want or ever expect to know can be horribly problematic. And here's why - after you learn the thing you didn't want to learn you then have to act on this knowledge. How was I to act on the knowledge of Elaine's pending departure? How was I to act on the knowledge of Kim's confusing sexuality? No matter the knowledge, the act can be big or small, but there will be action, because even choosing not to act is an act in itself. And these actions have a cascade effect which may then have its own terrible consequences, like finding out even more stuff you never wanted to know and forcing you to act on that as well. I mean, if Kim had been seeing another woman for the last two years, did I really want to know? What if it was four years? What if it was women AND men? What if it was women AND men at the same time? The possibilities were dizzying. And, on the non-lesbian front (but equally important at the time,} what if Elaine knew she was leaving BEFORE she met me? What if all the women in my life were hiding things from me? You can see how easily it can all snowball into a vicious cycle of unwanted awareness.

Knowing this, one may take the path of Pretending Not to Know, or PNK. At first PNK may not seem the obvious choice. But it can be a good one. At least until someone finds out you knew the "thing" and then employed PNK, and especially when it involves information the person may have deemed necessary to their own decision making. Imagine the consequences for a woman's best friend if she knows the best friend's husband is fooling around and Pretends Not to Know. One can bet that once the cuckolded woman learns the truth she will disinherit the best friend out of hand, even if she simultaneously chooses to stay with the playboy husband. It's a lose/lose situation. So there I was facing the vicious cycle; the same lose/lose situation. If I decided to act, what should that action be? Should I be relieved or frustrated? Should I be confrontational or passive? All of the above? Oh and by the way, is it even possible to turn someone gay?

So I wasn't having a stellar day. The woman I was in love with was leaving for good and the woman I used to be in love with turned out to be living an "alternative lifestyle." And despite what it may reveal about me, I must admit I found the prospect of Elaine's departure more heart rending than finding my wife in the arms of a woman. My illusions of Kim and me making things work had disappeared months before. Still, this bit of news about her liking girls certainly made an impression and was shocking in its own way, even realizing it didn't make much difference in the long run. Kim was gone, but as of that night I was confused about two relationships. For Elaine I was feeling a true sense of loss and it was pissing me off that the world just kept turning as if it didn't matter. For Kim I just had no fucking idea what I was supposed to think. We drove back to O'Hearn's in reflective silence.

Lesson Learned: Ignorance is Bliss.

The other lesson learned as a result of wandering away from O'Hearn's that night was that you just never know people. Or maybe it's just me that just never knows people. Regardless, in reality it appears that sometimes we actually know people, of course. Sometimes the grindingly boring person in the cubicle next to you is exactly that. But other times there may be all kinds of crap going on with the mild-mannered guy in that cubicle than would ever be imagined by his preoccupied workmates. In my case I discovered the woman to whom I had been married for nearly two decades was a homo. Who knew? Having been confronted with this new reality, my view of humanity has shifted unalterably, and from then on everyone started to look a little different.

Knowing this, however, didn't stop me from questioning my judgment for hours and days after seeing Kim lip locking another woman. How had I missed that all those years? How had she? Rationally, of course, I (mostly) didn't believe it possible for me to turn Kim lesbo from hetero. I (mostly) didn't, and don't, believe there's anything I or anyone else can do about anyone's sexuality, except maybe fuck it up. But my confidence in that knowledge was lost for the moment. It was later, after I failed to answer this and other questions, that I gave up asking them altogether and learned to live with the circumstances as they existed. But at that point I was far too close to the situation to be appropriately rational. As a result, I was essentially rendered speechless as Arthur shuffled me out of the bar, took my keys and deposited me in the passenger seat of my own vehicle.

"Well, that was a pisser." he mumbled as he started the engine. "Didn't see that coming."

"I guess the fuck not!" I can't remember if I was trying to be funny or if I was annoyed with Arthur's attempt at humor, but it felt good to swear.

"You know, a couple years ago you would have thought that was hot." Arthur smiled slightly and sounded nonchalant.

"What the fuck are you talking about?" Was he trying to piss me off? "Are you trying to piss me off?!"

"Of course not, I'm just saying under different circumstances you'd have found it a pleasant show." He was right.

"Where the hell are we going?"

"I left a perfectly good drink on the bar in there and I've got my mind set on finishing one more before going home. Why? Do you really want to go home? Right now?" His voice was even, his argument rational.

I was experiencing an infinite number of feelings and recognized none of them as the desire to go home. So I acquiesced, giving in to the logic of Arthur's position. Despite his vow never to drink and drive, a vow stemming directly from his second DUI, he drove us gingerly in the direction of O'Hearn's. Even in my tumultuous state, the significance and potential sacrifice of the act was not lost on me. Arthur was a good friend.

"Dude…thanks for driving."

"Cheers, mate. But don't get all teary about it."

It was probably one of the most touching moments we ever shared.

We arrived safely at O'Hearn's and in plenty of time for a night cap, which was taken mostly in silence. I suppose Arthur was giving me time to process the newly discovered snippet of information about my wife before trying to get me to talk about it. Of course, it was just as likely that he was uncomfortable with the situation and really didn't want to talk about it at all. Or didn't care. Or was already fantasizing about it. Regardless, the result was the same. We sat in silence drinking Scotch. Finally, as he neared the bottom of his glass, Arthur spoke.

"I don't suppose that bird, Elaine, would find this interesting…"

Was he suggesting I call her? I'll admit now that until that moment the thought of calling Elaine hadn't crossed my mind. I was still kind of pissed at her for her pending departure but perhaps found the shock of the scene distressing enough to drive the thought of her out of my head. If that was the case, it was the first time in weeks I had failed to devote myself to thinking about her almost constantly. Now she was back in my head, and Arthur's subtle suggestion seemed like a good idea. Maybe even a great one.

"That's a great idea. I'll give her a call." I felt lighter immediately, though the day's revelations had effectively unbalanced the universe.

"Well then, I'm off. Call her now and call me in the morning with a full report. And be careful. I'll take a hack." Hack is British for taxi.

Arthur finished his drink, slapped me on the shoulder and walked out the door. It was near closing time, and on a Friday night this meant a number of cabs would be lining up in front of the bar to swiftly carry the more avid party goers home in safety. I watched the door close behind him as I dialed. It took four rings for Elaine to answer.

"Hello?" Her voice had the dusty tone of someone who was sound asleep before the phone interrupted a good dream.

"Hey, Elaine. It's me. Did I wake you?" Of course I did.

"Yeah...yeah, but it's ok. What's up?" Her voice was getting stronger.

"Well, I found out my wife is gay." I paused for effect. "How was your evening?"

"What? What did you just say?" Now she was fully awake. I could tell.

"Well, first I told you my wife is gay and then I asked about your evening. Did you go out tonight? I did. That's how I found out my wife is gay."

"Jeez, Jason. I don't know what to say. Are you sure? You know I had a gay husband, right? But I never caught him. He was just a lot better than me at decorating the house. Plus one of his lovers called me one night and told me he was gay. How did you find out?"

"She was wrapped up with another woman in a gay bar."

"Jeez," She repeated. "Are you ok? Do you want to come over?"

I had been hoping for the magic question. I was feeling empty despite the scotch and the pleasure of Arthur's company. A physical and emotional booty call with Elaine seemed the perfect remedy, if for no other reason than to reaffirm of my own sexuality. I also figured the pleasure of her company would help fend off the black cloud that had been chasing me around all day. After all, even though she was part of my Bad News Friday for the most part her presence in my life had managed to do just that. Hold back the darkness, I mean. Elaine was the proverbial light streaming through the rain cloud, and now that I knew she was leaving the country my desire to spend time with her increased tenfold. The variable of her pending exit heightened my already sharp desire for her. Although she had been temporarily driven from my mind by the evening's events, the mere act of talking to her was calming my nerves. Of course I wanted to see her. I had to see her. I would deal with Kim's penchant for the fairer sex later. My time to spend with Elaine was now finite, and if she would have allowed me to move in with her for her last month or two left in the states I would have gladly succumbed (at least if I had no children.) Ominously, at the time I was clueless as to just how different her perceptions of our relationship were from my own. And that ugly monster of reality would rear its head soon enough. But, since ignorance is bliss, at that moment it didn't matter and I could continue to exist in my bubble of fantasy.

"Yes, please," was my simple response.

"Hurry," she said like I needed encouragement or coaching. "I'll leave the light on."

So I found myself driving to Elaine's. Again. Due to my inebriation, I realized almost immediately how dangerous was the exercise and relied heavily on my car's instincts and memory to get me there safely. Luckily for me the Chevy did indeed know the way and got me to the Secret Garden safely and without incident. As promised, Elaine left the lights on and I was able to see the frosty walkway quite clearly, gingerly making my way to her front door through the chill of the evening. My drive over had afforded me a few minutes of thoughtful reflection and this reflection led me to the conclusion that, at least on that evening, I didn't necessarily have to have sex with Elaine. So, by the time I arrived at the Secret Garden, I was operating under the warm conviction that just lying next to her and feeling her supple body against mine as we slept would be more than satisfying. In fact, I figured this was exactly what I needed. If

Elaine insisted on having sex then, well......so be it. But for me the sex would just be a necessary prelude to the post coital cuddling and a good night's sleep, if only as a reward for good performance.

I bound up the two steps to the porch, the front door opening as I alighted on the Welcome mat, revealing Elaine on the other side of the storm door. Her robe was untied and open, but only so far as to spark the imagination and allow me to see the wedge of smooth skin running from her neck to her panties, which happened to match her robe. Without a proper greeting I walked through the storm door and, wrapping my arms around her, started kissing her lips and neck. The robe didn't last long and soon my hands were grasping to remove the panties as well. For the moment she seemed to prefer me dressed and the feel of her nakedness pressing through my clothes aroused me further.

Now, even though things were moving quickly I wasn't as distracted as it may appear. The post coital cuddling was still on my mind. It just got pushed to the back burner. As any caring, giving man would in the same situation, I made a command decision to satisfy her needs first. An altruistic gesture, I know, but well worth it at the time.

And so our love making continued. I'm not sure how long it took but with Elaine's help I finally got my clothes off. Having them on with Elaine in the buff was just too painful. We bounced off the walls and furniture and even managed to slip in a sip of wine (which Elaine had poured prior to my arrival) while still fucking. It's amazing what a little creativity and a lot of determination can lead to. Intertwined, sweaty, and over-heated, it was easy to forget the world and just be there with her. I was hearing and feeling everything. Every touch of her body against mine, every sound; nothing was escaping me and her enthusiasm heightened my senses even further. I wanted to eat her. I wanted to tear her to shreds. I wanted to crawl inside of her and become part of her body. I couldn't get enough of the taste or smell of her. Her involuntary moans and heavy breathing were all the encouragement I needed to keep going until we were both wasted physically. I was so lost in this bout of escapism that to this day the intensity of the experience remains unmatched in my, admittedly, less than perfect memory.

We collapsed in the bedroom, where again I found myself basking naked in the cold moonlight. Elaine had her body compressed against mine and as our heat dissipated I found the energy to pull the blankets over us. I knew the sun would be up in a matter of hours but it didn't matter. At that moment I was getting exactly what I wanted. I could feel my whole "self" relax in anticipation of actually falling asleep with Elaine next to me for the first time. I began to doze with the smell of her in my nostrils and the pounding of her heart against my chest. I would soon be off to a peaceful place, or so I thought.

"Jason?" I heard her whisper. Her voice sounded far away. "Are you falling asleep?"

"Huh?" A grunt was the best I could conjure under the circumstances. I just wanted to go to sleep.

"Jason...." She whispered again. "You can't stay here tonight. I'm sorry, baby, but you've got to go home. I'm just not comfortable with someone sleeping over." Every word brought her voice closer and pulled me out of my dream haze.

"What? You want me to leave?" What the fuck was going on?

"Yeah... I do. I'm sorry but I didn't want you to fall asleep and then have to wake you up. Can I get you some coffee or something?"

Coffee? Did I want some coffee? I released Elaine, who had been trapped under my draping arm, and bolted upright. The magic of the moment disappeared in a whiff and just as suddenly all the confusion of the evening came flooding back. Nothing was making sense. Didn't let men sleep over? What the hell was that about?

"Are you saying you've never spent the night with a man?" I was incredulous. The "this sounds stupid" part of my brain was fully engaged.

"No, of course I have. Both my husbands, of course. And I've spent the night with men at their place, but never here. It's just a rule." She said this as she got up and put on her robe, which had somehow migrated upstairs from the living room. She was actually going to go make some coffee, which was the last thing I wanted. Coffee and a lonely drive home in the dark of the early morning were not part of the plan. Did Elaine not understand the plan?

"Ok...well, the thing is...I was really looking forward to spending a whole night with you. I thought that's what you wanted, too." I was suddenly embarrassed and began to ramble, sort of. I didn't seem to be able to stop the next part from coming out which, in hindsight, was over the top considering the circumstances and the fact Elaine had never expressed particularly strong feelings for me. I just assumed she had them, most likely because I really wanted her to have them. "You know, it's been such a weird day, you know? You told me you were leaving, my wife turned into a lesbian...and I was...I don't know. I think I was a lot sadder about the prospect of you leaving than I thought I would be. I think that...I feel...more for you than I expected. I think I'm falling in love with you, Elaine."

Holy shit! What was I thinking? The response to my emotional exposure was a blank stare. Elaine didn't move or really even change her expression though I seemed to have surprised her. She took a moment before answering, careful about what she was going to say.

"Wow, Jason. I'm amazed by that. You make me feel so good when we're together.... You know I'm sorry I'm leaving, too, right? I have a lot of reasons to stay, but I..." It was her turn to ramble and her voice trailed off. "I'll go make some coffee and we can talk some more, ok?"

"Ok." Disarmed by her reaction I didn't know what else to say. Plus, she really couldn't have been nicer in her rejection of my love and physical presence. I've since likened the feeling to what it must be like to ask someone to marry you and get a "no" or a "no way, Jose" or maybe even laughter, although that might be somewhat overstating the depth of the moment. Still, it's just one of those questions to which one should know the answer before asking. I didn't know what the hell I was doing by throwing all that at her. Did I think she would let me spend the night because I tried half-assedly to bare my soul? Because I told her I might be in love with her? Regardless, after she left the room I slipped my clothes back as I waged a silent argument with myself over the merits of one course of action over another. It occurred to me to push the idea of at least sleeping AT her house, if for no other reason than to sleep off the alcohol still running through my system. But I wasn't too far gone to recognize how pathetic it would appear for me to do so. Should I have coffee? Should I just leave? I opted for the latter. I had had enough for one day and was giving up. I got out of bed, finished putting on my clothes and headed back down the stairs where Elaine was busying herself in the kitchen.

"Are you ready for some coffee?" She seemed not at all disappointed to see me fully clothed.

"Not thanks, Elaine. I think I'm just going to head home. I'll call you tomorrow. Thank you for everything, tonight..."

"Jason. I really think you should stay..." I perked up. "for some coffee." Big letdown. "I want you to get home safe."

God knows I wanted a reason to stay. I needed a reason to stay. But it was clear to me that any further layover in the Secret Garden would be strictly temporary and highly regulated. There would be no more nudity or closeness or warmth or breath on my face. I had sobered enough to realize the truth by the time I pulled my underwear on and decided not to fight it.

"Can I get that to go?" Ok. I knew I couldn't stay but the coffee smelled really good.

"Can't you stay and have some with me?"

"No thanks, Elaine. I'll go ahead and get out of your hair. I really appreciate you letting me come over." The comment sounded disturbingly cordial considering what we had just done to one another but romantic words were nowhere to be found. Elaine dug through a cabinet and found a Styrofoam cup. In it coffee was dispensed and handed to me. After handing me the coffee Elaine pulled me to her and hugged me warmly. I returned the hug, sort of, and headed into the early morning without another word.

I didn't see Elaine as I climbed into my car. I closed the door behind me on the way out and felt fairly sure she had made her way back to bed already. Regardless, whatever was happening behind the door didn't matter. I was alone again and had been kicked to curb, so to speak. I mean, I did get laid. And there's something to be said for that. However, I wanted more from Elaine. More than she appeared ready to give. I didn't know why things were the way they were, and would come to spend an inordinate time trying to figure it all out. And eventually I pieced it all together, more or less. But that knowledge wouldn't make it any less weird or take the rejection away. At least I was able to put things in context. In the mean time I was left to drive home on empty streets, dreading what I might be walking into.

Angela the baby sitter was asleep on the couch when I got back to the house. A wave of anxiety washed over me as I contemplated her reaction to being unwittingly trapped in the Kubrick household all night AND at the thought of what it was going to cost me. Did I have enough cash to pay for 10 hours of babysitting? At today's babysitting prices?

"Angela..." I whispered repeatedly as I nudged her awake. She was less than half my age so I was being extra careful about where and how much I touched her, the consequence being it took longer to wake her up.

"Oh...hello, Mr. Kubrick." Angela's voice was dreamy as she slow brought herself up onto her elbow.

"Angela, I'm really sorry about being so late...."

"It's ok, Mr. Kubrick. Mrs. Kubrick called and asked if I could stay longer in case you guys came home late. I told her no problem."

Thank God! Assured I would not be receiving an angry phone call from Angela's father, I was almost happy to pay the $80 tab for her services. She gave the boys a good report and left the house, walking across the street and three houses down as I watched from the front door. It had been some time since I arrived home at this hour on a Saturday morning and it had never been alone. Kim had quit as my drinking buddy a couple years prior and after that I was always home within a few minutes of O'Hearn's closing. Maybe it was the coffee but I didn't feel that tired. With nothing better to do I pored over the contact list on my cell phone looking for a potential drunk-and-dial. Since his name started with an "A", Arthur was my first viable option. And of course I considered calling him but simultaneously felt he had already done his part for the cause that evening. Izzy was next on the list, followed immediately by Johannes. Two good choices, to be sure, but a strong possibility on both counts that I might catch them in flagrante delicto, so to speak, and did not want to disturb either in the middle of the activity in which I had earlier mightily strived. After staring at the phone for another minute or so I gave up the idea of bugging anyone at five AM and chose instead to wonder where the hell Kim had ended up, a question not attended to upon my arrival home due to the immediacy of the baby sitter issue and the underlying distraction of Elaine's rejection.

Kim, I assumed, had gone home with her new (not so new?) friend from the gay/lesbian venue. I didn't believe she knew I had discovered her there, and therefore her absence from the house appeared to be a challenge. Kim, in all our years together, had never spent the night away unless we were together. And even then the overnight absences were fewer than could be counted on one hand. Understanding this, I began to view her choice not to come home as a declaration. She had arranged for the baby sitter and then, without my knowledge, armed Angela with the possibility the parents might not coming home until very late. Obviously she wanted to claim her new territory without confronting me directly. She was changing boundaries. Indeed, changing boundaries she had set for herself, since I had never told her she could or couldn't do anything she wanted to. Her behavioral choices had always been her own, as they should be, and in reality are for any adult human being. All that was left for me was to react one way or another to her choices. Anti-climactically, I chose to go to bed. There was nothing left of the evening and, other than the boys, there was nothing left of the marriage. I wondered fleetingly (and amusingly) if Kim and I had the same taste in women, but for the most part sweating the details served no purpose other than to drive me insane. Exhausted, I climbed into bed.

I was truly spent, but not spent enough for a good, old-fashioned, brain race. The kind of race where thoughts flow across your mind not as floaty wonderments to ponder but more like dragsters racing from one side of the head to the other. The brain race allows insufficient time to contemplate the thoughts flying around, only enough time to recognize them and worry about them. Here's some of mine:

- What would I say to Kim when she got home? Do I draw her out or just tell her I saw her?
- I need to turn the heat down but I don't want to get out of bed.
- What would she say to me?
- Why are clowns so scary?
- What will Therapist Jim say when I tell him about Kim?
- Do animals have souls?

- Would Kim start giving the boys different books to read, like "My Two Moms."?
- Was Kim's Mom gay?
- I needed to polish my work shoes before Monday.
- Was Kim's father gay?
- Why does my ankle hurt?
- Why did Elaine kick me out of her house???

And there it was. The thought I got stuck on despite my exhaustion. I would later discover she had someone else she about whom she felt much more strongly than she ever would about me, which was part of the aforementioned 'piecing things together.' Obviously, this would have been useful information to have at the time but still wouldn't have fully explained the pre-dawn ejection from the Secret Garden. It made sense when she rushed off after day time sex. After all, she had a hectic job and a full schedule. I always knew she was just cramming me in to an otherwise busy day. But showing me the door with the lame excuse of not ever letting men spend the night was too ludicrous even for me to accept. A later epiphany would reveal the tremendous blind spot I had when it came to Elaine, but at the moment I pined for her alone in my bed. Elaine, who at first represented for me what a relationship could be, whose very presence in my life reminded me I was not alone in my desires and that I was worthy of an intelligent, attractive woman, had rejected me. And it was no small rejection. Had I been a mere dust bunny she would have swept me out the door snicker snack in order to remove any trace of me from her home. The thoughts raced again:

- Was I not really worthy of her? Did part of her actually hold me in contempt?
- Did the boys have a soccer game today? If so, that would suck.
- How was I to handle this new reality with Elaine?
- Was the rest of my life to remain one of persistent, semi-rejection, worth a good fuck but not worth time and real affection?
- Did Angela let the dog out in the last few hours?

110

- Was love drifting away from me? Would I ever know love again? Was I worthy of love?
- Was that last thought overly dramatic?
- Damn! What's up with my ankle?
- I want to live in a cave.
- I want to live in a cave with my recliner and flat screen television.

I finally drifted off to sleep with the remembrance of Elaine's body against mine in the moonlight. Unbeknownst to me I had been kicked out of the Secret Garden for good, and as I drifted off I held out hope to somehow make sense of everything that happened that evening and perhaps get another chance. It was a pipe dream.

CHAPTER NINE

Lost loves. Lost dreams. Regrets. When I woke some hours later my brain was filled with these less-than-inspiring nuggets of contemplation. Waking up hung over always leaves me feeling empty and agitated. Plus it can inspire unfortunate self-examination. How much money did I spend last night? What was I thinking? How much time was I wasting being hung over? Whose ass did I touch without permission? Common questions for the post inebriated, no doubt.

The sun streamed onto my semi-closed eyelids, gracefully altering my line of thought and forcing me to consider actually waking up. It also cleared my head just enough to allow the panic of the wasted morning to really set in, further increasing my anxiety. Still I managed to do nothing more than continue to lie in bed and listen for signs of life from the boys. Once located, I found the harsh sound of their escalating argument oddly comforting. It served notice of their safe presence within the household and that they weren't presently focused on their mother's absence. Or mine, for that matter. Now I could remain in bed with a little less guilt.

Feeling lonely and without resource to alter the mood, I stared at the ceiling and drifted in and out of a sea of disquiet and self-pity, wallowing in my perceived inability to be loved. Well, at least loved by women. Well…at least in the long term. Hmmm….I mean, I may not be model material, but I don't believe I'm ghastly to gaze upon. And I'd like to think I have an unassuming personality and am easy to be around. Add to those things a decent job and passable level of intelligence and you've got what many women would, or should, consider a "catch." So what was happening? What fatal flaw was preventing me from being worthy of love? Could it be self-indulgent narcissism? Was I only good enough to be a "boy toy?" Hell, under different circumstances I might have found the position of "boy toy" complimentary and ego boosting.

However, it had become painfully clear to me I would never find the role of booty caller satisfactory in the long term. Damn it! I was not an unthinking pair of shoes (testicles?) to be discarded for a comfy pair of slippers at day's end. I wanted to be more than a convenient cock, so to speak. Is that all I was to Elaine? Or was I the slippers?

Lying as still as possible so as not to anger the demon drummer beating in my skull, for the moment only the last twenty-four hours existed. Malingering in bed and only slightly distracted by the low-level chaos occurring a floor below me, I used the down time to review the highlights of the chosen time period and question each on multiple levels. I worked my way through what appeared to be the important moments and events, finally settling on the question, the age-old, boringly sophomoric philosophical stumper, "How did I get here?" But how did I? How had I reached that moment of confusing sadness? Still staring at the ceiling, I began to trace back through some of the major events of my life, like losing my virginity (a disaster involving pre-ejaculate and a partner only slightly interested in process.) Then high school graduation, which went only slightly better than my loss of virginity. Then there was college graduation, throughout which I was forced to sit next to a verbose classmate sporting breath so fetid I had to turn my head away during the unfortunate moments he chose to speak to me. Less horrifying things about my life occurred to me as well, like the fact that when I was a boy I wanted to be a fireman or an astronaut. At the time both occupations seemed terribly exciting and, admittedly, still do. Secret agent or pirate would have worked as well. So, considering my childhood dreams, how in the hell had I become Chief Credit Officer at a small bank in northern Kentucky? And did everyone's first time suck as much as mine? And why didn't that guy brush his teeth when he got out of bed the morning of his college graduation?

I figured I could now add "career choice" to the regret column, as I imagine about eighty percent of the population could on any given day. Maybe more. But while I don't think most of us "hate" our jobs, I do think almost all want more out of them, whatever "more" may be. The reality, of course, is the world needs only so many firemen and even fewer astronauts, so the employment track for most of us seems to be determined largely by the necessity to feed and clothe oneself, tempered with some combination of ability, timing, and desire. And luck, of course. I suppose it's possible these may be the criteria for love as well, especially the luck and timing parts, but the thought is frightening. Unlike the sight of my parents naked, love is something I never want to regret knowing, even if it doesn't last. It's also something I absolutely want "more" of, but adding luck and timing to the mixture makes it so random and improbable. What if I'm not naturally lucky? Or timely? On the bright side, statistically it appears most of us fall in love with someone living within a 50-mile radius of wherever we happen to be living, if we are to fall in love at all. I found this thought comforting. It certainly made things seem more hopeful. So, thinking as realistically as possible under the circumstances, I concluded my life would only be slightly less satisfying had I never become Chief Credit Officer of a small, Midwestern bank. Hell…maybe "more" satisfying. I imagine, however, never knowing love again would leave me feeling unspeakably empty. And 50 miles can be driven in less than an hour, especially if it's mostly highway.

Oddly, or perhaps not so oddly, unspeakable emptiness was exactly what I was feeling when I finally dragged my ass out of bed that morning. Still, after completing perfunctory morning ablutions but without being completely dressed, I managed to gently herd the boys into getting ready for their (mercifully) early afternoon soccer game. They either chose not to comment or failed to notice my late arrival, but Trevor was the first to mention his mother's absence, which hadn't really registered for me since noting it upon waking. He removed the tooth brush from his mouth long enough to make the inquiry.

"Dad? Where's Mom? Is she going to the game?"

What the fuck? Of course I "knew" she wasn't there but I had not contacted her and had no good answer to Trevor's inquiry. Was I becoming that self-absorbed?

"Uh, I don't think she's going to the game, sweetie, but let me give her a quick call and I'll find out." It was a band aid answer but it worked. Trevor went back to brushing his teeth. Alex finished brushing his and moved seamlessly on to flossing, an activity which generally occurred only when I happened to be watching. I scurried back to my bedroom and, locating the cell phone in my balled-up pants, dialed Kim's number. She answered quickly.

"Hello?"

"It's me. Where are you?"

"I'm ....at a friend's house."

"Why aren't you here?"

"I knew you'd be there." Kim's answer was stated plainly but I wasn't quite sure what she meant. Was she afraid to come home because she didn't want to confront me? Or did she stay out because she knew I would be home with the boys so she didn't have to worry? Did she even know that I saw her in the bar with another woman? With Trevor and Alex within earshot I opted not to explore further.

"Ok...Trevor wants to know if you're going to his game." I could talk plainly, but I could also talk through the kids, as opposed to asking her directly.

"Oh, shit," Kim muttered under her breath. "I wasn't thinking. Tell him not today. Tell him I'll be home by the time they get back from the game. Ok?"

"Oh...ok." I was startled, hung over, and experiencing a glaring lack of privacy. All of these factors worked to prevent me from finding out what the hell was going on with Kim so I let it go, as I had so many times and about so much of our relationship already. I hung up and turned to the boys.

"Mom will be home when we get back, but don't worry, I'll do enough cheering for both of us."

The boys' reaction was not one of confidence and the three of us left the house experiencing a bit of group gloominess, although for vastly different reasons. The ride to the game was quiet and quick and as I took a seat in the stands I resolved to pay complete attention to the action on field and cheer loudly whenever the situation called for it. In order to maintain this focus, and also to avoid questions about my familial status, I very nearly ignored the various greetings and queries offered me by other soccer parents. This probably came off as rude but I was resolved not to let my mind wander. About three minutes into the game, however, my failure in this resolution became apparent when a soccer ball arced its way over the protective Plexiglas wall in order to strike me square on the forehead. I never saw it coming. Fortunately, the glance from the leather sphere imparted no permanent damage and gave me and the surrounding crowd a good laugh, once they realized I was ok, of course. I took the hit as a sign from God that I should be living in the moment and redoubled my efforts to do so. God, of course, is infinitely wise and understood had I been paying attention to my sons' game I would have seen the offending missile, dodging it handily. After settling in for real, my increased concentration was rewarded with stellar performances from Trevor and Alex and a win overall. The boys had a good laugh about the incident as well and took their shots as we made our way to the food stand.

"Nice face ball, Dad!" Trevor laughed and Alex giggled.

"Yeah, Dad! Tough way to get in the game!" Alex stated as he took my hand, a gesture I found far more comforting than he could have imagined.

"You said it! And I think the ball gave me brain damage. What are your names again?" Most boys (and men) will laugh at anything involving brain damage, crotch shots, broken limbs, or people falling down. I got a half-hearted laugh for the poor attempt at humor.

We ate our snacks and rehashed game highlights while other soccer parents and kids stopped by our table to complement the boys and say hello. While still focused on my sons, or at least mostly focused on my sons, I did not fail to notice the goodly number of attractive soccer Moms milling about and found myself glancing at ring fingers. The exercise felt a bit peculiar. What did I think was going to happen and why, suddenly, was I focusing on marital status? If one of the comely Moms wasn't married was she going to rush over and have sex with me on the table? Doubtful, although in my imagination that kind of thing happens all the time. After the kids are sent off to play on their own, out of sight and ear shot of course. Despite my earlier lamentations concerning an inability to hold onto love, the attention being paid me by the Moms was boosting my confidence and I found myself feeling a bit freer than I had in some time. Maybe it was the blow to my head. No matter the cause, I was feeling foggy but unchained. What would or could take me by surprise next was anybody's guess. But the plethora of hot Moms was brightening my mood and giving me hope for the future. It's amazing how beauty can do that. I wondered how many of them might be secretly gay.

My vibrating phone interrupted the conversation. It was Izzy. I took the call as the harem dissipated.

"What's up, loser?"

"Just sitting here with the boys having a snack. They just had a hell of a game!" The comment drew smiles from my sons, as was intended.

"Excellent! Tell them I said congratulations!" Alex and Trevor had met Izzy, but I doubted they remembered her.

"You bet." I lied. I wasn't actually going to tell them, mainly due to the fact they wouldn't remember her and I would spend fruitless minutes attempting to get them to do so. "What are you up to?"

"Oh, you know, sitting around mostly. I'm trying to decide if I want to go out or stay in tonight." Izzy was fishing for a drinking buddy. "What are you up to tonight?"

"I don't have any plans. I had a big night last night, though." That wasn't a lie.

"Can you tell me about it or are the boys too close?" She asked discreetly.

"Too close. I'll tell you later, though, promise." That wasn't a lie, either. I was looking forward to it. "Did you want to meet up tonight?"

"Hell, yes!" The expected response.

Hours had passed since the boys and I arrived home and Kim still hadn't returned. Every now and again Alex and Trevor would inquire as to her whereabouts, to which I rendered vague responses such as "She's out and about" or "She's probably shopping." These seemed to satisfy them and they would then go back to the business of being preteen boys, which meant sports, video games, and annoying one another. Girls were on the horizon for them, but at the time neither seemed to carry any preoccupation with the opposite sex. I wondered if they knew what "gay" meant, other than being happy, or course.

Looking back, I realize I should have stayed home with the boys that night – for many reasons. However, my desire for immediate gratification demanded I spend the evening with Izzy. I wasn't about to allow Kim's absence to stand in the way of a good time, so I called Kim's parents and asked them if the boys could spend the night. Kim's parents were good people who had always treated me well, and Kim's father explained they had actually planned to call and see if their grandkids could be allowed to spend

117

the evening, so the timing of my request was serendipitous. My father-in-law let me know they'd be taking them to dinner and didn't further question Kim's absence after I provided the same "shopping" explanation I had been feeding the boys. It seemed a good, all-purpose excuse and I felt free to use it one last time as I left them with my children and my thanks. Having successfully compartmentalized my marital distress and Kim's continued absence, I climbed into the car looking forward to an evening with my beautiful, female friend. The lack of pressure would be welcome, and in her comfortable femininity I could hide from the problems I was having with other women.

I tried calling Arthur on my way to meet Izzy, but not to invite him out with Izzy and me, as I had often done in the past. I wanted her to myself that evening. I just wanted to check in and thank him again for looking out for me the night before, but his cell phone went straight to voicemail. Undeterred, I called his house phone and found myself in conversation with his wife, Gladys.

"Gladys! How are you? Is your husband available?"

"No he isn't, Jason." Gladys was American and Midwestern and so had no discernible accent. Her voice, however, did have a sort of scrapie sound to it. No doubt the result of 25 years at a pack a day. "He's out of the country meeting with someone about Iranian carpets or such. He won't be back for a few days."

"Hmmm. He didn't say anything to me about it last night. Did it just come up?"

"It came up quick, as usual. He just told me about it this morning. Needed to meet some Iranian all of the sudden to work out this carpet deal. Apparently he's going to try the import thing again. You know Arthur. We'll see...." Gladys' voice trailed off. She had been down this road with Arthur in the past.

"Well, you never know, maybe it'll work this time." I was trying to sound positive.

"Sure, maybe. We'll see...." She said again. "I'll tell him you called, Jason. And I'm sorry about you and Kim. Let me know if you need someone to talk to about it. I'm pretty good at this stuff. Just look how long I've lasted with Arthur." She said this without guile or humorous intent.

"I appreciate the offer, Gladys. I'll let you know. You take care and I'll see you soon."

Arthur had disappeared again. It was not unusual and I took it in stride. For all I knew he could have been a prisoner in some awful, third-world country by now, jailed for trying to export too many Persian rugs or for walking out on a bar tab. I declined to put too much thought into his possible circumstances, having learned that road led only to madness. Instead I made my merry way to Izzy, ready to regale her with news of my estranged wife's homosexual infidelity over a few drinks.

Izzy was at the bar when I arrived, sitting with a drink and surrounded by a murder of crows waiting for their chance to peck at her. She appeared to be having none of it, however, and must have swept aside a number of advances before my arrival. Men's reaction to Izzy tended to the visceral, but to approach her was something else altogether. Without beer courage most would never find the confidence for the attempt. She exuded composure and competence in the way one does when they know what they want – or at least know what they don't want. While she was not cold, for a man to storm her tower required their batch of equanimity to at least match her own, at least if one wanted a positive reaction to their daring play for her company. Izzy waved at me as I approached and the groan from the unattached males hovering around her was almost audible. I, quite naturally, was filled with schadenfreude at having facilitated the early demise of their misplaced hopes with Izzy. Adding to their pain, she stood up to greet me with a hug and a kiss on the cheek. It was going to be a great evening!

"Hey sailor, can I buy you a drink?"

"Always, and especially tonight. I have tales to tell."

Izzy ordered me a beer as the bartender floated by. "I can't wait to hear about it." She sounded enthusiastic.

"Hmmm…where do I begin…? Well, I got laid last night but then got kicked to the curb before dawn. Before that I found out Kim's a homo. Plus, somewhere in there Arthur bought me a drink."

Izzy did a double take and paused before answering. "Wow! Amazing!" She paused again. "That's certainly a lot to take in. So you're saying Arthur actually bought you a drink?"

"Yeah. Weird, huh? And then he drove me and my car back to O'Hearn's after he pulled me out of the lesbian bar!"

"That is amazing! What about his vow never to drink and drive? He must have really been worried. And where the hell is he tonight? I figured you'd bring him or Johannes along with you...."

Hmmm? How was I to explain to her that I wasn't fishing too deeply for male companionship that evening? I really did want her to myself, even if it would have been fun to have Arthur or Johannes along. "Johannes' got a new squeeze, as far as I can tell. He's been, shall we say.....preoccupied? And Arthur's out of the country." Though the facts were true I was still lying.

"Well, good for Johannes. All of us could use some of that kind of preoccupation. And you'll have to give me more than that on Arthur. But seriously, Jason, how are you holding up? You seem to be packing a whole lot of turmoil into a short time. What's keeping you going? Scotch? Beer? What's your secret?" She was only half joking. She was checking on my mental status and trying not to be too obvious about it.

"The beer helps, of course. But I think my mainstays are the kids and a general sense of confusion which prevents me from dwelling on any one thing for too long."

Izzy laughed. "Tell me how that works, exactly."

"Well...I guess it goes something like this: Since I don't know what's going to happen from one moment to the next I neither dread the future nor embrace it. At least not the distant future. On that I am ambivalent." I paused for a moment while Izzy stared, waiting for me to continue. "See? Any delusions I may have had about my own ability to control my life seem to be evaporating. I mean, I can decide what I'm having for breakfast, or what the boys have for breakfast, or what I'm going to wear for work, but all the big decisions seem to be being made for me. Does any of that make sense?" Wow! Things sure got heavy quickly. I hadn't even finished my first beer and suddenly I was sounding like a boneheaded Aristotle. But it was hard not to be honest with Izzy, especially with a drink in my hand. Indeed, I didn't know how else to act around her. Bare-all honesty had become a hallmark of our relationship and it felt good. Telling my male friends everything was good too but Izzy's warmth and femaleness were inviting in a way with which my other drinking buddies couldn't compete. Plus she was much hotter than them.

"Sure does. I gave up on control years ago, at least when it comes to what other people do. If you can do it too you might find yourself feeling a little better. Sort of the 'Give unto Caesar what is Caesar's' deal. Worrying about what kind of crap everyone else is into will just drive you nuts. But what we can do is cry on each other's shoulders for a while. I'll tell you what a shit my second ex-husband is and you can bitch about Kim." She smiled intuitively and gently adjusted my shirt sleeve, a move I would later understand to be flirting, but didn't know at the time.

"Well, hell yes. But I think we're gonna need more drinks if we're going down that road." My glass was nearly empty.

"It's on me tonight, Jason. I owe you a good drunk." She ordered another round from the bartender, who never seemed to be far away.

The hours passed with us stuck on the bar stools, moving only to go to the bathroom. We shared stories of passion gone cold, the heartbreak of love, walks of shame and hangover remedies. We solved a number of the world's problems, including curing the deficit and getting people off welfare. We opined on a range of topics encompassing work, the aerobic value of cycling (really fast, of course); is pork really the other white meat?; what qualities really do make men attractive to women (I'm embarrassed to say I had a goodly number of them, at least according to Izzy); and the erotic value of a well-rounded ass (Izzy read somewhere that in the deep recesses of a man's brain boob cleavage simulates butt cleavage, or the other way around, and was therefore erotic. I don't remember which since we were kind of drunk by then.) Izzy also shared her main complaint about men. She found them to be immature and generally not worth her time. I found her premise difficult to dispute though I could have said the same of many women I knew or had known.

It was a talk to remember as we huddled in the crowded pub ignoring everything around us, completely focused on what the other was saying and actually listening to what was being said. Through this odd act of listening I found out Izzy had been in love more than once and that her oft times hardball exterior had developed as a defense mechanism. She had bravely opened herself to joy and pain in the past and her reward had been pain more times than not. The information was communicated matter-of-factly and without a hint of martyrdom or regret. Yet she had become more cautious, and admitted that she would allow no more surprises. Her future loves would be known quantities, although she refused to elaborate on how the quantities would become known short of actually dating someone. Women are interesting creatures.

"Well, there's got to be a good one in this bar somewhere…" I meant a man for Izzy. My blood level alcohol was climbing and I wanted to sound positive.

"Oh, I'm sure there is," Izzy winked at me. "And he's sitting right in front of me."

Huh? Ok….so here's the thing: I was, and remain, clueless enough that this advance by Izzy went virtually unnoticed at the time. Only upon reflection would it occur to me that Izzy was, indeed, coming on to me. It was just that, at the time, I didn't think there was any way it could ever happen. After all, we had always been "just friends" and a good part of me considered her out of my league, at least from the attractiveness/dating standpoint. So, being clueless, I stupidly continued on as if nothing important had been shared.

"Oh, Izzy! You do go on!" I affected an effeminate aspect as I gave it my best Scarlet O'Hara. "You know you can do better than me!" In my brain I wanted this to be both a true and untrue statement.

Much to my amazement and probably that of every other man in the bar, without warning Izzy leaned over and kissed me full on. And it felt good. It was all warm and arousing and the focus I had been giving to what she was saying carried over into the kiss to the point where even the bar noise had diminished to be replaced by a sort of pleasant, white noise. And I'm not sure how long the kiss lasted, but it was long enough to convince me I needed to stop drinking for the evening. Things were getting blurry and not just with my vision. After all, I wasn't in love with Izzy in the conventional sense and probably never would be, but there I was letting her kiss me because she was beautiful and sensual and everything that a normal man could desire from a member of the fairer sex. But this was not a normal time.

"Damn." Was my simple response to the kiss.

"Damn? 'Damn' in what way?" Izzy asked as she took my hand in hers.

"'Damn' in a way that I really liked that and I'm not sure what to do next." I couldn't see myself but I could "feel" the idiotic expression on my face. Izzy didn't seem to notice. In fact, my answer seemed to please her.

"Good. Then leave with me now." It was almost a whisper, but it came across almost like an order - A sexy, why-the-hell-would-I-ever-say-no order.

"Uh...ok..."

We left the bar hand in hand. The darkness enveloped us as we walked toward Izzy's car and despite the fact she never let go of my hand Izzy seemed to bob in and out of my vision as if she had the ability to disappear and reappear at will. I'm sure my erratic sight could be blamed on alcohol mixing with a moonless night but the vision was simultaneously disconcerting and magical. Ocular issues notwithstanding I wasn't so drunk that it hadn't occurred to me what we were about to do was a bad idea. Indeed, the "feeling" of it being a bad idea started to spread through me before we hit the exit door. I didn't know what was happening but couldn't stop myself. Was I losing control of my behavior? Was I a latent sex addict? I wasn't sure but evidence of some sort of mental malfunction was definitely piling up. And what about Elaine? Were my feelings for her so unresolved or shallow that I would so easily jump at the chance for sex with Izzy? What about "fishing off the company pier?" That never seemed to work out. Was I Izzy's "known quantity?" But there I was, still married and getting more action than I had in years. Holy shit! The tornado of self-doubt and self-analysis was overpowering, yet I did nothing but sit there and stare at Izzy as she climbed into the car and started the engine. I was a coward.

Izzy took my hand again as she pulled into the street, pointing the vehicle toward her house. The feeling of her hand in mine was still pleasant but dread continued to creep over me. I had been to her house a few times before but never for sex. Beer, mainly. And maybe a glass of wine or the occasional cocktail, but never for sex. I glanced around as I sat in silence, my eyes alternating between the scenery whizzing by in the dark and Izzy driving the car with one hand. She was silent also, but I caught her occasionally glancing at me, utilizing peripheral vision. Perhaps she was afraid I was going to disappear. Or throw up. Either scenario seemed plausible at the time and sufficient reason to keep an eye on me. Who wants puke in their car? Or maybe she was having the same feeling of dread and was just as cowardly.

We did not speak during the whole of the drive. I suspect this was so because words might have expedited our exposure to our own stupidity, and far be it from either of us to alter a tragic course impulsively decided upon in a moment of weakness. No, we were decisive people, unwilling to admit a mistake even before it happened. And so we were done for. We were going to have sex if for no other reason than to prove we weren't fickle. Or maybe we were going to have sex because we both needed someone right then at that very moment. Nevertheless, we were done for.

Izzy pulled the car into her driveway without either of us breaking the code of silence instituted by mutual, unspoken consent on the way to her house. Izzy's home was one those houses where the first floor had brick on the outside and the second floor was covered with vinyl siding. It was small and cute but certainly no Secret Garden. Izzy's abode was situated in a rather typical suburban neighborhood of similar structures and small lots. It was the kind of neighborhood where the houses were close enough together that, if the mood struck, you could watch your neighbors perform their personal, or not so personal, day to day activities without benefit of binoculars or any other form of magnification. This fact was probably why Izzy kept her blinds shut most of the time. But I never asked.

As Izzy decamped I sat semi-frozen, wondering if the neighbors were actually were looking at us in this late hour. What would they think? And why the hell did I care? Izzy's voice startled me out of the moment.

"Are you coming in?" Her tone was thoughtful, almost as if she was hoping I'd say no. But I didn't. I was decisive.

"Hell, yes!" We were doomed.

"Awkward" is not really a strong enough word to describe the first minute or so in Izzy's living room. We got in the front door smoothly enough, only to find ourselves facing each other, feet planted firmly somewhere in the small space separating the sofa and coffee table. I was nervous and getting shaky. I was trying to hide it, of course. Serendipitously Izzy provided a quick distraction before I lost bladder and bowel control.

"Hold on…let me light a candle."

124

She slid out from behind the coffee table and returned momentarily with a candle, which she lit and set down before turning off the living room lamp. Instead of retaking the spot right in front of me, she sat down on the couch and pulled me down into a sitting position next to her. I don't know if it was the warmth of the candle, the alcohol, or just the fact that neither of us had backed down, but after all the doubt and dread I was still able to find my manhood at the crucial moment. Without a word I took Izzy's face in my hands and kissed her. It was a good kiss and Izzy was a good kisser and as it continued Izzy scooched her body over, pressing against me to where I could feel her breasts and the expanding and contracting of her chest as she caught air whenever my tongue wasn't in her mouth, or vice versa. Still on the couch, the clothes started to come off even as part of me worried about what we would do to the fabric if we didn't move to the bedroom. All the while another part of my brain was trying to distract me with thoughts of Elaine and wondering just what the hell was going on there, but those remained sufficiently suppressed for the moment and soon we were both shirtless. Wonderfully, Izzy's body was everything I imagined it would be after years of guessing. She really was stunning in her physical perfection. The flat stomach, her smooth skin; the definition of her wide shoulders and the curve of her lower back were enough to drive me over the edge before I was ready. But then Elaine popped up again, creeping around my head with a half-naked Izzy right in front of me. Damn! I alleviated the situation by picking Izzy up and carrying her to the bedroom which, thankfully, was on the same floor as the living room, thereby saving me from having to negotiate a flight of steps whilst drunk and carrying another human being.

Our lovemaking turned out to be…interesting. There were definite missteps and we did almost head-butt each other at one point but I would be lying to say it was not enjoyable. Izzy knew what she liked and clued me in when necessary. She also knew her way around a man's body and we made time to play with each before the actual intercourse. Izzy was giving and energetic and almost constantly on the move. She was loud, too. And the loudness started before we were joined, when we were still playing with each other. While a loud partner can be disconcerting, I found Izzy's vocalizations encouraging. Sort of like having sex with a cheerleader. I plan to rib her about it sometime in the future, when we can both laugh about it.

Still, things didn't seem to flow naturally, like we were reading a script for the first time, which in a way I suppose we were. But I don't blame either of us for the less-than-stellar sex. I truly believe it just wasn't meant to be for Izzy and me. We were in the friend zone for too long and now would be forever. And I'm pretty sure each of us was making something akin to a grocery list at some point, probably because it helped to keep us from thinking about the huge mistake we were making. I mean, her body felt amazing and it's always nice NOT to be rejected, but at times I found myself wishing it was Elaine's body pressed against mine and for all I knew Izzy might have been having a similar fantasy about some guy I didn't know and never would. No matter what was going through our heads during the act by the time we were done we both knew it was never going to happen again. I suppose there are some things one just needs to get out of their system.

When all was said and done we held each other for an appropriate amount of time before rolling over to go to sleep. We did not spoon but we did hold hands for some time while I listened to Izzy breathing, feeling happy not to be kicked out of her bed. At some point I began to mourn. I did not love Izzy romantically. Izzy did not love me romantically. She and I were there for each other that night but nothing would come of it except embarrassed conversation and the occasional awkward moment. So I mourned for things lost and things forgotten and other things I wasn't even sure I was mourning at the time. What the hell was I doing? From where I lay on the bed, facing away from Izzy, I could look out the window. I couldn't see anything but darkness. I tightened my grip on Izzy's hand and she returned the pressure. She would save me for the moment. She did not make me leave.

CHAPTER TEN

Here's the thing: Although it may not appear to be so, I actually work to keep chaos out of my life, even when I suspect I may be the cause of it. Intellectually I understand that life is messy and a lot of weird and unsettling stuff happens, but generally I've wanted no part of it. I enjoy the delusion that my life is a model of organization and efficiency, free from the harmful effects of the unknown or the unwelcome. In fact, I've tended to view those whose lives are messier than my own not only with something akin to pity, but also with a certain amount of contempt. For this I, at times, feel ashamed but it's the truth nonetheless. If I happen to find myself in conversation with a poor soul whose life seems out of control I always try to listen intently but simultaneously wonder how they could have let these things happen, as if they somehow wished ill fortune upon themselves. Now, there is no denying the impact our own choices on the course of our lives, and I was suddenly making a number of choices which seemed to invite disaster. In spite of this I still wanted to believe in complete control, but of course circumstance and this delusion did not really jibe. Whether it is the loss of a beloved pet, asteroids falling from space, or the pregnancy of a fourteen-year-old daughter, we seem to have little or no control over great swaths of our lives. I suppose it's possible the realization of this may be the beginning of a sort of freedom (for me it was the beginning of sleeping through the night.)

Unfortunately this level of heightened self-awareness did not exist for me at the time. Had I an inkling of it I could have, perhaps, hosed off at least a little of the muck in which I was mired. So, instead of waking from a troubled sleep wracked with confusion and guilt, wondering how I could turn back time or change things more to my liking, my energies could have been better spent trying to deal with the future. Alas, this was not to be. The hubris of believing in the ability to control the outcome of things external to myself was

deeply ingrained and not likely to surrender without much wailing and gnashing of teeth. So, for a time, I continued as a man in a bubble, roaming around in a confined space, thinking that space encompassed the whole world. I could see out of the bubble, as if it didn't exist, but I couldn't see much of anything inside it. Others could see into my bubble, however. Arthur could. And Johannes. And Therapist Jim. And maybe even Izzy even though she had, at least for the moment, become a bubble resident. On occasion the ones who could see into the bubble would clue me in as to what was happening inside. Well, mostly Therapist Jim. If asked, Arthur and Johannes would tell me what was going on but they weren't getting paid to do it and neither was in the habit of offering unsolicited advice. Later on, after I was legally divorced, both of them would indicate they thought I was in the shit long before I realized I was in the shit. When I asked them why they didn't bother to mention it at the time they both had the same response, "You didn't ask."
Izzy, on the other hand, never seemed to feel any compunction about citing my screw ups as soon as she became aware of them. But in other ways Izzy wasn't so different from my male friends. And one of those ways appeared to be her ability to compartmentalize her thoughts. I came to believe she had this capacity because, mercifully, in the weeks following our little tete a tete she exerted no pressure on me to "talk" about what passed between us that Saturday night. Indeed, she didn't bring up the subject at all, which is very man-like behavior. Perhaps, having been part of this particular failing, she was as anxious as I to forget it ever happened. Or maybe she just thought I stunk in bed and didn't want to confront me with it. Regardless, my bang with Izzy ended with a whimper, as evidenced by the following:

Aided by the earlier consumption of copious amounts of alcohol, I was able to fall asleep in Izzy's bed despite the misgivings that had permeated the entire sexual experience with her. Awakened early the next morning by neighbors one yard over involved in a heated, boisterous discussion on weed control, I made a quick exit with the excuse I had to pick up the boys. It was a lie, of course. I didn't actually need to pick them up. They were safely ensconced in the spare bedroom of their grandparents' house and wouldn't require picking up for many hours. Izzy knew this too (I had mentioned it the night before, when we were still talking,) but apparently didn't want to make things more awkward than they already were and didn't question the assertion. She was, and is, after all, a lady. And a friend.

Izzy's and my first contact following the escape that Sunday morning occurred the following Tuesday and went something like this:

"Hey!" Izzy called me to ask about the bank's recurring computer issue. "Are the evil hackers trying to break in again?" (You'll notice there's no mention of sex, feelings, or nudity of any kind.)

"Looks like it. Stephen says we may be down for a couple hours while they repair the firewall and reboot. Are you guys still operating?" (Her failure to mention sex, feelings, or nudity of any kind put me immediately at ease.)

"Oh, sure." Izzy didn't sound like she was going to talk about Saturday night at all! "It's like olden days, though. We're writing everything down on paper."

I laughed in a way that sounded natural enough. "Sounds tedious…Lunch next week?" I was trying to sound "breezy," which was becoming a habit.

"Absolutely. Call me on Friday so we can set it up."

And that's how it happened, embarrassment, shame, lies, computer hackers and all. That's how easily Izzy and I managed to get over the hump, so to speak. We did it with a stupid little lunch date. Unbelievable. Even better, over time an unspoken agreement developed. We seemed to silently agree to never speak of the "incident" again, and that worked just fine. Our unspoken agreement allowed each of us to act and think in a way that made our awkward act of sex seem less-than-real, sort of like a weird dream, thereby giving us the opportunity to just go back to being good friends. Therapist Jim disagreed with our failure to confront the issue, but to this day I feel the results speak for themselves. We are still friends and, for better or worse, have never again seen each other naked.

Having just lied to my best female friend about picking up the boys, I chose to run home for a shower and a nap. I was rather ripe and desirous of a shower and some alone time as well. I was out of sorts, riding an out of control wave of events and my level of uncertainty concerning these events was becoming…uncomfortable.

129

And it was only going to get worse. Lucky for me, however, I was still in possession of a sufficient reserve of arrogance to maintain the default mode of (at least) outward confidence. Everything in my life would turn out ok. There was no guarantee of this, of course, and never had been. Not for me or anyone. But I had enough history on my side to feed the false assumption of security. After all, until recently life had been firing on all cylinders, or at least appeared to be.

The house was empty when I arrived home. Still no Kim. What was that all about? I knew I would have to make another attempt to deal with that situation before retrieving Trevor and Alex but I was dreading it. Couldn't she just go away and leave me alone? Couldn't she just disappear and make my life easier? How was I supposed to untangle all the emotional threads left hanging all over our relationship? Even under the best of circumstances this wasn't a task for which I was very capable. Regardless, I managed to set the problem down long enough to get in the shower and take a few deep breaths. Relaxing as the warm water slid down my back, my mind wandered and I was confronted with a slide show of provocative images from the night before. While not necessarily unpleasant (Izzy has a beautiful body,) a tinge of guilt ensued. Then those (now shame-inducing) memories morphed into a naked Elaine. She was lying beneath me, telling me not to stop, breathing heavily and pulling me into her. I could feel her body pressed against mine. While the fantasy was not elaborate my reaction to it was that of any healthy, red-blooded male. I took it as a good sign that I was able to get a boner on such a stressful morning. Taking my time, I toweled off feeling only slightly cleaner than I had ten minutes earlier.

A wave of exhaustion washed over me as I got dressed. The last two days had been witness to enough surprises, bad decisions, disappointments and unintended consequences to last for months and I was feeling the effects. I was also feeling needy and alone and although I was unsure what kind of reception I would receive I decided to give Elaine a call. I hadn't spoken to her in over 24 hours, which felt like an eternity. Inexplicably some part of me was convinced 24 hours should be enough time for her to come to her senses about her feelings for me. But was it? Would she hear my voice and ask me to move to Prague? An unlikely scenario no doubt, but still a pleasant, frightening thought. I believed it more likely she wouldn't answer at all, engaged, I was sure, in some Sunday morning activity with her friends and not thinking of me at all. Or worse, laughing and telling jokes about the fool with whom she had been sleeping. I dialed the phone before the visions got too ugly.

"Hello?" Elaine answered. I relaxed somewhat upon discerning no laughter in the background.

"Uh...hi. It's Jason. I was just calling to say hello and see what you were up to." I quickly decided not to mention I slept with Izzy the night before and hoped she wouldn't pick up on it through the phone.

"Oh! Hello to you. I'm actually at home," Yay! "Packing for the move." Damn! "The movers are supposed to be here in a little while to take some of my furniture to storage."

"Movers? On a Sunday?" I was trying not to scream.

"I know! I had to pay extra but I've got to get everything organized and ready to go. I've only got a couple weeks. What are you up to?" Just another day for Elaine.

"Oh, just about to eat breakfast. I've got the place to myself this morning." But why did I say that? So that she wouldn't think I got laid the night before? Why would she care if I had the place to myself? And why did I care? She was rushing to leave town. Stupid! "Do you want some help packing?" Stupider!

Obviously I was fishing for an invite from Elaine. I wanted to see her and I didn't want to sound pushy or needy even though I was both. Besides, nobody likes to pack so who wouldn't want help with it? It would also prove to her what a true friend I was because only your best friends help you pack and move your crap. Average friends avoid it like the plague. Certainly, this thoughtful offer would prove to her how much she meant to me and how much I could mean to her. The simple act of packing a box would allow her to see my value as a friend and lover. It was fool proof.

"No, it's ok. Thanks for the offer, though." Huh? How was I to display my value to her if she wouldn't let me pack her boxes?

Undeterred, I decided to press on. "It's really no problem. I don't have anything else to do today and I'd love to hang out with you..."

"I don't know, Jason. After the other night I'm not really sure it's a good idea." There were more words, but the ones I heard were "I don't know." To me the phrase meant Elaine wasn't completely against the idea of me fumbling around with her undies and that I still had a chance. Emboldened by her lack of decisiveness I crafted my words carefully.

"Don't worry, Elaine. Friday was a rough night. I know I went a little overboard with the things I said to you about, you know, how I feel and everything." I was lying again. I really didn't think I went overboard at all. In fact, I figured I hadn't gone far enough. "How about I bring some coffee over and help you pack some boxes and you can tell me about the new job."

A pregnant pause emanated from the other end of the phone. "Well, I'll admit I could use the help but I really don't want you to get the wrong impression and I really don't want to hurt your feelings." She was beginning to crack.

"Don't worry, Elaine. I know I'm a little off balance right now," That was, perhaps, an understatement. "And I've been thinking that it's probably a good thing you're leaving for a while. I mean, I know I have a lot of shit to deal with here and, you know, you're kind of a distraction....in a good way, though. I just thought it would be nice to spend a little time with you before you leave and if that means I have to pack a couple boxes then so be it." I was trying to sound funny but I think that last part is what finally convinced her to let me come over.

I somehow doubt Elaine believed the part about me thinking it was a good thing she was leaving. I sure as hell didn't believe it and I'm a horrible liar, but she gave me the green light provided I bring some packing tape, coffee, and blueberry muffins. I felt manically elated but maintained a calm demeanor long enough to get off the phone, after which I allowed myself two vertical leaps to celebrate my good fortune.

Sycophantically purchasing the muffins, tape, and coffee, I felt heroic carrying the prizes up the walkway of the Secret Garden. The fact there was a moving truck parked in the drive barely registered, focused as I was on getting to the front door while the coffee was still hot. What did register was Elaine's absence. For the first time Elaine was not there to greet me either at the door or walkway. Now, it wasn't like there was a wealth of greeting history on which I could rely, and it did occur to me that she might be busy with the movers, but even the throes of unrequited love couldn't hide the way things "felt". The air was different…heavier. I made a note of it and kept moving. I was on a mission, after all.

I knocked on the front door (a thing I had never had to do before) and could hear a male voice telling the lady of the house that someone was knocking on the door. Elaine's voice drifted through the door but the words were indistinct. When the door finally opened I found myself facing off with one of the movers. Taken by surprise, I fell mute. The mover, on the other hand, had been given specific instructions by his customer.

"Are you Jason?" He did not appear to be too happy with his new job as butler.

"Uh…yes."

"She said to let you in and send you upstairs…" To his credit, he held the storm door open for me as my hands were full of coffee, muffins, and tape. I felt a bit guilty that I had not brought coffee for the movers as well.

"Uh…thanks."

I, like the mover, followed the lady's instructions without question and carried myself and the provisions up the narrow staircase and finding Elaine in one of the bedrooms. She was sitting on a stool sorting items and wrapping in newspaper those which were going to be transported in the box sitting directly in front of her. She looked smart and sexy in a pair of tight jeans and a white halter top, hair in a high pony. Lying behind her was a red flannel shirt she had probably been wearing before the heat from her labors allowed her to abandon it. For my part I was just happy to see her bare shoulders and arms. She did not get up to greet me, or even turn her head. My voice cracked the silence.

"Coffee?" I could have been talking to myself.

"I'd love some." Elaine answered pleasantly enough but still didn't get up from her stool. Instead I carried the coffee the last two steps and handed her the one with cream and sugar.

"Thanks. Is that the packing tape?" She was pointing at the bag in my left hand. She clearly regretted her decision to let me come over.

"Yup. Here you go." I handed her the bag, suddenly feeling terribly out of place. It seemed whatever was left of the recent winter was being preserved in Elaine's bedroom, just for me. "What do you need me to do?" I was sticking to conversational basics. The feeling of being out of place was quickly turning into a desire to flee. Other than the last time I tried to crawl into bed with Kim I couldn't recall ever feeling so unwelcome. Maybe it had been a bad idea to push for the invitation.

"If you don't mind you can pack all the books on the top shelf of the closet and take the boxes downstairs for the movers." Now she was pointing at the closet. She was cordial and cold.

"No problem." As instructed, I grabbed an empty box and started to fill it with books, but not too many. I knew I was going to have to carry it down the steps and books are heavy.

We sat in silence as each person in the house did their part to facilitate Elaine's departure from Cincinnati. Elaine had become an emotional fortress and the speech I had practiced on my way to the Secret Garden no longer seemed appropriate. I sat watching her from three feet away. I was not allowed to touch her. I knew that without having to be told. Our relationship had been short but intense, both physically and emotionally, and the void separating us shared that intensity. The fact that Elaine didn't need to tell me not to touch her, that I simply felt it, was a testament to her ability to project her desires out to the world. While being the recipient of those projections had not always been pleasant, they had never been this oppressive. Was she preoccupied or pissed off? Was it about me? Stupid question. I could only stay in my "cone of silence" for so long before trying to break the tension.

"So…when exactly are you leaving again?" I sounded a little mousy and I didn't like it. Plus I could hear the movers downstairs talking with one another and moving stuff around. Could they hear me?

"It's supposed to be in ten days if I can get everything arranged. I'm close to signing a lease on a flat now." I took heart that she took the time to string that many words together and speak them to me. I decided to broach my hot topic.

"Do you know yet exactly how long you'll be there?" I was trying to sound nonchalant but was failing.

"I don't know, Jason. It could be two or three years. It could be four. It depends on how things go." I was irritating her further but I felt an overwhelming urge to "define" our relationship and I needed her to quash my anxiety about her leaving. Elaine's and my affiliation had always been uneven. In many respects (maybe all) I needed her more than she needed me and the reality of her packing tilted things even further in her favor. The tilting was driving me off the edge.

"So…once you move, when will we be able to talk? I mean, how often can we talk?" I was really starting to sound pathetic. What could the mover's be thinking about my pitiable display?

"I don't know, Jason." Her frustration was palpable but I kept pushing.

"Once a week? Twice a week? I mean, I don't want to bug you when you're working and having, you know, sort of a 'chat' schedule might help with that." Jeez! Just knowing I said these things to her makes me sick to my stomach. I deserve nothing but scorn for sinking so low. Could I have sounded more needy and wretched? No wonder she was angry! She should have unpacked a knife and stabbed me with it. I would have.

But by now I wasn't at all concerned about eavesdropping movers. I was totally focused on getting something from Elaine that would never be forthcoming: A commitment to the future. If they were listening the moving crew had already judged me less than a man.

"How do I know, Jason? Why are you asking silly questions like that? We'll talk when we talk. I'm not going to be put on a phone schedule with you." Now she was really angry. Except for the sound of Elaine's voice the rest of the house had gone silent.

"Well…I guess I understand what you're saying. In that case maybe we could just make a standing day and time to call each other. Maybe just once a week. What do you think? Oh, and will we get to see each other again before you leave? I'll move my schedule…." I was begging to be stabbed.

"You know what?" She interrupted me. "You need to leave. Now." Her voice was calm but firm.

If I could go back and tell past-time Jason to just shut the hell up and pack some books I would definitely do it. Unfortunately that technology hasn't been invented yet so I am forced to recount my behavior, wincing with every word spoken. To my credit, after Elaine told me to go I did finally shut up. I sat in stunned silence for just a few seconds before standing up, dutifully picking up a box of books, and walking out the door of the bedroom. Elaine said not a word as I made my way down the steps, leaving the books in the living room with the movers before exiting the house and driving away. This would be my last ejection from the Secret Garden. I have never returned.

On the drive home I thought of calling one of my friends to relate the morning's drama but quickly nixed the idea. A few minutes of alone time in the car afforded ample time for the shame of my behavior to take hold. Certainly I wasn't going to call Izzy. That would just add insult to injury and she was already a big part of my shame spiral. Arthur was out of town and Johannes was probably having day sex with his new girlfriend. And even if he wasn't I had already decided to take the whole thing to my grave. I couldn't admit to them, or to myself, how low and how fast I had sunk.

Kim's car was in the driveway when I got home. The sight of it filled me with the desire to escape. I was in no mood to confront her about the last few days, resolve any issues or talk about her sexual preference and why she never told me about it. I really just wanted to sleep. The attractiveness of it had increased with every mile of the drive home but Kim's return meant no sleep would be forthcoming in the near term. Resolving myself to this, I turned the car off and scuffled into the house. Kim was sitting at the dining room table.

"The boys are with your parents." I offered this as a greeting.

"I know. I talked to Mom this morning. She says they can keep them until after dinner." Her voice was relaxed, which pissed me off.

"Did you tell them what you've been up to? I lied for you yesterday when I dropped Alex and Trevor off." I had lied for Kim for a few reasons, not the least of which was her tradition-oriented parents would never want to hear their daughter might be gay. That was a conversation I was more than happy to leave to her. I still wanted them to like me.

"No, I didn't." The question irritated her. Good. "They told me you said I was shopping so I left it at that. You and I need to talk."

"You think so?" I was being sarcastic because I was tired and was having a crappy day. "Where do you want to start? I'd like

136

to start with your girlfriend. You know – from Friday night at The Hot Spot?"

Kim didn't seem too surprised. "How did you end up in that particular bar?"

"Arthur and I decided to check out a different bar for a change and we ended up in that one."

"Great! The one night you and Arthur decide NOT to stay at O'Hearn's all night you end up in the only gay bar on the west side of town." Under different circumstances I would have found her observation amusing.

"Can you tell me what's going on, please? I know we're not staying married but you just disappeared. And are you gay?"

Here was her story: She was gay – or at least bisexual. She wasn't sure which yet. She knew Arthur and I had been The Hot Spot last night because we made such a ruckus as we left. The distraction was sufficient for her (and others) to catch Arthur shuttling me out of the bar. Knowing I had seen her, she then had some choices to make. One of them was that she wasn't going to come home that evening, mainly because she didn't want to deal with me. So she did, indeed, stay with the woman with whom I caught her exploring her sexuality. That woman was (and is) named Lola. Apparently Lola was (and is) full on gay. Oh, I also learned another bit of good news: Kim still felt nothing for me, nothing at all. She said she thought her lack of feeling for me was part of her inability to get aroused by men at all, so I shouldn't take it personally.

"And how do I not take that personally?"

"Well, because now you can believe you didn't have anything to do with me not wanting you, at least not directly. At least I don't think so...I don't think you 'turned' me gay...or bi...I guess. I mean...probably not. I think I've just been hiding from it for years."

"Well, I can't tell you how much better that makes me feel. I sure am glad I didn't turn you gay." I couldn't control the sarcasm. I did, however, opt not to tell her about the women I had been sleeping with or attempt to brag about how there were women in the world that did actually want me even if it was JUST for sex, or as a bed warmer, or whatever. She didn't need to know about my dalliances, which all happened to be heterosexual in nature and were therefore off topic.

"Alright, Jason. I get that you're upset. Look, we're both dealing with a lot right now and my new situation doesn't change anything between us when it comes to the divorce." She had a point here. The fact she was a lesbian shouldn't slow down the divorce process or induce us to give marriage counseling a second chance. "Even with all of this I was thinking there should be no rush for you to move out. As long as we can be civil to each other I don't see any reason for you to leave any time soon. I've decided to start working again and that would help us both save some money."

What the fuck was she talking about? Why would anyone want to continue living with the person they were divorcing? Granted, I had done little in the way of planning my exit, but it never occurred to me I wouldn't be leaving soon. I was ready for the freedom. My biggest concern was the effect it would have on the boys and I had already talked to Therapist Jim about it:

Me: How long do you think I should wait before I move out? I mean for the boys' sake.
Therapist Jim: Do you mean for their sake or for yours?
Me: Huh? I mean theirs. Why would it be about me?
Therapist Jim: Because your sons will adjust to you moving out whenever it occurs. It may take them a while, but you staying in the house with your estranged wife may be just as confusing for them, if not more so. And it gives them no resolution. You have to let them start moving on, too.
Me: Ok, I think I see what you mean. But, c'mon, this isn't about me!
Therapist Jim: Then why are you still in the house?

I really believe I should take Therapist Jim out for a beer sometime. He always has good advice and beer is cheaper than his hourly rate. But Therapist Jim had enlightened me to the whole moving out deal so I wasn't about to go along with Kim's idea that we should go on with our current living arrangement indefinitely.

"I don't think that would be a good idea." I was trying to keep my responses simple. I knew I couldn't explain it as well as Therapist Jim.

"Why?" Apparently my response was not sufficient to quell her desire for continued cohabitation.

"Because it's poisonous. The idea of it is poisonous. You know? We've made choices, it's time to move on."

"It doesn't have to be. I've read about divorced couples that still live in the same house. It would save money for both of us." She actually seemed serious and she really seemed focused on the money to be saved.

"I don't even know what to say to that, Kim. It's not just about money. It's about…it's about mental health, for God's sake. It's about not living in the past. Besides, this can't be good for the boys." I was getting exasperated. What the hell was she thinking?

"Oh, and divorce is?" She was starting to get snide.

"Of course not, Kim. But I think anything is better than what we've been doing." I wasn't sure I was talking about just Kim and me at this point, even though I was REALLY sure I didn't want to live in the same house with her anymore.

"Whatever, Jason. I don't care if you move out or not. I was just trying to think of something that would work for both of us." She walked out of the room and headed upstairs as she finished her sentence. I did not respond. I wasn't sure I trusted any of her motivations anymore but I was pretty sure my best interests were her last concern. Or else she was just nuts.

Moving day for me came the following weekend, which was unexpected but not unwanted. After my last conversation with Kim on the subject I was convinced I needed to move forward. Luckily the work week was uneventful. Also, it turned out if I didn't work very hard at my actual job I was afforded more than enough time to find an apartment and arrange for the move. As well, Kim was not being unreasonable about the furniture and I was able to take enough from the house so that I wouldn't have to buy anything right away.

Kim arranged it so that neither she nor the boys would be at the house while I was moving, which I thought was a good idea. I couldn't stand the thought of the boys watching the furniture walking out the front door and, God forbid, one or both of them offering to help. The mental image of it was enough to bring tears to my eyes. I had a moving crew all lined up anyway, consisting mainly of Arthur (who got back into town earlier in the week) and Johannes. I declined to request assistance from Elaine or Izzy. On the other hand Johannes' new squeeze, Angie (whom I had yet to meet,) offered to help as well, although she couldn't commit to the full eight hours for which I had reserved the truck. I couldn't imagine it would take more than eight hours to move a modest amount of furniture and an extremely limited wardrobe. Prospects for efficiency were improved by not allowing any beer drinking until AFTER the last item had been moved into my new place. Beer is fun but can be time consuming.

My crew arrived bright eyed and ready to go and after some initial discussion about what was to be moved Johannes took charge of the operation. With his engineering background and recent divorce he had invaluable expertise pertaining to the placement of items in the truck with regard to minimizing damage in transit and maximizing utilization of space. Arthur and I did as we were told, realizing that doing otherwise would have resulted in twice as many trips as the two it took to move everything. For my part I had anticipated the pain-in-the-ass factor of carrying furniture up steps and exploited this foresight by leasing a first floor apartment. All in all the whole "transition" took six hours and Angie didn't even show up until we were moving the last piece of furniture into the apartment. Once the truck was safely returned the four of us sat in my new living room and had one of the beers Angie brought for us (except for Arthur, who had gone back to his strict no drinking and driving policy.) I liked her immediately.

"Nice place, Jason." Angie mentioned, sitting as close as humanly possible to Johannes. I noted the two were generally touching each other in some fashion at all times which, as a side note, would have made moving furniture all the more difficult. But I'll admit this behavior made me a bit jealous. They were completely enamored of one another. "It's very clean and new."

"Indeed," I was trying to sound worldly for Angie's sake due to some sort of subconscious desire to impress a pretty girl. "I think it's a good place to start until other arrangements can be made."

I didn't know what those "other arrangements" might turn out to be. I had no plan and no clue as to what would come next concerning my living arrangements. I was damn impressed with myself for moving out so quickly (and not moving into a dump) but had put zero thought into what my next move was going to be. I was also a bit taken aback at the speed with which the "transition" had occurred. Was it really possible to change one's life so quickly? Later that evening I would spend a few minutes on this thought, lying alone in my new apartment listening to my new neighbors stomp around above me sometime past the witching hour. My conclusion was yes, life can change that quickly. And at the risk of sounding overly dramatic, I would also realize the sense of security that came with owning a tract house was an illusion. Listening to the muffled tones of rap music wafting through the ceiling from the party above, my epiphany was that everything was temporary. Even the Roman Coliseum would eventually crumble. In the face of that, what chance did I have? I would spend the wee hours trying to ignore the noise and fight off a rather aggressive existential crisis.

Whilst sitting with my friends in the living room, however, none of the above was yet a concern. The sun was up and the cable man would arrive any minute. Angie was easy going and a comfortable addition to the established troika. As I drank beer and listened to cross talk it occurred to me I probably could have asked Izzy to help with the move. Things were not really settled down with us yet and I didn't want to impose, but I imagine she would have jumped on board had I asked. Of course I didn't even consider asking Elaine. We had not spoken since my banishment from the Secret Garden. I had wanted to talk to her, of course, but decided to wait for her call, should it ever come. She had her own move to worry about and the unabated embarrassment over my behavior at our last meeting proved an effective deterrent. I didn't want to talk to her about moving ever again.

"Well, dude. I hate to move and run but Angie and I need to go shopping for dinner. We're having surf and turf. Be there around eight." Johannes was getting up to go and the matter-of-fact dinner invitation was unexpected but certainly not unwelcome. I had no food.

"Thanks, man! I'll see you then."

"Arthur, you and the wife are invited, too. We'll have plenty of food." Johannes was a good cook. I would find out later that evening that while Angie offered some support to him in the kitchen, her main function was that of hostess and official opener of the wine.

"I'll see what I can do, mate. I think she might have something planned for us tonight." Arthur smirked. "She gets a little lonely when I'm overseas."

"I hear you." Johannes wore a smirk as well. "You can always get that out of the way early and then come over. It'll be nice to get together." It was, too. Johannes had already invited other like-minded individuals. "The karaoke really gets going about 3 AM. And Jason, that's an ugly chair." He said, referring to my recliner as he departed. The consensus amongst the movers was that the chair was not an attractive piece of furniture. I liked it. It could recline to a nearly horizontal position.

Arthur lingered for bit after Johannes and Angie left and I gave him the thumbs up on filling his pockets with free beer.

"Are you going to Johannes'?" I didn't want to go alone.

"Perhaps. I'll see what's going on at home first." Arthur got a concerned look on his face. I had only seen that look when he was afraid he had missed last call. "So how are you doing with all this? Honestly."

I was touched by his concern. Arthur was almost never this emotional. "I'm ok, Arthur. And, honestly, I'm feeling kind of excited right now, like I just got out of prison. Not that I would know what that really feels like but I'll bet this is close. I'll admit that I'm not quite sure what I should be focusing on right now, but I'll figure it out."

"Getting out of prison is better." Arthur said this flatly and without elaboration. "Well, I would start with food, and maybe another lamp or two. When you have food and light you can focus on Alex and Trevor."

Arthur's point was taken. When I started getting the little things in order I could start to focus on the big things. God is in the details and all that. It also occurred to me the boys might want to go grocery shopping with me. This would be a fun activity for us and hopefully distract them from the fact their father had been downsized. I sat in my easy chair and made of list of things I needed, finding that listing one item often forced me to list another. You don't buy salt without pepper. You don't buy laundry detergent without dryer sheets. And certainly you don't buy pop tarts without a toaster. I did not have a toaster. I moved that to the top of the list. My financial condition made the toaster a major purchase and would require budgeting.

I was surprised to find myself exhausted after my day of moving and list making. The cable guy had come and gone so I allowed myself the respite of a nap in the chair everyone hated, reclining it to its full glory. I woke a couple hours later with a mind to go to Johannes', the choice made easier by a bare cupboard and empty refrigerator. Johannes' usually invited couples to his house but my rumbly stomach rendered me little worried about being a third, fifth, or even seventh wheel. Arthur did not show up at Johannes' that night. Perhaps he was worried about the drinking and driving or maybe he and his wife never made it out of bed. There were, however, six other couples besides Johannes and Angie, making me a fifteenth wheel. Normally I might have found the situation uncomfortable but Angie, who seemed to sense my unease, silently took control and kept me amply supplied with food and drink and introducing me to the guests I did not know. Even with me as her charge she found a way to keep touching Johannes. The other couples weren't quite so clingy, which gave me the opportunity to engage them socially and poll the room on the pros and cons of touchy-feeliness. Half of them admitted they were jealous of Johannes' and Angie's desire to be in constant physical contact with each other. Guess which half.

Johannes had bought the house just a few months prior after his own period of post-divorce apartment dwelling. The floor plan had a nice flow to it with the kitchen in full view of the family room, which is where most of the couples were hanging out. I was free to move about the cabin, so to speak, and the distraction of new faces and new stories was welcome. Johannes' efforts produced a steady stream of epicurean delights and as we ate Angie played the sommelier, regularly opening and serving bottle after bottle of wine. The free flowing food and drink helped to spread Bacchanalian joy throughout the house and though the noise level never achieved high school party decibels a good time was being had by all.

Considering my wine consumption I should have stayed overnight in the spare bedroom, but I left soon after the karaoke began. Despite the lack of consensus regarding constant touching, the couples did make a point of singing with each other and I was lacking a partner. Yet again I used the boys as an excuse to make my exit, arriving home well after midnight but also well before dawn. So, after some muffled Led Zeppelin and a bout of the aforementioned existential crisis I drifted away, telling myself I should call Elaine. I fell asleep before I could dial.

I woke the next morning to loud knocking. Holy shit! I forgot to set my alarm and Kim was dropping off Alex and Trevor. It was ten in the morning and I smelled like the inside of a wine bottle. As quickly as I could I pulled on the pair of pants I had earlier abandoned to the floor, grabbed a clean t-shirt and patted my hair down as I rushed the door.

"Good moooorning!" I greeted them loudly. Kim was standing behind them, scowling. "Thanks, Kim. I'll bring them back in the morning." She said goodbye to the boys, turned on her heel and walked away, taking her scowl with her.

"Hey, Dad! What are we going to do today?" Alex asked as he and his brother began investigating their new space. "Can we play hide and seek?" Having so few items with which to fill the apartment, there was a plethora of empty spaces in which to hide.

"Sure! I thought we could also go grocery shopping. What do you think, Trevor?"

"Sure." He seemed more apprehensive than his younger brother. Later in the "divorce process" I would discern Trevor lacked the adaptive skills of his younger brother. I believe this is at least partly a function of age. The younger ones haven't set everything in stone yet. Alex, having just turned ten, was very accepting of the changes being made in his life as it came to his parents. Trevor, hurtling toward pubescence and with the attendant rush of hormones, probably didn't appreciate another wrench being thrown into his already uncertain frame of reference on life.

"Well then, let me grab a shower and we'll get going." I didn't usually shower up for the grocery store but I could smell myself. It was unpleasant.

While showering I was treated to a solid stream of questions about the apartment as the boys continued their explorations. I couldn't see them through the shower curtain (expertly installed by Angie the day before) but could hear them tearing in and out of the bathroom as they discovered each nook and hidey hole the apartment had to offer. When I was done I could tell Trevor's anxiety level had somewhat decreased and the boys were raring to go to the store to buy things for their room, which currently lacked beds. They didn't seem to mind, however, and were looking forward to camping out in their sleeping bags until proper bedding could be requisitioned. On the way out to the car they took note of other boys in the complex, especially those which looked close to their age. I was feeling more comfortable by the minute.

Our shopping excursion went smoothly and was completed without any screaming or tantrums. The boys were well behaved also. Unlike the normal willy-nilly behavior common to our food super-store trips, they were respectful and reserved and weren't asking for random items at every turn. I wasn't sure how to deal with it. I had prepared to say "no" over and over again but when it was rendered unnecessary I found myself falling into an equally respectful silence. It seemed my sons were growing up. I wasn't sure how to feel about it. With everything going on between their mother and me it was a foregone conclusion that our relationship was going to change. There was just no way to know how or, for that matter, how much control I would be able to exert over the changes. I had heard parents of older children talk about this phenomenon – that as their children got older the parents role became one more of observation than actual participation - and found the thought slightly depressing. But I took comfort remembering how I never really stopped needing my own father, even after he died. Yup, if I had anything to say about it they would need me until long after I was dead.

We arrived at the apartment with the trunk of the Malibu chock full of useful and tasty items. Without me asking, Trevor and Alex grabbed bags and carried them into the building and I began to wonder if Kim had briefed them on expected behavior beforehand or if they just felt sorry for me. I doubted the former and didn't like the thought of the latter. It was, however, quite nice not to have to carry everything myself. I thanked them with a reward of pop tarts heated in the brand new toaster, which were consumed whilst they watched a workman scrub the inside of the empty apartment complex pool. They were excited the pool was so close to where they were standing.

"Can we swim in it?" Alex was ridiculously innocent.

"Of course! But I think we should wait until they put water in it. Don't you?"

"You know what I mean, Dad!" He had a big smile on his face and so did Trevor. And so did I. I felt they had given me a huge gift and we wiled the rest of the day away exploring the complex, renting movies on pay per view, and putting things where they belonged. It was the best day I had had in months.

Elaine was on hold. That's what Emily had just told me. This was unexpected. I told Emily I would take the call.

"Hello? Elaine?"

"Hey, Jason. How are you?" She didn't wait for an answer. "Listen, I'm just calling to let you know I'm leaving for Prague on Sunday and was hoping you and I could get together before I leave."

What? Did she just say she wanted to "get together" before she left? After the way I behaved at our last encounter? "That would be great. Friday night?" Oh God, would she actually find the time to see me the Friday before she left for Europe?

"I'm sorry, Jason. I can't Friday." Of course not. "As you can imagine, I have a lot to do before I go and I've made plans with some other people." People she didn't want to introduce me to, I imagined. "I was thinking you could meet me at the airport for coffee before my flight."

What the fuck? Even in that moment of confusion I had to hand it to Elaine. She sure knew how to keep me off balance. But I still had some pride left in me. I wasn't going to be the slobbering puppy, grateful for the random pat on the head or for any scrap thrown my way. How could I force her to let me have more meaning in her life?

"Well, I guess that would be ok. What time?" This wasn't the way. But I really wanted to see her before she left. Forgive me.

Elaine was beautiful and beaming sitting across the small table from me at one of the many airport coffee shops. Her excitement about her new journey was tangible. She was at the airport waiting to start the next chapter of her life's journey. I didn't really know why I was there. I wanted to reach across the void and touch her but feared she wouldn't allow it. The situation gave me approximately 23 minutes to explain myself to a woman who had come to mean so much to me and whose feelings were not reciprocal. What was I allowed to do? What was I allowed to say?

"So...how long is the flight?" Even I am astounded at my ineptitude and lack of grace.

"It's about 12 hours with the layover in Paris." She couldn't keep herself from smiling.

"Well, you know I'm sad to see you go. I wish things were different." Still inept but at least more to the point. Considering she had to leave in just a few minutes I hope she appreciated the brevity of the sentiment.

"I know, Jason. I really do appreciate you coming down to see me off. I wanted to see you before I left so...you know, so we didn't leave things..." Her voice drifted off but I knew exactly what she was trying to say. I had played the fool at our last encounter and she was giving me the opportunity to replace the memory. Unlike me, she was graceful. Too bad she didn't love me.

"I hear you, Elaine. Thank you." This was the extent of my speech. We sat together, fingering our coffee cups, staring without talking. The silence carried enough information to make actual words seem trivial. Finally she glanced down at her watch.

"I have to go."

We stood and hugged each other. It was a good hug and sincere. When I released her she picked up her bag and walked away. I did not sit down until after she was no longer visible. I should have left the airport but was immobile, overcome with a sense of emptiness. Even now I'm not sure how Elaine had so quickly come to fill that emptiness. It really didn't make any sense, but somehow she had. And now she was gone. It was not a good day.

CHAPTER ELEVEN

Naturally, I spent the next few days in a funk. On the one hand I was still feeling the sense of freedom that came with having my own place; on the other hand I wasn't enjoying it as much as I had hoped. Trevor was settling into the "two home" routine better than his brother, but so far Alex was at least acting like he wanted to be at my place when he was there. Even with their compliance, however, my mood after Elaine's departure made my time with them more trying. I found myself having to constantly redirect my attention to them when they were at the apartment, reminding myself they needed me to help them adjust to their new life. And I wasn't always up for this. At the time it seemed preferable to spend at least a few evenings wallowing in self-pity, crying into a beer and allowing myself to sink into immobility. I should have been grateful to my sons for the distraction they provided when we were together, but I must admit I felt a bit of resentment at their intrusion into my self-pity. I wanted to be left alone, at least for a little while, to sort things through.

Elaine did not call. I had given her 48 hours (a time frame with which she was unaware) to settle in before trying her cell phone, but I opted not to leave her a voicemail when she did not answer. I didn't want to sound desperate, even if I was feeling so. How does one emotionally span four thousand miles? I have no idea. What I did know was that any message I would have left her at the time would have fallen flat and most likely provoke a number change on her part. So I let it go. Her cell phone knew my cell phone and would tell her I called even if I didn't leave recorded words behind. Maybe it was time to move on.

Work, much like my sons, helped sustain my sanity with the distraction of "keeping busy." The workload had picked up and, with nothing better to do, I went ahead and threw myself into it. When the world hands you lemons... Whether I was feeling it or not my revived work ethic was making an impression on my boss AND my assistant. In the weeks following my departure from the house and Elaine's departure from Cincinnati the occurrence of Stephen and Emily complementing me in the same day was becoming less a rarity and more an expectation. Indeed, it was close to becoming commonplace. It seemed my failed love lives had borne not-so-rotten fruit and become a boon to my employer, but I wondered how long I could keep it up. Did I have to be in dire straits to be a super-productive employee, or could I keep it going when once again blessed with happiness? I wasn't sure because when I really thought about it I realized it had been years since I was really happy, through and through. Oh, I had my moments, of course. As noted earlier, I'm not really given to melancholy. In fact, I'm often the 'life of the party', so to speak. But one thing I am really good at is self-delusion, and that was the skill that got me through the last five years of my marriage. Hell, maybe the last eight.

I soldiered on, leaning on Izzy when we both had the time for me to lean on her. It's funny how easily a job can detract from your social life, if you allow it to do so. But even with the flurry of work completion I still managed to find time to listen to Emily complain about the boyfriend du jour, make weekly to semi-weekly visits to Therapist Jim, put my new apartment together and cruise internet porn. Therapist Jim knew all about the goings on with Izzy and Elaine (and the porn) and I like to think he found me entertaining, even though he would never say so in those words. Well, at least not to me. As far as I knew he could have been regaling his wife nightly with tales of my antics. I may have been fooling myself but he seemed to get a little excited whenever I came around. I mean, he never said anything like "I really missed you" whilst embracing me warmly, but I figured the lack of that particular form of expression was a product of shrink training. I imagine therapists are generally discouraged about behaving this way toward their customers, or touching them in general. But even if he didn't go over the top with me emotionally I think the fact I wasn't a serial killer or suicidal or anything like that made me easier to be around. My belief was he viewed me as a delightful, though cautionary, tale as opposed to someone who might cause him grave concern every time I ventured back out into the world after spending fifty minutes in his office.

Indeed, we had what I would consider a very lighthearted conversation in our first meeting after Elaine's departure.

Me: Elaine left about thirteen days ago. (It had been two weeks since our last session.)

Therapist Jim: And how do you feel about that?

Me: Well, at first I felt pretty shitty. And then after the first few days I felt just kinda shitty. Hmm…and I suppose just a light veneer of shittiness for the last couple of days.

Therapist Jim: What's your shittiness level today?

Me (giggling because my shrink just swore in front of me): I guess, maybe, three or four on a scale of ten?

Therapist Jim: Then it sounds like your recovering like a normal person. (I hate being called normal, even when it's supposed to be comforting. I've never been sure what "normal" is supposed to be.)

Me (now feeling suspicious because of the "normal" comment): I suppose so…. I'm thinking I might give up on her and make a fresh start. What do you think?

Therapist Jim: I think it's probably a good idea. You might actually think about staying single for a while, letting your wounds heal and adjusting to your new life. (Unlike your typical movie shrink, Therapist Jim didn't mind giving me his opinion once in a while.)

Me (still suspicious): Hmmm…intriguing thought, but have I ever told you about how lonely I feel when I'm alone?

Therapist Jim: Yes you have, Jason. But that's my point. You need to get used to being alone, at least a little. It would give you a chance to learn about yourself before becoming part of a couple again.

Me: Hmmm…interesting, but I see a couple problems with your theory, Doc. I mean, what if I spend all this time learning about myself only to find out that I'm really not a very good person? I mean, what if it turns out I don't really like myself? Or that I'm not very interesting? And what if it's not just lonely being by myself, but also boring? Unbelievably, unremittingly boring. It seems to me if I follow your advice I might be stepping into a minefield.

Therapist Jim (perhaps with just a touch of sadness): We'll follow up with that next week.

Me: Really? You're going to cut me off now? I think I might be having a breakthrough.

Therapist Jim: You're not having a breakthrough. Trust me.

I walked out feeling gypped. It was all about the coin with Therapist Jim. I was sure a life changing epiphany was in the offing given just five more minutes on the couch. But considering my current relationship status and my personality generally, I didn't deem Therapist Jim's "being alone" theory even remotely plausible. Still, as I saw it he had done his job. I felt unburdened as I headed back to work and was feeling excited about having the boys that night. I hadn't seen them in two days and was feeling their absence from the mostly-empty apartment. Thinking on that fact, it occurred to me there might be something to this whole "alone" thing, although I couldn't quite put my finger on what that "something" could be. On the one hand, in their absence, my heart had grown fonder, if indeed it was possible for me to love them more. On the other hand, I was pretty sure I had learned absolutely nothing about myself while knocking about my empty apartment for two days. And maybe that was a good thing in light of my desire to avoid the self-loathing that would no doubt accompany all that alone time and "getting to know myself." It was best not to dwell on such things.

Work was in its state of controlled chaos when I got back from my hour with Therapist Jim. I arrived ready to dig back into the stack but was interrupted by Emily before I had my suit jacket on the hangar. "Stephen told me to tell you to come and see him as soon you get back. Cool?"

"No problem." I guess I could have replied "cool" but it would have made me feel silly. I hung the jacket up, walked into Stephen's office and plopped down in a chair across the desk from him.

"Emily told me I had to come and see you." I tried to sound morose, like I had been ordered to appear in front of a magistrate - or my mother.

Stephen smiled. "Just wanted to see where you stood on the Engler Steel request and to thank you for all your hard work lately. You've got us caught up almost single handedly." There he was again with the complements. How I had ever gotten along without them I'll never know.

"Well, I guess marital failure has enhanced my work ethic." And it had. "Engler will take one more day. I'm waiting for up to date receivables."

"How's all that going?" Stephen, like almost everyone I knew, had gone through his own divorce a few years before and things had gotten ugly.

"As well as can be expected. Did I tell you she's gay?" I had begun to make a point of telling anyone who would listen that my estranged wife was gay, even if I had told them before.

"On numerous occasions. Are you seeing anyone?" It's possible Stephen was tiring of hearing about my gay wife. "Anyone who's NOT gay?"

"No...not really. I mean I'm not really seeing anyone. But I was seeing someone. I mean I'm not now seeing someone who's not really gay. Not anymore. And the someone I was seeing isn't gay. Well, I don't think she's gay, or even semi-gay for that matter… But no. I'm not seeing anyone. Not anymore…gay or otherwise." Jeez! That was a tough question. Elaine had been gone for a couple weeks and I definitely wasn't going to tell Stephen about Izzy's and my carnal knowledge. "But I'd like to. I figure if my wife can date another woman why can't I?"

"Funny." Stephen delivered it deadpan. "But you can't date other women, gay or otherwise, because Kim is a woman. And women don't care if you're separated or not. If she catches wind that you're seeing someone she will find a way to make you pay for it. I know it sounds like a double standard but I suspect she'll try to roast your balls."

This was not the first time I had been presented with this theory of female retribution. Not even the first time by Stephen. He seemed to bring it up nearly as much as I brought up the "my estranged wife is gay" scenario. But the first person to clue me in to this potential hazard was a retired divorce lawyer from whom I had sought advice when things with Kim started to decline. During our meeting the (male) attorney offered me a number of pieces of advice and harped on the fact I should never hire a female lawyer as they would, he believed, always relate to the wife and never really be fully committed to protecting a husband. He, like Stephen, also admonished me concerning dating outside the failing marriage. He told me that if I was going to do it to not get caught. He told me

Kim would not react well even though the marriage was in the shitter. Not even if we were separated. He told me revenge would be exacted even if the divorce were final. I asked why this was so. He responded it was "just something about women" and explained even though his evidence was anecdotal it constituted an absolute truth, like the existence of gravity. When pressed he explained the phenomenon could not be explained scientifically, only that he had observed it on numerous, devastating occasions.

"Hmmm… This sounds like something with which you've had some experience." I leaned forward, resting my chin on my fist for intellectual effect, staring at Stephen will all the intensity I could muster.

"Well, hell yes, Jason! My last wife tried to turn my son against me because she was pissed off that I was dating and she wasn't! At one point he wouldn't come to my house for two months because of the bullshit she was feeding him. And that was just one of the tricks she pulled." This was the most animated I'd ever seen Stephen.

"Why did she do it?"

"I don't know, Jason. Maybe because she's a conniving, vindictive bitch who thought it was fun to use her child to score points against his father. Maybe she thought she could get more money out of me if she had one of the kids full time. Who knows? I'm just telling you to watch out."

"Noted. And thanks for the heads up. I promise do my best to keep my act together until this thing plays out." I walked out of Stephen's office feeling off balance, hoping my nose hadn't grown enough for Stephen to notice. Would Kim try to use the boys to manipulate me? It wasn't like she hadn't done it in the past. We in the "door mat" club are used to being beguiled by the fairer sex. I would have to keep my guard up...from now on.

As I made the short trip back to my office I caught Emily making a weird, stern face at me, motioning toward my office with her head. I didn't know what the hell she was doing so my pace continued unabated. Upon entering my office I discovered the reason for Emily's palsitic movements. A rather large gentleman was sitting in one of the chairs on the opposite side of my desk. I had no idea who he was.

"Can I help you?" I sat down across from him as he stood up. He was holding an envelope.

"Are you Jason Kubrick?"

"Why yes, yes I am. What can I do for you?" I was trying not to smile but it was all so curiously formal. I felt like I had been thrown into an old episode of "Dragnet."

"These are for you." He handed me the envelope. "You've been served." He turned and started walking out the door.

"Hey! Wait a minute. What is this?" He was walking out my office door.

"Divorce papers." He did not turn as he replied. He walked past Emily's desk and headed downstairs. Emily apparently heard my question and the envelope man's response and shot me a look of sympathy, which I found disconcerting. I was used to Emily being self-absorbed, not sympathetic. Well, I found Emily's sympathy AND the fact I had just been served with divorce papers disconcerting.

I didn't even know people got "served" anymore. Obviously "people" did, but I'll bet the sender of the server has to pay extra for it. If that were the case, it appeared Kim was sparing no expense to get the ball rolling on the whole divorce thing. I had to admire her decisiveness even as it pissed me off. After all, technically she was still using "my" money to pay for the human intervention. I would find out later in the day Kim had found a job in her chosen field of nursing. For that I would eventually be eternally grateful, but at the moment I was still wondering how much the server dude cost me.

One might think the loop I'd just been thrown for might have tossed me off my game at work. It did not. Indeed, so much weirdness was already occurring around me the serving of divorce papers seemed minor by comparison. After the initial shock diminished I relegated the experience to the emotional minor leagues. Besides, in a way it was comforting to know there was some movement, no matter which party instigated the procedure. I should have been expecting something like this anyway, but had gotten so wrapped up in work the whole 'destruction of my marriage' thing had somehow been moved to the back burner. This did not appear to be the case for Kim. Obviously she was determined to move forward and, much like the revelation about her job, I would eventually be happy one of us took the bull by the horns. So I reviewed the divorce filing, got the name and number of Stephen's divorce attorney and made the call. Without emotion and with great efficiency I made an appointment with my new attorney, Jim Randolph, and negotiated a retainer. The whole business took about eighteen minutes, inclusive of the part where I found out divorce attorneys prefer their specialty be referred to by the ironic term "family law". Would that all such endeavors be so simple. Of course, the eighteen minutes was the easy part. The tough parts would come later.

I was just hanging up the phone after speaking with my new "family lawyer" when Emily buzzed in. "Jason, there's a person named Elaine on hold for you." Now that surprised me.

"Thanks, Emily." I picked up the phone and hit the button as calmly as possible. "Elaine?" I have to say I was patting myself on the back for the ease with which I made the transition from talking to the family lawyer to talking to my would-be love interest. I mean, I hadn't heard from Elaine since she flew away and here I was fielding her call right after what should have been a traumatic occurrence. I was Mr. Smooth.

"Hey, Jason! How are you doing?" She sounded bubbly and maybe somewhat drunk. It was much later in the Czech Republic and the bars were probably just getting going.

"Hey…Elaine! You out doing a little drinking?" Mr. Smooth…

"I am. This is a great town! I'm out with some new friends and they taught me how to ask for beer in Czech. What are you up to?" She was definitely drunk.

"Nothing as fun as you!" Huh? I was trying to sound as bubbly as she and it was killing my sentence structure. "You know I've tried to call you a couple times…"

"I know, sweetie, but things are crazy here with the transition and all. I've been working 12-hour days just to get things going." Her voice had lost part of its "fun" sound. "Hey, I gotta go. I just wanted to say hi."

Drunk-dials were supposed to be more fun, at least for the drunk person. "No problem, Elaine. How about if I try you this weekend." Well, that was kinda smooth.

"Sounds good, Jason. Ciao!" A couple weeks in the Czech Republic and she was already speaking Italian.

I promised myself I would call her next time I was drunk, figuring that day wasn't too far off. I also found odd comfort in the fact that Elaine, indeed, called ME in her inebriation. Of course, it's possible she was just working her way down her list of contacts and I was the only one who answered. But it's also possible she was thinking of me at that very moment and that thinking of me resulted in an unstoppable urge to hear my voice. Either way I was willing to take what I could get. I hung up the phone and went back to business, smiling with self-satisfaction. SHE called ME. Awesome! (Pathetic.)

Somewhere in the middle of the pile of work, meetings with process servers and lawyers, and calls from long lost friends I remembered I had no cash for the weekend. Perhaps my mind longed for the mundane. To get some cash I had two choices. I could write a check and cash it at the teller line or I could walk outside to the drive up automatic teller machine. The risk of attempting the latter was I would have to stand there in the "drive thru" lane, fumbling with the ATM, hoping no one would actually attempt to drive through while I was standing where a car should be. I chose the former. Nowadays writing a check to get cash seems a quaint anachronism but somehow is still superior to risking one's life. I fished my check book out of my brief case and headed downstairs to the branch.

Most days I enjoyed loitering in the lobby and today was no different. It turned out I wasn't the only person in the world taking care of their banking needs before the weekend. The lobby was full of people milling about waiting for their turn at the teller line and, as was my habit, I found myself innocuously casing the room looking for interesting people at which to stare, silently making guesses as to their business with the bank. I noticed a couple in their seventies looking around also. I was ninety nine percent sure they were there to roll over a certificate of deposit. This is the kind of thing older couples generally do in bank branches. There were also some employees of local businesses there to make deposits for their employers. These people generally dressed in their work clothes and tended to look relieved at being given the opportunity to be out of their work place for a few minutes. Then there were younger people. This demographic was tech savvy and tended to come inside the bank only to open accounts or apply for auto loans. The place was hopping.

I was still at my guessing game when my gaze fell upon the Russian girl I had noticed a few times before. According to my inside sources (the tellers) her name was Katarina. By all accounts she was in the bank quite regularly and kept a number of personal and business accounts through which she was always moving money in one direction or another. She was sharply dressed in heeled black boots, tight jeans and a short-sleeved, button down Oxford, a wool coat resting over one arm. She was slim and tone with green eyes and a thick mane of brunette hair, which is the particular trait on which I was focused when I noticed she was staring at me staring at her. Embarrassed, I not-so-smoothly looked away, pretending I wasn't actually doing what I was doing. I gave myself a ten count before sneaking a peek, only to find her still staring at me, smiling. What to do, what to do…? I smiled back. I figured I might as well. She had me dead to rights and there was no way to fool myself into believing otherwise. But she didn't just keep smiling. She also gave up her place in line to come over and talk to me.

"Hi." I couldn't hear the Russian accent yet. "You work here, do you not?" There it was. "I have seen you here before." God! She was so cute with the hair and the accent and an amazing ass.

"Yes. Yes. I work upstairs…on the second floor. I work on our commercial side. You know, making loans to businesses and stuff." Smooth. "I've seen you before also. Are you here every day?" It was a stupid question but I was feeling tongue tied and she had great skin.

"I am here often. My partners and I keep most of our accounts with this bank but we have a few others. I like this bank." She meant better than the other banks. I was really glad she liked my bank. Her lips were thick and her shiny, red lipstick showed them off as they formed words into sentences.

"Well, that makes me feel good!" I was enthusiastic. Really. "Sometime you'll have to tell me about your business and why our bank is so awesome." Was I being overly flirtatious? Did I just ask her out on a date of some kind?

"I would love to. When would you like to get together?" I guess I did ask her for a date. Did she think it was a date? Or was she trying to make an appointment?

"Uh...it's up to you." I punted. "When would you like to get together?"

"How about tonight? I will buy you a drink...unless you do not drink. If you do not we can have coffee." She touched my shoulder while offering to buy me a drink, or coffee. Was this really happening? I mean, I was picturing her naked already but was it really ethical? I rationalized that it must be ok as it would severely limit my potential dating pool if I cut out all coworkers and bank customers. I wasn't in the mood to be limited.

"Ah...sure, sounds good. Oh no...I'm sorry. I can't tonight. I have my kids." Stupid kids.

"How about tomorrow night?" Wow! Was my luck turning?

"Tomorrow would be great. I am free then." Before falling back into line Katarina proceeded to give me her cell phone number, instructing me to call her that evening so we could make plans for Saturday night. I, on the other hand, wandered back upstairs without cashing a check. I ended up using the ATM on my way home.

I picked up the boys at "Kim's" house on my way home from work. They were boisterous and looking forward to the bowling I had promised as an evening activity. In truth I had forgotten about the promise until they started asking me about it. Their excitement was infectious and by the time we got to my apartment I was as excited as they. So after a quickie spaghetti dinner and a change of clothes we were off to the Western Bowl to throw balls at things without getting into trouble for it. Every boy's dream.

Western Bowl had been around since before I was born and is a landmark on Cincinnati's west side. Its 68 lanes seemed to stretch on forever and besides a full-service bar there was a billiards room and a Mexican restaurant. Western Bowl also employed valets to help its patrons with everything from getting the scoring machines going to keeping drinks full. The boys liked coming because it was big enough for them to run around between frames and on Friday and Saturday nights they had "Cosmic Bowling." During "Cosmic Bowling" the regular lights were turned off in favor of black light, serving to bathe everyone and everything in an eerie glow. Watching neon balls appear to defy gravity as they floated down the blind alley was always fun to watch and added to the boys' thrill of the evening. This night wasn't particularly busy and we were able to get on a lane quickly. The boys each selected a ball from the many racks lining the walls while I unpacked my own shoes and ball. Once things got going the only challenges were keeping them focused on alley etiquette and responding to seemingly infinite requests for soda and candy.

"Dad, can I have another pop?" That was Alex. He had already burned through two and we were just finishing our first game.

"No way! How about water?" I like water.

"No thanks." He was temporarily glum. He didn't like water as much as me.

I expected Trevor, being the younger of the two, to wander more between frames and to require regular reminders when it was his turn to bowl. Trevor, however, proved more focused than his older brother and his game improved to the point he barely needed the bumpers that had been erected by the valet to prevent gutter balls. I was fairly impressed by this because he still used two hands to throw the ball and regularly risked losing control of it on the backswing. Indeed, twice during the evening Trevor actually did throw the ball back at his brother and me, teaching us to pay more attention while he was holding a ball.

All in all it was a fun and leisurely event. The boys were relaxed and full of smiles, which had a parallel effect on me. The place was so big it easily sheltered any number and types of people on a Friday night. A few lanes down on our left a group of teenagers bowled slowly and loudly and were obviously having a great time. Down a little further was an overweight couple with three overweight children who didn't seem terribly excited to be bowling. Risking a karmic backlash, I cruelly assumed this was the most exercise they would get all week. A group of women inhabited the two lanes directly to our right. I was pleased with this because at least half of them were worthy of the "eye candy" label I had secretly attached to each. Beyond the ladies were more teenagers and a couple who were so stereotypically 'trailer park' I thought someone must be filming a sitcom. It was certainly a diverse crowd although the boys didn't seem to notice. They were too busy alternately insulting or encouraging each other as we ooohhhd, aaahhd, and high-fived our way through three games. We left the alley feeling lighthearted and stopped for ice cream on the way back to the apartment for good measure. As usual, Trevor and Alex had a game the next morning. This one happened to be scheduled earlier than usual so I had them in bed soon after we got home.

"Dad, do you think you and Mom will get back together?" Trevor asked this without agenda. This is the fantasy of children from divorced parents.

"No, sweetie. I don't think so." And even though I understood the fantasy the answer made me sad. I wasn't said because I wanted to be with Kim. I didn't want to be with Kim anymore. I was sad because I had to answer the question at all. I had to confirm for my youngest son that his mother and father were over, that his world had been permanently altered. For his part, the answer didn't seem to have the same effect on Trevor, so I assumed he asked the question simply to confirm a conclusion he had already drawn.

"Are you going to marry someone else?" He yawned as he asked, adding to the matter-of-fact aura displayed in his last question.

"I don't know, sweetie. I hope…maybe someday." I really did, too, but how was I to explain to a 12-year-old the depth of my belief in love everlasting despite the fact I currently had no proof of its existence. Maybe I was selling him short.

"I hope so too, Dad. Just marry somebody nice, ok? Goodnight." With that he rolled over and closed his eyes. I'm sure Alex heard the whole exchange (they were in bunk beds, after all) but he did not join in on the questioning. Nor did he seem upset by what he had heard. He did, however, ask for an extra hug before saying goodnight and I tucked his covers in twice. Everyone processes things in their own way.

I walked to the living room disturbed by the poignant simplicity of Trevor's request. All he wanted was that I marry someone "nice." They didn't have to be pretty or a good cook. They didn't have to be smart or funny. Just nice. It's possible Trevor's definition of "nice" included all of the above but I doubt it. I find it difficult to believe a 12- year-old's version of "nice" would mean anything more than the obvious. It certainly wouldn't include all the layers of crap adults consider when picking a mate and of all those things "nice" might actually sit beneath "hot", "sexually compatible", and "not crazy." Thinking on this, it's also possible Trevor had his sights set too high, but I would hate to think so. I would like to believe if Trevor followed his own guideline he would end up being happier than his father when it came to his relationships with women, even if he didn't end up with the hottest girl he could find. Perhaps as a defense mechanism, my brain reminded me there were plenty of mean, ugly girls, too. And that's right around when the phone rang.

It was a text message from Katrina. "Are we still good for tomorrow night?" I responded in the positive and we spent the next few minutes messaging back and forth about where we would meet and at what time. I did not, however, allow her intrusion to interfere with my musings. Indeed, I wondered if Trevor would approve of her. After all, she seemed nice, but I could have been allowing her beauty to feed a desired perception. The fact she was beautiful would probably escape Trevor. He was approaching young manhood but almost-13-year-old boys rarely if ever appreciate beauty in females past the age of fifteen. I knew he found some of the girls in his class to his liking and had his share of the middle school version of girlfriends, but that's as far as it goes for most boys his age. He and his brother would have many opportunities in the years ahead to make the mistakes I was currently making. When they do then maybe I will tell them all about my own. For the moment I allowed myself a modicum of excitement about the impending date with the comely Russian. I also fell asleep on the couch, thereby making us late for the Saturday morning soccer game. It turned out ok, though. The coach was very nice about it.

CHAPTER TWELVE

I found myself fairly nervous as I prepared for my date with Katarina. Kim had picked the boys up from their soccer game so I found myself with an inordinate amount of time to prepare for the evening. Way too much time. Nearly twelve hours, in fact. There was so much time between the end of the soccer game and the beginning of the date I was forced to create jobs for myself to make the clock move faster, which is no easy task for an apartment dweller, even a brand new one. There's, like, no yard work and/or home improvement to be undertaken in a rental, at least not if you don't want to change things back a year later. I passed the time as best I could, including masturbating twice. And while masturbating didn't burn significant time off the clock, the last thing I wanted was to go fully loaded on a first date with an incredibly attractive woman. I suspected I would appear "strained" regardless and felt it beneficial to lower my testosterone level. (Having forgotten nearly everything I'd ever learned about biology, I really have no idea whether or not this goal was accomplished.) In addition to the masturbating I went shopping and purchased some wall hangings, a skillet, an appropriately "fun" shower curtain for the boy's bathroom, and a bed skirt for my bed. Incidentally I would later discover the final item to be an exasperation to Trevor, who believed bed skirts to be unmanly. I, on the other hand, found the canvas colored box-spring covering preferable to the exposed, brushed steel bed rails. Twenty years of marriage to someone who paid attention to such things had not been completely lost on me.

My efforts to kill time paid off when the big moment arrived. Finally the clock marked the sufficient passing of hours and minutes for me to leave my apartment and arrive at Katarina's at the prearranged time. I hopped in the Malibu and went on my way, being careful not to wreck the car or get pulled over for speeding as either occurrence would have invariably made me late. With so much time on my hands earlier I had an ample span to map the path to Katarina's apartment in Newport, Kentucky, coming up with at least three viable routes. In the end I chose the quickest, of course, and double checked it against the GPS I kept in the car. I also found it useful to employ some personal knowledge about the chosen byways in order to allow for projected traffic flows, possible bottlenecks, and other suspected hazards. As mentioned, I had a lot of time to kill before the date. The high level of planning paid off, however, as I arrived at Katarina's with four minutes to spare. I gave myself a pat on the back for perfect timing. Four minutes was early enough to be respectful but not so early as to interrupt any last-minute date prep that might be occurring on her end.

Katarina answered the door wearing skinny jeans and a short-sleeved sweater top appropriate for the cool, early spring evening but also sufficient to show off her toned arms and smooth skin. She was not wearing shoes, however, and I remembered once being told by Izzy that some women wait to choose the evening's footwear until they see what their date is wearing. When first told of this I thought it amazingly considerate and foresighted and was impressed when I saw the maneuver put into practice by the beautiful Katarina. I was wearing a pair of leather, sort of faux hiking boots and watched as Katarina went to her hall closet and pull out a pair of brown leather boots. Although they weren't almost-hiking-boots like my own, once she slipped them on we looked as if we had somehow planned to dress similarly, a trick about which I've never forgotten.

"It is nice to see you outside your office." She said this as she placed one hand on the back of my neck and pulled herself up to kiss me on the cheek. I told myself it was a European thing and she probably did it with everyone but the thought did not prevent the skin on my neck from tingling where she touched it.

"I think so, too." I said and then awkwardly took a shot at kissing Katarina on the cheek as well. My lack of experience was apparent and I found my nose smashing into her left ear. So, instead of an actual kiss I managed only a line of slobber on her cheek. She did not embarrass me by pointing out the failure.

"I am ready whenever you are ready." She said with her Russian accent, adding the second "ready" to the end of the sentence as no American would. She was adorable.

Katarina led me out of her building and, once in the car, we made the journey to Arnold's Restaurant in downtown Cincinnati. Arnolds had been around for 150 years and touted itself as the oldest bar and grille in the city. It was only a ten-minute drive from Katarina's apartment in Newport across the Ohio River. Besides its proximity to our starting location, the restaurant had other features to recommend it for a first date, like good food and a unique dining area in what used to be a stable for a carriage house. Upon entering the 160-year-old building we were told it would be a few minutes until we were seated so Katarina and I retreated to the old barroom for a before dinner drink. I had a Black Russian in her honor and she had a Cosmopolitan in honor of girlie drinks everywhere.

Katarina and I used the time to delve into each other's history and as she spoke I found myself unable to take my eyes off her. I'm pretty sure I wasn't falling in love with Katarina as that part of me was shamelessly being held in reserve for Elaine. But I was definitely falling in lust with her. Plus she was smart. She laughed at all of my jokes and when I talked about banking her eyes didn't glaze over at all. Indeed, she seemed quite interested in my work and asked pointed questions about how everything operated. In my experience this was unusual but I took it as another sign of her powerful intellect. I found out Katarina had grown up in St. Petersburg and went to university in Moscow. She came to the United States to manage an export-import business for the Moscow-based company for which she worked and was very happy to be here. For my part I summarized my childhood in Ohio but somehow my stories of high school sports, cow tipping, and family vacations to Tennessee didn't sound nearly as exotic as growing up in the old Soviet Union. Still, Katarina seemed to hang on my every word and by the time we were on our way to a table we had at least a cursory understanding of each other's backgrounds. And I had as yet failed to uncover any "deal breakers." I mean, she didn't appear to be a hermaphrodite or to be sporting a vestigial tail. And I must admit, at that moment at least, those were the only things I could think of that would have been actual deal breakers. Well, maybe not the tail.

"I like this place!" She was looking around at the old brick walls as we were led to our table. We were in the part of the restaurant where horses were kept in the "old days." On dry summer nights the area was open to the sky but, still being early spring and chilly, an opaque, temporary roof was still in place.

"I'm glad! I like it too. They have live music later, you know, if we decide to hang around." We were sitting twelve inches from the stage and a sign announcing what time the band would start playing so it's possible Katarina could have already figured that out on her own. I was feeling nervous, chatty and excited. Telling Katarina what was written on a sign directly in front of her face wouldn't be the most fatuous thing to fall out of my mouth that evening. At one point I found myself describing a persistent wart with which I had been plagued as a boy and at another told a gripping tale of excessive flatulence experienced as a younger man during a trip to the grocery store. In the right setting it was all very interesting stuff, no doubt, but probably not my best first date material. The fact I had been on so few first dates in the last twenty years may have contributed to my awkwardness, but in truth I'd never been very good at them. In my life before Kim if my date couldn't manage at least sixty percent of the conversation I was in trouble.

On that night, however, my graceless ramblings did not seem to turn my date off. Katarina seemed interested in everything I had to say, even though her life had already been far more intriguing than my own. I mean, the Iron Curtain came down during her childhood and then she moved to a whole new country. I suggested I would have liked to experience just a little of her childhood to know what it was like and Katarina pointed out that, had I had the opportunity to do so, I might not have noticed much of a difference from my own childhood. Her parents, like my own, were devoted to their children and she did not want for anything that really mattered.

"Besides, children do not know anything about politics or economics. They only know about what is right in front of them." Of course she was correct. Hell, most adults don't know anything about politics or economics either, which is one of the reasons they ended up with communism in the first place.

Katarina was worldly and seemed to take most things in stride. I believe part of her nonchalance existed as a result of having the experience of living in two so vastly different countries. She probably found being too ideological counter-productive to living a happy life. It was also possible she really just didn't give a crap

165

about a lot of things about which other people make a big stink. Either way she was so confident and comfortable with herself one had to be careful what was asked lest one get a brutally honest answer. At least she appeared to be so. Like any of us, Katarina had secrets and it would take more than one date to discover them. In the mean time I found myself completely immersed in her bubble. The wine we ordered disappeared quickly but the food was eaten slowly due to the number of words we attempted to shoehorn between every mouthful. We polished the food off by the middle of the second bottle and allowed the table to be cleared without ordering dessert. Having finished the dinner stage of our date, I was at a loss about what do to next. Having used up so much time planning the route from Katarina's to Arnold's, I had failed to plan any after-dinner activities.

"Umm…would you like to stay and listen to the band?" According to the sign the band was going to start in about fifteen minutes, but as yet there was no indication anyone intended to play music. The stage was devoid of humanity, musical devices, or amplifying equipment of any kind.

Katarina glanced at the stage. "You know, it is a beautiful evening," She could tell because we could see through the temporary roof. "Will you walk around the city with me? Perhaps we could stop for a drink at another bar?"

"I think that's a great idea." Her demeanor was infectious. As we stood to leave she took my hand and led me out of the restaurant. Her hand was soft and full of electricity. I was ready to go anywhere she wanted.

"I like Cincinnati," she said as we emerged into the out of doors.

"What do you like about it?" I wasn't challenging her. I really was interested. I like my city, too, but always wanted to know why other people did.

"It is clean." I made a mental note to teach her contractions, and maybe point out that some parts of the city were cleaner than others. "And it is pretty. And the people who live here are very nice."

"I'm glad you think so. I think those things, too." We were just standing in front of the restaurant. "So…which direction do you want to go?"

"Let us walk toward the river."

And we did, holding hands the whole time. While I was conscious that with every step the distance between us and my car was growing, I was also conscious of the fact Katarina's hand was still full of electricity. I wondered how she did it and quite naturally found myself wanting to touch other parts of her as well. For the moment, however, I was more than happy to walk with her and listen as she pointed out things she liked or didn't like about this building or that and how the city seemed to be constantly changing and yet stayed the same.

"You know, some of these buildings are over 100 or 150 years old, like the one where we just had dinner." I rounded the potential ages because I couldn't actually tell her for sure how old any of them actually were, except for Arnold's, and that was only because of the research I conducted earlier in the day.

"I know, Jason, but you must remember how old Moscow is." She smiled while gently reminding me what's old to Americans by comparison often seems new to those from other parts of the world.

"Good point." I smiled back at her and she squeezed my hand, weakening my knees ever so slightly. "Let's stop in here for a drink." My temporary inability to walk with confidence made our location in front of the Righteous Room bar serendipitous.

She looked up at me, eyes shining. "Or we could go back to my apartment and have a drink there. I will do whatever you want to do."

What? What did she say? Was she saying she would do whatever I wanted as it concerned where we were to have a drink or was she saying she would do whatever I wanted ONCE we got back to her place? I wasn't sure if I was losing something in translation or if I was merely a victim of wishful thinking. Regardless, for the moment I took the safe route.

"Uh…let's do that…the apartment. I mean, let's go back to your apartment. For a drink…" Smooth, as always. The Righteous Room would have to wait.

She smiled up at me as she again took my hand, making our way back to the Malibu in relative silence. Perhaps we were both contemplating what would happen once we returned to Katarina's apartment. At least that's what I was contemplating, and hoped she was doing the same. She continued to hold my hand on the drive back across the river. I don't know if it was because we were out of the elements and the heat in the car was set too high but I was sure her skin felt warmer than it had earlier. Of course, it's probable my skin was warmer as well. My blood was pumping pretty hard by then and as we drove across the Big Mac Bridge (thus nicknamed because the shape and color of the steel support structure is reminiscent of the golden arches of fast food fame) I again contemplated touching more than her hand. I rationalized she wouldn't have invited me back just for a drink, although in the past I had been burned by such rationalizations, especially in college. The lesson learned from those experiences was to never assume anything more was going to happen than had already happened. In other words, don't count on getting laid just because you're invited up. The assumption is both ungentlemanly and frustrating if things don't work out as hoped. When we arrived at Katarina's I was excited, of course, but simultaneously tamping down my expectations, telling myself this was a first date and not to be disappointed if I didn't get to see her naked.

It didn't take long to discover Katarina's intentions. She barely finished locking the door before unbuttoning my shirt without asking permission or, indeed, even saying a word. Her fingers turned out to be quite nimble and before I knew it my shirt had disappeared over the back of her couch, not to be seen again until the next morning. Taking the cue I gently pulled her sleeveless sweater over her head (I didn't want to stretch out the fabric,) revealing her black bra and flat stomach. Joyously, it turned out the skin underneath her shirt was as smooth and glowing as the skin she had already made available to me. I dug in quickly. The smell and taste of her was arresting. Before I knew it we had sunk to the carpeted floor, wrestling around as we fought buttons, belts and zippers in our urgent quest to remove the remainder of each other's clothing.

Katarina was an intense lover and at times quite literally found a way to wrap her body around mine, forcing us to move as a single unit as we rolled around on the floor. We tumbled this way and that, sat up and laid back down as if we were one creature, our bodies pressed together tightly, our skin becoming so slick with sweat we began to glide over one another. Even then we still managed to find good hand holds on one another, like climbers confidently scaling a rock face. I don't think any part of our bodies were ever more than three inches apart even as I tried to move around in my attempts to explore more of her. And it turned out it wasn't just her hands that were full of electricity. Everywhere her body touched mine I could feel her energy pouring in, penetrating until I lost track of everything but the two of us. In addition to her tremendous physical energy Katarina was fabulously vocal which, I admit, frightened me at first. I had never been with anyone with such ecstatic volume and though I don't speak Russian, I'm fairly certain at least half of what came out of Katarina's mouth was in her native language. It's also possible she was speaking in tongues. Regardless, at the time I wouldn't have understood her exclamations had they been spoken in English, although it's possible her neighbors would have if they chose to listen. Surrounded by Katarina's body, redolence and furor it was easy to get lost. So I let myself get lost. And it felt astonishing.

At the end we found ourselves staring at the ceiling, catching breath as damp skin chilled from the slight draft flowing over the floor of the apartment. I wasn't immediately cognizant of the time or date or even of my location, happily contemplating the paint pattern floating above me. At the moment the draft felt good and although Katarina wasn't currently in my field of vision I could feel her arm pressed against my own. There was none of the awkwardness that accompanied the sex with Izzy and none of the post-coital emptiness I experienced with Elaine. I just felt…relaxed. I was the first to speak.

"I'm just, uh…can you point me to your bathroom?" I also felt like peeing. I'm a born romantic.

She appeared bemused. "It is the second door on the left." She used just enough energy to vaguely point to an area somewhere in the direction our heads were aimed and before going vertical I rolled over to kiss her. Katarina took the opportunity to pull me back down to her, which felt wonderful but forced me into the awkward position of having to extricate myself from her grasp without appearing too anxious to do so. I really did have to pee, after all. Had I been thinking more clearly I would have allowed her to attach herself to me again, carrying her into the bathroom hanging on me like a baby koala bear. In the end I made it there alone.

While in Katarina's bathroom I resisted the urge to check out the medicine cabinet, figuring any knowledge of rashes or infections rendered at that point would only serve as a buzz kill. I was forced, however, to hunt for a new roll of toilet paper and was surprised at what I found UNDER the sink. A safe. Yes, a safe. As I sat contemplating its existence I could not find a reason any average person would put a safe in a bathroom. The thing took up half the space in the cabinet and looked heavy. Naturally, I wanted to know more about why it was there but the material need for toilet paper and the stress position in which I found myself, bent over exploring the under-sink area while my ass hovered over the toilet, only increased the sense of urgency to complete the task at hand. I decided to take on one challenge at a time and made a mental note to ask Katarina about the safe later.

I finally found a roll hidden under a cozy, an item with which I had little experience. The cozy was hiding in plain sight and appeared to me, as I imagine it would to most males, to be just a knitted item randomly left under the sink because its owner could not find a better place for it. Katarina had a safe AND a toilet paper cozy in her bathroom. I found the incongruity perplexing. If I kept searching what else would I find?

The opportunity to interrogate Katarina on the origin of the safe was cut short upon my exit from the water closet. Katarina was waiting and as I emerged she attacked me with the ferocity of a bobcat, throwing me off balance and forcing us through the open doorway to what I assumed was her bedroom. As I was not in control and had no idea where we might alight I was pleased to find a bed situated perfectly to catch our fall. Though I wasn't given much time to look around, the state of the bed and bedroom revealed much about Katarina's personal habits. Indeed, it was possible what I thought was a bed was actually just a pile of flotsam, some component of which, incidentally, was working to stab me in the left kidney. Considering what was happening at the moment, however, I couldn't find it in me to care all that much. As with the safe, I took note of the surrounding debris and only focused my attention on the crap pile long enough to shift whatever was poking me to a less offensive position. Round two could then continue, interrupted only if one of us felt the need to move this or that item out of way, or move each other to a more convenient position. However, even those efforts failed to enable us burrow down to an actual set of sheets.

"I would like you to spend the night." Did she really? We were now staring at the ceiling of the bedroom, which was very similar to the ceiling in the living room. I was exhausted and wanted to stay but wondered where we might actually "sleep."

"I'd like that, too, but…would we sleep in here?" What a stupid question! What an idiot! I couldn't have blamed her for kicking me out right then. Why did I care?

She smiled with understanding. "Yes, Jason, but I will clean the bed first."

"Oh, well, sure. That'd be great." How lucky was I?

Katarina giggled as she shoved me off the crap pile and began the process of revealing the actual bed. Though I had no idea to where anything from the pile should be relocated I still made sure to offer to help, which was the gentlemanly thing to do. My offer was politely declined. Standing with my back to one of the bedroom walls and with nothing better to do I took the opportunity to ask Katarina about the safe. Apparently I felt I hadn't asked enough stupid, mood killing questions for one evening. Luckily Katarina was as gracious about answering the "safe" question as he had been about answering the "bed" question.

"Oh, yes." Katarina stopped folding a garment when I asked, appearing to ponder the question for just a moment. "That was here when I moved in. I don't know why it is there. I do not even know the combination." She told me this while she hung up the pair of pants she was holding. "Would you like to pour us a glass of wine?"

"I'd love to."

I complied with Katarina's request and found her in bed when I returned with the wine. By now there was nothing left on the bed but Katarina and what most of us would consider normal bed-type items, but not everything had been put in its place. There were still piles of clothing around the room, rising from the floor like rumpled stalagmites but as none of them would pose a problem should I later make a trip to the bathroom in the dark, I ignored them and slid in next to Katarina. We sipped wine and talked for a bit but were asleep before we knew it. I remember waking twice. Once for a bathroom trip and again when Katarina pulled me to her in the dark. Her energy flowed into me even at three in the morning. The heat of her kept me warm.

Naturally, the first thing I did after pulling away from Katarina's apartment building the next morning was call Arthur. Our relationship had always been such that I knew few details of his sex life with Maureen. Regardless, I was pretty sure I was presently having more than him in this area, so me calling Arthur to brag about my evening with Katarina may have had an element of showboating. On the other hand, as far as I could tell Arthur had actually come to enjoy my stories of errant love, or at least tolerate them.

"Who'd you shag this time?" His voice was deadpan but less so than usual.

"Is that what you think? That I only call you to tell you sex stories?"

"Is there another reason to call me at eight in the morning on Sunday?"

"Hmm...I can't think of one. Her name is Katarina and she's Russian." I was trying not to sound overly excited as I gave Arthur a not-too-specific play by play of the evening. In these situations men are generally not in the habit of providing excessive detail about emotions, cute things that might have happened or other such niceties. Rather, they tend to focus on shapes, sounds, and other relevant highlights more gratifying to the male psyche. If called for it is also appropriate to provide the number of "innings", but only should there be more than one.

"Three last night and once more this morning before I left." I realize this all sounds very childish but it's a piece of young manhood most men never seem to lose, even if it gets somewhat buried by layers of civility. I'm sure the smile plastered on my face was being received loud and clear on the other end of the phone.

"Cheers, mate. Congratulations. Where did you meet this one?" Arthur was duly impressed.

"At the bank."

"Really? At your bank? When was this?" Arthur sounded truly interested. "Any idea what her last name is?"

Arthur was asking more questions than usual and almost sounded anxious. "Yes...at my bank." What other bank would I be frequenting? "But you know what? I can't think of her last name right now. Is that bad? I know I've seen or she said it or

172

something…" Now I was sounding anxious. "Holy crap! How do I ask her what her last name is now? I mean, I've already slept with her. Four times! Any ideas?"

"Well then," Arthur paused to think for me. "Alright, here's what you do. The next time you see her work it into the conversation that you are having problems pronouncing her name. I'm sure she'll volunteer to help you say it properly. It's subtle enough. I'm sure it will work."

I was sure it would work also and told him so. Embarrassingly, it didn't occur to either of us the easiest path to Katarina's last name was through the bank, where I could have found it in the system or simply ask one of the tellers. Instead we developed an overly elaborate scheme to answer a simple question which could have easily been exposed by other means. An example of great minds thinking alike, no doubt. Even so, I was glad for his help with my dilemma-of-the-moment and with that settled I said my goodbyes.

"Alright then, but do me a favor, Jason. Be careful with this one." Arthur sounded cryptic and had an odd tone to his voice. "And make sure you call me when you figure out her last name. I want to see how you handle this one." That sounded more like him and I made a mental note to honor his request.

I signed off leaving Arthur's curious warning hanging in the middle of my car like an old air freshener. In the past the only time Arthur had ever sounded so murky was during drunken rants about the cultish origins of the Nazi Party but his words continued to needle me as I wound my way through traffic. Why should I have to be any more careful with Katarina than I had been with any of the other women in my life? Did he just not like Russians? And was his problem with me or her? I mean, I was obviously incompetent with women, but not hateful, and other than throwing some hurt feelings into the universe had I really done any permanent damage to myself or others? I comforted myself with a "no" answer as I arrived home and went about straightening my apartment. Still, I couldn't shake the low level discomfort. Arthur had never been given to drama, so why start now? I decided I could wait to follow up with him later which, when coupled with the simple redundancy of housework, helped clear my mind. Once cleaned the apartment wordlessly invited me to take a nap in it, an offer to which I happily complied. I was out in minutes, sleeping the sleep of the innocent.

I woke to a sense of inappropriate movement. The apartment should have been quiet but it wasn't. It was a shuffling noise, like the sound someone makes when they're trying not to make any noise. I waited for the first moment of panic to dissipate and gather myself before deciding what to do. I must have been asleep for hours. The sun was sinking and the apartment had gone dark except for some light leaking from the kitchen over the back of the couch. I couldn't remember if I left the light on before nap time but that was definitely the room from which the hushed noise was emanating. I made the extremely brave choice to peak over the edge of the couch. It was Katarina, preparing to cook in my kitchen.

"Katarina?" She looked great in a tank top and short, black skirt. But what the hell was she doing in my apartment? "What the hell are you doing in my apartment?"

"Hello, sleepy head! You caught me making you dinner!" Any misgivings she might have had about breaking into my apartment were not apparent, focused as she was on preparing the evening meal.

"Katarina, how did you get in here?" I was still peeking over the back of the couch. Admittedly I was already admiring her legs as they extended to the floor from her skirt.

"I wanted to surprise you but no one answered when I knocked on your door. When I tried to open the door it was unlocked and I saw you sleeping on the couch so I was trying to be quiet." While offering this explanation she simultaneously smashed the contents of a large pan with my potato smasher. She had great triceps.

"Ok, then. I have another question. Why did you just let yourself in and how did you know where I lived?" The second part of that question hadn't occurred to me until just then.

"Jason, you left your wallet at my apartment last night. I tried calling you but you did not answer. I believed you would want your wallet so I looked through it to find your driver license and I went to that address to find you and give you your wallet." Katarina smiled. "I did not know it was your old address. Kim told me how to get here after I told her about the wallet." She said all this matter-of-factly, like she met her boyfriends' estranged wives every day. "She was not very pleasant."

"Holy crap! You met Kim? What did you tell her?" My surprise at finding Katarina unannounced in my apartment was replaced by the surprise of her encounter with Kim. Hindsight being twenty/twenty, I should have suspected something like this would have happened eventually.

"I told her you left your wallet at my apartment and I was trying to return it to you. She did not ask any questions. She just told me how to get to your apartment. We did not talk much but I think I understand why you left her." She smiled as she said this and put whatever she was smashing on a burner. "Are you hungry, Jason? Do you like steak?"

"I love steak." And I was hungry. The surprise of Katarina's encounter with Kim was now replaced by a rumbling in my stomach and a concordant craving for meat as the pleasant smell of cooking steak wafted about the apartment. Somehow everything was suddenly right with the universe. Katarina's explanation of how she ended up in my apartment made sufficient sense for me to stop wondering about it. And I knew Kim was going to make me pay for Katarina's unexpected visit. I just didn't yet know how. In the mean time I wasn't going to let these distractions get in the way of a tasty meal.

Before long Katrina was pulling the steaks from the oven, adding a smoky texture to the wonderful smells she had already created in the apartment. I had long been off the couch and in the kitchen, kissing the cook and aching for the meal to begin. I had slept for hours and felt energetic. As I embraced Katarina I was not too hungry to notice she felt as wonderful as she had the night before, so I lingered with her tight against me until she was forced to push me away in order to finish the dinner. I offered to help but setting the table was the only useful thing left to do. After completing the task I sat down for the most ample meal I had yet consumed in my new digs.

"I've got to tell you, Katarina, when I first woke up and saw you there I was ready to throw you out. I had a vision of you standing over me with a knife..." I was trying not to talk and eat at the same time but it was difficult because I seemed unable to stop shoveling food in my mouth long enough to do so. "But after I

smelled the food I felt a lot better. And you had a good story, too."
I opted to not mention the skirt as a reason for letting her stay.

"I am sorry about startling you, Jason. I felt I wanted to do
something nice for you. I will try not to startle you again in the
future but I cannot guarantee this. I think this in my nature." She
smiled as she said this but even then I didn't think she was really
joking. I would find out later just how serious she was being.

"Do you have any plans tonight?" I finally got around to
asking this after I cleaned my plate.

"Yes I do, Jason. I plan to stay here tonight." She was
completely matter-of-fact, as if she had no doubt as to my position
on the matter or the eventual outcome of the evening. I did not
disabuse her of the notion and we continued chatting as we finished
dinner. Clearing the table as a team, we discussed following dinner
with a movie.

"What kind of movies do you like?" I asked while I searched
through the pay-per-view categories, fearing she would insist on a
chick flick.

"Do you know the movie called Titanic?" Aaaargh! "I do
not really like that kind of movie. I like science fiction movies."
Was she the perfect woman?

Katarina plopped herself down against me on the couch and
we viewed the movie attached at the hips and shoulders. Despite her
wonderful smell and the feel of her cuddling against me I was able to
concentrate just enough to get through the movie. It helped that I
covered her legs with a blanket. Of course I was excited when the
movie was over, and not just because I was going to get to sleep with
Katarina again. It was also the first time a woman had slept in my
apartment, which somehow cemented my new existence. I was
taking the milestones as they appeared.

CHAPTER THIRTEEN

There are many things I do not understand about relationships and many things I will never understand, especially if it's my relationship. So, while I'm great at pointing out problems in my friends' relationships, figuring out what's happening in my own fishbowl has figured to be far more problematic. Despite that failing, over time I have come to understand the sense of shame involved with losing your mate to another. It's truly a horrible feeling to know, or even suspect, someone else is getting the best of the person you once had. It is as if you're being told you're not good enough. It sucks. I don't want to sound overly dramatic, but it sucks so much it can lead to suicide (at least in French films. And this may be true of French society as a whole, including the part of French society that is not involved in film making, although I can offer no scientific proof one way or the other. Regardless, my point is that it sucks.)

What I've observed in these situations is that the offended party tends to act in one of two very distinct ways: Either they fight to keep the person who is slipping away or, in an act of revenge, go find someone new for themselves. In my experience, which is admittedly entirely anecdotal, it is rare indeed for the injured individual to withdraw either emotionally or physically from the fray, thus allowing the chips to fall where they may. And I imagine this sort of surrender is almost always the best option. After all, cloying attempts to keep lovers in a fold from which they so obviously want to escape often serves only to further push them away. In my humble estimation we would certainly be better served to let the transgressor figure things out for themselves. If you love something set it free and all that.

Here's another thing I've come to believe: ego is at the core of the problem. I believe our egos, because of their need for approval, force us to reject an otherwise logical course of action because we don't want to feel, or actually be, rejected. When our sense of worth is on the line it's nice to have that sense of worth ratified by someone other than ourselves, be it our original love interest or someone new. It is sad but true we too often rate our value using someone else's scale.

I did not understand consciously how my 'sense of self' (or sense of worth or humanity or whatever) felt diminished by the situation with Kim...or the situation with Elaine...or the situation with Izzy. All of those situations were acting on me in different ways and I was working hard to ignore all of it even though it was obviously getting me nowhere. At the very least I was acting out in a way indicating at least some part of me knew what was going on. Unfortunately, the part of me that realized something was going on refused to reveal it to the rest of my otherwise semi-functioning brain. I don't know why this was so. Maybe my brain was trying to protect me from myself. Or maybe it just wanted to have some fun before I came back to my senses. Regardless, I had been diminished, laid low by rejection and failure. It was humbling and I was refusing to grasp how humbling it was or how humbling it would become. In the meantime my ego responded to its perceived humiliation by bedding as many women as possible, or so it appears. It's anybody's guess.

Katarina left early the next morning. Like me she had a job to which she must attend, albeit one I didn't yet fully understand. While I had definitely enjoyed the evening with Katarina I did not feel particularly sad to see her leave that morning. Though I was generally oblivious to the underlying pathology of my behavior part of me was nevertheless aware of a need to regroup, and for that I would need some alone time. The other part of me, the part that wasn't feeling a need to regroup, wanted to take Katarina back to my bed and touch her some more, smell her skin, make her breakfast and maybe even sing her a love song or write her a poem. The conflict between the self-aware part of me and the not-so-self-aware part of me was rather irritating, as inner conflicts often are. Still, the bizarre desire to sing her a love song or write her a poem (as opposed to the more rational and physically satisfying act of making her breakfast) did not diminish and I found myself getting ready for work whilst simultaneously cruising the internet for a song that would give voice to that particular feeling of manic elation. Ultimately my search yielded nothing and served only to delay departure for work, so I tried to let it go. I slipped on my suit jacket silently wishing computers had evolved sufficiently to read peoples' minds, or at least my mind. Once safely on the way I began my morning ritual of flipping around the radio dial in what was generally a fruitless attempt to avoid commercials and the inane chatter of local morning shows. Having no desire to listen to sardonic dating advice from a thrice-divorced, childless disc jockey with a face for radio, I finally settled on an oldies station which prided itself on playing "more music." I wasn't sure to what standard they held themselves when it came to "more" but at that point it was "more" than could be found on all my other dial presets. Serendipitously, the universe rewarded my frustrated persistence by finding and playing for me (through the guise of a humble DJ) the song I was seeking earlier when I didn't know what song I wanted to sing. Ironically, it was Songbird.

For you, there'll be no more crying
For you, the sun will be shining
Because I feel that when I'm with you, it's alright
I know it's right

It is a beautiful song from my teen years, the kind of song that somehow finds a place to stick in the fevered psyche of the teenage brain. And just as it did back then, the plaintive honesty flowing from Christine McVie hit me like a brick. I knew the words and silently sang along with her and the rest of Fleetwood Mac.

To you, I'll give the world
To you, I'll never be cold
Because I feel that when I'm with you, it's alright
I know it's right

I was dumbfounded. How did she do it? How did Ms. McVie drill down to that level of emotional simplicity? While I sang the words I felt shamed and jealous. How long had it been since I had felt anything so raw and easy? I found myself spiraling downward, crying. I was losing. I was losing things that mattered and I didn't know how to stop it. The mania of the early morning had been replaced with an inexorable rush of melancholy. The

179

stupid song was ripping the plastic off the empty space I had been achingly working to ignore and, as a result of those efforts, had done nothing to productively fill. I realized I wanted desperately to sing the song, this song, with someone...for someone. I wanted someone to sing the song to me. I wanted someone to feel it the way I was feeling it at that moment and feel it for me. It was all very selfish, unexpected and overwhelming. Damn Christine McVie.

> And the songbirds are singing
> Like they know the score
> And I love you, I love, I love you
> Like never before

Holy shit!

To what lengths was Christine willing to go to destroy me? Had I ever loved anyone in this way or had I just gone through the motions, unaware of the shallowness of my existence? How was one song able to throw me into such a fit? The existential crisis had come on so rapidly I was lost in it in a matter of minutes. I wanted to strip down and just ...feel. But I didn't know where to begin. I had allowed layers of crap to pile on over the years and didn't know how to get out from underneath.

> And I wish you all the love in the world
> But, most of all, I wish it from myself
> And the songbirds keep singing
> Like they know the score
> And I love you, I love, I love you
> Like never before

The song ended three minutes later with me having been run through an emotional meat grinder. It ended as I pulled into the bank's parking lot. I was therefore forced to pull myself together. To this day I have not had a similar experience and I certainly didn't want to keep reliving it at the time so once I got in my office I threw myself at the pile of work. I did not take time to reflect upon what the hell just happened, pausing on my way in only long enough to greet some branch personnel and my assistant Emily, none of whom seemed to take notice of my agitated state. I figured this was just fine. The last thing I wanted to do is try to explain an event I didn't understand myself. That's why I had Therapist Jim. Besides, I didn't really want to understand, or I wasn't ready to understand, or something along those lines. So, as quickly as I could, I put my whole morning commute into a little box and put it high on a shelf to be taken down and, like so many other things occurring at the same time, examined later. And being at work helped with all of that. Work was great because it helped me ignore everything else. Plus it paid the bills.

Relative to the unexpectedly distressing drive to work the rest of my day remained largely uneventful, broken up only by Emily carrying work files in and out of my office or by the occasional snack break. Stephen spent the day locked in his office on conference calls and so did not have time to converse with his underlings. I was more than content to keep my head down, nose to the grindstone, and spent no time at all in self-examination. I suspected if I learned anything more at that point it would end up being more depressing than the information already available. So why bother? It was far easier to keep flailing about like the proverbial bull in a china shop, not noticing or caring about the mindless destruction occurring all around me.

I did get two non-work-related phone calls that day. The first was from Elaine and the second from Katarina, both of whom I had mostly managed not to think about thanks to my diligent efforts to not think about anything that might be affecting me deeply. Elaine called first, right before lunch time.

"Jason! Hello!" She sounded so happy to have me on the phone. I wasn't buying it.

"Hello Elaine. How's it going?" I wasn't feeling very enthusiastic. I was angry with her and hungry as well, which served to worsen my mood. And despite my efforts not to think about anything but work, at some point that morning it did indeed pop into my head that Elaine was at least partly to blame for my drive time funk.

"It's going well. I'm getting ready to go out to dinner and…we hadn't talked for a while. I wanted to talk to you before it got too late here. How are you doing?" She sounded unsure of herself, a situation with which I was unfamiliar, at least from her. For some reason it pissed me off even more. "I miss you."

"Huh?" I was not prepared for the last sentence. She had made a habit of avoiding me, or at least that's how things appeared, and I wanted to be angry about it. If she kept saying things like that I was going to lose my righteous indignation. "I miss you too."

"Thank you for saying that. It means a lot to me." I had no idea where any of this was going. "So are you divorced yet?"

"Nope. Not yet. We're working on it." Her question made me feel guilty, like I had to defend myself for not being divorced yet. What the hell did she care? It wasn't like I was going to see her any time soon. "Why do you ask?"

"I don't know… I guess I was thinking I'd like to see you. I was fantasizing about you flying to Prague." She sounded sober. What was she hiding?

"That's…kind of you, Elaine. I don't know exactly what to do with that but I think it's nice of you to say that to me. I don't think it's something I can do right now. I mean, I know it's not something I can do right now. I've got too much going on here." That was no joke!

"Oh." I could hear the disappointment expressed in just one word. "Do you think you'd like to come, you know, eventually?"

Well, damn, Elaine! Of course I'd like to come to Prague and see you. Why the hell wouldn't I want to do that? I was angry again, but all I said was "I would if I could." Somehow she still picked up on the anger.

"You're upset now. I'm sorry I've upset you. Is there anything I can do?" I wondered how serious she was because there were a million ways for me to answer that question, none of them realistic. Yes, I thought, yes. You can leave Prague and come back to Cincinnati to be with me. You can call me every day until I'm through all the crap I'm going through, and then you can call me every other day until you move back. You can keep inviting me to come there even if I can't go. You can feel about me the way I feel about you and tell me so. You can tell me you love me…

"No…no. I'm fine. It'll all work itself out in the end." One of the last things you want to do with someone you care about, and who cares about you, is make them feel bad when they're six thousand miles away and can't do a damn thing about it.

We talked for another ten minutes with Elaine sounding concerned the entire time. I wasn't ready to open up to her so I diligently avoided any topic outside the weather, eastern European architecture or Czech beer. It was a completely dissatisfying conversation on both ends of the phone.

"Well, hey, I'm heading out now." I didn't know if she was heading out of the apartment or just heading out of the conversation, but the affect was the same. "Can I call again this weekend?"

"Of course. I'll be around." Unless I'm sleeping with Katarina or someone else, but even then I might still be around because I always seemed to have plenty of down time between sleepovers. It was very confusing.

"Alright, sweetie. Have a great night."

"You too." I said this with as much conviction as I could muster.

Elaine hung up, leaving me alone in a void. The end of the phone call sufficiently sucked all the air and inspiration out of the room. I was left sitting and staring at a portrait of the bank's founder hanging across the room from me. He was staring right at me and though his visage was wise he offered no comment on my current situation. I was close to asking the portrait for advice when I was again interrupted by Emily, who rang in to tell me Katarina was on the line. Things were getting interesting.

"Hello!" Katarina's voice was too cheery for the mood I was in.

"Hey! How are you?" I faked it.

"I am having a good day and spending much time thinking of you. May I see you tonight?"

"Oh...I'm sorry Katarina. I have the boys tonight." I wasn't sorry.

"That is fantastic, Jason. I would love to meet them. I could make dinner for all of you." Katarina was persistent. I, on the other hand, was not keen on the idea of introducing her into my son's lives, especially after observing disastrous results from similar attempts by a couple of my friends. It doesn't play well with the kids to have a string of women tromping through their lives while they're adjusting to a divorce. It was more important I reinforce my relationship with them at this juncture. Besides, I really wasn't up for playing host and I suspected if I let Katarina into my apartment she wouldn't leave without much wailing and gnashing of teeth. She had proven herself to be creative and persistent in finding ways to be

183

around me and I did not relish the idea of explaining to Trevor and Alex why Daddy's new friend was going to sleep in his bed with him. It would occur to me later this conversation with the boys would be much easier than the one their mother was eventually going to have to have with them concerning her sleep-over friend(s). Imagining their questions on the topic made me shudder and giggle simultaneously.

"No, I'm sorry Katarina. I can't make it tonight. I'm not ready for the boys to meet anyone I'm seeing. I hope you can understand." I really meant it when I said it, too.

"I do understand, Jason. I know that they are going through a difficult time, like you."

She really sounded like she understood, too. "Thanks for understanding, Katarina. Perhaps we can do it a couple nights from now?" I was already making plans to shorten her name to "Kat." Four syllables is at least two too many.

"Of course, Jason. What are you making them for dinner? I'm sure it's something special." Kat sounded sincere. It was marvelous to have her empathize with my situation.

"Hmm. Good question. I hadn't thought of it. I'll have to stop at the grocery on the way home and pick something up. Maybe hot dogs." My mind was suddenly in full dinner mode and had engaged my stomach. Hot dogs sounded good. Maybe some macaroni and cheese, too. "Oh, and may I call you Kat?"

"Call me what?"

"Kat. You know, short for Katarina."

"Yes, Jason. You may call me Kat." She sounded bemused. "I enjoy hot dogs as well, but had I come over I was going to make you lasagna. Do you like lasagna as much as you like hot dogs?"

My mouth started watering when she said lasagna. "Yes, Kat. I do. It's one of my favorite things."

"Mine too. Do your children enjoy lasagna as well?" I saw where this was going but my resistance had melted somewhat. I had a vision of me relaxing with the boys while Kat made dinner for all of us. I might even get them outside for a game of catch. Not making dinner seemed to provide me with all kinds of free time. Still, my resolve had not crumbled completely.

"Yes, they do, almost as much as me. But I really am serious about keeping them out of my dating life for now. I don't want things to get any more confusing for them." Or more confusing for me, for that matter. "Maybe we could do it on another night."

"Of course we can. But I was thinking…what time do they go to bed? I would love to come over later and have a drink with you." It went on like this for another ten minutes or so. She would make an offer to come over and I would counter. Each time she made the suggestion the timing and nature of the visit was slightly different but it always involved that evening. I would have received less assertive treatment at the hands of used car salesman behind on his monthly quota. Before I knew it I was agreeing to let her come over and make dinner.

"Ok, Kat. We'll see you at seven." And it better be the best damn lasagna I've ever eaten. The self-loathing commenced before I hung up the phone. Why was I so weak and how was I going to explain this to the boys? I decided I would introduce her as a friend and try to keep the touching to a minimum. I was also determined to shove her out the door sometime between Trevor's bed time and my own, although I was already distrustful of my ability to do so. Katarina was a firecracker. My life experience to that point left me defenseless against someone like her. I knew I would eventually pay the price for my lack of sophistication in such matters but like nearly everything else going on I managed to compartmentalize the future dread and get on with the business at hand. Katarina was coming over and I was going to eat lasagna and try to explain it all to Trevor and Alex in a way that didn't make me look like an ass.

I have a theory on why people ask advice of certain other people when they are under duress or unsure of what they're doing. Well, I'm pretty sure it's really someone else's theory (probably Therapist Jim's) but I've claimed it as my own regardless. It goes like this: People ask advice from people they suspect will reinforce the decision they've already made. For instance, if a married person was on the verge of sleeping with someone other than their spouse, that person would talk to the friend who would tell them what they wanted to hear, be it advice to stay out of the pants of the new love interest or to dive headlong into said pants. In the same vein, an alcoholic doesn't call their AA sponsor to invite them out for a drink. For my part I appeared to be in a losing battle to Katarina's fawning interest and I needed someone to tell me what I should be doing, even if I already knew what I should be doing was calling

Katarina back and telling her to stay home. It was probable either of my best friends, upon questioning, would reinforce this knowledge and prompt me to do what I already knew to be the right thing. But while both were enigmatic in their own way I had known Johann to change his position on this subject or that in the space of five or ten minutes, which made the solicitation of his advice on the matter rather dicey. I needed someone who was going to be firm in their rejection of Katarina and support of me. I called Arthur.

"It's Monday evening, mate." He sounded confused.

"I know it's Monday evening, dude. Is that a problem?"

"No...no. I just don't think you've ever called me on a Monday before. Completely unexpected." He still sounded confused.

"Really? I'm sure I've called you on a Monday at some point. I mean, we've known each other for years. How can I have not EVER called you on a Monday?" The topic was distracting.

"Don't know, but I am ninety-nine percent sure we've never talked on a Monday evening. Go ahead, though. This was bound to happen eventually."

"Are you drunk?" I was serious.

"No. Not yet. I've had a couple beers but I'm not drunk. Just stunned. I'm wondering what could have prompted this shift in the universe." I was sure he was drunk but plowed ahead regardless.

"Well, this particular shift was prompted by the Russian girl I told you about – Katarina."

"What about her?" He sounded perkier.

"Well, we've been spending some time together, which has been fine, but now I feel like she's trying to invade my time with the boys. They're with me tonight and I let her invite herself over to make dinner."

"What's she making for dinner...on a Monday?"

"I think you're missing the point here, Arthur. The point is I feel like a dumbass for not telling her to stay away tonight. I'm looking for some advice here. I don't think we've reached the point of no return, you know, time wise, and I need your opinion. Should I call her and tell her not to come over? The prospect of introducing her to Trevor and Alex is stressing me out."

Arthur was silent for a few moments more than was usual. I suspected his mind had wandered while I blathered about my personal life. He broke the silence just as I was about to ask him if he was still there.

"Hmmm…. I thought you liked lasagna?"

"Dude! You're not helping me here. Whether or not I like lasagna has nothing to do with it. Do I tell her to stay home or not?"

"Not if you want to have a good dinner." Arthur was laughing on the other end of the phone. The sound of it lowered my anxiety level. "No, mate, really. I think you should let her come over. I think the boys will be fine. Just don't grab her snatch in front of them and everything should work out."

"Really, Arthur? You're telling me you think it'll be ok for Katarina to come over as long as I don't grab her crotch in front of my children? Thanks for the heads up." I was trying to sound annoyed but felt myself smiling as well. Perhaps the situation wasn't as dire as I believed it to be. Or perhaps my powers of rationalization were sufficient to overcome any valid internal objections I might be having to the scenario of a domestic evening with my two children and a Russian woman they've never met.

"Well, listen, if you really don't want to do it then don't do it." He was still chuckling. "All I'm saying is one dinner made by a strange woman isn't going to send the boys running to the shrink's office."

"Well, I suppose you're right. I didn't have anything planned for dinner anyway."

"Listen, Jason. If you think about it you can try taking notes about the evening to look at later. Hell, I'll even go over them with you if you feel like. It might help you put things in perspective." The whole thing sounded odd. Arthur had never been touchy-feely.

"Are you actually telling me to 'journal' my experiences? Who are you and when are you scheduled for the sex-change? When's the last time you wrote down your 'feelings'?"

"I don't, of course. But everything's right as rain in my world. Your world, on the other hand, has gone to the shitter. It's my understanding that when people write this crap down it helps them organize their thoughts and understand their impressions. It might actually help you, Jason." Arthur sounded serious, almost empathetic. It was odd.

"Well, I guess I can think about it but right now I have to get the boys ready to meet their new Mommy. I'll let you know how it goes."

Arthur was laughing again. "Can't wait to hear about it. Cheers."

I hung up the phone resolved to my next big task: Telling the boys what I knew (and was willing to tell them) about the woman who was feeding us that evening. I envisioned a number of scenarios, each ending badly and at least one where they decide they never want to talk to me again. In the end I figured I would wing it and keep it as positive as I could. I called the boys into the living room for a family chat.

"Alright guys, here's the thing." Even as I said it I was still trying to formulate what 'the thing' was without sounding diffident. I pressed on. "Ok, the thing is I'm having a friend over tonight."

Trevor piped in. "Is it Mr. Smythe?"

"No, sweetie, it's not Mr. Smythe. It's someone you don't know. It's a different friend. A woman named Katarina."

Alex looked excited. "Is she your girlfriend?" He was obviously adjusting quickly.

"Well, no. I wouldn't call her my girlfriend. She's a friend and she's a girl. She's just coming over to hang out and have dinner with us." I felt like I was back in high school. Defining relationships for a ten-year-old is a lot like defining them for your parents when you don't know the answer yourself.

"Oh. Ok. What are we having for dinner?" Alex was jumping right in while Trevor looked a little anxious.

"Lasagna, I'm pretty sure. Katarina is going to make it for us. What do you think Trevor?"

"It's ok, Dad. I like lasagna." He smiled at me but the look on his face was not one of total acceptance. "When is she getting here?"

"Soon, I think. I hope it's soon. I'm starting to get hungry."

As if on cue Katarina knocked on the apartment door. We all gathered by the door for her entrance and the boys greeted her with a sheepish "Hello" when she walked through. It was already going better than I had imagined.

"What handsome boys you are! You both must have many girlfriends!" Katarina knew how to work a room.

188

The boys' sheepishness continued as their faces went scarlet. "No, not really." They said this almost simultaneously as Katarina maneuvered into the apartment laden with grocery bags ostensibly holding the ingredients to tonight's dinner. I relieved her of her burdens as she continued buttering up my sons.

"Well I am sure that it is only because the girls at your school are too afraid to talk to you. You make them shy when you are so good looking." The boys continued to share embarrassed smiles. They were falling for it hook, line and sinker. I couldn't blame them. After all, who doesn't like it when a beautiful woman tells them how good looking they are? I imagined, however, that Katarina had never been one of the wall flowers she was describing for my sons.

The three of us tagged along with Katarina to the kitchen as if tethered to her. I deposited the bags of food I had liberated from Katarina on the counter and watched as she continued her conversation with Trevor and Alex. Their normal coloring had returned and while there appeared to be some sort of invisible barrier keeping them from getting too close to Katarina they were also rapt with the conversation. This made me happy and I was able to sit back and relax a bit rather than play the role of ambassador.

"Now who would like to help me make the dinner?" She was staring at Alex and received his immediate approval. "Trevor, what do you like to do before dinner?"

Trevor thought for a moment. "My Dad and I used to play catch before dinner."

"Then you and your Father must play catch and Alex and I will start making food. Unless you, Alex, want to play catch also."

"That's ok." Alex blushed again. "I think I'd like to help you."

Trevor and I retreated to the hall closet to get a baseball and mitts before making our way to the grassy area behind my apartment building. By the time we were out the door Katarina already had Alex pouring ingredients into a mixing bowl. He looked contented and did not pause in his labor to acknowledge the exit of his father and brother. For our part, Trevor and I found the simple act of tossing the ball back and forth as relaxing and bonding as we always had. It had been a good six months since we had undertaken the activity and by the time we were done we were joking and talking as if there was nothing unusual about having a beautiful stranger making us dinner.

While the food cooked the four of us spent more time talking. The boys opened up and asked Katarina a number of questions about Russia and how she ended up in the United States. I did not interrupt or interject as Katarina told them anecdotes of her childhood and family. The boys couldn't take their eyes off her. By the time the food was ready the conversation had gotten quite lively and the liveliness continued throughout the meal. Things had gone so well none us realized it how late it had gotten while we ate and jabber-jawed.

"Alright guys, time for bed." I was still sipping some of the wine Katarina had brought with her.

"C'mon, Dad, it's not that late. Can we please stay up?"

"Nope!" I did not consider Trevor's request for even a moment. I wanted to get them to bed so I could shoo Katarina out the door and I didn't want to do it with them as a distraction. And it really was late. "Go on, guys. Time for bed."

Going against type, Trevor did not pursue his request and he and Alex left the table and trundled off to their bedroom. I told them I would be in to kiss them goodnight in a minute and turned my attention to Katarina.

"Thank you very much for dinner, Kat. It was the best dinner we've had in the apartment."

"You are welcome, Jason. I look forward to making more of them for you. I will clean the dishes while you tell your sons good night, yes?"

"Oh…don't worry, Kat. I'll just leave that for the morning. It's late and I'm sure you want to get home. Cleaning up is the least I can do after such a great dinner." I was trying to be smooth and not hurt her feelings. It was, after all, a great dinner but I still didn't want her to stay the night and it would have been terribly rude to just come out and say it right after finishing the meal. I'm a better host than that.

"Do not worry, Jason. I will stay the night with you and we can clean the dishes together." She smiled as she rested her chin one hand, beaming at me from across the table. I was at a loss. I really didn't want to be rude but she didn't seem to be taking the hint.

"No, it's ok Kat. I really can clean up on my own." It was time to pull out the big guns. "The thing is, well… You know, I haven't had anyone stay overnight while the boys were here. I'm not sure they're ready for that. Or that I'm ready for that, for that matter. Do you understand?"

"How many women have spent the night here when your sons were NOT here?" She was being provocative and didn't miss a beat. I was taken by surprise by the turn in the conversation. "Ummm, well…none, except for you. You are the only woman who has spent the night in my apartment." And that was the truth.

"Do you believe Trevor and Alex do not like me?" She was still smiling, probably because she had just taken control of the conversation.

"No…I mean yes, I think they like you. In fact I think Alex has a big crush on you."

"Then I think you should ask them how they feel about it. No?"

The simplicity of her statement belied the complexity I was feeling about asking it. Would the boys get it? Or would they just view Katarina's stay as sort of an adult sleep over? Suddenly I was no longer concerned with why I didn't want her to stay the night. I wanted to know how my son's felt about it.

"Hmmm… I'll go ask them now." I got up from the table and swooped down on the boys, who were not in bed yet. "Guys, can I ask you a question?"

"Sure, Dad." Alex responded as he pulled on a clean t-shirt.

"Katarina wants to sleep here tonight. How do you guys feel about that?"

Trevor stopped tugging at his blanket and looked at me. "Where would she sleep?"

"In my room." I did not hesitate with my response. I didn't want to cue them to what I thought.

Alex crawled into bed. "It's ok with me, Dad." He said this matter-of-factly and seemed very relaxed. The boys knew where baby's came from but I wondered if either of them would assign the baby making act itself to idea of Katarina sleeping in my bed. It didn't appear so. Perhaps because the last people any offspring can imagine having sex are their parents.

"Trevor? What do you think?"

"I think it's fine, Dad. Do you think she'd make us breakfast?" Apparently Trevor's thoughts had little to do with human sexuality.

"I'll ask her, Trevor." I was smiling at his focus on food. "I don't know what her schedule is but I'll definitely ask her. Well, alrighty then." I bade them good night and went back out to find Katarina cleaning the dishes. She couldn't have been sexier.

"You were right, Kat. They're just fine with you staying. And so am I." I said this as I hugged her from behind and slipped my hand underneath her shirt. Her skin was warm and her taught body felt wonderful as I pressed against her. My arousal was immediate and she responded by turning herself within my arms until she was facing me.

"I think we can finish the dishes later. No?"

"Yes." I picked her up and carried her into the bedroom, making sure to close and lock the door behind me. Our lovemaking that evening would be relatively tame so as not to disturb my children. Although far less vocal, Katarina was as aggressive as ever, gripping me so closely it became difficult to tell where her body ended and mine began. It was as if she thought she might fall off a cliff if she let go too soon. It felt wonderful. I was an idiot.

CHAPTER FOURTEEN

I woke the next morning to the heat of Katarina's body pressed against mine. I found it pleasant but confusing, surrounded as I was by the haze of an early morning. Sunlight was just beginning to poke through the slats of the venetian blinds, apparently in amounts insufficient to wake Katarina. Other than the slow up and down movement of her rib cage, she remained motionless beside me, lying on her stomach in what looked to be an otherwise uncomfortable position. Our clothing had not been reapplied before we drifted off to sleep the night before so I took in the view while I had the opportunity. Katarina was indeed beautiful and the effort required to drag my ass out of bed and into the shower without touching her was no less than herculean. I tiptoed my way to the bathroom so as not to wake her.

Fortunately it was not as difficult to get Katarina to leave in the morning as it was to get her to leave at night. She had a job and we all left the apartment together, me to take the boys to Kim's and Katarina straight to work, or so I assumed. I did not ask before we kissed goodbye between our parked cars outside of the apartment building. Katarina smelled heavenly. I don't know how she did it. All I had in the bathroom was some generic shampoo and a bar of Dial soap. She smelled like neither, so either she had packed in her own morning-after supplies or she just naturally smelled that good all the time. I pulled her close for one last aromatic encounter before jumping into the driver's seat of my car. The boys were already buckled in the back, leaving the passenger seat empty.

"What's going on, guys? How come nobody's up here with me?" I was looking at their quizzical expressions through the rear-view mirror.

Alex piped up first. "We figured Katarina would ride up front…with you." I was momentarily taken aback by the idea my sons had actually thought far enough into the future to anticipate another butt might be filling the seat next to me. Amazing! Then it occurred to me they had discounted the obvious – Katarina had arrived at our apartment under her own steam.

"Oh. Well, guys, that was very nice of you but did you forget a little something?"

"Like what?" Trevor was now looking back at me through the rear-view mirror, like he was staring at it instead of at the back of my head.

"Like the fact she drove here on her own?" Duh!

"We knew that, Dad." Alex sounded exasperated. "But we thought you were going to give her a ride to work or something."

Ok, they were more logical than I had given them credit, although I had no idea why they thought I would give Katarina a ride into work. I chose not to pursue it. It was enough they seemed comfortable with the whole situation, although I foresaw a nasty call from Kim later in the day. I did not believe she would take too kindly to the idea of her sons being exposed to the wanton sexual proclivities of their ne'er-do-well father. I planned to spend some time preparing a suitable response to the inevitable cranky phone call.

"Again, guys, that was very nice, but let's change the topic. How did you sleep last night?" The question was posed mainly to determine whether or not the sounds no doubt emanating from the master bedroom the night before had disturbed them. Or perhaps generate questions with which I didn't want to deal, i.e. "Were you having sex with Katarina last night?" I didn't feel ready for those questions even though I had put myself squarely in the cross hairs for just such an interrogation. I waited for an answer with bated breath.

"Fine, Dad." This was Trevor's standard answer to that particular question. It was a mixture of bored repetition and contrived distraction easily achieved by most 12-year-olds and it was exactly what I wanted to hear. If Trevor had been aware of any shenanigans his answer would have been more guarded and self-conscious. I dodged the bullet. The rest of the drive to Kim's house was pleasantly uneventful and I felt calm as we said our goodbyes and watched as my sons walk into my old house.

By the time I got to work I hadn't really come up with a strategy to deal with the inescapable phone call from Kim. This would have been a good use of my long drive in. Instead I spent the down time listening to talk radio or Bob and Tom, the latter having far fewer commercials than the former. Though I hadn't utilized the drive to formulate a strategy, I DID obtain a decent grasp on the news of the day and a few jokes to tell around the office. I felt full and productive as I walked past Emily's empty desk and to my own, sitting down silently and making a mental note to write Emily up for her tardiness. This, however, would largely be an exercise in futility. The write ups were having little effect on her behavior, probably because the consequences of the bad behavior were never more than another write up. I had started writing a to-do list when my errant assistant came bopping through the door carrying a dozen roses. She seemed quite pleased with herself.

"New boyfriend?" I asked dryly. Emily went through boyfriends like most of us go through underwear.

"Yes, as a matter of fact." She was beaming at me with a sly smile. "But these aren't from him and they aren't for me. They're for you!"

"Huh?" I really was surprised. I had never received flowers at work before. Indeed, I don't believe I had ever received flowers at all. Ever.

"They're for you! I just went downstairs to get them from the delivery guy. You owe me two bucks for the tip." She handed the flowers to me over my desk. I received them gingerly, as if the vase might burn my fingers, and set them down in the middle of my desk blotter. What was I to do with them?

"There's a card. See it?" Emily was becoming exasperated with my lack of procedural knowledge. I grabbed the card from its plastic holder and opened it. It said, "Thinking of you, Katarina."

"So who are they from?" Emily was far more excited than I.

"Um, just this lady I've been seeing." I felt like a 13-year-old getting ribbed by his friends for having a girlfriend.

"So who's the lady? She must think you're pretty special if she's sending you flowers."

"Her name's Katarina. We've been on a couple dates." What little excitement I had about receiving the flowers was waning under the duress of Emily's oversized excitement, which seemed to siphon mine off. "Hey, listen, can you go check if there's any inter-office mail for me downstairs? One of the branches was supposed to send me a bunch of financials on H & H Tooling." I really needed Emily to leave.

"Sure, but I'm still going to have questions later." She seemed to understand I was trying to get rid of her. I wasn't giving her enough credit.

After Emily left I contemplated the flowers for a moment, wondering what my next move should be. I was definitely attracted to Katarina and she had all the qualities I wanted, at least at the time. At first I figured I should just go for it but I was quickly reminded of earlier disasters. Izzy's phone call interrupted my ruminations. I decided to be brave and answer.

"Hey, Izzy." I had her on speaker phone.

"What's up, big fella? Are you busy? I haven't heard from you in a while." She sounded relaxed on the other end of the phone. To Izzy "a while" could mean a few days or a few weeks. In this case it meant more than a few days.

"Keeping busy, for sure. You guys have been keeping me hopping with all the loan applications." I should have told her about Katarina right away but our relationship had been permanently altered. Now I felt guarded about sharing certain types of information with Izzy that in the past I would have just blurted out. It would take months and months before we'd be able to rebuild that part of our relationship.

"What've you been up to outside of work? How are the boys? Are you dating anyone?" I liked how she slipped the most awkward question in at the end, like I might not notice.

"Oh, you know, making the apartment livable. Trevor and Alex seem to be doing fine and Kim hasn't been making trouble. And, yes, I've been on a couple dates." I was proud of myself for telling her the truth. Between answering the phone and my bout of honesty I felt sure to receive a good shot of Karma from the universe.

"Really? What's she like?" Izzy was trying to sound nonchalant.

I decided to continue with the honesty bit. I didn't see a point in hiding from Izzy what I would eventually tell her anyway. "She's Russian. I met her in the lobby here. She's a bank customer. We've been on a few dates."

"Oh. Ok….so you must like her. Has she met the boys?" Her voice had taken an edge. I wanted to get off the phone but wasn't sure how I could get away with it at this juncture.

"As a matter of fact, yes. She met them last night. They seem to like her. She made dinner for us at the apartment and Alex helped out. We had lasagna…." Aaargh! Why was I giving so much detail? I could feel the tension spike right through the speaker phone.

"Hey, sweetie, Todd (her assistant manager) just walked in my office. I gotta go. I'll call you later." That was it. I had hurt Izzy again.

Johannes told me once that, theoretically, white lies were ok if you were protecting someone's feelings. I countered that any lie was bad because of the inherent, negative effects on the fabric of the universe. And besides, what if they found out you lied to them? Then their feelings are hurt twice. But by the end of my conversation with Izzy I was starting to believe in the potential efficacy of a few well- placed white lies. And Johannes generally seemed happier than me, so...

I went back to the business of approving or turning down loan requests, preoccupied with thoughts of Katarina and Izzy. The thoughts concerning the former were, on balance, quite pleasant. Thoughts of Izzy, however, were turning dark. For some reason I was working really hard to destroy our relationship and wondered how I could stop. Limiting contact with her would have the same effect as all the other stuff I was already doing to her, so I dismissed the idea straight away. Perhaps flowers? It had taken me years to learn the power of flowers and what the act represents to women. I stopped what little work I was doing in order to order daisy's (Izzy's favorite) from a local shop. On the card I had the flower order taker write this: Always friends. Thick and thin. The simplicity of it was grand and I admit I was very impressed with myself. My hope was that the daisies and card would constitute a lethal, friend-retaining combination. All I had to do was sit back for a day or two and wait for the adoring phone call. I gave myself a few more moments of self-congratulation before going back to work.

"Ring, ring, ring!" This was Emily letting me know I had a phone call. It was something new she was trying. It was not being well received.

"Jason?" It was Katarina. I felt annoyed and turned on at the same time. Mainly turned on.

"Hey, Katarina! How's your day going? And hey! Thank you so much for the flowers! You are the first person ever to give me flowers." That was true. No one had ever given me flowers. Maybe I had just never deserved them.

"My day is going fine. I have been thinking about you all morning and would like to meet you for dinner tonight. Would you like that as well?" I giggled internally at her odd syntax before reminding myself that her English was a bazillion times better than my Russian.

"Yes, I would like that." And I would. Our conversation lasted long enough to make plans for the evening. At the end I shifted smoothly back into work gear but spent the rest of the day with the vision of a naked Katarina floating in my head. I'm sure it made me more productive.

Arthur called to chat at the end of my work day, somehow timing the call to catch me just as I climbed into my car. I made a mental note to search for a hidden camera at the earliest opportunity.

"Your timing is impeccable."

"Generally." I laughed at his dry delivery. To the best of my knowledge Arthur had never tried stand-up comedy but perhaps he should have. "Plans tonight?"

"Yup. I'm having dinner with Katarina. What was your plan?" Shamefully, I was prepared to cancel plans with Katarina had Arthur proposed something interesting enough to make it worth my while. I really did desire to see Katarina but Arthur and I had not gone for beer in weeks and weeks. I missed it.

"Beer at O'Hearn's." Arthur's plan was not as elaborate as I hoped but it certainly did sound inviting.

"Well, how about I meet you there now and I'll have a late dinner with Katarina?" Why was I asking for Arthur's permission? Arthur was not one to get upset if things didn't always go his way, especially the little things.

"I'll see you in thirty?" He was probably already in his car.

"Yup." I hung up the phone happy I was about to spend time with my friend but now worried Katarina would be pissed off at the change in plans. To my great relief she was not upset and agreed to move the dinner back. I was unaware that such women existed. My experience with them, though meager, implied a generally negative reaction to any attempt I might make to alter a dinner plan in order to make time for beer with a friend. Had I hit the jack pot with Katarina? It struck me there was so much about her I didn't know. She was obviously one of a kind. I needed to make a concerted effort to figure out how she came to be. And if I discovered all Eastern European women shared similar traits I would definitely have to scout out a job in Prague.

Prague. I didn't wonder how that particular city popped into my head. Elaine continued to sneak into my thoughts at odd moments. I mean, the connection between Katarina and Eastern Europe was obvious but if it was her I was keeping in mind I should have come up with Moscow or St. Petersburg. Elaine, through no fault of her own, was still competing for my attention. By now, however, with Katarina in my life and the physical separation from Kim complete, I found it easier to not think about Elaine if I chose to. Of course, I often chose to not choose to not think about her, but the problem with thinking about her was that my thoughts were often unrealistic. I was still having fantasies about jumping on a flight to Prague and visions of what reuniting with Elaine would look like. In my head it involved tears and hugging followed by a nice dinner and lots of sex, followed by some sort of "happily ever after" scenario. It was all good stuff but very distracting, so at that moment I decided to let all of it go long enough to be happy about Katarina's reaction to my request for a dinner delay. Still, I went ahead and made a mental note to call Elaine the next day and hope the conversation would be less uncomfortable than the last one.

I left work feeling thirsty. On my way to O'Hearn's it occurred to me I could have simplified my evening somewhat by inviting Arthur to meet me at a satisfactory downtown drinking establishment, of which there were many. That way I could have just crossed back over the river to pick up Katarina after I was done with Arthur. I was already in a suit so I wouldn't have had to change for the date, however, in order to rationalize my lack of efficiency I told myself that I did, indeed, need to clean up and change before meeting Katarina. I just needed to make sure I left O'Hearn's with sufficient spare time to accomplish all these things. Arthur was getting out of his car as I was pulling into O'Hearn's parking lot.

"Howdy, stranger!" (I couldn't come up with anything better?)

"Hello, Jason." Arthur's greeting was not as homey as my own and he got right down to business. "Let's have a beer." He actually did sound kind of excited about that.

"My thoughts exactly."

The bar area was already half full with after-work-drink patrons and would get busier within the hour. We took a couple bar stools and ordered. It felt good to be sitting with Arthur at O'Hearn's. It felt like an age since we had been there together. While we sat I brought Arthur up to speed on all my active female relationships and he described his trip to Iran in search of Persian rugs. It appeared that, although he made a few contacts, he did not expect much to come of them. So, since there was little to tell from his end, my woman troubles were arguably far more interesting than Arthur's recent travels. After I paid for the beers Arthur began asking me about Katarina, a topic on which he seemed to place some importance.

"What does she do for a living?" I was almost sure he had asked me this question before but couldn't remember.

"Import/Export, as far as I know. I think she might do some real estate also. She's told me some stories about how they buy cars here and ship them back to Russian because it's cheaper than buying them there. BMW's and what not. I have no idea why it would be cheaper to ship a car from the U.S. to Russia than shipping one just a few countries away. Maybe it's taxes and stuff. I'll have to ask her about it." I made a mental note to have a nerdy and very unsexy conversation with Katarina about country-to-country tax rates and the cost of overseas shipping. "Maybe you can tell me why. You do all that import/export stuff, right? Is it cheaper to ship to Russia from here than from Germany?"

"I have no idea. I don't do Europe. I know the Arabs like the big American cars because of the big American air conditioners and engine cooling systems. How long has she been here?" He sounded matter-of-fact but by now we had spent a lot of time on Katarina's job and citizenship status. I was getting bored. I wanted to talk (brag) about her shapely ass.

"I don't know, dude. A couple years, I think. We haven't talked about it that much. She sorta came out of nowhere but so far it's going well. The boys even like her. Plus she seems to be the most tolerant woman I've ever known. She didn't even have a problem with delaying dinner tonight so I could hang out with you."

"Oh, well then. That IS special. You know, maybe she didn't mind moving dinner because she really doesn't give a wit about you." Arthur smiled. "You know, Jason, I tend not to dwell on your personal life but don't you think this is moving pretty fast? The sex is one thing, I get that. But she's at your apartment already? Making dinner? Aren't you just a little concerned?"

"Maybe you're just jealous." I didn't really believe this. Arthur was never jealous of anyone. "Anyway, if you really want to meet we could all go on a double date. We could even get Johannes to come. I think things are going good for him and the new girl."

"I'll ask Gladys, but I still want you to keep an eye on her. You've got a big blind spot for a nice piece of ass and I don't trust those Russians, even if they're not commies anymore." Arthur paused. "What's Therapist Jim say about all this?"

"All what?"

"You know, all the stuff with the birds. Have you talked to him about it?" He seemed concerned.

"Uh, nope. Not really. I mean, I haven't been to see him in a while." And I hadn't. I made another mental note to set up an appointment with Therapist Jim. Although I hadn't talked to him in weeks I was suddenly feeling the urge to, probably as a result of Arthur's interrogation. No matter the reason my time with Therapist Jim, although costly, always had a centering effect on me and I figured I could use some centering. "I'll give him a call on Monday."

"Don't do it on my account. I'm just making conversation. You do seem to like him, though, and the way you've been bed hopping you could probably use his time." Sometimes Arthur sounded vaguely insulting. But since I didn't want to be insulted my brain converted the tone of his voice from one of disapproval to one of concern.

We talked for a couple of hours on topics ranging from world politics to the beef stew waiting for him at his house. I noted, however, Arthur regularly rolled the conversation back around to Katarina. When I jokingly confronted him with this revelation he mumbled something about attractive Slavic women and started talking about the dearth of affordable Persian rugs in the Cincinnati area. I didn't pursue the topic, figuring he was just fishing for more sex stories in a blatant attempt to live vicariously through my sex life. When the time came to depart I was feeling relaxed and a little buzzed. Despite his new obsession with my Russian girlfriend my time with Arthur was as fulfilling as always.

"Remember to keep your eye on the new bird." He was saying this over his shoulder as he opened his car door. "I mean it."

"Don't worry, Arthur. I'm keeping a very close eye on her." I was flippant and Arthur did not respond. Maybe he didn't hear me.

The Malibu made its efficient way to Katarina's apartment in Newport. The sun was close to setting as I headed south on I-75 and the last light of the day cast a red glow on me and everything around me. I was glad I wasn't getting to Katarina's too late in the evening as there was still plenty of time to have a nice dinner, a few drinks and some conversation. The trepidation I had experienced earlier in the day over seeing her that evening had melted away under the influence of alcohol and the setting sun. And I was feeling something close to elation by the time I arrived, which is what I should have been feeling all along, of course. Of course, this is what any man should feel when he is about to meet with a special lady friend, so I let go of Arthur's assertion about things moving too quickly. So what if she wanted to make dinner for me and my kids? Maybe that was the norm in Russia.

"Come in, Jason." Katarina greeted me at the door in a strapless "little black dress" covered by a long-sleeved jacket and wearing thigh high boots. My response was simple.

"Wow." I hugged her and crossed the threshold. She was pleased by my reaction.

"I wore this for you, Jason. I am glad you like it." I liked it.

We left her apartment and headed back across the river into Cincinnati. I knew Katarina had never been to Mt. Adams, which was and is one of my favorite parts of the city. We did not talk much as I wound my way up through Eden Park. I noticed Katarina spent most of the drive looking out her window. I assumed she was taking in the view of the city as our elevation increased or perhaps she was just lost in thought. However, she got more talkative after we parked and started walking around. St. Gregory Street was bustling with bar-hopping revelers and the energy of it was infectious.

"Where are you taking me?" Katarina asked this after we parked the car.

"I'm taking you to the Blind Lemon."

"And what is the Blind Lemon?" She had such a cute accent.

"The Blind Lemon is a little bar that will have a guitar player tonight, but even with the guitar player we'll still be able to talk. From what I understand it was a speakeasy during prohibition." It took a moment for it to occur to me there was a good chance that Katarina had never heard of prohibition and, by extension, had no idea what a speakeasy might be. So I spent the remainder of our walk explaining both, finishing my lecture on the unintended consequences of prohibition as we gingerly moved down the stone steps into the Blind Lemon. "And that's how we ended up with our crime becoming better organized into groups."

"That is interesting." Katarina sounded distracted. "There is much organized crime in Russia, also."

"So I've heard."

The inside of the Blind Lemon is small and rectangular with a low-slung drop ceiling. The table cloth covered tables are kept close together to accommodate as many people as possible in the tiny seating area but there is also an inviting outdoor patio which is very popular on warm evenings. On this night the patio was full so Katarina and I were shown to a table for two inside. Our table was one of a number positioned along the banquette running the length of one wall, each with a wooden chair opposite the padded bench. Since the tables are placed only inches from one another in order to obtain ingress and egress the table has to be pulled in and out by the host. It is quite cozy and the arrangement makes it a simple task to eavesdrop on your neighbors or to be eavesdropped upon. Katarina and I were seated at the very end of the banquette against a half wall on the other side of which the guitar player is located during the winter months. Being given the choice, Katarina took the seat opposite the bench, giving me the view of the bar over her right shoulder. As she sat down she removed her jacket, revealing her bare shoulders and arms. The soft lighting complemented her dark complexion, giving her skin a gentle glow.

"You look quite lovely tonight." The words emerged without forethought, an unchoreographed reaction to her physical presence. Absurdly I found myself wondering if she was wearing underwear and how, exactly, I could subtly discover the answer.

"Are you wearing underwear?" Subtle, as always.

Katarina's gaze was fixed on my own and she answered without hesitation. "Of course not." Perhaps subtlety wasn't her strong suit either.

"Thank you." I was careful to form the words lest the sudden onset of cotton mouth and loss of facial control make them unintelligible. My tongue had expanded to twice its normal size.

"You are welcome. Do you like my boots? I bought them just for you."

Did I like her boots? Was she being rhetorical?

"Yes, very much. Thank you again." I was pleased my response didn't emerge as a series of clicks and grunts, at least I didn't think it did. Judging by Katarina's smile I assumed I had formed actual words, but a change of topic was in order.

"So...I need us to talk about work or the weather or anything that doesn't have to do with sex or else I'm not going to make it through the first drink. Any ideas?" Katarina looked a bit crestfallen. Should I have spent more time complementing her amazing taste in clothing? Probably, but if anything had become apparent to me over the last few months it was that I was generally a failure at making women happy. I think it's because I miss the small things. Or perhaps the big things. Or perhaps both. I tried to recover. "I mean, Katarina, you look amazing. You look so amazing that I'm completely distracted and if I could I would take you right here in the middle of this bar, but since we're not going to get away with that I need you to help me think about something other than ripping your clothes off."

Katarina smiled at me and looked much happier. "In that case, Jason, I think we should talk about work. Maybe our jobs are exciting enough to get us through a drink or two."

"Maybe...we'll see." I was skeptical and though I wanted nothing less than to devour her I allowed myself to be a little excited at the prospect of grilling her about her work. I had been trying to get to the bottom of Katarina's job situation for a couple weeks and the most I had gotten so far was the same old import/export crap I had been hearing from Arthur for years. There had to be more to it than shipping a couple BMW's back to Russia. Katarina, however, got the jump on me.

"Are you in charge of all the money?" She smiled as she asked the question but the cultural divide was sufficient to make me wonder if she was being serious.

"Well, no, not really. I mean, I'm sort of in charge of some of it. You know, because I'm one of the people who can approve loans. Is that what you mean?" Did I even know how to explain my job to someone who wasn't a banker? Honestly, it's not that complicated but I was being overcome by some sort of early-stage dementia resulting from Katarina's dress code and high pheromone count. I should have turned the tables and started asking her about her job. Instead I found myself hoping she wouldn't ask me too many questions since it was beginning to look like the explanation might not make much sense to her.

"Do you know many bankers in Russia?" Dumbest question ever but the dementia was getting worse.

"No, not many." She was still smiling, apparently delighted by my plight. She reached across the table and took my hand in hers. "At least none like you, Jason."

Call it banker's intuition or simply a lack of self-confidence, but under the circumstances I found it unlikely Katarina had never met a banker like me. What mattered at the moment, however, was that I wanted to believe it. I wanted to believe that a woman so beautiful and exotic actually found me special. And the desire to believe was enough. It was enough to distract me from her bare skin and it was enough to draw me into her circle. The size of the room and close proximity of the tables makes it easy to people-watch at the Blind Lemon. For the rest of the evening, however, I would reside contentedly within the cocoon Katarina built around our table, a cocoon fabricated with touch, laughter, words and long, meaningful stares. I stood about as much chance of escaping her as I did of becoming President of Uzbekistan.

"Would you like another drink?"

"Yes. Thank you. I like it here, Jason. I like being here with you." She really seemed to mean it.

"I like being here with you, too…you do mean the bar, right?" It suddenly occurred to me that she might have been talking about the United States, not just the bar.

"Yes! I mean the bar, at least for right now." She was laughing at me again and it didn't bother me at all. In fact, I was starting to like it. "Later I will like being in bed with you, and I will like it better than being here with you. And I will like how you kiss me and how you feel inside of me."

Katarina put her hand on my leg and began to slowly move it upward. The table cloth provided some level of camouflage for her maneuver but a persistent onlooker would no doubt see what was going on. Again, I didn't care. It felt wonderful and sexy and I assumed if anyone noticed it would inspire more jealousy than antipathy, so I let her hand roam. And when the server came over with our drinks she paid us no mind, no doubt having seen it all before. With her had still meandering, Katarina turned our conversation back to my job.

"Jason, may I ask you more about your work?"

"Really? You want to talk about banking right now? You don't think it'll be rather…unsexy?"

"I told you Jason, I think bankers are sexy. Besides, I wanted to talk to you about my money, which I always find interesting." She giggled at her joke and squeezed my leg. "You know my company has checking accounts with three different banks. I do not like this arrangement but I worry to keep all of the money in one bank."

I resigned myself to talking about work, at least for a few minutes. "Why do you worry about having it all in one bank?"

"It is probably silly but I worry the money will be stolen or the bank will go out of business."

"You don't really have to worry about either of those. If the bank got robbed we wouldn't charge it against your account. Plus there's not much chance of us going out of business, at least not in the near future. And I promise to call you right away if it looks likely to happen! We have plenty of money and the computer hacker who was attacking our system seems to have gone on vacation or given up, so I can assure you we're pretty safe and solvent."

Katarina's hand inched a little further up my leg and she smiled.

"Then I would like to bring more money to your bank, Jason. You make me feel safe." At this point her hand had reached what I imagined was its intended destination. Between that and the idea of bringing a big depositor into the bank I was feeling pretty good about myself.

"That's great, Katarina, but considering how amazing you look tonight and the way you keep touching me you should feel anything but safe. What else would you like to know?" I only asked to be polite. I still didn't want to talk about banking at all.

She eased herself back into a more upright position and took a sip of her drink. "Can you help me move money into your bank?"

This was one of those moments where it seemed something was getting lost in translation. The way she asked the question almost seemed to imply she wanted me to physically help carry money into the bank. "Uh….I guess so. How do you want me to help you? You know the easiest thing to do would be for you just to write a check and deposit it."

She took another sip of her drink and leaned forward, giving me an even better view of her cleavage. "I will do that Jason, but I have other money to deposit and I need to be able to have money deposited right from Russia. Can you do that?"

"How are you doing that now?" Now I was actually getting a bit interested. The only really efficient way to move money from one country to another was to have it wired. Surely any bank with which she was dealing would have told her the same thing.

"It gets moved around electrically." I didn't ask but I'm sure she meant electronically. "If I send a car back to Russia the money goes from a Russian bank to a Swiss bank and then they send it to a bank in New York and then they send it here because the bank we are using cannot take money from out of the country. It takes a long time for us to get paid and I would like it to be faster. Can you help me?"

"Well, I guess I can. I'll have to check things out tomorrow to see what I can do. Honestly, though, I don't know everything about our wiring policies, which is scary because they let me sign off on the big ones all the time!" I was trying to be funny but the reality was exactly as I described it – I really wasn't very familiar with my bank's wiring practices. "Can we talk more about it tomorrow?"

"Of course, Jason." Katarina leaned across the table and, placing her hand on the back of my neck pulled me toward her for a kiss. Her hair fell around my face and her redolence surrounded me. I was lost in her.

We spent the rest of the evening talking quietly, trying to learn as much about each other as we could. We stayed at the Blind Lemon long enough to have the table next to us empty and refill at least three times. Finally my anxiousness to bed her again overcame the egotistical pleasure in being seen in public with such a woman. With her permission I ushered her to the car and back across the river to her place. Our lovemaking that night was as it had been except for its intensity. Looking back, I remember wanting her more that evening. I wanted more of the physical, of course, but I also wanted more of…her. I wanted to consume her as I had wanted to consume Elaine months before and was ready to give her anything in return. Without really being aware of it, I was giving myself over to her.

CHAPTER FIFTEEN

Here's something I think I've learned but I hope is wrong: We all want to be loved but many of us don't feel worthy of that love. Oh, we may do our own daily self-affirmation but deep down it's most likely all doubt with a touch of self-loathing. This lack of worthiness may stem from low self-esteem, lack of self-confidence, personal history with the opposite sex, some combination of all those things or other hyphenated conditions yet to be discovered. Had this epiphany materialized at the time it would have been a good topic to bring up with Therapist Jim. Or rather it would have been a good topic to bring up with Therapist Jim had I still been making bi-weekly visits. For some reason my schedule kept getting in the way of my pursuit of mental stability and self-knowledge, or at least that's what I told myself. Certainly, the first step to reconnecting with Therapist Jim would have been to make an appointment, but for weeks I had failed to make even that meager effort.

I remember a girl on whom I had a crush in eighth grade. Andrea Thomas. She had red hair and a slim but developing figure and to this day I can still picture her face. She sent my junior high hormones blazing and although I managed to strike up a conversation with her occasionally (largely because she sat right next to me in a number of classes) I couldn't get up the nerve to ask her "out." Of course, "out" in junior high parlance is the rough equivalent of "going steady" when one is slightly older. As going "out" with someone may last just days or even hours, it represents an element of exclusivity without the emotional consequences inherent in the more intense relationships that occur later in life. The main impediment to asking Andrea to go "out" with me was fear. Fear of rejection. The fear was sufficient that when I was one day unexpectedly confronted at my locker by a delegation of Andrea's girlfriends on whether or not I "liked" her, I responded in the negative. This turned out to be the wrong answer and the last shot I would ever get at Andrea Thomas. Taken completely by surprise, I failed to grasp that Andrea might be experiencing the same fear of rejection as I and therefore sent her envoys to test the waters. Sadly, my self-confidence was so lacking I took the question as an attempt to make me the butt of a joke. Surely Andrea's friends were not simply assessing the situation on Andrea's behalf, but rather attempting to make me her fool. How could Andrea, with her beautiful red hair and perfect skin be interested in a gangly, four-eyed geek? It would be too late by the time I found out Andrea's true intentions, and though eighth grade romances tend to be short-lived, it would have been nice to not have Andrea permanently stationed in the "regrets" column of my life's balance sheet.

Lucky for me more aggressive women than Andrea Thomas would eventually wander into my life. If there weren't I may well have ended up alone and childless, living in a one-bedroom apartment nursing my hatred of the happy to this day. The first of these female go-getters turned out to be Charlotte Smith, who sat next to me in French class in ninth grade. Charlotte was unabashedly pro-Jason Kubrick and made it known in no uncertain terms she wanted me to ask her to the ninth-grade dance, which I did. I was rewarded for the effort with my first real kiss, which occurred on her parent's porch at the end of the evening. Charlotte and I didn't make it out of ninth grade as a couple but she represented the first in a mostly fortunate trend. From then on nearly all of my successful encounters with women would be initiated by them. But even with the apparent plethora of women who desired my company in some fashion, I never really came to understand why they would want it. To quote the great comedian Rodney Dangerfield, "I wouldn't want to belong to any club that would have me as a member." Of course, there are aberrations blessed with bullet proof egos and an aptitude for chatting up the opposite sex, even from a youngish age. I've never been one of those. But I don't believe this condition of befuddlement as to one's attraction, or lack thereof, to the opposite sex is isolated to the space I happen to occupy. Sad-sackiness aside I think most of us, even the bullet proof, harbor the seeds of inter-sexual inaction. Luckily for our species, there are methods with long histories of success that have helped mankind overcome this inaction. These include various types of desensitization or immersion therapy but the preferred method for many, including myself, is simply the consumption of copious amounts of alcohol. Despite its inherent hazards, alcohol consumption seems to be the least expensive and most effective way to overcome one's fear of the opposite sex, and the fearless behavior attempted while under the influence often creeps into sober interactions as well, thus further bolstering one's chances of getting what he or she wants. I admit I have only anecdotal evidence to support my thesis. But it's worked well enough for me.

So here I was waking up next to a beautiful woman whose desire for me I found inexplicable. Did she want me just for me? Possibly. Did she want me because she truly found bankers sexy and me particularly so? Doubtful. Did she want me because I was a nice guy and she'd discovered that's what she really needed in her life? That sounded plausible. These questions and more were going through my mind as I stared at Katarina's bedroom ceiling. She was still asleep, her bare back pressed against my side, breathing quietly, the heat of her willowy body flowing over me. The lonely depths of me didn't want to question the veracity of her feelings for me. To do so held the potential of discovering an ugly truth which, upon the knowing, would therefore deny me her presence in my life. And if there was a time when I needed someone like Katarina in my life it was then. I mean, I barely had sufficient time to decipher what happened in my marriage, why I was so easily rejected by Elaine and why I screwed over Izzy. I wasn't ready to add any more "female" problems to the list, and Katarina's devotion was giving me as much emotional warmth as her hard-working internal furnace was giving me physical warmth. I just wasn't ready to take on the additional burden of actually decoding the ins and outs of my relationship with her. In the inimitable words of Paul McCartney, I just wanted to "Let It Be." I closed my eyes and let Katarina's heat wrap around me.

The next day found me chipper and ready to work but no closer to solving life's mysteries. Katarina and I spent the day before naked and in bed, mostly. We were occasionally forced by hunger to stray out for food and drink, noting the spinning of the earth only by the waxing and waning of the sunlight streaming through her bedroom window. Interrupted periodically by text messages from my sons or her business partner, we each answered promptly in order to keep outside disturbances to a minimum and relieve some of the attendant guilt stemming from doing nothing productive all day. I retained some of that guilt as I unloaded my brief case and turned on my work computer. From past experience I understood the faster I dove into my work day the faster the guilt would be alleviated. To that end I had left Katarina's apartment before sunrise in order to arrive at the office earlier than usual. As yet mine was the only office on the floor in which a light was burning and the branch downstairs was devoid of life as well. Alone and in "nose to the grindstone" mode, the sound of my phone ringing nearly startled me out of my chair. It was Katarina.

"I miss you this morning, Jason. I want you back in my bed." Her voice had the sound of early-morning-just-woke-up-still-in-bed-and-naked.

"You know I'd love to be back in your bed," I could feel myself smiling. "But we have to work sometime. Or at least I do." I made sure the last sentence sounded jokey.

"I know you are right, Jason. I must go to work also." She sounded sincerely disappointed. "May I see you later today? Will you have lunch with me? I have to come to the bank for business anyway."

"Anything I can help you with? And lunch would be great."

"Yes, Jason. I need to open another account. Can you do that?" Now she sounded alert. She must have gotten out of bed.

"I can do that…whatever you need." Technically, my job no longer involved opening accounts or even dealing with customers directly, and hadn't since I moved to the credit side of banking. I was still allowed to open them, however, or at least suspected that was the case. And bringing more business into the bank was a feather in the cap of whoever managed to do it.

"Then I will come to see you at eleven? And then I will buy you lunch."

"Eleven will be fine. And thank you in advance for lunch." Katarina had hit on two of my current weaknesses – her and free food.

With the conversation over I refocused on the tasks at hand. As coworkers began to stream in the building started to breathe with life. And if anyone noticed the uncharacteristically early start to my day it was not brought to my attention, my presence being noted only by the greetings of random passers-by. Stephen, who was nearly always at work before me, wandered in after the branch opened looking slightly hung over.

"Rough night, soldier?" I wandered into Stephen's office to amuse myself. It was rare to see him like this.

"You could say so." He was slightly hunched over his desk with his chin resting on one hand. "The wife and I decided to go out for a night cap and ended up having four or five. Maybe six. We took a cab home and had to go back and get the car this morning."

"Well aren't you just the solid citizen. Is that why you're late?"

"Nope. I'm late because we needed to sleep in, so how about getting the hell out of my office so I can get some work done." He sounded gruff but not too serious. "Or maybe I'll just take a nap on my couch…"

"I think either would be fine." I was working hard not to laugh. "I'll cover for you if you want to crash. Quick question, though. Am I still allowed to open deposit accounts?"

"Well, you're an officer in the bank and you know how to do it, right?" I nodded in the affirmative. "Good. Now get out, please."

I couldn't say no to such a pleasant invitation to vacate Stephen's office so I went back to my own. Emily did not acknowledge my passing. Her head was down as well and I couldn't tell if she was asleep, intently reading or texting. Probably the latter. It was possible I was the only one in the vicinity who had their wits about them. It was a self-satisfying moment, broken only by the sound of Izzy ringing in to my office phone.

"Hey, Izzy. Good timing. Guess who's hung over?" Our communication had been working its way back to something resembling normal.

"Emily?" This response normally would have been the correct one.

"Nope"

"You?" This was another strong possibility.

"Nope. Wrong again. It is our fearless leader, although Emily might be. I can't confirm that at this time."

"No shit!" Izzy was laughing. "That's weird. Did you get the dirt?"

"Only that he and the wife went out for a few drinks and things got a little out of hand. He's banking on a mid-day nap to relieve some of the sting. How's your day?"

"Not as interesting as yours, I'll bet. What else is going on over there?" She sounded loose and easy going. The tension between us seemed to be gone completely.

"Not much. Katarina is coming in to open a business account today. She's supposed to take me out to lunch."

"Oh, really? Where are you going for lunch?" The tension was back. What was I thinking? Izzy didn't want or need to know any of my goings-on with Katarina. I could feel myself sweating.

"Oh…you know…just somewhere around here. No big deal." I was consciously trying to reduce my exposure to this conversation but Izzy was having none of it.

"You know, you could send her to my branch to open those business accounts. It would look good for me and I could meet her in person." I was still sweating despite the wave of cold erupting from my office phone.

"Thanks for offering Izzy but I'm sure I can handle it here. Plus, you know, we've got the…lunch…thing…." My words were faltering. I needed to get off the phone. "Oh, hey, Izzy. Stephen is calling. I better talk to him. I'll let you know how he handles the rest of the day!" Stephen was not calling and I was definitely not going to call Izzy back that day.

"You'd better." Izzy hung up, leaving me to wonder what I'd "better" do. Her tone indicated a myriad of possibilities that had nothing to do with Stephen's hangover. Regardless, I was happy to have escaped the phone call.

I let the rest of the morning flow past without really taking notice. After the phone call with Izzy I buried my head in work in order to give myself something to think about that didn't involve women, emotions, or close interpersonal relationships. That was the simple beauty of my job. I could sit in my second-floor office and never actually meet the people for whom I was making potentially life altering decisions. I either granted a loan request or denied it based on the customer's ability to pay, their time in business, their asset base and any number of other factors, none of which involved my personal feelings for or against them. I could do my job and never touch or even know the people my decisions were affecting

214

and it was exactly what I needed at that moment and at many others. The messiness of interacting with the other humans in my life did not play out at my desk. Indeed, I could avoid it altogether quite simply by not answering my phone and leaving my door shut. I could be isolated for hours at a time, the isolation interrupted only by the need to eat or void my bowels. And although a text or call from my child or a loved one might be welcome, I could count on serene loneliness returning at the end of the call. My musings on the topic were occurring in the back of my head as I threw my focus at the files in front of me. Yet the blessed solitude was brazenly interrupted by Emily, who respected no boundaries, if indeed she noticed them at all.

"Katarina is downstairs for you." Her voice was not nearly as tense as Izzy's had been. In fact, Emily was sounding giggly again, like we were sharing a secret. Maybe we were.

"Thanks, Em. Let her know I'll be right down, please." With that I stood and left my office to retrieve Katarina feeling not nearly as happy as I thought I should. As I walked down the steps the sense of unease was unmistakable, but I rationalized this sense of misgiving was not so much a result of Katarina's arrival as it was a byproduct of my conversation with Izzy. I wanted things to be right with her but I didn't know how to make that happen, hence the vague feelings of anxiety taking root in my chest and stomach. The fact Katarina's arrival coincided with the end of the conversation with Izzy was merely an unlucky synchronism, or so I told myself. Why would the sight of Katarina standing expectantly in the lobby bring me anything but joy? She of the long days of nudity and attentive, unbridled sex could bring me nothing but goodwill. And there she was wearing tight jeans, a form fitting short-sleeved shirt and knee high, heeled boots. She was a vision of fashion and carnality all rolled up in a Russian doll. The doll kissed me on the cheek when I reached her, drawing the attention of the tellers and a couple customers.

"Is that ok?" I think she was only asking to be polite. I don't think she gave one whit about bank protocol as it concerned employee's public displays of affection.

"Of course." I was smiling but felt my face flush slightly. Not even Kim had ever kissed me during work hours. Of course, that could have been because she was gay. Who knows?

I took Katarina's hand and led her to the elevator without asking her about taking the stairs, the use of which would have removed us from public view more quickly. She did not object to the elevator and never let go of my hand, gazing at me with her beautiful smile. Emily did not stop staring as I introduced her to Katarina and I assumed had he not been sleeping on his office couch Stephen would have been out of his office trying to make it look like he wasn't gawking as well. After a quick exchange of pleasantries I led Katarina into my office and shut the door behind me.

"I'm so happy to see you at work!" I was, indeed, feeling more upbeat about her arrival than I had ten minutes prior. "Shall we get those accounts open and grab some lunch?"

"Of course, Jason, but…first things first." Katarina was staring at me from across my desk in the same way I would occasionally catch her staring at me from across the bed.

"Um…what did you have in mind?" Writing this I realize now it sounds like a bad line from a porn but I couldn't come up with anything better.

"I want you to come sit on your couch with me." Like Stephen I had a couch in my office. I glanced at my office door and was relieved the mini-blinds were already closed, thereby relieving me of at least one task that might cause suspicion on the other side of the blinds.

"Um…ok." I wanted to play along but the words weren't coming. I did, however, make my way to Katarina, who was already on the couch.

Without a word she began to undress me, starting with my tie. At the moment I was participating in no way other than to let her do whatever she was going to do. I had never done anything like this at work and was stunned and excited by what was happening. Before I knew it there was nothing left on my body but socks and Katarina had managed to strip down to nothing. As she straddled me she wrapped her arms around my neck, burying my head in her chest. I pulled her head back by her hair as the scent of her skin again overwhelmed me. My mouth worked to take in as much of her as possible. Soon the location of our love making didn't matter and even the soft moaning emanating somewhere from deep inside of Katarina didn't register as something I needed to fear. She just kept working her magic, sliding her body rhythmically over mine until all

I could see was her. I didn't come to my senses until after I finished (which is when all men come to their senses.) Even then part of me wanted to keep her naked as long as possible, thinking the world would be a better place if Katarina never wore clothes.

"Wow. Thank you for that." I was still holding her against me, fighting the competing urges of taking her again and wanting to put my clothes on before we got caught. "And this sounds weird, but shall we go ahead and open those accounts now?"

Katarina started laughing as she pulled herself slightly away from me. "You are funny, Jason. And thank you, too. You must know that I want you all the time. But certainly let us do our business as soon as possible!"

I don't know why it was suddenly so important to stay on a schedule. I was feeling uncomfortable, I think largely because I had never been naked in my office before that day. But no one was going to disturb us and should someone have attempted to drop in unexpectedly they would have found the door locked, thanks to Katarina's foresight. Still, for some reason I wanted to get things moving. As soon as we got our clothes back on I quietly unlocked the door and began filling out papers with Katarina. She opened the accounts with $8000 in cash. I thought it unusual for someone to carry around so much money but in previous discussions of her business she told me how she would often pay for cars in cash as it eliminated the step of waiting for a check to clear. Not a great reason but it seemed good enough for someone like me who had little experience in the export of vehicles to foreign countries. Regardless I took her money, passport and signed papers downstairs to the teller windows, and deposited the money. The teller who did the work, Cindy, didn't bat an eye despite the large amount of cash, probably because it was me doing the opening. But I found her confidence and lack of inquisitiveness comforting, especially because I felt ready to break out in a cold sweat the entire time I stood waiting for her to finish her part of the work. Katarina, on the other hand, was unfazed and spent the time jabber-jawing with Cindy.

With the inexplicably painful experience of opening Katarina's account behind me, I was happy to get her out of the bank and into a restaurant, which represented the last step necessary to getting her on her way back to her job and away from mine. I'd figured out early in my marriage to Kim I didn't enjoy the convergence of the two worlds of home and work and Katarina's entrance into my life hadn't changed my position on the matter. My sense of relief upon exiting was palpable though Katarina either did not notice or chose not to comment. Regardless, we made it safely next door to the Macaroni Grille to eat our meal. It was my weekend with the boys and although I wasn't consciously limiting their exposure to Katarina I was somewhat relieved when she told me for that weekend she could only stay at my place through Saturday night. She was leaving town for work on Sunday, she explained, and would not be back for four or five days. I didn't recognize it as such at the time, but I've come to believe the arrival of this circumstance meant the universe was trying to help us out. It would seem the universe felt we, or at least I, needed a chance to regain some perspective. I didn't take the hint.

Trevor and Alex were boisterous when Kim dropped them off Saturday morning. Katarina was still asleep in the bedroom when they arrived but I did not try to quiet them down. I was happy to see them happy and happy Kim actually brought them to my place. It had become habit that I almost always ferried the boys back and forth between residences. I managed to get Kim to bring them this time only by countering her passive aggressiveness with even more deft passive aggressiveness. The conversation went something like this:

Kim: "So what time are you picking up the boys?" Note her assumption. I could hardly blame her, however, since I had been falling for this trap for months.
Me: "Oh. Sorry! I've got an early morning thing. You can bring them over any time after nine, thanks."
Kim: "Uh….ok…"

Kim had always sucked at asking me directly for favors and I sucked at making her, so she could do nothing but agree with my assumption the way I had been agreeing with hers. Of course, I suppose I could have just directly asked her to bring the boys over, but this was more fun. I also figured this method was better for conflict avoidance, which might have been Kim's position as well. Nevertheless I got what I wanted and saved gas in the process.

Upon entering the apartment the boys threw their backpacks down in the middle of the living room and took positions at the pass through window in the kitchen.

"Hey, Dad, can we have some breakfast? We didn't eat at Mom's." Apparently Trevor had chosen himself for the task of food gathering.

"Why didn't you eat at Mom's?" I was having one of those holier-than-thou moments divorced parents get when the other parent has obviously failed in one of the basic tasks of parenting. Unlike Kim, I thought to myself, I would NEVER allow my children to go hungry.

"She asked us but we didn't get hungry until we were on our way over here." Trevor burst my ego bubble as quickly as it had been inflated. Ah well, maybe Kim wouldn't starve them either. At least not on purpose.

The three of us decided pancakes were an excellent way to start the day and we gabbed and shared stories from the week as I labored in the kitchen. I made them aware of Katarina's physical location and slumbering condition and agreed it would be a good idea not to wake her up until the pancakes were finished. Since moving out I had learned to make a number of food items the boys and I liked, but my favorite and theirs was pancakes from scratch. Pancakes from scratch take but a few minutes longer than pancakes from a box but are superior in taste and texture. Plus the extra prep time lends itself to quiet conversation. Once the concoction of pancake ingredients was sufficiently soupy I recruited Alex to pour the batter and put Trevor in charge of flipping. What resulted were pancakes of a variety of shapes, sizes and colors that would each prove tasty in their own way. While they were working on the second batch I snuck out to wake Katarina.

"Wake up, sleepy head." I was holding her hand and speaking barely above a whisper, wondering why I was speaking just above a whisper when the idea was to wake her up. Thankfully Katarina stirred before I was forced to reassess my tactics.

"Good morning…" She looked lovely with tousled hair and no clothes.

"Good morning. Breakfast is almost ready. Would you like to join us?"

"Of course, Jason. Thank you. I will be out in just a moment."

"Sounds good, but I do think it's a shame to make you put clothes on." Katarina smiled at the comment. I really wasn't concerned she would saunter around in the buff in front of my children. Well, not as long as she knew they were there.

When I returned to the kitchen the boys had set out plates and seemed anxious about pleasing my overnight guest. All eyes were on Katarina, adorably dressed in one of my t-shirts and a pair of my boxers, as she took the first bite.

"These must be the best pancakes I have ever eaten!" The boys smiled ear to ear as they dug into their own stacks. It was quite a contented scene. Katarina was patient and forthcoming as the boys again peppered her with questions about her childhood and family in Russia. And she made a point to grill them about their interests. I was left mainly to observe and enjoy their interaction.

"Trevor, do you have a girlfriend?" Katarina was leaning toward Trevor with a wry smile as his face flushed red.

"Oh...I don't know. I might..." Trevor's voice trailed off as he tried not to answer.

Alex decided to clarify the situation for all concerned. "He wants to ask Leslie Borgman to be his girlfriend but he's afraid she'll say no."

"Alex! I told you not to tell anyone. I'm never telling you anything again!" Trevor's face was even redder, if that was possible.

"Well, Trevor, let us talk about Leslie and see if she likes you or not, hmmm?" Trevor shook his head in the affirmative. "Does she talk to you in your class when the students are supposed to be listening?"

"Ummm, yes, I guess so."

"And does she talk to you in the hall way? Does she always seem to be around?"

Trevor was gaining confidence. "It seems like it. What does that mean?"

"It means you should ask her to be your girlfriend and she will say yes. I know this to be true. Do you believe me?" Trevor nodded again. It occurred to me this woman could get any man to believe anything she said, and that after listening to the back and forth with Trevor I was as convinced as he that Leslie Borgman would indeed say yes should Trevor pop the question. "So if you like her Leslie must be a very cute girl, yes?" She had Trevor in the palm of her hand. Had he had any real secrets he would have revealed them immediately.

"Well, I think so."

"And what else to do you like about her?" Before long Katarina had Trevor blathering about what sports Leslie played, where she lived and her part in the school play. She managed to find out more about Trevor's love life in 15 minutes than I had in a month. I realized I would have to get better at communicating with my own kids or at least keep Katarina around to do it for me. At the moment my mood was such that I was very open to the latter, which seemed to have positive implications beyond just getting to better know my children. I continued to listen as I cleaned up the evidence of our morning labors from the table and kitchen. Katarina made it a point to engage Alex as well, finding out his teacher's name, with whom he usually ate lunch and what he liked best about school. We were all under her spell by the time the last plate was placed in the dishwasher.

As I walked into the office that Friday morning I felt lighter than air. Katarina was due back that evening and the week had thus far unfolded without crisis. I didn't have the boys that night and was sorry I didn't for more than the usual reasons. The interaction between Katarina and my sons had grown natural and easy going and they had begun to look forward to her presence at dinner as much as I did. Trevor was especially pleased because Katarina's assessment of Leslie Borgman's affection for him turned out to be true. They were now officially "going out." And this was an easy enough arrangement mainly involving texting and talking more at school. Since Trevor was years away from driving I did not worry about an unwanted pregnancy. There would be plenty of time for that later.

Emily appeared before me as I set my brief case down. "Joyce needs to talk to you about those new accounts." She acted as if it was no big deal, at least to her, but the fact the branch manager needed to talk to me about the only deposit accounts I had opened in years had a slight chilling effect. I had the sinking feeling my crisis free week might be in danger of ending.

"How come?" I tried to sound unhurried, keeping my focus down on my desk. Surely Emily noticed my discomfort as I methodically started turning a big pile of paper into smaller piles of paper.

"I don't know, Jason. You probably did something wrong." What? What could I have done wrong? "You know, probably got a signature wrong or something like that. You said you hadn't opened accounts in a long time, so...."

Emily's facile assessment of the situation caused me to brighten. Maybe she was right. She was certainly right about the opportunities for mistakes for someone who hadn't opened accounts for years. Rules change. Laws change. Forms change. That was probably all that was wrong. Joyce was simply reviewing new accounts from the week before and found a glitch in the paperwork. No problem.

"I'll handle it, thanks Em. If she calls up here again please tell her I'll be down in a few minutes." The strain in my voice was miniscule relative to a minute before.

"Okey dokey, smokey." What? Was Emily trying on a new catch phrase? I didn't ask because I wanted her to clear out of my office and worried the answer to such a question would take considerably longer than I was prepared to listen. My lack of curiosity was rewarded by Emily's quick exit but I walked to the stairwell as if walking on pins. Why was I so nervous? I was nervous because there was part of me that understood I should have done a better job checking out Katarina's business and what they did with their money. Although not unheard of small businesses don't generally keep their money in different banks unless they are suffering from the "don't keep all your eggs in one basket" virus. Mostly it's just an accounting hassle.

Joyce waved me into her office as soon as she saw me in wandering across the lobby. She didn't look overly concerned or upset and I took this as a good sign. I plopped down in a chair across her desk from her.

"Hey Joyce, Emily said you needed to see me?" I think I sounded pleasant enough.

"I do, Jason. It's about that accounts you opened for Auto International last week. Have you been tracking that customer at all?" She was holding the account documents in her hands but not looking at them.

"Well, no...not really. I mean, they've had accounts with us for a while, right? Katarina...um, Ms. Smolenska asked me to open up a couple more last week." My antiperspirant appeared to be failing. I wondered if Joyce would notice.

"Katarina? The girl you've been dating?" I was having problems discerning the meaning behind Joyce's smile. Was she amused by my awkward attempt to misrepresent my relationship with Katarina? And if that were the case, was it because she thought it was "cute" or because she was suspicious? "She's a cutie, huh?"

"Well, I think so." I tried to smile, too. Was she toying with me?

"Listen, Jason. I know it's not really your job so maybe it's not surprising that you haven't paid much attention to this company, especially considering your relationship with....Ms. Smolenska." Joyce winked at me in a way that exuded familiarity and understanding, but I sat frozen in anticipation, knowing that whatever was coming was not going to be good. "But I need to tell you, they move a lot of money around and bring in a lot cash. Not enough to where we have to report it, at least not until now. After you opened that new account the transfer volume increased to where we've had to report it to the Feds." She stopped smiling and lowered her voice before continuing. "And you should know I've reported it to Stephen. You may want to talk to him as soon as you can. There's a good chance you're involved in a money laundering scheme, maybe with the Russian mob. We've seen it before. Do you understand?"

CHAPTER SIXTEEN

I did understand, but I didn't believe what I was hearing. I understood my legs were turning to mush, my sweat glands were busy emptying themselves into my arm pits and I was finding it difficult to breathe. And I was barely controlling an urge to run out of Joyce's office. What Joyce was telling me was that she suspected I had, wittingly or unwittingly, either become involved with or was a member of a money laundering operation. But how could this be possible? It couldn't be possible. I knew it couldn't be possible because I'm a good person and stuff like this doesn't happen to good people. Right? Meanwhile the office continued to spin around me as the implications of what Joyce was stumbling to articulate pounded me in the chest like riot control bean bags.

Convinced I would go flying from the chair at any moment, I kept my fingers locked on its arms. I knew it wasn't bolted to the floor but needed it to be. At some point my brain stopped working but, once revived, escape was again its overriding impulse. And at some point it became obvious my brain didn't understand I wasn't a criminal or that I could even be mistakenly involved with criminals. But what if my brain was right? If, indeed, my brain was right about me being a criminal (which, as would later be revealed, it was) it was still failing to understand the futility of flight or the part my crappy financial position played in that futility. To escape this type of thing one had to run fast and far. With ignorant prescience I had often joked that, had I been blessed with the character flaws necessary to make it possible, the minimum amount I was willing to steal was ten million dollars. My rationale was that if one was going to steal money it should be of sufficient amount to get out of the country post haste and settle in a place with no extradition treaty. The few hundred dollars I had in savings was barely enough to get me to Chicago, let alone Brazil.

Feeling trapped I could do little else than sit speechless, hoping Joyce didn't notice the panic exuding from my every pore. Everything was moving in slow motion, like it does in the midst of a car wreck, but the extra time this adrenaline burst allowed for a proactive reaction was wasted. I was in no condition to do anything proactive. What it did do, however, was make the next ten seconds seem like ten minutes. I felt I had been motionless for so long Joyce would surely begin to think I had suffered an aneurism or been overtaken by some other malady of commensurate proportion. I had to find a way to make my mouth move.

"Thanks for the heads up, Joyce. I'll get with Steve ASAP." Did I really say ASAP? I was trying to sound matter-of-fact but the acronym just sounded stupid. Despite the jello-legs I managed to get up and walk out of Joyce's office without collapsing, striding somewhat unsteadily toward the patiently waiting elevator, its doors open and inviting.

If Emily acknowledged me as I shuffled past her desk I did not notice it. I wasn't sure if she yet knew what was transpiring but I knew if she didn't she soon would. News travelled fast between the floors. My shame would soon be public knowledge. At the moment all I wanted to do was make it to my office and shut the door. The office didn't represent a safe haven, indeed, far from it. It was, however, a place where I could think, at least for a few minutes. When I got there it occurred to me I didn't know if Stephen would want to see me immediately or even if he was in the bank. I hadn't seen his car when I arrived earlier. If he wasn't there it was possible the universe had granted me some sort of short term reprieve. Would it give me time to fix things? Did I even know how to fix things? First things first. I needed to find out if Stephen was in without drawing attention to the fact I was trying find out if Stephen was in. I took the chance that Emily was still in the dark as to my new status as King of the Shit List and dialed her extension.

"What's up, Jason?" Her voice seemed to indicate she had not yet been made privy to the new grist in the rumor mill.

"Hey, Emily, do you know if Stephen's in this morning? He's not answering and I'm too lazy to walk over there." Did I sound natural? Breezy? Doubt it.

"Nope. Stephen called and said he wouldn't be in today. He's sick or his wife's sick or somebody in his family is sick. I'm

225

not quite sure." Emily's incompetence was working in my favor for a change. But now what? I was probably safe for the day. I figured if he was overly concerned Stephen would have already attempted to contact me. At least if he was not dealing with some type of family emergency or other serious occurrence. I mean, money laundering is a super big deal. I was sure if Stephen thought I was helping Katarina launder money he'd be knocking down my door. I dialed Emily's extension again.

"Hey, Em." I was probably trying too hard to sound natural but Emily didn't seem to notice. "Are you sure you don't remember why Stephen's not in today?"

"Nope. I just remember somebody saying something about somebody being sick. He didn't call me."

"Okay, thanks Emily." I didn't expect Emily to know any more than she had already related but my need to do "something" overrode my knowledge of well-established work habits. Having no practical experience on the laundering side of money laundering (until now, of course) I knew I would need some outside advice. However, in addition to my own ignorance as to the ins-and-outs of money laundering I also lacked the acquaintance of anyone who might currently be involved in the field, let alone gotten themselves out of a money laundering pickle. I had no idea to whom I should turn. So, lacking ideas and or anything resembling what could otherwise be construed as a plan, my mind went manic. Myriad thoughts rushed through my stupid brain, not the least germane of which was some theory I had heard a couple weeks before on the radio. The theory went something like this: In a crisis, 10% of the people involved will do exactly the right thing, 10% will do exactly the wrong thing, and the other 80% will wait to be told what to do. At the moment there was only one person involved in my personal/professional crisis: me. That being the case and considering there was no one yet available to tell me what to do, I was confident I would find a way to be included in the 10% that make exactly the wrong decision. Finally a light bulb lit over my head, dim though it may have been. I did indeed know at least one person involved in a money laundering scheme: Katarina. And at the moment Katarina had at least two of the three qualities I was looking for in an advice giver. She had experience with problem (money laundering) and she would answer when I called. The third quality was trust, which was sorely lacking. So, if I called her, in which 10% would I end up? To the best of my knowledge Katarina had, as yet, not worked her way out of a money laundering pickle, so would calling her be the right thing or the wrong thing? In a blessed moment of clarity, I realized it didn't really matter. She couldn't make things any more abysmal, which meant at worst the outcome of the phone call would be neutral. And at the very least she'd have the opportunity to give me some sort of explanation. Whether or not she would take that opportunity was a different question altogether.

As I ruminated on the call to Katarina I was caught short by the growing pile of evidence pointing to a loss of intestinal fortitude. What happened, after all, to my balls? Why was I hiding in my office, the cowardly anti-hero, instead of taking the bull by the horns? The thought seemingly popped in from nowhere, but it was a powerful epiphany. When, exactly, had I given up my manhood in favor of panic, fear, and indecision? And I wasn't just including the last thirty minutes of my life as proof of my lack of valor. To get to that moment I had to have suffered a series of degrading incidents, trickling though my life over the course of months or (more likely) years, unremarked and unnoticed. They must have gone unnoticed because had I been paying attention I most certainly would have made the adjustments necessary to keep me from arriving at such a dark place. Wouldn't I? If so the question remained: Through what series of unfortunate events had I arrived here, at my desk in a cold sweat, worried that a generally incompetent underling would find out about my predicament and perhaps judge me as a result? My hands stopped sweating and my breathing steadied as I searched within for the person I believed myself to be, as opposed to the person I had presumably become. For good measure I took some time to flog myself for having arrived at this cowardly moment, believing from past experience it would work to steel my nerve. I imagined Arthur ordering me to "sack up", advice I had never felt compelled to give to him. Luckily my self-loathing-cum-flagellation did the trick and before I knew it was picking up the phone to call Katarina, who I was sure had grown horns and a tail since last I'd seen her. Perhaps she had even developed a taste for human souls. I couldn't be sure.

"Jason?" She sounded normal to me, not at all like I imagined a destroyer of worlds would sound.

I dove right in. "Katarina.... What the hell is going on? Bad things have been happening to me at work today. Bad things because of you. Tell me what's going on. What have you gotten me in to?" I sounded more demanding than plaintive, a tone with which I was pleased.

"What do you mean?" Her voice was edgy but controlled.

"You know exactly what I mean. You've been laundering money through the bank and

I helped you do it. Why the fuck would you do that to me?" I was going to have to be careful. I was starting to sound needy. From the other end of the phone I could only hear breathing. "Katarina, just tell me what's going on."

"Jason....Jason I am sorry..." Her voice trailed off.

"What are you sorry about? Please, Katarina. Tell me something!" There was the neediness again.

"Jason...I am sorry that I made you involved. I did not know I would care about you and that maybe you would care about me." Annoyingly I still found her English-as-a-second-language somewhat beguiling.

She went on from there and told me the whole story. She was doing the bidding of some faction of the Russian mob and, of course, the business of shipping cars to Russia after buying them in the U.S. was just a way to convert dirty money. She told me everything had been going fine for a couple years but then the volume of money began to increase. To cope with that her little group in Cincinnati initially thought to bring in a computer hacker. The hacker's job was to probe some of the smaller banks in the area to see if they could hide money somehow, but were surprised at how difficult that proved to be. In the end they just decided to expand on their existing modus operandi - keep multiple accounts at different banks and move the money around until no one would question where it came from. And everything was just peachy until the volume of laundry increased again.

Katarina and Friends knew that banks had limits on the cash they were allowed to handle in a transaction before they had to report it. To keep the dollar amounts under that limit she and her cohorts were forced to expand into banks with which they were unfamiliar, posing more risk to their operation. So, while Katarina was not a classically trained femme fatale she did possess sufficient self-awareness to know the opposite sex found her highly desirable. The group, with her acquiescence, decided to use this to their advantage. She then chose three banks at which she would attempt to identify and attract a male executive with the characteristics the cabal found suitable. I just happened to be the first person identified as having these all-important attributes, the selection of which demonstrates the genius of simplicity. The desired attributes were thus; 1) The target must be a branch manager or higher in the organization, 2) The target must be vulnerable to Katarina's charms. That was it. When I asked Katarina if the target at least had to be a man I was told no; that, quite frankly, she just believed a man would be easier to manipulate. Although untimely and inopportune, my first instinct was to protest her assertion on which sex was easier to enthrall. Certainly women were as susceptible as men to this type of come on. But I let it go without saying a word, walloped by the realization that such points of order had been rendered moot and a waste of time. I must admit, however, that despite everything that was happening, the byproduct of Katarina's admission to bisexuality produced a fleeting yet pleasantly powerful image of Katarina with another woman. Unfortunately this otherwise agreeable vision didn't stand up for long against the truth of Katarina's accusation of moral weakness. Man or woman, she had chosen well. Katarina's operation had been successful and she had found her stooge. Unfortunately for Katarina and her mates the stooge's coworkers were smarter than he. The dominoes would begin falling soon.

At some point during her recounting of the attempt to launder money through my bank Katarina began to cry and again express her regret for getting me involved. As I recall this was also around the time when I reached the end of my attention span. I cared for Katarina and, perhaps astonishingly, part of me wanted her to be ok, but by then I wasn't much inclined to feel bad that she felt bad about screwing me over. I made a half-hearted attempt to make sense of the words squeezing their way out between sobs but provided no words of my own to provide her any comfort. I mean, what was I going to tell her? That everything would be alright? That we could hook up again after we got out of jail? Was I going to tell her I loved her? Nope.

"Katarina…I have to go…. Good luck. I mean it." Those were my last words to Katarina. I would see her just one more time, but the circumstances would preclude us from striking up a conversation.

My conversation with Katarina left me feeling buzzy and unsatisfied. It had done nothing to help me solve my most immediate problem. Yes, my (now ex) lover came clean with her artifice, but while she provided intelligence heretofore unknown to me that intelligence did little to unravel the ball of yarn in which I was trapped. In light of this my next call was to another (ex) lover whose experience might be useful. I called Izzy. Initially, at least, I did not find the sound of her voice reassuring.

"Holy shit, Jason. What the fuck is going on over there?" Evidently the rumor mill had begun exporting product.

"I think I've gotten myself into some pretty big trouble, Izzy. Bigger than I know how to handle." As I confessed the entire story to Izzy I found my voice to be remarkably calm. I don't know if the initial shock had begun to wear off or because talking to Izzy always seemed to make me feel better, even when faced with jail time. As far as I could tell Izzy was listening attentively on the other end of the phone. She did not interrupt, gasp in surprise, or give me a stern talking to. She merely listened until I finished my tale of woe. And then she asked the question for which I called her to get an answer.

"What are you going to do?" Her tone was humorless, which was to be expected, but also distracted, like she had been reading the newspaper at her desk while I rambled on about my poor judgment. Perhaps Izzy had already decided she did not want to hitch her wagon to a sinking ship, or maybe she had finally had enough of me, or both. Who could blame her?

"Well...I was hoping you could help me with that. I have no idea what I'm supposed to do." I never wanted to hurt Izzy and she had to know that, but it sure didn't sound like My Drinking Buddy Izzy on the other end of the phone. I had a feeling if there was such a thing as Vindictive Izzy I was about to meet her.

"Well, Jason," She paused and I was sure I heard the sound of newspaper ruffling. "I don't really have anything for you." Damn! Did she already call the police on me? Was Izzy aware of and trying to collect a reward for my capture?

"You 'don't have anything' for me? What the hell, Izzy? You know what, if you want to treat me like shit right now that's fine. I probably deserve it but I don't have time for it. I'll try to call you later and you can be bitchy to me until you get it all out of your system. How about that?" I really was pissed off.

"No…wait, don't hang up. Please Jason." Her tone changed. "Listen, I only caught wind of this a few minutes before you called and I guess I was, or I am, angry. I'm angry because you're so stupid and you never had to be."

"I know I'm stupid, Iz. Don't you think I know that? How could I not? And I know things haven't really been right between us for months and I'd love to fix that but right now I need help, ok? Just tell me if you can think of anything that might help."

There was a long pause before she spoke again. I could discern no paper rustling. "I'm sorry sweetie, but I've got no experience with this sort of thing. If I were you I'd probably go ahead and turn myself in. Maybe get a lawyer and try to make a deal." Her voice grew softer as she continued speaking. "You know I love you, Jason, but I don't really know what I can do for you right now, even though I want to do something. I really wish you had come to me with this before now. I would have given you the right advice. Maybe you'd even have taken it." She paused again. Her voice had lost all of the sense of agitation it had conveyed at the beginning of our conversation. She now sounded as if she were close to tears. "It's all so weird, isn't it?"

"I guess 'weird' is one way to describe it. 'Surreal' would be another." I knew she was talking about more than just what had happened that day, I just didn't have time dive into it with her. "But listen, thanks for answering the phone. I've got to go but if you think of something please call me."

"Hey!"

"What is it, Izzy?"

"Listen, this may not help with the big picture but I think you need to get out of there right now, at least if you're not going to turn yourself in. You caught a break with Stephen out. I don't think anybody will make a move without his ok and, besides, he probably won't turn you in until he has a chance to talk to you anyway. You might be ok but I wouldn't take any chances. You should go home and ride out the weekend there. You know, 'out of sight out of mind.'"

I didn't have to spend much time thinking about it to realize Izzy's assessment was spot on. "You're right, Iz. I'll get out of here now."

"And call Arthur."

"Why?" I only asked because I wanted to know why SHE thought I should call him. I would have done it without any prompting.

"I don't know. He's just got all that weird life experience. Maybe he knows something that will come in handy."

"Thanks, Izzy…thanks. I promise to call you when I've figured something out." I would, too.

"Call me even if you don't. I do love you, Jason. You know that, right?" Izzy's words were heartfelt. I could not give her the response she deserved because the response she deserved would have taken hours, maybe days.

"I know, Iz. I love you, too." I hung up the phone and scuttled out of the office without pausing for pleasantries. I imagined, as I walked out of the building and into the parking lot, dozens of eyes boring into the back of my head. True or not I did not turn to find out, believing such an action would make my exit somewhat less dignified, as if that were possible.

I did not listen to the radio nor call anyone as I drove back to Western Hills and though the distance home appeared to have increased from what it had been the day before my trek did not pass without incident. Not long after merging onto I-74 from I-75 I noticed a white Buick coming to a complete stop on the shoulder of the highway. Being an older model Buick I naturally assumed the driver would be well past retirement age and, recalling my vow from months before not to pass on an opportunity to help a stranded driver, I worked my way across the lanes and pulled in behind the disabled LeSabre. My view of the interior of the Buick confirmed I was correct in my assumption concerning the age of the driver. A mane of thick, gray hair was clearly visible.

"Ma'am? Ma'am?" I tapped the window gently so as not to frighten the car's single inhabitant, a well-manicured lady in her mid-70's. She was smartly dressed, as if she had just come from some sort of board meeting or breakfast appointment. She looked at me and rolled her window down a crack. "Ma'am? I just saw you pull over. Is there anything I can do to help?"

"I think I've got a flat tire. It felt like one of the tires started going flat a while ago. I was just going to call my husband to come and get me." She brandished her cell phone to make her point.

"Well, if you like I'll go ahead and check out your tires while you're calling your husband. Shall I?" I was speaking into the crack she created between the door frame and the top of the window. I was somewhat insulted by her distrust but really couldn't blame her. She couldn't be sure I wasn't a pervert or thug despite my attire. I was a criminal, after all. Although had I told her I was only a money launderer I feel confident she would have lost her fear altogether and volunteered to look at her tires with me. White collar criminals aren't very intimidating.

"Sure, dear. That would be fine." She waved permission with her left hand and focused her attention on her cell phone. In my best don't-get-hit-by-a-passing-car manner I gingerly paced around the LeSabre. A visual inspection revealed four new tires, none of which was sans oxygen.

"Ma'am?" I was back at the crack. "I don't think there's anything wrong with your tires. They all look just fine to me. Why did you think one had gone flat?"

As far as I could tell she still hadn't got hold of her husband. "Well, I hit a bump back there and the car, well, the car just didn't feel right after I hit the bump." She paused. "I know that sounds silly but I didn't want to take any chances."

"I don't think it's silly, ma'am, but I think you're ok to drive home. Maybe your husband can check them again for you." Though my ass is not overly large I couldn't escape the feeling it was hanging out into the highway, just waiting to get sliced off by a fast moving vehicle. Indeed, I was being buffeted by the turbulence created by passing vehicles. As a result I huddled close to the car and the window crack, shifting my weight from foot to foot attempting to lower my ass' profile.

"That's very kind of you, young man. I think I will do just that. Thank you very much for your help." She seemed sincere even as she eliminated the crack through which we had been communicating.

"You're welcome!" I yelled back through the closed window. I felt good about my behavior. I had lived up to a promise I made to myself and maybe garnered some good karma even though the lady really didn't need any help. Of course, any good karma I had coming would probably be too little, too late and likely be overwhelmed by all the bad karma. Nonetheless I arrived home feeling calmer than I had all morning.

My otherwise smallish apartment felt cavernous. Perhaps it was because I was not used to being there in the middle of the day. Indeed, the energy level of the whole complex was truant. Gazing out the glass doors I half expected to see a tumble weed roll by. Regardless, I plopped down on the couch and took stock of the day so far. It wasn't good and no amount of rationalizing was going to make it better. It occurred to me to call Kim to let her know our sons' father may well be in jail soon. It was Kim's weekend with them but the possibility of a sudden onset of jail time made me anxious to see them in person. Whether I made the effort to see the boys or not I knew I should definitely clue their mother in to the possibility she might soon have full custody. And over the course of the next hour or so the idea of "putting my affairs in order" took on very real meaning, not just as a line one sees in movies when a character is about to leave on a long journey or make the ultimate sacrifice. I went through all the things that might be left as loose ends should I be unceremoniously hauled off to jail and came to the conclusion that, luckily, I had few assets with which anyone would have to deal. Indeed, divorce had simplified my life through a sort of Francis of Assisi cleansing, although the giveaway was somewhat less than voluntary. Regardless the effect was similar. My lack of possessions was actually a load off my mind. I figured the few items left could be dealt with from a jail cell or by friends and family.

I had yet to consult Arthur. Perhaps it was because he was no longer a banker or because he had never struck me as savvy in the handling of money. He was, after all, a notorious cheap skate and it's possible, after quietly accounting for this fact, I subconsciously deleted him from my list of possible helpers. On reflection, however, it suddenly seemed calling Arthur was the only logical thing to do. I had in fact given Arthur a key to my new digs soon after I moved in. He would at least have access to the apartment should the worst occur. His phone rang three times before he mercifully picked up. I did not think he might not be available on a Friday before lunch until the moment the phone started ringing.

"Jason…how are you?" Arthur sounded distracted, like I had caught him in the middle of something.

"Arthur, have you got a minute? I've got a lot to tell you." I wasn't sure how else to introduce a discussion my transgressions to my best friend.

"Of course, Jason. What is it?" I could tell whatever he was doing had been set aside.

Arthur gave me his full attention. Barely skipping a beat, I launched once again into the story of my impending downfall. Arthur listened attentively, interrupting only occasionally to ask questions like "This is the Russian bird, right?" Some questions were more pointed than others, like when he asked me how many people were involved on Katarina's side of the scheme. There were a couple times during our conversation I could have sworn he was taking notes. He made no mention of it, he just seemed generally focused on the details of the story. At the end, as with others, there was silence on the other end of the phone.

"What do you think? I mean, shit Arthur, I know there's nothing you can do here but you've got a key to the apartment and if I'm hauled off I need you to take care of anything in here that needs to be taken care of. And if you've got any advice here…." I let my voice trail off as Arthur's silence continued a few moments longer.

"Let's get drunk tonight." The statement was matter of fact and closed ended. I wondered if what I had just told him was registering in the way I had hoped.

"Sure. Why not. O'Hearn's?" I acquiesced easily. Arthur's solution was no worse than anything I had heard or thought of that day. It also had the advantage of simplicity.

"Of course. Hang in there, Jason. I'll see you at eight." Arthur hung up. I looked at the clock and I had exactly eight hours to kill before the ingenious plan of meeting at O'Hearn's to get drunk was to be fully implemented. I could think of nothing better to do in the intervening hours than to sleep, thinking this would stave off round two of the panic attack that had begun in Joyce's office four hours earlier. And was that only four hours ago? It seemed an age had passed since that moment. Exhausted but knowing sleep would not come easily I foraged for a sleeping pill, undressed and crawled into bed. Maybe when I woke up everything would be different.

Things weren't different when I woke. I got up anyway, mostly because lying in bed any longer seemed anathema to me. Going to O'Hearn's to meet Arthur meant I was at least doing "something", something other than waiting for fate to come calling. And if fate were to find me on that day better it find me in my favorite bar than sulking in bed. I dressed for an unspecial evening and made the short drive to O'Hearn's, finding Arthur waiting patiently on a bar stool.

"You're turn to buy." He said flatly. I took the stool next to him, noting the beer in front of him was nearly full.

"Fine. Am I buying that one there or the next one?" Why not buy beer all night? The dent in my newly formed legal fund would be slight as a result. Regardless, the fund existed only as a concept. Since moving out of the house months prior I had succeeded only in creating a "general fund" from which all my expenses were paid. The fund was also known as the "checking account."

Arthur turned slightly to face me. "Both."

"That's fine, Arthur, but I might be coming to you for a loan next week." But considering his job hopping and entrepreneurial failures I sincerely doubted Arthur had the wherewithal to contribute to my legal fund. I ordered the beers and let it go.

"So…." Arthur had something like a grimace on his face. "Sounds like you're in a bit of a pickle. Any plan of action? Any tactical or strategic maneuvers in the offing? Is there anything you haven't told me that you should have?"

But for Arthur's serious demeanor I wouldn't have otherwise taken his questions seriously. But he was serious so I considered each one. No, I told him, I hadn't formulated any plan of action or developed any "maneuvers" which might lead to a beneficial conclusion. Indeed no one, including Katarina, had thus far been able to offer me any real advice beyond turning myself in. "And, honestly Arthur, what could I possibly have not told you that I should have? I mean, how the hell am I supposed to know what I 'should' be telling you?" I probably sounded a little angry and for that I will always feel some regret. He really was trying to help.

"I don't know, Jason. I suppose I mean anything Katarina might have done or said in the last few months that would be relevant to your…current dilemma." Arthur locked his gaze on my own. "What things might have you forgotten? Were there things that happened or things of which you were aware that may have seemed like nothing at the time but might now seem relevant?"

The earnestness and odd professionalism Arthur displayed gave me pause. What had I missed? I wasn't sure, but with his permission I launched into as thorough a history of my relationship with Katarina as I could manage. Trying to recall as many details as possible, I gave him an almost day to day, blow by blow story line. As we drank I shared such things as wall hangings in her apartment to my impression of her partners and my own concerns about possibly having a hand in something…untoward. Throughout my commentary Arthur paid close attention and asked pointed questions. I couldn't remember a time when Arthur had been so focused on anything I had to say. Ever. But while that thought crossed my mind it did not coincidentally occur to me to ask him why he was suddenly taking such an interest in my travails. I just figured he was engrossed because to date it was certainly the most interesting thing I had shared with him about myself. Hell, I figured it was probably the most interesting thing that had ever happened to any of his friends. All I really knew at the time was that Arthur had suddenly become a genuinely good listener, and a genuinely good listener was enough. I had abandoned the hope that anyone in my current circle of friends could provide me with any useful insight apropos navigating myself out of the legal dilemma in which I was soon to be embroiled. Having coming to my senses after spending much of the day in a panic it was the only logical conclusion. And by the time I rendezvoused with Arthur the opportunity to lay it all out for prosperity's sake seemed productive relative to the rest of the day. Whether he knew it or not that was Arthur's gift to me that evening. No matter what happened next, Arthur was now the vessel carrying around the truth of my story, or at least the truth of my side of it. In fact I was so relieved by the opportunity to unburden myself that I didn't question Arthur's last words to me:

"Don't tell anyone else anything about this." We had just completed a man-hug (part handshake, part chest bump) in the parking lot. My reaction was uncomplicated.

"Ok."

I left O'Hearn's feeling calmly resigned to my fate. In less than a day life's prospects had changed from being rather blandly unknown to somewhat dreadfully sure. I had never been one to do much planning when it came to long term prospects. My life had tended to move along well enough for the last forty plus years to make it easy to assume it would continue to do so for the next forty. On the drive home, however, I found myself regretting not having been more proactive in identifying and achieving some life goals. This clarity of thought was, no doubt, brought on by the very real threat of incarceration, a condition to which all the goals I never set for myself would be subordinate. But I wasn't sure which seemed more bleak: The idea that I might soon have to abandon my life's ambitions or that I had no real ambitions to abandon.

By the time my head hit the pillow none of my philosophical ruminations on the meaning of my own life seemed to hold much water. In less than a day I had managed the five stages of grief and made it to "acceptance" (though I may have skipped "bargaining") and was as content with my new reality as I was ever going to be. The evening's sleep was disturbed only by the wailing of sirens rushing past on the main road near the apartment complex. I was relieved when they did not terminate their call in front of my building.

Kim generously allowed me to take the boys to lunch the next day. Per Arthur's instructions I did not to tell her anything, instead explaining my unusual request resulted simply from missing them and not wanting to wait until Monday to see them. All of this was true, of course, and she didn't act suspicious. Since establishing a schedule with Trevor and Alex and (finally) ironing out many of the details of the divorce our communication level had drastically diminished. We shared a sufficient level of mutual respect to feel confident each was treating the boys well and not exposing them to Bacchanalian orgies or satanic ceremonies. And I had ceased to care which sex she preferred or whom she may or may not be dating. For her part she appeared to share this apathy when it came to my love life. This impassivity regarding each other's life and livelihoods made it easy to avoid telling her about my newfound affinity for lawlessness, the knowledge of which might give her a good reason to rethink our shared-parenting agreement.

My lunch with the boys at the local Big Boy was as distraction-free as I could manage. They were boisterous but I made no effort to calm them down or get them to sit still until they began to disturb the people in the next booth over. Their bouncing around was rattling the shared seat-back between the booths. Our impromptu lunch had not interrupted any plans the boys may have had and they seemed happy to get out of the house, where they were apparently doing nothing more than playing video games and watching TV. At one point I found myself overwhelmed by this simple bit of information. I had been a bad example for them before I left the house, allowing my own unhappiness to turn me into a stereotype. Over the last year or so with Kim I regularly found myself in front of the television in the recliner, a la Archie Bunker, when I should have been interacting with my children. Now they were following suit in their own way and whether or not that was actually the case was irrelevant. Thoughts like that haunted me during lunch and on the drive back to Kim's house and despite the fact that in the grand scheme I truly believe I am a good father, it didn't matter much on that day. All the mistakes I made with my sons, real or perceived, were being amplified by the possibility that most or all of our interaction over the next few years might occur behind tall fences and razor wire. Upon dropping them off I hugged them until they complained of an inability to breathe and watched quietly until they were in the house. I decided to spend the rest of the weekend alone.

CHAPTER SEVENTEEN

It was Monday morning. I was greeted with the appalling clatter of a poorly tuned AM radio station emanating from the clock/radio. I felt confident I had slept because I was not awake when the alarm clock sounded, but it was an instance where I couldn't be sure of the actual volume of sleep achieved. If not for the surety of that first confused moment of waking I would have assumed I spent the entire evening either staring at the textured ceiling or ruthlessly adjusting the bedding. An impractical attempt to masturbate, undertaken hours before in order to aid in the effort to sleep, failed as I was unable to concentrate long enough to complete the act. I had foregone pacing around the room, which had never been my thing. Whenever I saw someone doing it in a movie I assumed it could only serve to wake them further. In the end I opted for tossing, turning and staring, broken up only occasionally by a fitful sleep. The high probability of walking into a hornet's nest was really putting a damper on things. I was crawling out of bed just as the phone rang. It was Rita Standwoegen.

"Rita?"

"Good morning, Jason." Her voice was as professional as ever. "Do you know what's going to happen at work this morning, Jason?"

"I have a pretty good idea, Rita, but we can compare notes if you want. And I'll even go first. I think I'll get arrested as soon as I hit the parking lot." I probably sounded sarcastic but didn't want to be.

"I don't think so, Jason. I don't think they'll arrest you right away. I don't think they'll arrest you at work. But I'll be honest with you Jason, I don't know." Those last three words were probably the most difficult Rita ever had to vocalize. I loved her for it. "I recommend you don't go to work until I can find out more. I'm sure I can find out something that will help you."

"Rita, I can't tell you how much I appreciate what you're trying to do, and I'll be honest with you too. I'm going to go ahead and go to work and let the chips fall. Honestly, I'm tired of waiting to see what's going to happen. I'm ready for it to happen, no matter what it is. But, damn Rita, how did you learn all this?"

"The same way I learn everything, Jason. People tell me things. I just wish you had come to me sooner. I could have been more help." I was sure that was true. She probably knew all there was to know about money laundering, amongst other things, and probably how I could have gotten out of it. Now it was too late.

"Thanks, Rita. Not calling you was just one more thing I did wrong. I know you don't believe in this sort of thing, but my karma is finally catching up to me. And I'm as ready as I'm ever going to be. I'll call you from the klink though. Promise."

"I understand, Jason." She paused for moment. Was Rita Standwoegen getting choked up?

"Call me. I'll help you however I can." The phone went silent. I hadn't really understood the particulars of my relationship with Rita, as I hadn't with so many others.

The drive to work was rainy but uneventful. The gray haze wrought by the lightly falling but steady sprinkle confirmed the dread which had kept me up the night before and was growing with each mile. If there were any events worthy of note along the highway they occurred beyond the limits of my attention. I took grim pride, however, in not driving off the bridge as I crossed the river, a whim dismissed without too much difficulty by some combination of hopefulness, cowardice, and fear of being even a worse father than I already believed myself to be. Regardless, the engineers that designed the bridge did not make it easy to simply drive off the side. There was concrete and steel all over the place. Somewhere in the long night before I had chosen to face the day in the same way I knowingly took an ass-beating one night in college. On an evening of late night drinking my ridiculously drunk and obnoxious friend thought it funny to harangue a group of conspicuously large males on the other side of the bar. Drunk and absurdly outnumbered, we stood little chance in the physical confrontation that occurred behind the bar after closing. Even as it was happening I knew we deserved the beating, he for being an ass and me for being stupid enough to stand with an ass. Unsurprisingly, our friendship did not survive post-graduation.

Except for the presence of Stephen's car, the parking lot looked exactly as it had Friday. I imagined, as I pulled into an empty space, numerous faces on the other side of the tinted glass of the building glaring out at me, waiting to see what I would do or what would be done to me. Would I actually make my way in to the bank, only to be served my just deserts as I had that night in college? Would I panic and bolt out of the parking lot, to be viewed later by my former coworkers as a mug shot on the local news? Or perhaps as a cautionary example in a bank training film? They couldn't know and neither could I. I was just performing the same movements I had for years and waiting to see how different things had become. I grabbed my briefcase from the back seat of the Impala and strode to the front door. I had few illusions about what would happen once I got inside and therefore did not acknowledge the stares and whispers. My weakening legs held out long enough for me to get to the elevator, where I relished the very few moments that passed between the door closing on the first floor and opening on the second.

Emily became visible as the doors slid open, and looked up at me with no apparent alarm. "Stephen wants to see you." After passing me this simple instruction her head went back down to her lap, her text conversation taking precedent over my doom. Or perhaps she was spreading the word of my doom on the available social media. I didn't stop to find out, tossing my brief case to the couch in my office as I walked past the door toward Stephen's office. As I walked the world slowed down again, so much so I swear I could hear Emily's texting as her nimble fingers whisked over the keyboard of her phone.

Stephen was slump-shouldered in his chair, elbows on his desk and chin in his hands. This was usually his posture when he was displeased or hung-over. At the moment I assumed "displeased" but quietly hoped for "hung-over." I plunked down in a chair across the desk from him, as ready as I could be for what would come out of his mouth.

"Morning, Stephen."

"Morning, Jason." He signed heavily and leaned back in his chair. "Jason...before anything else happens I want you to know

242

that I've always enjoyed working with you and I think you were doing a great job, at least until I found out what's been going on." He paused but I didn't interrupt. It didn't seem like a pause where he intended that I speak. He was obviously struggling.

"Listen, after I was told everything on Friday I made some calls, trying to figure out what I should do. I guess I was hoping there was some way I could make all this disappear because, you know...I really do like you. Honestly, I don't know how or why this is happening or what to do about it, so like I said I made a bunch of calls trying to figure out what I should do."

He was starting to ramble but I still didn't interrupt. I felt a morbid desire to push him, to get him where he was going, but decided not to guide him in any way. Anything I said at that point would have sounded petty. It was all too little, too late and apparently I had found some dignity over the weekend, or perhaps reached the last stage of grief – acceptance. Regardless I sat there staring at Stephen, waiting for him to get to wherever he was going which, despite my curiosity, was becoming increasingly difficult. He was droning on, scattering poorly organized thoughts all over his office. Getting fired had to be less painful than watching Stephen at the moment.

"And you know...I even talked to the wife about it. She's always been a good sounding board for me and I, well, you know, I like you and all....and she likes you too and I thought, you know, women are good at the whole emotional thing compared to us, men, I mean. Well, generally they are, but maybe not always. But you know what I'm saying, right? I mean about the woman/man thing. Anyway I asked her what she thought and why you might have made this sort of mistake and she told me it was probably just for sex." Oh God! Make him stop! Any hankering I had to hear Stephen out deserted me as he stumbled through a speech he obviously wasn't qualified to deliver. I felt compelled to step in and help him lest we sit there like that for another hour.

"Alright, Stephen. I get it. I fucked up and you did a lot of soul searching and you came to a conclusion, right?" I sounded ungrateful but I was ready to leave. "So where are we? What happens next?"

My abruptness startled Stephen out of his half-assed castigation of my behavior. He stared blankly at me before answering. "I called the police and they're picking you up today.

Or you can turn yourself in, either way. Whatever you do though, I can't let you back into your office or leave you to wander around the bank. You have to leave now." Stephen had always had somewhat of a hangdog demeanor and his expression now was more doleful than ever. He looked like he could use a hug.

"I appreciate the heads up, Stephen. I think I'll just go turn myself in. Thanks for being a great boss." I turned to begin my perp walk out of the building, pausing long enough to grab my brief case out of the office I was just told I was no longer allowed to be in. I also stopped to goodbye to Emily, who was now busy polishing her nails.

"See ya, Jason." She said this without diverting her attention from the task at hand, in such a way it appeared she still didn't have a clue as to what was happening right in front of her boss. But others took note of my exit. The stunned and dismayed faces greeting me on my way in to the building just moments earlier were just as stunned and dismayed as I exited. Not a word was spoken, or at least none that I heard. There would be plenty of time for gossipy jabber jawing as soon as I was out of ear shot. By the time I hit the door I desired nothing more than to be away from anything bank related and let fate run its course.

Sometime during my extremely short work day it had begun raining in earnest. Though I had been warned of the possibility of this by a local radio meteorologist I had not bothered to take an umbrella or rain coat into the bank. (I did have an umbrella in what had been my office but couldn't imagine a way to retrieve it without even more embarrassment.) Accompanied by cracks of thunder the downpour was already creating rills which flowed freely over my shoes once I stepped off the cement walkway onto the tarmac of the parking lot. To avoid getting struck by lightning I tried to make myself as small as possible, walking with my head tilted downward. Though a ridiculous presumption with regard to my potential electrocution by Mother Nature, this downcast posture also served to help me discover, and thereby avoid, the deeper streamlets. The rain was coming down so hard by the time I made it to my car I was sure I had gained five or ten pounds of water weight. Fumbling with the keys and intensely absorbed in an effort to keep some patch of me dry, I was startled upright by a figure popping into my field of vision. It was Arthur, of all people.

"Jesus, Arthur! You scared the shit out of me! What the fuck are you doing?" I couldn't figure out what Arthur was doing in my parking lot in the rain, putting himself between me and the dry interior of the Impala. It was really annoying.

"I'm here to save you, mate. Now get in the car and shut the fuck up." He delivered the sentence in the monotone deadpan with which he delivered nearly all his sentences. Wanting to get out of the rain I complied immediately, crawling in behind the wheel as Arthur slid into the passenger seat next to me.

"Now what?" I didn't really know what to say. He was acting so weird and the last four days had denied me a good measure of my ability to be surprised, or so I thought.

Arthur considered me for a few moments before speaking, just staring at me from across the arm rest. "Well then, Jason. Before I tell you what's about to happen I want you to understand you're a total dumbass and that you don't know how unbelievably lucky you are to have a friend like me." He paused here, perhaps for effect. I was still at a loss for words; however considering the context of our conversation I assumed he knew it was judgment day for me.

"You'll get no argument from me, Arthur, on either point, but I still have no idea exactly why you're here or how a part time carpet importer is going to help me out of this jam. I mean, are you here to spirit me out of the country? 'Cause that would be ok, except that I would miss the boys….and you too, of course. Still…"
Maybe leaving the country would be better than going to jail. The boys could always visit me, just like they would if I was in jail, with the added benefit of them not actually having to go into a jail.

"No, Jason, I'm not going to help you run away. I'm going to help you become a hero." He paused again. He was really drawing this out.

"And just how are you going to make that happen?" I found his insinuation annoying. Obviously he failed to understand I was resigned to my fate and his presence was interrupting the deliverance of said fate. "Arthur, can you just tell me what you're talking about? Please?"

He started the car, put it in gear and drove out of the parking lot. "I'm not who you think I am, Jason. I'm not a carpet importer. I have never actually imported any carpets at all. The truth is that I work for Interpol. You know, the International Police. And my job for the last few years has been to track part of the money laundering activities of the Russian mob." During his confession Arthur never took his eyes off the road.

"What? What the fuck, Arthur? Are you messing with me?" Though I had at times thought Arthur to be rather dull witted I had never thought him insane. "Umm, I'll tell you what, buddy…why don't you just take me back to my car so I can turn myself in like a good citizen." If it hadn't been raining so hard I would have asked him to let me out on the side of the road.

"Listen to me, Jason. I'm going to help you. I can help you." Arthur's serious tone and the fact the rain was still coming down in sheets were sufficient to convince me to sit tight and hear him out. I nodded my acquiescence and Arthur began to explain to me that, indeed, he was currently employed as an undercover Interpol agent and had been for some time. He had been assigned to the money crimes unit of the agency for years, apparently, and had been working this particular assignment for a couple years while his employer was busy putting all the puzzle pieces together. He worked undercover because the Russian mobsters were/are known to be particularly violent. If they knew of him and his activities anyone he knew would potentially be in harm's way, including me, his wife, and even Johannes. I sat dumbfounded as he described his job to me. Were there cameras watching us? Had I been thrust into the middle of a new reality show?

"How did you know they were going to approach me?" I slyly glanced around the vehicle to see if I could spot the hidden cameras.

"I didn't, well, not really. We knew they were probing the banks in this area for potential laundering either through hacking or direct contact. It was simply a stroke of luck that Katarina approached you personally. I didn't know anything about it until you told me about her, so I started paying more attention. We've never had anyone that close so we decided to let the thing 'run its course', so to speak. Whether you know it or not you've been a treasure trove of useful intelligence. We've been making arrests all morning."

Arthur was driving north on I-75 and we were getting close to the Ohio River. Despite a touch of light-headedness, no doubt caused by an overwhelming sense of surrealism, I was still managing to absorb most or all of Arthur's words. Did he just say they had been making arrests all morning? I was coming around to believing what he was telling me. What choice did I have? Either he was telling me the truth or he was certifiable, but none of my experience with Arthur had lead me to believe he could either be insane OR a secret agent. Regardless, I chose to believe the latter. After all, the idea of Arthur as secret agent was more exciting and, at least in my head, would lead to a healthier outcome for me.

"Um….so who are you arresting? And who's doing the arresting? And what have I done to help you with all this?" I felt like I was yelling as I competed with the rain pounding Arthur's car. And the yelling only added to the sense of surrealistic ridiculousness surrounding me like damp smoke, yet Arthur seemed as confident as ever.

"Well then." Arthur paused, apparently to organize his thoughts so he could answer my questions in order. "Besides Katarina we are arresting eight of her compatriots, four in Cincinnati and four more in Chicago. The arrests are being made by our partners in U.S. government agencies like the FBI and Treasury, and you helped every time you answered my questions about Katarina."

My heart dropped with a pang of regret at hearing Katarina's name in the context of being arrested. Intellectually I understood her to be a prime suspect and likely conduit to important parts of the money laundering "operation." My feelings for her, though perhaps comprised predominantly of passion and lust, were real enough. However the possibility she didn't share them and had probably only been using me help her gang pursue their felonious interests weren't factoring at the moment. Having committed time and energy to our relationship I was loath to think her capable of evil deeds, even though the proof was sitting in the car next to me. No one wants to think they could make such crappy decisions regarding someone looming so large in their personal life and I was no different despite the preponderance of evidence to the contrary. Indeed, even the most facile examination of my recent personal history would indicate I am gloriously incapable of making good decisions concerning intimate relationships with women, and so I shouldn't have been at all surprised that my newest girlfriend had turned out to be a gangland criminal. Yet somehow I was.

"So what are we doing now? What happens next?" I decided not to say anything to Arthur apropos my sadness at Katarina's arrest. He didn't need more evidence of my, shall we say, foibles? Besides, considering what was happening at that moment around Cincinnati and Chicago and all the work that had gone into it my shortcomings seemed refreshingly irrelevant.

"Now you meet some more agents and answer some more questions." He said this just before he turned into the parking garage located under the Federal Building in downtown Cincinnati. "There are some U.S. Treasury boys that have some questions for you, too. As I said, I'm turning you into a hero."

I didn't even know there were U.S. Treasury agents, or any other types of agents, in Cincinnati. I love my city but never thought of it as a place where such people were needed or housed. But there they were, tucked away in their drab looking offices as Arthur led me through the halls to a conference room. I kept quiet about this amazement and scolded myself silently for allowing myself to feel it. I was not there on a tour of the building. I was there because I had gotten caught up with criminals. International criminals. Again, I chose not to mention any of this to Arthur. I'm sure he already thought me a fool. Instead I followed a step behind him, like an obedient dog. Other than his initial reprimand in the rainy bank parking lot he made no further negative comments regarding my behavior or circumstance. He was all business now, intent on putting me through my paces with his people and their American counterparts.

As we entered the conference room I couldn't for the life of me figure out what I could provide to them that I hadn't already provided to Arthur. I mean, he already knew everything I did. The room was appointed in the sterile way one might expect of a government-owned meeting space. The walls were lined with pictures of people I didn't recognize plus one of the President. There were also a couple of plastic plants situated in the corners of the room intended, I imagine, to soften the utilitarian feel but serving only to add to it. Official looking people sat waiting for us, standing and introducing themselves upon our arrival. I didn't, and don't, remember any of their names but through the course of the day they helped me discover I knew a lot more about Katarina's operation than I thought I did. In addition to the crowd already waiting, a series of additional "interviewers" shuttled in and out of the room, mostly Americans but also a couple of guys and gals with accents whose origins I couldn't always discern. It made for a long day but Arthur stayed in the room with me the entire time, rarely saying a word. Rather, he sat opposite me at the other end of the rectangular table, which had seating capacity for ten, leaving the seats immediately to my left and right available to the questioners. We ate a taxpayer provided box lunch and my new friends were quite liberal with the bathroom breaks provided, of course, I was accompanied by one of their number to the toilet. Perhaps they thought I would make some attempt to contact Katarina or some other person of ill-repute. I had no such aspirations, desiring only to get through the day providing as much help as I could. I also was hoping to sleep in my own bed later, as opposed to a jail cell.

And then suddenly it was all over. I had apparently given them all the information they needed, or at least all the information they determined I could provide. After taking some notes on a legal pad the man who turned out to be the last of my inquisitors abruptly stood and announced we were finished.

"Thank you, Mr. Kubrick. You're free to go." He said this without flourish as he picked up his writing materials and exited the conference room. Within moments the room cleared, leaving Arthur and me with the fake plants and pictures of mysterious government functionaries (plus the President.)

Arthur stared at me from across the mega-table. "Shall we have a beer at O'Hearn's? I'll buy."

I knew then Arthur must have been pleased with my performance for the day. Whether in the guise of secret agent or rug importer Arthur, at his core, was still a cheap bastard. As we left the room he took the lead, guiding me out of the maze of hallways, non-descript doors and faux plants. I felt exhausted, but nonetheless quietly counted my blessings and amazing luck. When the elevator arrived the door opened to reveal my would-be co-conspirator. I was startled, naturally, and could do nothing but stare. Katarina looked small, poised as she was between two beefy agents, her hands cuffed behind her back and her eyes puffy as if she'd been crying. It was uncomfortable to see her in this way, in this forum, or at all, having already presumed I would never see her again. Arthur needlessly positioned himself protectively between Katarina and me as she and her entourage exited the elevator, as if one or both of us would do something stupid given the opportunity. Nothing of the sort happened, of course, and no words were exchanged. I did, however, receive a long look from her as she trod past, and felt sure I saw remorse in her swollen, bloodshot eyes. Perhaps not. Maybe it was just regret for getting caught.

Arthur drove directly to O'Hearn's and used the drive time back to the west side to explain how things were going to work going forward. I listened as intently as if I were receiving instructions on disarming an unexploded missile.

"And everything's going to be fine." This was his closing statement as we pulled into O'Hearn's parking lot.

"Really?" I was skeptical and hadn't shaken the feelings of abject criminality. "We'll see, I guess. Maybe I can get my job back? Regardless, Arthur, I don't know how to thank you for everything you did for me today." This was the tenth or fiftieth time I had thanked him since getting on the down elevator at the Federal Building. "I can't even imagine where I'd be right now if you didn't have my back. Actually I can imagine…so thank you again." I went on like this right up until we ordered the first beer.

"It all worked out in the end, Jason, for everybody." Well, maybe not Katarina and her friends, I thought. I kept the thought to myself.

Arthur bought all the beer that night. And dinner.

Flying over the Atlantic Ocean is something I had never done before today, though it was definitely something I had always wanted to do, and even vaguely planned to do at some point in the not too distant future. What I did not plan for was a working trip. But here I am on my way to Prague on assignment for my new employer, Interpol.

Here's what happened: Despite being exonerated due to Arthur's efforts to save me from myself, I was still out of a job. Apparently money laundering is still a terminable offense even when, ostensibly, you're doing it for the good of the planet. But it was ok, because it turned out Arthur didn't just save me from going to jail, he also set it me up to look like a hero. On the way to O'Hearn's that day he told me the whole story. Or at least his part. Arthur told his bosses that he and I had come up with a scheme for me to work undercover just for him. He told them he decided to run a little side operation on his own in order to keep the project as secure as possible, just in case there were any leaks in the organization. The only people who knew what we were doing were Arthur and me, so I was the "agent" and Arthur was my "handler." It was all very covert, you see, and obviously went just as planned because, as a result of our efforts, a goodly section of the Russian mob's Midwest money laundering operation had been dismantled. The extra-special bonus derived from Arthur's cover story was that I wasn't the only hero. Arthur, who evidently was already well respected by his employer, was promoted to bureau chief or station chief or some kind of management position, the name for which I'll memorize soon enough. And here was the beautiful thing about Arthur's efforts on my behalf: I'm quite sure Arthur hadn't given any thought to the potential consequences of his behavior on his own career, at least not in a positive sense. After all, he put his whole career at risk to help me and told me a month ago he would have been pleased to just not get fired for his unauthorized actions. And here he was getting promoted for being a real go-getter (at least as it pertained to international law enforcement.) I couldn't have been happier for him and told him so right before he offered me a job.

Now, the job offer was certainly another happy surprise, but my reaction can best be described as muted. I mean, it was exciting to think about working a job so potentially full of intrigue, but Arthur as my boss is something I had never considered. For years Arthur was my friend who never seemed to have a job for very long and was frugal to a fault with regard to financing his recreational activities. But even after all he had done for me I was going to have to put some work in at changing my perceptions and the conceived "idea" of Arthur that had become so ingrained. In the end I of course responded to the offer in the affirmative and, having deep experience with Arthur's thrift, decided to make the salary negotiation a priority, though I didn't really have a leg to stand on. Had they offered me minimum wage I would have taken it. Regardless, when he gave me the job description I was hooked and now, just several weeks later, I find myself on the way to the Czech Republic and my first real assignment. My role in this particular enterprise is to scour the financial records of a small bank in the Prague and look for activity that would indicate the mob was running the same scam they ran on me and my bank (only in a different language.) I realize, of course, that scouring financial records doesn't sound particularly exciting in a James Bond sense but I couldn't have felt more blissful. After all, my life had been going down the shitter and here I was working for the International Police helping to fight international crime. Who'd of thunk it?

The time away from the boys has been difficult, but they'll be fine staying with Kim while I'm gone. They're proud of their father, and not just for the fake police work arranged by Arthur. It turns out working for the International Police scores a ton of points with pre-teen boys. I've promised to email them every day and buy them something made in the Czech Republic. I promised Johannes the same thing. And Izzy. And Rita. Of course, I didn't tell any of them the real story, even though I suspect Rita knew nearly as much as Arthur. Nor did I tell their Mother, believing that doing so would have only given Kim a reason to start a custody battle. Some lies make sense for everyone.

In the couple months since becoming a hero I've made an effort to curb my carnal desires. I'm proud to say the effort has been largely successful. Indeed, I have been celibate since my last time with Katarina and only gotten drunk once with Arthur and Johannes, which was a celebration of my new job and so can hardly be counted against me. In the future I intend to be less reckless, but even as I tell myself this I am reminded that God has heard many promises made under duress, and that these types of promises often don't last longer than the period of duress, although they may serve to moderate the bad behavior for a while. So, what I need to do from now on is make myself worthy of all the people who watched over me during all the shenanigans. I'm thinking it's the least I can do for them and my sons. The excitement level may lower somewhat as a result, but that remains to be seen. I've got my first assignment waiting for me and I've still got Elaine's number programmed in my phone.

She doesn't know I'm coming.

63796766R00141

Made in the USA
Middletown, DE
05 February 2018